DISORDERLY CONDUCT

DISORDERLY CONDUCT

THE VLS FICTION READER

EDITED BY M. MARK

Serpent's Tail
London and New York

PUBLISHED BY SERPENT'S TAIL

In the United States:
401 West Broadway #2
New York, NY 10012

In the United Kingdom:
4 Blackstock Mews
London N4 2BT

Library of Congress Cataloging-in-Publication Data
Disorderly conduct: the VLS fiction reader / edited by M. Mark.

     p. cm.
  ISBN 1-85242-245-9
  1. Short stories, American. I. Mark, M.
PS648.S5D57 1991
813'.0108—dc20   91-24274

British Library Cataloguing-in-Publication Data
Disorderly conduct: The "VLS" fiction reader.
  I. Mark, M.
  813[F]

   ISBN 1-85242-245-9

Printed in the United States of America
Set in Bodoni Book
Designed by Laura Lindgren
First printing 1991

10 9 8 7 6 5 4 3 2 1

Acknowledgments

I'm grateful to members of the *VLS* Fiction Advisory Board for their stalwart and inspired support. This book wouldn't have happened without Elizabeth Alexander, Marcellus Blount, Margo Jefferson, Patrick McGrath, Albert Mobilio, Ann Snitow, Sharon Thompson, and Lynne Tillman.

Thanks to Peter Ayrton and John Hampson at Serpent's Tail in London, for proving again and again that a small publishing house can flourish, even in perilous times, if it's run with audacity and intelligence.

And thanks, for their encouragement and admonitions (not to mention their hard work), to friends and colleagues in New York—to David Schneiderman, of the *Village Voice,* for getting *VLS* up and running, and to many others for keeping it lively. Here are a few of them: Wes Anderson, Sally Cohen, Stacey D'Erasmo, Michael Ellerin, Mark Gates, Judy Hottensen, Cecil Hurdle, Perry Janoski, Walter Kendrick, David Kim, Kim Klein, Jon Larsen, Scott Malcomson, Maria Margaronis, Rebecca Martin, Carole Oster, Linda Nelson, Brian Palmer, Jon Pareles, Patience Parker Pierce, Alma Rodriguez, Ralph Sassone, Karyn Seltzer, Polly Shulman, Lisa Steinmeyer, Rochelle Stolzenberg, Sylvia Topp, and the writers who have filled *VLS*'s pages during the past ten years.

Without the invaluable skills of Laurie Muchnick, Ira Silverberg, and Laura Lindgren, *Disorderly Conduct* would have lived up to its name in more ways than one. They've made editing this anthology a pleasure.

Contents

Introduction

For ten years, the *VLS* staff has occupied a gentrification-resistant pocket of downtown Manhattan, where we spend our days attempting, in an enthusiastic if somewhat ad hoc manner, to provide writers of promise with the readers they deserve. Though we're usually too busy to contemplate our image in the publishing world, we get occasional messages from uptown. Last year, when the National Book Critics Circle invited me to be on a panel with the literary editors of the *New York Times* and the *Los Angeles Times*, my role was clearly to represent the upstarts and mavericks of this world. Or maybe I was supposed to provide comic relief. "*VLS* refuses to be solemn about literature," the moderator said. "It's a publication that breaks all the rules." Listening to the other panelists talk about obligations and restrictions, the weight of history and responsibility, I felt increasingly glad to be an outsider. There's freedom in editing a magazine that's not an establishment institution—freedom to be opinionated, eccentric, outrageous; freedom to write about what captures your imagination in any way you please. One of the many advantages to being an upstart is that you get to make things up as you go along.

We don't feel obligated to review every big new book that comes our way or print every big-name writer who sends us a short story. In fact, we're committed to the periphery—to books published by small and scholarly presses, literary books from commercial houses, writers whose talents have been inadequately recognized, writers who unsettle the folks in charge of big bucks and bourgeois proprieties. Of course, if something smack in the middle of the mainstream strikes our fancy, we feel free to tackle that as well. But the mainstream can look after itself; those on the margins need help from their friends, especially these days, when repression has been renamed "responsibility" and the demands of the marketplace distract publishers from the rigors and pleasures of the life of the mind.

If the *VLS* is perceived as a rule breaker, it's partially a consequence of my naïveté. Ten years ago, when the *Village Voice* backed haphazardly into starting a literary magazine, I didn't know there were any rules to break. One spring morning, in the shy, ladylike fashion for which I'm justly famed around the office, I was giving our advertising director a hard time: because he didn't sell enough publishing ads, there wasn't enough editorial space in the weekly book-review section. (The *Voice*, countercultural inclinations aside, is emphatically not a nonprofit publication.) To my surprise, he suggested I put together a prospectus for a monthly literary magazine—which seemed a transparent attempt to keep me quiet.

Emboldened by skepticism, goaded and enlightened by friends, I began to cook up my dream magazine: a mix of short reviews and long essays, criticism and fiction, written by people who love books, make a habit of questioning conventional wisdom, and understand that a sense of humor will see us through many an intellectual *crise*. According to the prospectus, *VLS* would publish precise and rigorous thinking, without the usual shroud of dull prose; the language, like the ideas, would be vivid, pointed, full of life. "The *Voice Literary Supplement* is a quirky, iconoclastic magazine that provides a home for critics who refuse to stay in the middle of the road," I wrote, prematurely and grandiosely, then filed the project under Wishful Thinking.

Two months later, I got a shock: our crack advertising team returned from the American Booksellers Association convention with numerous pledges of ads. We were on our way. In those early, heady days, the tiny *VLS* staff often resembled Mickey Rooney and Judy Garland planning a backyard theatrical. We got the first issue out by the skin of our teeth, and the second; readers seemed to like them. The magazine grew so steadily that in 1988 we inaugurated a new improved jumbo colossal national edition. We have systems now, and grown-up staff meetings, and orderly procedures.

Well, not all that orderly. We like to keep things a little messy, a little loose; categorical imperatives make us irritable. Last year, reading *The Paris Review Anthology*, I came across a 1953 letter by William Styron, who was in a swivet because the other *PR* founders had edited a manifesto he'd written; I felt grateful that I'd never drawn up a detailed public declaration of editorial principles (which causes me to ponder, somewhat belatedly, the wisdom of writing this introduction). Styron's letter makes it clear that he and his colleagues thought hard about the distinction between criticism and fiction before deciding to give predominance to the latter. At the *VLS*, by contrast, one thing led naturally to the next: both our essays and our short stories are about the way we live now.

Deciding to publish fiction every month was easy; making it happen was trickier. Because few magazines with a circulation of over 100,000 regularly run short stories, we found ourselves inundated by manuscripts. The Fiction Advisory Board rode to our rescue. Board members do the first read on all fiction submitted to the *VLS*—a daunting task which they accomplish with grace and skill. They also share with us their ideas, their expertise, and their enthusiasm. Stories they've recommended have appeared in O. Henry Award and Best American Short Stories volumes, and now twenty-five of them are gathered here. From the fiction published since 1986, we could easily have put together several anthologies: off-kilter coming-of-age stories, oddball domestic dramas, tawdry tales of fin-de-siècle New York. Instead, we went for breadth. An embrace of diversity is as close as we get to a manifesto.

So: eclecticism. A mix of well-known and unknown writers, high and pop cultural references, sly and serious voices, brutish Anglo-Saxon cognates and highfalutin litspeak. Beyond that, generalizations are hard to come by. This is not a minimalist volume, though our stories have more in common with the minimalists' plain syntax than with the intellectualized fanciness they reacted against. It's not a collection of shapely bourgeois set pieces—neither the cool, hard-edged sort associated with writing workshops nor the neo–nineteenth-century variety advocated by Tom Wolfe. These stories don't traffic in brat-pack sheen (our writers do, however, know their way around sex and drugs and rock and roll) or Lower East Side grit (they don't subscribe to the notion that you have to write from extremes—what

Albert Mobilio calls the Junkie Psychotic Living in a Garbage Can School). There are no stories about writing stories (okay, there's one). There are no numbered paragraphs. If forced to identify a common thread, I'd suggest, with a certain amount of hedging, that these stories might be considered outsider fiction—which means, among several other things, that they're outside prevailing literary trends.

By "outsiders" I don't mean glamourous rebels in black leather. Many of these stories are about lonely, anxious people trying, with humor and ingenuity, to put together acceptable lives at the nasty tail end of the twentieth century. They feel exiled, even from friends and lovers; home is not a cozy place. Some of them are misfits; most are smart and self-conscious. "These stories share a voice," one of our fiction board members said, after reading the anthology selections. "Whether marginal or benighted or ironic or befuddled, the characters have a sharp-tongued tendency that makes them seem urban even when they don't live in an urban context." The voices in this collection tend to be prickly but personal, even intimate—sources of warmth in a cool fictional climate. We're back in the land of storytelling, miles from the conceits and constructs Barthelme and Gass used to dazzle us with. Our writers are investigating experience, and though they understand that it's no longer possible to speak the truth, they're willing to risk some temporary half-truths.

What I've just written makes *Disorderly Conduct* sound considerably more tidy than it is. Every generalization, viewed from a certain angle, applies to a maximum of four stories. That's fine with me: too much coherence brings manifestos to mind, and anyway I like to be surprised. The month after we sent this anthology to the printers, the *VLS* played with genre, publishing two splendidly creepy gothic tales. The month after that, who knows? Maybe, to be perverse, we'll engineer a revival of numbered paragraphs . . .

M. Mark
New York City
April 1991

DISORDERLY CONDUCT

First Season in Hell: Medea

Kathy Acker

I was asked to write a version of "The Tell-Tale Heart" by Edgar Allan Poe. In "The Tell-Tale Heart," one man murders another man for no reason at all. But I am sick of men murdering men, especially for no reason at all. It happens all the time. I am interested in women murderers.

I asked myself, who was the first woman murderer. We live in the Greco-Roman civilization. The first mythic, therefore historical, woman murderer was Medea.

Imagine: there is a boy named Arthur Rimbaud. Arthur Rimbaud is totally madly in love with Paul Verlaine and Paul Verlaine's in love with him, only Paul Verlaine has this *wife* and *child*.

All the rest are the words of Arthur Rimbaud:

There was a king, in Greece, and he was tired of his wife. He married another, *younger* wife. This wife didn't like the first wife, so she decided to murder the child of the first wife and the king.

This was her plan to murder the child: She ruined all the seed corn so the people began to starve. When the king asked the gods why his people were starving, the gods, bribed by the *younger* wife, replied that the people would stop starving if he killed his own child.

The king took his child to a place in order to kill him. Just as he was about to murder his child, a gold male sheep flew by, snatched the child up, and took him away to Colchis. Far away.

When the child grew up, he killed this ram and gave him to the King of Colchis, Aeëtes.

King Aeëtes's daughter was Medea, the witch who will never tell us what she knows and we can never know.

Now when Jason came to Colchis in order to steal the fleece of the dead golden ram, he first stole Medea's heart, made her forget her family, her homeland, her duty. She lived only for Jason and his adventure: she defeated her own father, killed her own brother and scattered his cut-up limbs in the sea, and had Jason's father sliced up and boiled alive—all for the sake of what Jason wanted. Adventure. She gave Jason two children. Then he told Medea he was going to marry someone else. Medea complained. Jason told Medea that because she was protesting his actions, she was exiled. Medea was a brat like me. She wasn't going to be exiled and become nothing and suffer any longer because of her loving a man who was incapable of love, because of *her loving a man more than he loved her.*

Here is a confession by a friend of mine, Medea, who's also in Hell:

"Oh husband. Divine husband. My Lord, please listen to the saddest of your maidservants. I no longer know what to do. I want to suicide and I don't want to suicide. I'm out of my mind. My mind is mad. I'm drunk.

"My life has stunk and stinks like your dead fish.

"Oh, please, forgive me, I didn't mean to say that, Jesus Christ, of course, everything is good. What are these stupid tears? And there'll be tears and tears—tears'll build up into reality—this is what I hope!

"I was born submissive to You, Lord, and I've let another man beat me up and reject me all over the place. Now I need friends to take me away from this pain, but I have no friends. I fought Fate—You—by loving a human man, so now I have only pain and torture as lovers.

"I don't have to cry all the time. I can do whatever I want because Jason exiled me set me free he doesn't care about me—

"I am the slave of a husband out of Hell. This husband likes to make women about whom he doesn't give a damn fall in love with him. He's just that kind of guy. Because he thinks he's powerful, he thinks he's a man. A real King. But I who've lost my reason my sense cause of this man, I who'm now *dead to the world:* I'm not going to let myself be murdered. I'm not going to let him kill me.

"How can I describe him to you? I no longer know how to say things out loud: I just cry. I need a (real) husband.

"I used to be uninterested in men . . . I was always a kid . . . his romanticism seduced me . . . I left everything to follow him . . .

"This is the sort of thing my husband said cause he was a romantic: 'Love has to be continually reinvented. But all women want is security. As soon as a woman's secure, that is, married, she becomes celibate. There are women who don't care about security and like sex—I see these women being happily devoured by brutes who are as sensitive as logs in burning funeral pyres—

" 'My race,' said my husband, 'came from far away . . . Vikings . . . the first heroes . . . who slashed into their own bodies then drank down their own blood. I've inherited this love of blood, of tattooing, I'll be as ugly as one of them, *for I know who I am.* Don't show me your treasures, for I'd vomit over your antique Persian rug: My jewels're stained in blood. I don't have to work . . .' he said as he took me, we rolled over each other on the kitchen floor. I fought my demon.

"Nights, always drunk, both of us, he dragged me out on to the public street. There, or inside, he tried to frighten me into dying with his violence. 'This time he's going to thrust the knife into my heart— But that's not right!' In those days, in those nights, he wanted to be thought a criminal.

"He used to talk a lot about death—when he was being tender. He wasn't able to realize that he loved until that love had died; he wasn't able to realize that he had loved until he felt guilt and repentance.

"In a dirty hole in the city, we would drink ourselves deeper and he would begin to pity himself. Back on the public street he kicked me down then against a tree dog piss had stained, then lifting up my body, hugged me. It was raining lightly. Then he strangled me until I passed out and when I came to became angry at me for letting him strangle me: every gesture of his muscles revealed the gentleness of a girl at her catechism.

"That night I followed him whenever he let me. I had to.

"Followed him into strange, complicated actions, very far, bad and good actions. But I was never allowed into his world. What was I to him? A fantasy. I gave him *another* identity. Whenever I lay next to him in a bed and it was night, I was too excited to fall asleep, too unwilling to lose a chance that I might be allowed to enter his life. Since he wanted fantasy, what I wanted didn't matter.

"I asked myself if there was any chance he would change. Would he want to transmute this fantasy into reality? No. Change, for him, was fantastical. Yet I was, and still am, a victim of his charity.

"I was in him as if he were the palace. A desolate palace. The palace had been shut down so that no one could see that a person as desolate as me was in it. I depended on him, but who could love the dependency of someone as lonely and sad as me?

"So sadness is always renewed while perception dulls: I no longer saw the world. The world forgot me. Only his charity existed. When he kissed and hugged me *as if he liked me*, I entered a sombre room named 'Heaven.' In this room I was deaf, dumb, and blind and I never wanted to leave. Here, I took the habit. We were two children freely wandering in and massacring the *Paradise of Sorrow*. We were together. But after he had penetrated me, Verlaine said, 'All this is going to amuse you after I'm gone. When your arms'll no longer hang around my neck, when you'll no longer rest inside me, when your lips'll no longer touch my pupils. Because I'm going to have to go and not come back. There are other people I care for: I have duty. Although that isn't exactly what I want ... darling.' I saw myself—he had just gone—suicide. I looked up at Verlaine. I begged him to never leave me. He said he wouldn't. I made him promise this twenty times. I knew it meant as much as when I had said I didn't want him to leave his wife.

"Sometimes I forget this insoluble mess and dream: he'll save me, we'll travel; we'll hunt in the deserts, we'll sleep on the pavements of strange cities, carelessly, without his guilt, without my pain. Or else I'm going to wake up and all the human laws and customs of this world will have changed—thanks to some magical power—or this world, without changing, will let me feel desire and be happy and carefree.

"What did I want from him who hurt me more than I thought it possible for two people to hurt each other? I wanted the adventures found in kids' books. He couldn't give me these because he wasn't able to. Whatever did he want from me? I never understood. He told me he was just average: average regrets, average hopes. *What do I care about all that average shit that has nothing to do with adventure?*

"Did he talk to God? No. I should talk to God and tell God that I'm living in the bottom of an abyss and, here, there's no prayer.

"As for talking to him—he mocks me, avoids me, denigrates me. 'Once upon a time,' I would say to him, 'you were as wild as me. You thought that all straight men were the playthings of Nature in a grotesque delirium. You laughed at straight men, hideously, for a long time. Hiding, you became so perverted, you had to become straighter than a straight man. If you had acted less perversely, you wouldn't have had to become so straight—get married—and we could have stayed together longer. Your tenderness to me was mortal. But I'm a slave to you. I'm mad.

" 'One day perhaps—miraculously—you'll disappear, you'll die, but then, since I don't believe in murder, I'm going to go with you: when you go to heaven, I'll be there to witness your Assumption. Ours is a strange kind of marriage.' "

These ended Medea's words.

Medea killed the woman Jason was about to marry and then she killed the children Jason had given her. She couldn't kill Jason. As she sat on the palace roof amid flames as fierce as her love, a chariot of snakes carried her away from Jason and into safety. Jason wandered homeless from city to city and everyone hated him. Medea didn't die but became immortal and reigned in the fields of Heaven.

But I, Rimbaud, I love Verlaine.

A Bastard out of Carolina

Dorothy Allison

I was named for and by my aunt—Aunt Dot. My mama did not have much to say about it, since, strictly speaking, she wasn't there. A carful of them had been going out to the airport to meet some of the cousins. Aunt Dot, Uncle Lucius, and his wife were squeezed into the front and Mama was stretched out in the back, sound asleep. Mama hadn't adjusted to pregnant life very happily, and by the time she was eight months gone, she had a lot of trouble sleeping. She said that when she laid on her back it felt like I was crushing her; when she laid on her side it felt like I was climbing up her backbone; and there was no rest on her stomach at all. The only comfort lay in the fact that Uncle Lucius's Chevy had the back seat jacked up so that it could easily cradle little kids or pregnant women. Moments after lying down there Mama had fallen into her first deep sleep in eight and a half months. She slept so hard, even the accident didn't wake her up.

My Aunt Dot insists to this day that what happened was in no way Uncle Lucius's fault, but I *know* that the first time I ever saw Uncle Lucius sober was when I was seventeen and they had just removed half his stomach along with his liver. I cannot imagine that he hadn't been drinking. There's no question in my mind that they had *all* been drinking . . . except Mama, who never could drink, and certainly not when she was pregnant.

No, Mama was just asleep and everyone else was drunk. And what they did was plow headlong into a slow-moving car. The front of Uncle Lucius's Chevy accordioned; the back flew up; the aunts and Uncle Lucius were squeezed so tight they just bounced a little; and Mama, sound asleep, flew right over their heads, through the front windshield, and over the car they hit. Going through the glass, she cut the top of her head, and when she hit the ground she bruised her backside, but other than that she wasn't hurt at all. Of course, she didn't wake up for three days, not till after Granny and Aunt Dot had signed all the papers and picked out my name.

I am Dorothy for my Aunt Dot, and Earleen for my mama—Ruth Earlene. It's lucky I'm not Mattie Earleen like my granny wanted. But Mama had always promised to name her first daughter after her sister Dot, and Aunt Dot thought her child should just naturally carry Mama's middle name since they had come so close to losing her.

Other than the name, they got just about everything else wrong. Neither of them could write very clearly, and they weren't really sure how to spell Erleen, so it wound up spelled three different ways on the form. As for the name of the father, Granny had forgotten it as soon as she had run him out of town for messing with her daughter, and Aunt Dot had never been sure of his *last* name anyway. They tried to get away with just scribbling something down, but if the hospital didn't care how a baby's middle name was spelled, they were definite about having a father's last name. So Granny gave one, and Dot gave another, the clerk got mad, and I was certified a bastard by the state of South Carolina.

Mama always said it would never have happened if she'd been awake. "After all," she told her sister, "they don't ask for a marriage license before they put you up on the table." She was convinced that she could have bluffed her way through it, *said* she was married firmly enough, and no one would have questioned her.

"It's only when you bring it to their attention that they write it down."

Granny said it didn't matter anyhow. Who cared what was written down? Did people read courthouse records? Did they ask to see your birth certificate before they sat themselves on your porch? Everybody who mattered knew, and she didn't give a rat's ass about anybody else. She teased Mama about the birth certificate with the red stamp on the bottom.

7

"What was it? You intended to frame that thing? You wanted something on your wall to prove you done it right?" Granny could be mean where her pride was involved.

"The child is proof enough, and ain't no stamp on her nobody can see."

As much as Granny didn't care, Mama did. Mama hated to be called trash, hated the memory of every day she'd ever spent bent over other people's peanuts and strawberry plants while they stood tall and looked at her like she was a rock on the ground. The stamp on my birth certificate burned her like the stamp she knew they'd tried to put on her. *No good, lazy, shiftless*—she'd worked her hands to claws, her back to a shovel shape, her mouth to a bent and awkward smile—anything to deny what Greenville County had tried to make her. Now a soft-talking black-eyed man had done it for them—set a mark on her and hers. It was all she could do to pull herself up eight days after I was born and go back to work with a tight mouth and swollen eyes.

Mama waited a year. Four days before my first birthday and a month past her sixteenth, she wrapped me in a blanket and took me along to the courthouse. The clerk was polite but bored. He handed her a form and asked for a two-dollar fee. Mama filled it out in a fine schoolgirl's hand. Though she hadn't been to school in three years, she wrote letters for everyone in the family and was proud of her delicate, slightly arched script.

"What happened to the other one?" the clerk asked.

Mama knew he meant the first birth certificate, so she kept her eyes down on the battered pine counter.

"It got torn across the bottom."

The clerk looked at her more closely, turned a glance at the blanket-wrapped bundle in her arms.

"Is that right?"

He went to the back and was gone a long time. Mama stood, quiet but stubborn, at the counter. When he came back, he passed her the new certificate and stood to watch her face.

It was the same—identical to the other one. Across the bottom in oversized red-inked block letters it read ILLEGITIMATE.

Mama drew breath like an old woman with pleurisy, and flushed pink from her neck to her hairline. "I don't want it like this," she blurted.

"Well little lady," he mouthed at her in a long slow drawl. Behind him the other clerks—all women—stood in the doorway, their faces almost as flushed as Mama's but their eyes bright with an entirely different emotion.

"This is how it's got to be. The facts have been *established*." He drew the word out long and loud so that it hung in the air between them like a neon reflection of Mama's blush—*established*.

The women in the doorway shook their heads and pursed their lips. One giggled to the other, "Some people."

Mama pulled her back up straight, bundled me closer to her neck, and turned suddenly for the hall door. "You forgetting your certificate," the man called after her, but she didn't stop. Her hands on my body clamped so tight I let out a high thin wail. Mama just held on and let me scream.

She waited another year before going back, that time taking my Aunt Dot with her and leaving me with Granny. "I was there," Aunt Dot promised them, "and it was really my fault. In so much excitement I just got confused . . . what with Ruth looking like she was dead to the world, and everybody shouting and running around . . . you know, there was a three-car accident brought in just minutes after us." She gave the clerk a very sincere direct look, awkwardly trying to keep her eyes wide and friendly. "You know how these things can happen."

"Oh I do," he said, enjoying it all.

The form he brought out was no different from the others. The look he gave Mama and my aunt was pure righteous justification. *What'd you expect?* his eyes laughed at them. Aunt Dot came close to swinging her purse at his head, but Mama caught her arm. That time she took the certificate copy with her.

"Might as well have something for my two dollars," she said. At seventeen she was a lot older than she had been at sixteen. The next year she went alone, and the year after. The same year she got married, and talked for a while of having my stepfather adopt me, but that came to nothing when a friend told her she could live with him seven years and get the same result without paying a courthouse lawyer. That sounded good but gave her still another idea, and a few years later, when she got a settlement from another car accident, she used a piece of it to hire a lawyer for a few hours.

"I'm sorry," he told her, handing half her money back. "The way the law stands there's nothing I could do for you. You just wait a few years. Sooner or later they'll get rid of that damn ordinance. Mostly it's not enforced anymore anyway."

"Then why," she asked him, "do they insist on enforcing it on me?"

"Now, honey," he sighed, clearly embarrassed that she felt she had to say anything. Didn't she know how considerate he was being? He wiggled in his seat and then passed the rest of her money across the desk.

"You don't need me to tell you the answer to that. You've lived in this county all your life and you know how things are." He gave a grin that had no humor in it at all. "By now they look forward to you coming in."

"Small-minded people," he told her, but that grin never left his face.

"Bastard!" Mama almost hissed, and then caught herself. She'd sworn never to use that word again.

Mama quit working honky-tonks as soon as she could after her marriage. A year in the mill was all she could take; the dust in the air got to her too fast. After that, there was no choice but to find work in a diner. The tips made all the difference, though she knew she could have made more money if she'd stayed with the honky-tonks or managed a slot as a cocktail waitress. There was always more money serving people beer and wine, more still in hard liquor, but she'd have had to go outside Greenville County, and neither she nor her new husband could imagine doing that.

The diner was a good choice anyway, one of the few good ones downtown. The work left her tired but not sick to death, like the mill, and she enjoyed the people she met there, the tips, and the conversation.

"You got a way with a smile," the manager told her.

"Oh, my smile gets me a long way." She laughed and no one would have known she didn't mean it. Truckers or judges, they all liked Mama, and when they weren't slipping quarters in her pocket they were bringing her things, souvenirs or friendship cards, once or twice a ring. Mama smiled, joked, slapped ass, and firmly passed back anything that looked like a down payment on something she didn't want to sell.

Family is family, and even love can't keep people from eating at each other. Mama's pride, Granny's resentment that there should be anything to consider shameful, my aunts' fear and bitter humor, my uncles' hard-mouthed contempt for anything that could not be handled with a shotgun or an ax handle—all combined to age Mama fast and painfully. There was only one way to fight off the pity and hatefulness. Mama learned to laugh with them before they could laugh at her and to do it well.

"Where you keep that paper?" they'd tease her.

"Under the sink with all the other trash," she'd shoot back, giving them a glance so sharp they'd think twice before trying to tease her again.

"Put it away," Granny started telling her. "If you stopped thinking about it, people would. As long as it's the only thing they can hurt you with, they're gonna keep on using it."

The preacher agreed. "Your shame is just between you and God, Sister Ruth. No need to let it mark the child."

Mama went as pale as the underside of an unpeeled cotton boll. "I got no shame," she told him, "and I don't need no man to tell me jackshit about my child."

"*Jackshit,*" my Aunt Dot boasted. "She said *jackshit* to the preacher. Oh! An't nobody says nothing to my little sister, an't nobody can touch that girl on what's hers. You just better watch yourself around her."

You better. You better. You just better watch yourself around her.

Watch her in the café, laughing, pouring coffee, palming tips, and frying eggs. Watch her push her hair back, tug her apron higher, refuse dates, pinches, suggestions. Watch her eyes and how they sink into her face, the lines that grow out from that tight stubborn mouth, the easy banter that rises from the deepest place inside her.

"An't it about time you tried the courthouse again, Sister Ruth?"

"An't it time you zipped your britches, Brother Calvin?"

An't it time the Lord did something, rained fire and retribution on Greenville County? An't there sin enough, grief enough, inch by inch of pain enough? An't the measure made yet? Mama never said what she was thinking, but her mind was working all the time.

Mama was working grill at the White Horse Café the day the radio announced that the fire downtown had gone out of control, burning the courthouse and the hall of records to the ground. It was midway through the noon rush. Mama was holding a pot of coffee in one hand, and two cups in the other. She put the cups down and passed the pot to her friend Patsy.

"I'm going home."

"You what?"

"I've got to go home."

"Where's she going?"

"Trouble at home."

The cardboard box of wrinkled and stained papers was tucked under the sheets in the bottom of Aunt Shirley's chifforobe. Mama pulled out the ones she wanted, took them into the kitchen and dropped them in the sink without bothering to unfold them. She'd just lit a kitchen match when the phone rang.

"You heard, I suppose." It was Aunt Dot. "Patsy said you took off like someone set a fire under you."

"Not me," Mama replied. "The only fire I got going here is the one burning up all these useless papers."

Aunt Dot's laughter spilled out of the phone and all over the kitchen.

"Girl! There an't a woman in town going to believe you didn't set that fire yourself. Half the county's gonna tell the other about how you burned down the courthouse."

"Let them talk." Mama blew at the sparks flying up. "Talk won't send me to jail. The sheriff and half his deputies will know how I was at work all morning, 'cause I served them their coffee. I can't get me into any trouble just 'cause I'm *glad* the goddamn courthouse burned down."

Of course nothing is ever settled that easily. Years later, after Mama and I moved to Florida, it turned out to be quite difficult to prove I'd been born.

"Two pieces of identification—one of them a birth certificate," the passport clerk insisted, and then allowed as how affidavits might be acceptable. Mama went to the courthouse and swore to it, but one witness, even the most vital one, wasn't enough and there wasn't money to go back to Greenville. It all had to be done by mail. Witnesses who weren't relatives were finally found, and I was just glad to get it settled. Still the friendly clerk insisted that if there had *ever* been a birth certificate, then somehow, somewhere, there had to be a copy. He was so determinedly friendly, he traced hospital records till he found one.

It came to Mama's house addressed to both of us. When I got home, she was sitting there with it at the table, drinking coffee and looking down at the bold red print. I sat down with her and read it over. It didn't bother me much. I had, after all, grown up with the stories—how Granny had run my daddy off, dragged Mama home and only found out I was on the way after he was settled with another woman two counties away. It was a family legend, and I'd developed a mystique 'bout being a no-count *bastard* out of the state of South Carolina.

But there was no way to pretend it didn't bother Mama. I tried determinedly to be casual about it.

"How's my name really spelled?" I asked her. "It's spelled every whichaway here."

Mama lit another cigarette, ignoring the one dying in the ashtray. "What you complaining about? It gives you a choice, don't it? Just pick the one you want."

She pushed her hair back in a gesture so familiar it hurt me, tapped her cigarette on the side of the ashtray, and stared at the paper in my hands as if it might take flame from her glance. When she let the smoke trail out her nose, her shoulders slumped down, and I recognized for a moment a weight so old I'd never imagined her without it.

She looked back up at me, and the light in her eyes glinted brightly.

"You know who else is a bastard?"

She looked old, so old I could barely answer her. I drew breath deeply and felt my own age waiting for me.

"Well, who?"

"Just about every firstborn child I know."

I laughed, looked her in the eye, and felt my heart hurt from loving her—one more time not being ashamed of either of us. She laughed back, her shoulders loosening, and her hands sweeping up to stroke at her temples, a woman with absolutely perfect timing.

" 'Course, not all of them have a paper to prove it."

The Visitor

Russell Banks

In late April of a recent year, I drove from my home in New York City across New Jersey to deliver a lecture at East Stroudsburg University, which is located in Pennsylvania at the southern end of the Pocono Mountains, not far from the Delaware Water Gap. I arrived a few hours earlier than my hosts expected me, so that, once there, I was free to drive thirty-five miles further north to the small town of Tobyhanna, where my mother and father lived with me and my brother and sister for a single year, 1952, when I was twelve, my brother ten, and my sister six.

For the five of us, the year we lived in Tobyhanna was the most crucial year of our shared life. It defined us: we were that family, we have remained that family. The following summer, my mother and father got divorced, and from then on, although we were the same, everything else was different. Not better, just different.

Looking back, I see that both my parents were careening out of control with rage, frustration, and fear. For years, my father had been plotting ways to leave my mother, whose dependency and hysteria had imprisoned him then, as later it would me. For her part, my mother had been just as busy trying to keep him from leaving, which only made him feel more trapped today than yesterday. He was thirty-eight; his life was skidding past. And he thought he was somehow better than she, a more important person in the overall scheme of things than she, and he acted accordingly. This made my mother wild.

My father was a plumber, and he had been hired by a New England contractor as superintendent of all the plumbing, heating, and air-conditioning installation in an enormous Army shipping and storage depot then being built in Tobyhanna. It was one of the first big postwar military bases commissioned by the Eisenhower administration. My father was the company's man sent down from Hartford to run its largest out-of-state job, an extraordinary position for a young journeyman pipe fitter with no more than a high school education, a man whose biggest job up to then had been adding a wing to the Veterans' Hospital in Manchester, New Hampshire. But he was bright, and he worked hard, and he was very good-looking and lucky. People liked him, especially men, and women flirted with him.

He was a heavy drinker, though, starting it earlier every day. And with each additional long night's stay at the bar in Tobyhanna, he turned increasingly nasty and sometimes violent. The job he held was, in fact, way over his head, and he was terrified—not of being fired, but of being found out, and not so much by other people, as by himself.

I drove my car into Tobyhanna, a poor bedraggled batch of houses and garages and trailers strung along a winding two-lane road abandoned long ago for the Stroudsburg-Scranton highway, and saw at once the bar where my father used to spend his evenings after work and as much of his weekends as he could steal from the house in the woods where he had established his nervous wife and three children. It was a small depressing impoverished town, despite the presence of the Army depot—or perhaps because of it.

I drew my car up to the bar on the main street, shut off the motor, and went inside. It was dark, dirty, and damp, smelled of old beer, sweat, and pickled hard-boiled eggs, with a jukebox at the back, a U-shaped linoleum-covered bar that ran the length of the room, and several dim flickering neon beer signs in the window.

I ordered a beer from the middle-aged woman behind the bar, whose exact round dun-colored double—her twin, I thought, or surely her sister—sat on a stool on the other side of the bar. She sat next to a man with a tracheotomy who was talking to her in a harsh electronic moan.

A second man was perched on a stool a ways down from me—a scrawny fellow in his mid-fifties whose arms were covered with badly drawn tattoos. His head was wobbling on his neck above a bottle of beer, and he seemed not to notice when I sat down.

The place had not changed a bit in the thirty-four years since I last entered it. The doubling image of the round woman behind the bar and the woman sitting by the man with the hole in his throat acted like a drug or a mathematical formula or a vision, instantly doubling the place itself with my memory of it, matching my arrival in Tobyhanna today with my memory of a Saturday in winter, when my father drove me and my younger brother into town with him—ostensibly to pick up a few groceries or some such errand. It's no longer clear to me why we three males left the house and hearth for town that day, just as it was not clear to me why I decided to drive north from Stroudsburg, when I more easily and pleasantly could have strolled around the college campus for a few hours, killing time. There was a powerful need to go there, but no remembered reason.

I remember my father bringing my brother and me straight into the bar with him, and I remember his cronies—soldiers and construction workers—buying my brother and me Cokes and potato chips. They teased us and praised us for our manly cleverness, our clever manliness, because we were little men, while down along the bar my father leaned over a friend's shoulder and talked intently into his ear, then smiled at a fat woman (or so she looked to me) with bright red lipstick sitting next to him and patted her forearm affectionately and soon switched his attention completely over to her, leaving his male friend to drink alone for a while. I watched this take place.

The bartender waddled over to me, picked up my nearly empty bottle and studied it and set it back down. "Want another?"

I shook my head no.

She lit a cigarette, inhaled furiously, a large red-faced woman smoking like a steamship, and she studied my face the way she had examined my beer bottle. "You're not from around here," she stated.

"Last time I was in here was thirty-four years ago," I said.

She laughed, once, more a bark than a laugh. "It hasn't changed."

"Nope," I said. "It's the same."

The man next to me at the bar, his head wobbling like a heavy flower on a stem, was alert, more or less, and watching me now. "You ain't old enough to've been in here thirty-four years ago," he growled.

"I was only a kid then. With my father. My father brought me in here."

The man sat up straight and swept his arms around and then pointed at each of the four corners of the dingy room. "This place, it hasn't changed," he said. "Where are you from?"

"New York City."

"Hah!" he laughed. "This," he said, waving his arms again, indicating the three other people in the bar as if they were a place, "this is the way to live! You never lock your doors here. It's safe," he proclaimed. "Not like, not like your goddamned New York City."

I nodded in agreement, got off my stool, and made for the door.

He called after me, "Hey, buddy! You're welcome!" He grinned through loose red lips and broken teeth and started to cackle at his joke on me and then cough and finally wheeze and whoop with joy, as I hurried out the front door to my car.

On our way home from the bar, me in front in the passenger's seat, my brother in back, my father had said, "Listen, boys, let's just say we spent the time at the depot. In the office. I should've gone over some drawings there anyhow, so we might's well say that's what we did, right?" He looked over at me intently. "Right?"

"Sure," I said. "I don't care."

I peered out the window at the gauze curtains of snow falling, the houses that occasionally flashed past, the dark shadows of trees and of the Poconos closing off the sky. I didn't care.

My brother didn't say anything, but my father never asked him to. I was the one he worried about; I was the one my mother would interrogate.

The house itself had not changed. Except for the coat of blue-gray paint, it was still the same two-story farmhouse with the long shed attached at the rear and the weatherbeaten, unpainted barn across the circular drive. The two stone chimneys at the ends of the house were matched by the pair of huge maple trees next to the road. Hanging from one of the trees was a small wooden sign. RETTSTADT'S RESTAURANT, it said. SERVING DINNERS FRI. TO SAT., 5 PM TO 9 PM. I could not imagine who would drive all the way out from Tobyhanna—five miles through the woods on a narrow winding hilly road, passing barely a dozen other houses on the way, broken-down and half-finished bungalows and trailers set on cinderblocks among car chassis and old refrigerators and tires—for dinner at Rettstadt's.

I looked at my watch, 4:45, and drew my car off the road, pulled into the driveway, and parked by the back porch, facing the door that, when we lived there, opened into the kitchen. By now my limbs felt weak and awash with blood and my heart was pounding furiously, as if I were at the entrance to a cave.

By the time my father and brother and I arrived home, the snow was coming down heavily, and my father told my mother that the snow had slowed him up, he had got stuck twice, and besides, he had to spend quite a while at the office at the depot working on some drawings for Monday. That was why we were so late getting home from town.

My mother looked at him wearily. It was the same old story, the same old challenge tossed down, the dare for her to take him on one more time: either believe the liar or enrage him by forcing him to tell the truth.

I know from photographs that my mother was a pretty woman—small, blond, precisely featured, with lively hazel eyes and a sensitive mouth. "Petite," she liked to say of herself. People said she looked like beautiful women—Claudette Colbert, Ann Blyth, Bette Davis—and she did. Not like any one of them, but she belonged to that particular caste of beauty. I remember her that afternoon as standing before the stove, a ladle in hand, a steaming pot before her—but that, too, is a generic image, like her beauty. It was a Saturday afternoon, it was snowing.

My brother dodged around her and disappeared like a mouse through the living room, toward the stairs and the unused bedroom on the second floor, a kind of attic in the back where we had set up our electric trains. My sister—I have no idea where she was, possibly in the kitchen, possibly with a friend for the afternoon: country children often visited each other on weekends; it made the driving back and forth easier for the parents. I hung around by the kitchen door, as if waiting for orders from one or the other of my parents. They were looking angrily at one another, however, and did not seem to know that I existed.

My mother said, "I know where you've been. I can smell it on you. I can smell her, too."

My father's face reddened, and he glowered down at her from his full height, which, because my mother was small and I was only twelve years old, seemed a considerable height, though he was never any taller than six feet, which turned out to be my height as well. He began to shout at her. It was at first a welling up and then an overflow of anger, wordless— or no words that I can recall—a kind of sustained roar, which she answered by letting loose with shrieks, cries, calls, wails—again, with no words that I can recall now and surely could not hear then, for the tone was all one needed in order to understand the sad rage this man and woman felt toward each other, like a pair of beasts caught side by side, each with a limb in the jaws of the same cruel trap, and at first they scream and bite at each other's face, and then they begin to gnaw on the flesh and bone of their own trapped limb.

What in 1952 had been the kitchen was now a restaurant dining room, the floor covered with bright green indoor-outdoor carpeting, the walls paneled over in imitation pine with five-and-dime framed pictures of a trout stream with a deer bending its head to drink, a barn and silo and waves of grain, a covered bridge with throngs of fall foliage behind it. I smelled food cooking, and I walked through the door that had once led to the woodshed behind the kitchen and discovered that it led now to a large open room filled with stainless steel counters, dishwashers, sinks, and stoves. I saw in the far corner of the room a small man in white pants and T-shirt scrubbing utensils in a sink. He saw me and waved, as if he'd been expecting me. He was in his late fifties, I guessed, square faced, short, thick bodied.

I said, "I'm not here to eat, don't worry."

He smiled and nodded. "We're not set up yet, anyhow. Too early, friend."

"Yes, well, I'm not here to eat," I repeated. "I used to live here."

He squinted across the room at me. Then he pursed his lips and pronounced my last name. My very name.

"Yes!" I said, astonished. "That's right!" I did not know this man, I had never seen him before. I felt my father loom up beside me, huge and red and full of heat, and I looked automatically to my left, where I felt his presence most, and leaned away from him, then recovered and stood straight and regarded the small man in white before me.

He put down the spoon he'd been scrubbing and took a step closer. He said my father's first name and his last. "The plumber. Right? The plumber?"

"Well, yes. My father. I'm not him, though. I'm his son."

He examined my face for a few seconds, as if he did not believe me. He was looking at a gray-haired man in his late forties, a man nearly a decade older than my father had been in 1952. I was, however, more likely my father than my father's son.

I told him that my father had died five years ago.

He was sad to hear that and asked what he died of.

"Liver," I said. "He pretty much drank himself to death."

He nodded. "Yeah, well, those construction guys. They all hit the booze pretty hard. I ran the food concession for the job your dad was on, down there at the depot," he said. "I was a kid then, just out of the service. I knew your dad, what a guy he was! Memorable. He had what you call real personality, your dad." He wiped his hands with a towel and stuck one out to shake. "George Rettstadt," he said. "I bought this place a few years after your dad lived here. He rented it, right? Brought your mom and the kids out from someplace in New England for a while, right? C'mon and look around, if you want. I've made loads of changes, as you can see," he said, waving his arms at the four corners of the room, just like the drunk at the bar.

I agreed. There had been a lot of changes. But even so, it was the same house, and it smelled the same to me, the light fell at familiar angles through the maple trees and tall narrow windows, rooms opened into rooms where they always had. Rettstadt had turned woodshed into kitchen and kitchen into dining room, he had covered walls and floors and he had lowered ceilings, hung brass lamps and tacky pictures. He had altered the whole function of the house—though he still lived in it, he assured me, upstairs. The living room was now a large second dining room that was for private parties, which he said was most of his business. "You know, Lions Club, Boy Scouts, stuff like that. Reunions, weddings, like that."

Rettstadt walked ahead of me, pointing out the changes, while I saw only the house that lay hidden beneath this one, the white house under the blue one, the drab decaying farmhouse in the woods where a young man had stuck his unhappy wife and bewildered children while he drove into town to work every day and to drink every night and tried to invent a man he could never become.

On that snowy Saturday long ago, while my mother shrieked at my father and he bellowed back, barking like an angry dog at her small spitting face, I finally darted past them and fled the kitchen for the bedroom upstairs that I shared with my brother. It was a corner room with a pair of long windows on one side and our twin beds on the other. I remember lying on my bed, the one nearer the windows, reading a comic book, probably, with my wet feet on the clean bedspread, my arm crooked back to support my head, when suddenly the door flew open, and my mother was hovering over me like a great bird, clutching my shirt and yanking me up beside her on the bed.

"Tell me!" she cried. "Tell me where you went! Don't you lie to me, too!" She raised her hand and held it, palm out, a few inches from my face, as if she wanted me to read it, and she said, "Don't *you* lie to me, too, or I swear, I'll go crazy. Tell me where you went all afternoon. I know he took you to the bar in town. He did, didn't he? He didn't get stuck in the snow, and he didn't go to the depot. He just went to the bar. And there was a woman there, I know it. Tell me the truth."

I did not protest, I did not hesitate. I nodded my head up and down, and said, "We went to the bar in town. Nowhere else."

She smiled, wiped the tears from her cheeks and stood. "Good boy," she said. "Good boy." She turned and left the room. I lay back down trembling, and in a few seconds the buzz of the electric trains from the attic room in back replaced the buzz in my head, and I believe I fell asleep.

When George Rettstadt asked me if I wanted to see how he'd changed the rooms upstairs, where he said he had fixed up a large apartment for himself and his wife, I felt my chest tighten. "No," I said very quickly, as if he had invited me to look steadily at a gruesome object. "No, that's okay, I'm in kind of a hurry, anyhow," I said, easing toward the door. "I wanted to walk around the yard a minute. I wanted to see where my brother and sister and I used to play. You know."

Rettstadt said, "Sure, take all the time you want. Look at whatever you want to look at, everything's unlocked. We never lock our doors out here, you know." He opened the door, we shook hands, and I stepped out, breathing rapidly.

I did poke into the barn, but there was nothing about it that spoke to me. I stood inside the dark cluttered building and it was as if I were resting, idling, conserving energy for a more strenuous enterprise to come.

A moment later I had walked around the back of the house, crossed through the tangled brush and crumbling stone walls in the gathering dusk and had come to stand next to the house on the far side, just below my old bedroom window.

My father's heavy footsteps on the stairs had wakened me. He swung open the bedroom door, and I knew instantly, as if I had been standing downstairs in the kitchen between my mother and father, what had happened between them when she had returned from my room armed with betrayal, and with utter clarity and an almost welcoming acceptance, I knew what would happen now between him and me.

Violence produces white light and heat inside the head, and it happens both to the person who administers the beating and to the person who is beaten. It is never dark and cold. It happens at the instant of violent contact, before pain is felt, or fear, even, or guilt, so that pain, fear, and guilt come to be seen as merely the price one pays afterward for this extraordinary immolation. It's as if violence were a gift worth any price. Beyond the light and the heat, it's a gift that engenders gorgeous dreams of retribution that last for tens of generations of fathers and children, husbands and wives—it shapes and drives fantasies of becoming huge as a glacier and hard as iron, fast as light and sudden, like a volcano.

When you are hit in the head or slammed in the ribs and thrown to the floor by a powerful man, you find instantly that you are already halfway into a narrative that portrays your return to that moment, a narrative whose primary function is to provide reversal: to make the child into the

23

man, the weak into the strong, the bad into the good. Listen to me: you are locked into that narrative, and no other terms, except those present at its inception, at the very opening of the drama, are available for the reversal—and, oh! when that happens, I have risen up from my narrow bed in the upstairs corner room I shared with my brother in Tobyhanna in 1952, and I overwhelm my dead father's rage with an awful crippling rage of my own.

I eventually moved away from that spot beneath the window of the bedroom and got into my car and drove back to Tobyhanna and then on down to East Stroudsburg University, where that evening I gave my lecture to a small gathering of students and teachers, who seemed appreciative and expressed it with good-natured gentle applause. Afterwards, we ate and drank a little wine in a local restaurant, and I drove home to New York.

I will not go back to the house in Tobyhanna or to the bar in town, just as—after having been there once—I have not returned to any of the other houses we lived in when I was growing up, or to the apartments and barrooms in Florida and Boston and New Hampshire, where I first learned the need to protect other people from myself, people who loved me, male and female, and utter strangers, male and female. I go back to each, one time only, and I stand silently outside a window or a door, and I deliberately play back the horrible events that took place there. Then I move on.

I have traveled a lot in recent years, and consequently I have completed almost all my journeys now. When I have returned to every place where someone beat me or I beat someone, when there is no place left to go back to, then for the rest of my life I will have only my memories, these stories, to go to—for the heat, for the light, for the awful endlessly recurring end of it.

The Black Hand Girl

Blanche McCrary Boyd

My mother hadn't wanted me to go to Harvard Summer School because of the Boston Strangler. "I just hate to think of you like that," she kept saying, "with your face all purple and your tongue hanging out. Why can't you be a normal girl and get a tan?"

The Dean at Duke University probably had not wanted me to go to Harvard either. At Duke I was viewed as a troublemaker, partly because of hypnosis.

When I was in high school I had learned to hypnotize people by accident. "Look deep into my eyes," I said to my cousin Sister-Girl one night when we'd been watching an evil hypnotist in a B movie on television. I said this with great conviction, and Sister-Girl looked at me in great fun. Then something peculiar happened: Sister-Girl seemed to drift toward my eyes. "I'm going to count to five," I whispered, "and when I get to five you'll be in a deep trance." I whispered because I was afraid. There was a current between us as certain as the electricity in a doorbell I'd once touched.

Sister-Girl's eyelids fluttered. She was a sweet, lumpish girl everyone loved. I counted to five and her eyes closed. "Can you bark?" I asked.

"Yes," she said.

"Will you do it?"

"Yes."

"Be a dog, then. Bark."

Her eyes remained closed, but Sister-Girl's lips pulled back from her teeth. She began to make little yipping noises. I recognized our neighbor's Pomeranian.

I counted backward from five and Sister-Girl woke up. "I don't think we ought to tell Momma or Aunt Rose about this," I said.

During my senior year in high school I developed a different technique, no longer hypnotizing through eye contact, which scared me too much, but with a lighted cigarette in a semidark room. My favorite trick remained making people bark. Sometimes I told them what kind of dog to be, and other times I asked, after they were barking, "What kind of dog are you?" The answer might be, "I'm a German shepherd," or "I'm a Lhasa apso." I knew I shouldn't be doing hypnosis, especially at parties, but at Duke it made me popular and feared.

College caused me authority problems. There were rules against women wearing pants to classes or to the dining room, and rules against wearing curlers in public; there was even a "suggestion" against women smoking cigarettes standing up. Soon there was a new regulation concerning hypnosis.

The Dean's note came right after second semester began. For my audience I wore a madras wraparound skirt, a Gant button-down shirt, and a cardigan that had leather patches on the elbows. I even wore a panty girdle and hose. The Dean would see that I was a normal, healthy sorority girl, not a troublemaker.

Dean Pottle was at least forty years old. Her hair was brown and she was wearing a brown tailored suit. Her skin was pocked, as if she'd once had acne. She was smoking a cigarette and seemed quite friendly as she invited me to sit down across from her.

"Ellen," she said comfortingly, "we have had a report that you went to Dr. Hillyer's class in the medical school wearing nothing but a bathing suit and carrying a bottle of champagne on a silver tray."

I tried to think of how best to reply. "I'm not in the medical school," I said, "so I didn't think the regular rules would apply. Anyway, it was Dr. Hillyer's birthday, and some of his students asked me to deliver the champagne. It seemed harmless enough. I would never have agreed to do it if I'd known the class was at eight-thirty in the morning, I can assure you of that."

When the Dean said nothing, I continued with less confidence. "I wore my trenchcoat over my bathing suit until I got to the door of the classroom, and I put it right back on as soon as I gave him the champagne."

Her eyes seemed less affable. "The same trenchcoat you've been wearing to your regular classes?"

I nodded.

"Is it true you've been wearing your trenchcoat to classes with nothing under it?"

"It certainly is not true, Dean Pottle. I wear a slip and a bra. I even wear hose."

"Ellen, you do know about the dress code, don't you?"

"I'm within the dress code, Dean Pottle. It just says you can't wear pants, it doesn't say you have to wear skirts. Also, a slip is a kind of skirt, isn't it?"

The Dean was trying to look stern, but I began to suspect she might like me. "Do you think of yourself as an unusual girl?"

I nodded miserably. "Listen, Dean Pottle, would you mind if I smoked too? I'm very nervous."

"Go ahead. You have a tendency to bend the rules a bit, don't you think, Ellen?"

I lit a Winston. "I don't know."

"Let's start with the hypnosis."

"There was no rule against hypnosis."

The Dean took a final meditative drag on her own cigarette and crushed it out in a brown glass ashtray.

"Anyway, there's not much to it," I said. "To hypnosis. I saw it on TV one night. I say corny stuff like 'Look only at the tip of my cigarette, your eyelids are getting heavy.' Most people are just dying to go into a trance."

The Dean was staring at the smoke curling from my cigarette.

"Hello?"

With effort she looked up at me. When she didn't speak, I continued, "I tell them, 'Look at the glowing ember of the cigarette. Let your mind relax.'"

The Dean looked back at my cigarette. She seemed like a nice enough person. She probably thought the rules were dumb too.

"Your eyelids will close by themselves."

Her eyelids lowered quietly, like dancers bowing.

I counted slowly to ten. "That's good. You're feeling very good. Just rest now."

A manila folder with my name on it was lying on her desk. In it were my college application, my board scores, and a handwritten report on the hypnosis incidents. The conclusion said I had difficulty accepting discipline and was on academic probation for poor grades.

I replaced the folder and said in my most soothing voice, "When you wake up, you'll feel great. You won't have any memory of this trance. No memory of it at all. You'll think Ellen Burns is a nice, interesting girl with no problems. Nod your head if you understand me."

The Dean nodded.

I was curious to know what kind of dog she might be, but someone could walk in, and I wanted to put this unexpected opportunity to use. Several acquaintances of mine were going to Harvard for the summer.

"When you wake up, I'm going to ask you about recommending me for Harvard Summer School, and you're going to think that's a wonderful idea, in spite of my academic record. You'll say that Harvard is going to help me with my authority problems. Do you understand?"

She nodded again.

I counted slowly backward from ten to one, then said, "Wake up now."

The Dean's eyes opened. "I feel great. You're a wonderful girl, Ellen, with no serious problems."

I put out my cigarette in her brown glass ashtray. "Dean Pottle, I wanted to ask you about Harvard Summer School."

I had made several unsuccessful attempts to lose my virginity at Duke, and Harvard had begun to seem like a possible solution.

My roommate at Duke was named Darlene. Darlene was an angular, good-looking girl with sharp cheekbones and black hair cut in a smooth pageboy that swayed when she moved.

She had been coaching me on the loss of my virginity. In high school I had read an article that said sperm could swim right through your underpants, so whenever I got close to intercourse with a boy, I imagined microscopic tadpoles swimming desperately through cotton fibers the size of the columns at Stonehenge. And I was distracted by other thoughts: germs swim back and forth between mouths; the tongue is a muscle and disappears down the back of the throat, so what is it attached to?

"I want to be normal," I kept saying to Darlene. "I want to lose my normal virginity. Normally."

"I'll fix you up with Don. He doesn't have any experience either. You can learn together."

"Darlene, how could that be a good idea?"

"Trust me, it's a good idea."

Darlene arranged for Don to take me to dinner at a restaurant called Chicken in the Rough. The restaurant's logo was a long-legged chicken in a tam-o'-shanter swinging a golf club. Sitting in one of the dark red booths, I felt as if I were in a dentist's waiting room.

Don was a melancholy boy with dark, dramatic looks. His thick black eyebrows moved when he chewed. When he bit into a chicken leg I pointed at the tiny string of meat hanging from the bone. "That's a ligament. In the fourth grade they told us that you could see what ligaments were when you ate fried chicken."

He looked uncertain.

"I only eat white meat," I said.

"Why are you telling me this?"

"Once the top of my mouth started getting loose. I could move the skin with my tongue. So I went to the dentist and said, 'The roof of my mouth is rotting off. I have some terrible disease.' He looked in my mouth and said, 'Do you eat soup?' So I said of course I eat soup. 'Do you drink coffee?' Yes I drink coffee. 'Well you're drinking it too hot.' I was kind of disappointed, you know? I thought I had some rare disease."

Don put down his chicken leg. "I don't know what Darlene said to you, but we don't have to do anything. We really don't."

"Could we drink some beer?" I said.

So, while the fried chicken and fried potatoes congealed in their grease and the salad wilted in its pool of dressing, Don and I drank a pitcher of beer, and I began to relax. Don was a good enough looking boy, although he lacked the wildness I found compelling in Darlene's boyfriend, who had taken the mike away from the singer of a black blues band at a fraternity party and sung a version of "Put Your Head on My Shoulder" called "Put Your Legs Round My Shoulders."

Don had been raised by his grandmother in Greensboro, North Carolina. When he graduated he wanted to be a newspaper reporter in a small Southern town. His grandmother's lifelong wish was to meet Lawrence Welk, and some day Don hoped to arrange that for her.

"I have to go to the bathroom," I said.

In the bathroom I confronted the most serious obstacle to the loss of my virginity: under my skirt I was wearing a panty girdle. I hadn't meant to wear the girdle, but when I was dressing I kept hearing my mother's voice saying *any woman looks better in a girdle,* so I'd put it on experimentally, and it felt so secure, so bracing, I'd left it on. Now I didn't know what to do about it. I considered taking it off, but it was too bulky for the pocket of my trenchcoat.

What I did have in the pocket of my trenchcoat was a Norform vaginal suppository that Darlene had given me to insert "just before intercourse." It was supposed to lubricate me, a word which made me feel like a car. But when was "just before intercourse"? After I peed, I inserted the suppository and pulled the girdle back into place, feeling deeply relieved: the girdle meant I couldn't make love, but the suppository meant I sincerely wanted to.

On the way out of Chicken in the Rough I stopped at the bar in the front room and downed a double shot of bourbon, neat. "I never met anybody like you," Don said.

"I'm just normal," I said, feeling a rush of love for the shot glass. "I'm normal for me. Really."

The November night was inky blue, the air clean and brisk. Don put his arm around me as we walked. The bourbon warmed my blood and the Norform melting made me feel odd. I stopped Don on the street and kissed him on the mouth the way I thought someone in a movie might kiss.

Soon we were in the dormitory parking lot, leaning against a stranger's empty car, still kissing cinematically. Then we were in the back seat of the same car, half lying down. Just when the kissing was getting boring, Don put his hand up my skirt. I had never had anyone's hand up my skirt before.

His fingers moved tentatively up my legs. "My god, what's this?" he said, encountering the girdle.

I wanted to explain, but I felt too dizzy.

His hand wandered around the flesh of my thigh, then moved inward and upward. The dissolved Norform was all over the crotch of the girdle. "My god, you're wet," he said.

I tried to hold still.

"Okay," he mumbled, sliding two fingers awkwardly up the leg of the panty girdle. When he touched me something flashed in my head, and my hips pushed hard against his hand.

"Oh my god, oh my god," he said, pulling his hand free.

"I'll take it off," I said. "No problem. No problem, really."

Don was still crouched over his hand. His fingers glistened in the darkness. A lump appeared behind his knuckle and swelled while I watched.

"It's ... it's growing," I said.

"It's sprained," he said.

Don's hand was not sprained, but he had broken a blood vessel behind his knuckle. Overnight the blood spread under his skin, turning it puffy and greenish. By the end of the week his hand had turned black, with a dark red palm.

Apparently Don told no one about the girdle, perhaps out of kindness, perhaps to save face, but he did admit to Darlene's boyfriend that his injury was "sort of sexual."

"*Sort of* sexual," Darlene's boyfriend kept saying to her. "*Sort of* sexual."

I became famous almost overnight. Boys I had never heard of called me, and Don followed me to several classes. "We'll try it again. We've got to try it again." He looked vulnerable, stunned by love, extending his black hand.

I never wanted to see Don again in my whole life, so when my mother telephoned and said, "Why don't you fly home this weekend and get measured for your hand-sewn human-hair wig?" I felt relieved at the chance to leave school.

My mother met me at the airport in Charleston, just before midnight on a Friday. She was wearing purple toreador pants, a gold lamé shirt, gold lamé slippers, a stroller-length mink coat, and large dark glasses. "I don't want anyone to *recognize* me," she whispered, looking uneasily around the deserted airport. "That's why I have on the *glasses.*"

For two years my mother had been addicted to diet pills. "*Ambars,*" she would say in a singsongy voice, "I was a different person before I found *Ambars! The am* stands for amphetamine and the *bar* stands for barbiturate! The amphetamine speeds you *up,* and the barbiturate slows you *down!* You don't have any *app*etite, but you're not *nerv*ous!"

Before my mother found diet pills, she did not speak in italics and exclamations, and she was not wiry and loud. Before she found diet pills, she was heavy and depressed. Now she liked to scrub the tiles in the bathroom with a toothbrush, and she had fired the maid because she said it felt so good to push the vacuum cleaner around and polish the silverware herself. She liked to get down between the tines of the forks. "It takes *patience,*" she said. "I have lots of *patience!*"

Her arms vibrated as she embraced me. "Doesn't it look real?" she whispered. "Isn't it *astounding?*" She patted her French twist.

Her hair was so smoothly arranged that no false scalp showed, but the elegant twist looked odd: My mother's real hair is naturally curly.

The next day I was staring at myself in the beautician's mirror. "Thank you, Momma." Like Momma's wig, Aunt Rose's wig, and Sister-Girl's wig, mine was set in a French twist.

The four of us were standing around the beauty parlor. We had a monolithic look, like a gang. "The French Twist Gang," Sister-Girl said quietly, meeting my eyes in the mirror.

Sister-Girl had become large and statuesque, a natural blonde with a sweet smile and a quiet manner. A year older than me, she had declined college graciously, as if she were not hungry for dessert.

Her mother, Rose, was my mother's sister. "We all look alike in these wigs," Rose said, "but I'm the inflated version." Rose didn't care for the diet pills because they made her heart hurt.

Rose was built square, "like a refrigerator," she said cheerfully, and she wheezed almost all the time. "There's just not much room for air in there," Sister-Girl had once remarked.

After my wig fitting, we all went shopping, and I bought a garter belt. "I'm not wearing girdles anymore, Momma," I said. "Don't ask. I'm just not, no matter what."

The wig not only changed how I looked, it changed how I felt about myself. When I got back to school, boys stopped pursuing me. Perhaps they no longer recognized the black hand girl. I abandoned not only hypnosis but parties, and my study habits improved. By the time I went to Harvard Summer School, I had been taken off academic probation. Dean Pottle thought it was her confidence in me that had "turned me around."

At Harvard Summer School I met the man I would eventually marry. On a sticky Saturday night in a drugstore in Harvard Square I was buying a new copy of *Peyton Place* because the pages of my copy were falling out. Nicky Sommers was buying a book called *Thinking About the Unthinkable,* which I assumed was pornographic. It turned out to be about nuclear war.

My copy of *Peyton Place* was worn out because, in the long afternoons in my apartment in Back Bay, while my roommate, Dottie Plant, was out waitressing, I had discovered masturbation.

When I was wearing the wig, I dressed like a Duke sorority girl and studied calmly, but when I was not wearing the wig a certain wildness seemed to overtake me. So I wore my French twist almost every day and I was making very good grades. Dean Pottle was going to be proud.

My wig got gummy with dirt, and I had to give it up for six days to have it professionally cleaned. Without the wig I began to wear white lipstick. I combed my hair out straight, drank scotch on the rocks while I studied, and imagined I was a beatnik like the ones I'd seen in *Time* magazine. I was at Harvard and no one in the South need ever know I was behaving this way.

Sexually, I began to experiment. I read the sex scenes in *Peyton Place* and drifted into them like hypnosis, my old teddy bear clutched tight between my legs. I felt bad about my teddy bear, who was not holding up well under this assault, but as long as I didn't touch myself directly, I was sure I couldn't be doing anything wrong. Then, one afternoon when it was too hot in the apartment to wear a lot of clothes, the situation got out of hand, so to speak. I bled and it wasn't my period. The word masturbation came to me. I realized I had deflowered myself.

I was getting my wig back on Monday. On Saturday night, since I was ruined anyway, I went to a drugstore in Harvard Square in my white lipstick, my black jersey and tight black jeans, to buy a new copy of *Peyton Place.* I was standing furtively behind the paperback rack when this greasy, stringy-haired boy in Levi's that looked like they hadn't been washed in weeks said to me, "Are you from down home?" He had an unmistakable Southern drawl.

I didn't answer, of course. My mother's warning about the Boston Strangler had made a vivid impression on me, so vivid, in fact, that when I tried to swear off *Peyton Place,* fantasies about the Boston Strangler had drifted in to replace them.

"Southerners look different," the boy continued. I looked at him out of the corner of my eye. "We walk different, or something."

It seemed unlikely that the Boston Strangler was a Southerner, so I looked him full in the face. "Where are you from?"

"Texas." He had a nice smile and crooked teeth.

"Texas isn't the South," I said. "Texas is the West."

If I hadn't agreed to go drink beer with Nicky Sommers, I wouldn't have told him funny stories about Sister-Girl and Aunt Rose, and if he hadn't laughed so much at my stories I wouldn't have drunk so much, and if I hadn't drunk so much I wouldn't have ended up back at my apartment with him. When he kissed me I put his hands on my throat. "Squeeze just a little bit," I said, "I want to see how it feels." If Dottie Plant had been home I wouldn't have ended up on the sofa with him, and if he hadn't been lying with his skinny hip jammed against my tight black jeans, I wouldn't have drifted into *Peyton Place.*

Your nipples are as hard as diamonds, the irresistible man in *Peyton Place* had whispered.

Do it to me, the woman whispered back.

Nicky unbuttoned my shirt and cupped his whole hand over my breast.

"Diamonds!" I shouted, and we both began to shudder. I was extremely embarrassed and shut my eyes tight.

"Hey," Nicky kept saying, "hey," only it wasn't as if he expected an answer.

I was breathing like I'd been running.

"Wow," Nicky whispered. "You had an orgasm."

"I certainly did not." I was trying not to cry.

"Wow. I never gave a girl an orgasm. Hey. Wow."

When Nicky arrived at my apartment for our first real date on Monday night, he had cut his hair and shaved so close his jaw looked raw and scraped. We were going to dinner at a restaurant where, Nicky had promised, the menu would be written in French.

Nicky was wearing a suit and tie, and on his feet were grown-up, lace-up, men's shoes. In his hand was a bouquet of daisies.

I had picked up my wig from the cleaners. I was wearing a blue dress, a garter belt, hose and high heels.

"Your hair looks great that way," Nicky said.

We stared dumbly at each other, like people who have fallen in love.

Pulling Proofs

Bruce Brooks

O ne evening eight months ago, Buzzy and I were giggling over glasses of yellow champagne, celebrating her first day as my "cohabitor" (her word), when she brought an especially snappy laugh to an upbeat stop, rubbed her bubble-invaded nose to compose herself, and solemnly pulled a package out of a nearby suitcase I had thought was emptied. To my expectant eye, the package had all the markings of a large tin of smoked oysters I had openly admired that afternoon during our first official joint grocery binge. I had already presented to Buzzy a bottle of Spanish olives stuffed with almonds and a set of Scandinavian measuring spoons, which I had snatched from shelves and hidden beneath paper products in our burgeoning cart as she looked the other way. Certainly she could have snuck me a gift the same way. I smiled, and reached for the package with a gracious nod.

As soon as I touched it, I knew it was not the tin of oysters. Nevertheless, I enjoyed the tender excitement a mysterious gift brings, and placed the thing on the table to open it.

Now, I like to unwrap gifts with patience, peeling away my illusions about them as they peek out from layers of paper. But this package would not be toyed with. The instant I touched it, the tape let go, and the stiff white paper sprang open like a box lid on a spring. And there it was: a black paperback book with gaudy gold letters all over it. I nodded my thanks with a tight-lipped smile, and rotated it so that I could read the title. Buzzy delivered a serious little speech. "Toby. If you are going to live with me, live with a woman, then really, you simply must know this book. You have to *read* it, Toby. If we were twenty, or even twenty-five, it wouldn't matter. But we are both thirty, and we can't afford to fool around many more years, and, well, this book sort of provokes adult considerations of the way people contend. It's all in there, Toby; it *matters.*"

I grunted soberly, and did a fine job of hiding my disappointment. You see, not only had I set my sights on smoked oysters; I had also hoped briefly that the package would *not* contain a book. Buzzy had never given me a book in the months that we had known each other, and I had been quite happy about her restraint. It's not that I have anything against reading. I read quite a lot—I subscribe to five printing journals, two quarterlies of science and technology, a chapbook series of nature poems, and an ice hockey magazine. I *love* words. I am, after all, a printer. Who could possibly appreciate language more than a printer?

But books make bad gifts. What the giver extends as intimate code, the recipient can easily find to be detached artifice. Too often, a person depends on a book to communicate to a friend something that could simply be said without the unnecessary intrusion of a third voice using words unnatural to either party. Books are especially dangerous when they are presented to mark an auspicious occasion: they do not transmit layered significance very precisely. The reader cannot feel his work is done when he has figured out what a sentence is trying to convey, and what an author means behind it; he must go on and construct some numinous intention at a third remove.

This can make a book an enemy. I have flung my frustrated disdain on quite a few masterpieces because they served as important gifts. In my life I have hated *The Little Prince,* which my grandmother gave me when I discovered at age six that I liked cutting up sweet potatoes and watching them sprout in water; *Great Expectations,* which my fifth grade teacher gave me shortly after I was orphaned at ten; and *The Autobiography of Benjamin Franklin,* which the same eager grandmother presented to me on the occasion of my formal apprenticeship to a letterpress printer, at seventeen. Now, from Buzzy, there was another.

I thanked her, and promised to read it right away. But I was not optimistic. I disliked the book from my first glance at its cover, which had been designed by a typographical dunce who flaunted his incompetence, in the hope of being "fresh," by breaking half a dozen timeless laws of graphic design and good taste. Gold cartoon letters with fake ligatures and bogus serifs had been crammed into a flush-right jumble so grossly unfit for the book's title that the last of the three words had to be *hyphenated,* for crying out loud:

THE

GOLDEN

NOTE-

BOOK

I pitied Doris Lessing, the author, for being made to bear the bad impression her novel's silly cover implanted. I was certain no one could begin to read this book with a perfectly open mind. However, I promised Buzzy I would do just that, and did not bother her with my misgivings.

I tried to keep my word: the next day I started reading *The Golden Notebook.* I made myself a pot of cocoa, put on my red mukluks with the navy blue manatees embroidered on the toes, took the telephone off the hook, and curled myself into an armchair. These preparations were necessary—if I were to read intelligently, my concentration had to be coddled by comforts and silence. Perhaps this is because I rarely read long books. Buzzy reads constantly, and her attention has an uncanny durability. I always admired the way she used reading to make full use of the moments that slip away in the course of a day: she reads while waiting for her coffee to cool, while listening to records of chamber music (she says the complexity of ensembles containing more than six instruments demands her full attention, however), even while flossing her teeth if she happens to have a heavy limp book that can be propped open while her hands are occupied. I once measured her progress through an old gift edition of *Seven Pillars of Wisdom* by yards of discarded waxy string instead of by weeks (131 yards for 658 pages).

All of this amazes me. If I am to skim an article on the new laser-sensitized papers or the comeback of Bodoni typefaces, I have to retreat to the printery behind the apartment, where the distractions surrounding me at least bear a relevance to the material I peruse. As for novels—the only one I have finished in the past ten years is a replica second edition of *Tristram Shandy*, which was notable to me only because it was so innovatively printed.

So I set myself up carefully for *The Golden Notebook,* and cracked it open. Right away, I had trouble getting started; I had to read the first page four or five times, to get my mental wheels spinning. But then I felt myself settle and relax. A certain attentive ease came over me. The process felt very smooth, and Lessing's story suddenly caught me: these two women were talking, and then a man came in, and the three of them shifted into a new discussion and talked, and then the man suggested they all go skiing. So they put on bright clothing, dressing right there in the same room, and then they went out in the snow and set out across the countryside. It was lovely country. They kept talking all the while about abstract aspects of relationships. Then they came upon a pond and saw a manatee in it. While they watched the manatee, two people appeared and skied over to say hello, and lo and behold the two newcomers were Buzzy and me! *Well, hello!,* I thought, *Look at us right here in this book!* But then some part of my awareness performed the realization that our presence did not really fit with the act of reading the novel, and my mind made a little twist, and pulled me awake.

I blinked. The pond was gone. I stared at the black and gold cover of the book, which had closed in my lap as soon as I slipped into sleep. I thumbed through the first few pages and found that I had made it up to page three. I yawned, vowed to do better the next day, and went out to the printery to finish up a stationery order that was to be picked up that afternoon.

The next day I tried again. This time I spread the book out on the cold white enamel of the kitchen table, next to a steaming cup of black coffee. I leaned over it with my head in my hands; the cold enamel stung my elbows, keeping me alert. I cut into the novel with determination. This time I made it up to page five, where everyone starts saying "*Well?*" in italics. "*Well?*" says one and then "*Well?*" says another, and so on.

Well, it really put me off. I mean, "well" is hardly the sort of word that deserves italic emphasis. Lessing and her publisher were constructing a cheap reliance on typography for articulations that ought to have come from textual substance; such dependence not only indicated a shortcoming of the story but tended to devalue the impact of italic typefaces. Soon everything would get italicized, and emphasis would be sought from a new fillip—squiggly underlines, perhaps, or oversized asterisks.

This sort of carelessness typified the liberties writers and publishers took with print these days, without a thought to the fact that they were ruining the equipoise of type and idea upon which their business depended.

I slammed the book shut and stormed out to my printery. On the Linotype in twelve-point Goudy I dashed out a sardonic letter to the editor of *Printing Impressions* on the general escalation of italic abuse. When I had finished, I read it over, and decided that perhaps it might make a fair article if I revised it coolly. I spent the next hour expanding and rewriting it, pulled a clean copy on a sheet of twenty-four-pound rag, slipped it into a manila envelope after drying, and walked to the post office to send it to the magazine. (Three weeks later I received a notice of acceptance and a check for $300.) I never quite returned to my reading that day.

In the next few weeks I gave *The Golden Notebook* numerous chances to fascinate me. I tried to read it in every possible situation conducive to concentration. I read it stretched out in a hot bath laced with sandalwood oil, and I read it sitting upright in a ladder-back chair. I read it by the pink light of the sun at dawn, and the yellow light of a kerosene lamp at midnight. I read it in a starched shirt and corduroys. I read it naked. I read it with prevailing moods of zeal, wrath, adoration, skepticism, lightheartedness, profundity—each of which I whipped up beforehand in the hope that bringing a definite bias with me might give Lessing and her characters a little extra something to snag.

Nothing worked. In about six weeks I reached only page forty-nine, at which point someone named Molly says, "The point is, these letters were interchangeable. Discounting handwriting of course." Letters interchangeable! Discounting handwriting! As though the sense of words could ever be transmitted without formal contribution of the letters in which they were rendered! As though such complementary articulation could ever be discounted! I was outraged. I ran out to my Linotype and wrote a scathing critique of contemporary graphic disregard; I sold the piece to *The Letters Review* for $500, but I never really returned to *The Golden Notebook*.

At first, Buzzy asked me how my reading was progressing. I always said something like, "Oh I'm plugging away!" But after a couple of months we began to develop our own intricacies of contention, and did not need Doris Lessing to provoke adult considerations for us.

It wasn't that we had fights, or anything like them. Instead, we had peculiar moments—of disengaged concern, misaligned enthusiasms. Pleasant things were our worst foes: enjoyments we began together we finished apart. Buzzy had particular trouble with laughter. Her trouble thus was frequent, because almost every time we were together for more than ten minutes we reached some moment of shared amusement and started laughing. But suddenly Buzzy would stop cold, with a wrinkle in her forehead—to think.

The first few times this happened, she included me in her deliberation. It seems she has a need to test what should be her best moments, by introducing a detached intellectual challenge to her happiness at the height of its spin: *Stop,* she thinks to herself, *and consider: are you TRULY enjoying this?* Of course, the act of challenging the fun is enough to spoil it, and she must answer, *No, I guess not.* I suppose what she loses in gaiety she gains in discernment; but the gloom on her face always makes such a benefit seem a queer prize at best.

I soon understood that Buzzy's interior parsing of mirth was beyond my ability to help, however sincere my wishes for her success. When she started studying herself in the middle of one of our laughs, I would hang around only long enough to ascertain that my presence was useless, and I would leave, giving her a hopeful squeeze.

I decided the best action I could take was to provide Buzzy with enjoyments that might survive her challenges. I had to ignore the irony that by amusing her I was setting the scene for despondency. So I started working hard to make her happy. I took care of all the small chores Buzzy found annoying—watering the plants, sweeping the floors, washing the clothes, straightening the pictures on the walls, discarding the junk mail. I closed the printery at four o'clock every afternoon so that I could have a good dinner on the table when Buzzy came home from the birth-control clinic where she worked as a counselor. I baked breads. I brewed beer. Outside, in my shop, I took on a dazzling rush of jobs and got up before dawn to handle them, whipping through posters and stationery and business cards and pamphlets so that Buzzy and I could spend bright Saturdays in elegant Georgetown shops, buying good things for our home. We purchased two puce chairs from Denmark, three cerulean rugs from Pakistan, a clear glass teapot from France. The complete Duke Ellington recordings from 1929 to '41, and a boxed set of Bach harpsichord partitas, with scores. A food processor. A halogen lamp. A waterbed. But nothing helped; Buzzy kept sulking, and we continued our odd misfires, which we never quite succeeded in discussing.

This brings us up to the day before yesterday. I woke up in the morning and found Buzzy up a full two hours earlier than usual. She was dressed. She even wore her overcoat. She said, "Good morning," but I could not reply right away because I saw to my surprise that she was packing a suitcase.

"I'm going to New York for a couple of days," she explained. I stared at the tangle of tights and underwear she pushed into her small valise. "I'm sorry, Toby, but I just have to think about my situation here, by myself. My mother's out of town up there, so I'll have the house to myself. I just have to think, pin a few things down. About me, about you, too. I'm not altogether sure that our . . . system here is really *functioning*, you know? There never seems to be very much to show for our time spent, or something . . . I think I expected more of a sense of *context,* more of a feeling that living together, a man and a woman, was a *muscular* sort of thing. I don't know, I just want to think a few days. I hope you understand. I'll be back in a couple of days, probably, and we'll see what signs there are, okay? Maybe . . . you could try and do some thinking too. Men, women, how they fit together, us, you, me . . . "

We kissed briefly and she left.

I had a lot of printing to do, so I was unable to devote my attention to Buzzy's proposal that I do some thinking until late afternoon. I closed the shop, returned to the apartment, and tried to begin thinking while preparing a smoked salmon loaf. No luck—I guess if I am chopping celery, I have to be *chopping celery,* not musing upon the musculature of cohabitative contexts. Once the salmon was in the oven, I sat down and devoted myself to thinking.

Nothing came. I changed chairs, put on a sweater, closed the curtains. Nothing. My intellect could not be pressed into an engagement with the items Buzzy had raised. There was no fascination with the mechanics of relationships. I could gain no general entry into the matters of system and function—my mind was like one of the noble gases, refusing to mingle molecules with the substance of the issues. When the bell on the oven timer signaled that dinner was ready, I gave up in relief, thinking *Geez, this is as difficult as reading that novel Buzzy gave me.*

The thought stopped me in my tracks. *That novel Buzzy gave me.* What was the title? I remembered that the book had been about muscular adult relationships, fairly rippling with context. I spooned out some salmon loaf and thought about the fat novel. Where was it? If I found it, I might be able to read it by the time Buzzy returned. At the moment this seemed easier than thinking about Buzzy's points—more efficient, even. Perhaps a careful assimilation of the book could accomplish what the thinking might: perhaps I could consider in the novel exactly the issues Buzzy wanted me to consider relative to our particular situation. Who knows what I might learn from the book?

She had given it to me at the beginning of our life together, but maybe it was not too late even now.

The Golden Notebook—that was its title. I sprang up from my salmon after a couple of bites and went to look for the book, its trashy gold and black cover flashing in my mind's eye. In a few minutes I found it at the bottom of a stack of printing journals, in an antique brass bucket beside one of the puce chairs. I sat down eagerly to read it.

But no, this time it did not take long to realize it was still impenetrable. I simply could not keep the page and its depictions before me—my vision and mind kept slipping off. Yet I was determined, and I had no time to experiment with sandalwood baths and cocoa and the light of dawn: I was down to my last forty or fifty hours, and I had to get 666 pages of print behind my eyes. How could I force myself to do it?

The answer was not long in coming: I simply had to set the whole novel in type.

Perfect! My problem with the novel was an inability to maintain concentration, so I would take it to my Linotype, where I am professionally conditioned to concentrate on *every single letter* of the text I am setting. I am an absolute wizard of focus once my fingers start dancing over the feather-touch keys, once the brass matrices start clacking as they assemble at my command, once the galleys start filling with bright inches of silvery type. Not one comma of Doris Lessing's masterpiece would escape me now. I would see it all.

I ran out to the printery to check my supplies. I had plenty of lead, though I really only needed a couple of pigs: I could dump each galley back into the Linotype crucible as soon as the galley was full because I did not need to keep the type to print anything. Pure composing was all that mattered. I turned the crucible on and ran back into the apartment to gather supplies while the lead in the pot melted. From the bedroom I grabbed a sweatshirt, from the living room I grabbed *The Golden Notebook*, and from the kitchen I grabbed a loaf of fresh sourdough bread, a slab of the salmon loaf, and a jar of instant coffee. There was a hot plate and water in the printery. I was all set for a long haul at the Linotype—I did not intend to stop composing until I popped the last period on page 666.

In two hours I whizzed through seventy-nine pages, filling six galleys. It went so smoothly and rapidly that I did not stop to recycle the lead, but shoved each galley onto the rack and hung a spare pig on the metal feed mechanism. I was setting in eight-point Schoolbook Oldstyle, in double columns of thirty picas each. The Schoolbook seems tiny at first glance, and many people complain that it is illegibly old-fashioned, but they are simply weak readers with no ocular determination. Every year, Schoolbook Oldstyle finishes at the top in exhaustive tests run by the Institute of Visual-Verbal Communication in Chicago, consistently outpointing all contemporary eight-point faces in a dozen indices of technical readability. In Schoolbook Oldstyle, *The Golden Notebook* would be easier to *read* than it was to read!

When I stood up to stretch after the eighth galley, I found myself pulling a proof of the first page out of habit, instead of sliding the type directly back into the pot. I glanced at the proof. It was *gorgeous*. That was when the idea came to me:

Why not pull a proof of every galley and put together a handmade copy of the book as a gift for Buzzy?

The pure beauties of the first galley proof inspired me. The Oldstyle characters stood out so clearly that the paragraphs seemed to sing, and the noble proportions of the double columns gave the text a legendary quality—as if Toby Hutch's *Golden Notebook* were descended from William Caxton's *Morte d'Arthur*!

I read the proofs of the first six galleys and corrected the few mistakes. Before pulling final proofs I had the inspiration to add a double hairline border to the margins. This was a stroke of genius: the rule gave a contained bit of dash to the classicism of the print. I knew I had a very special project on my hands. This book was truly going to "matter," as Buzzy had said eight months ago.

I had to hurry. First, I needed some fine paper. I put on my sweatshirt, locked the printery, and jogged six blocks to the shop of a papermaker with whom I do a little business. He spent three years at a guild school in Wessex, England, and his small, varied lots of paper inspire in me the sort of raptures some people feel in the presence of great paintings. I often buy odd packets of his paper for no specific printing purpose, purely in the spirit of aesthetic collection. He has a similar appreciation of my craft, and has commissioned several sign and text jobs from me simply so he could savor the impression.

His shop was closed. He lives upstairs, so I rapped on his door. He opened it and told me it was after midnight. I told him I needed some precious folio stock. He thought for a moment, then took me downstairs and showed me exactly what I wanted: a thirty-pound mock vellum the color of buttermilk, with a deckle edge like duck down. The opacity was unassailable, the life of the hue eternal. My friend had just made it during the previous weeks, so he had enough to stock my project. I bought one hundred folios for $100 and returned to my printery.

The next few hours passed in a flurry of interdependent processes. My printery became an aviary of folio wings unfurled over clothesline for drying. I had a palette of inks spread out on the lockup stones, for I had come up with a chromatic scheme: a little way into the text I found that *The Golden Notebook* was composed of not one but six narrative strains—one straight descriptive narration and five different texts representing five notebooks written by one of the characters. The notebooks are referred to by the colors of their covers: red, yellow, blue, black, and gold.

Naturally, I leapt at this chance to lend a complementary graphic distinction to the text. I decided not to print the words of each notebook in the indicated shades of ink, but rather to adjust the color of the border rule enclosing the words. So the contents of the red notebook were now bordered by a double hairline of nazdarin crimson, the yellow notebook by a seventy percent cadmium, the blue by a deep indigo, and the black by a very pale gray that accentuated the ebony richness of the print's ink. For the gold notebook, which came later in the text, I planned a gilt ink enclosure.

The proofs of the notebook pages thus required two separate impressions, one for black text and one for colored border, and this new intricacy slowed me down a bit. Nevertheless, I made good time in my progress through the book: in twelve hours I had blazed through 280 pages.

As I set the type and pulled the proofs I grew increasingly excited at the prospect of presenting the book to Buzzy. The gift would mean so much to her! Here she had given me a flimsy, ill-pressed, off-center pulp thing with a hyphen on the cover, and she was going to get it back as an aesthetic masterpiece composed precisely for her. If the shabby paperback had been "important," certainly the handmade edition would mean a thousand times more. I could envision her turning the pages slowly, scanning the graces of the Oldstyle, tracing with her soft fingertips the neat impression of the hairline rule, shivering with the structural resonance of the double columns. With every new proof I realized this book would be the apotheosis of my *giving*—it was composed of so many expressions of my particular insights, my private tendernesses, my unique inspirations, all mingling and reflecting in a layered richness that I offered for Buzzy's patient exegesis.

In addition, Buzzy would have the happy knowledge, as soon as she saw the book, that I had consumed every letter of *The Golden Notebook*—that I had read it not once but *twice*, in setting it and then proofreading it. Thus she would be able to feel secure that I had assimilated whatever it was she had wanted me to get when she gave me the thing.

Such inspirations kept me going hour after hour. I fell asleep only once, at page 422, for perhaps half an hour. When I woke up I made a pot of coffee and ate some salmon smeared on a chunk of bread. This refreshed me, and I raced through the next three galleys in record time. I was animated by the strange amphetamine of pure productivity, a vitality that springs naturally from the processes of printing. I grew more exhilarated with every brassy clack of the mats. I burned with boosted zeal at every rumble of the proof press. The folios dried, folded their wings, and nested on a clean imposing stone. Others flew up in their place. The discarded pages of the paperback book (I tore off the sections I set) filled a wastebasket. I sped on.

Finally, after more than thirty hours, I tapped out the last word on page 666—"separated"—and set the last period. Quickly I pulled the last proof and noted with satisfaction that I had finished a string of five galleys without a single typographical error. It was done. *The Golden Notebook* was finished.

While the final folios dried, I planned my binding. I wanted to stitch the folios together and bind them in a stiff cover backed with rich gold lamé fabric. I oiled my stitching press, warmed my bindery glue, selected my stiffest chipboard. In a pan of water, inks, and Varsol, I marbled endpapers for the inside covers. Now all I lacked was the gold cloth. A walk to Georgetown would provide that.

I locked the printery and set off briskly in the chilly night air. The moon sat high and white, the wind blew with the gentle force of breath. I was invigorated, giddy with accomplishment. But when I found the fabric store at Q and Wisconsin dark and locked, I realized suddenly that it was about two in the morning—and my zest puckered. I had forgotten all about store hours in my haste to meet the deadline of Buzzy's return. It was late. It was *too* late. I could not wait until morning, now—she would be back in the morning, and I would have nothing to show for my weekend but red eyes and a mess of paper and chipboard.

Without a proper binding, the whole book was worthless. A printing masterpiece must combine perfections—the magic depends on the uncanny consonance of all elements, inks contrasting with papers, the limpness of riffling pages contrasting with the stiffness of covers that swing like gates, the tiny intricacies of the type contrasting with the monolithic face of solid color on the cover. I knew I had no dignified fabric at home. I did not even have a cheesecloth with which to bind the book. No stores were open. I looked around the dark streets, and faced the cold fact that my project—perhaps even my life with Buzzy!—was doomed.

And suddenly I was tired, terribly tired. My sense of purpose vanished. I wandered. From the looks I received from the few people I passed in the strange streets, I gathered that I must have been moaning or mumbling, but I did not care to listen or stop. I just walked, turned corners, lingered in alleys. I was adrift. My printery was forgotten.

As I said, I passed a few people now and then. I did not look at most of them very long, because they all seemed dull and dark and ugly. But then, after I had wandered for perhaps an hour, I found my gaze lingering on a young blonde woman who crossed the street in front of me, passed beneath a streetlight, and entered a small bar. It took me a few seconds to focus on the aspect of her appearance that had attracted my unwitting attention; but by analyzing the memory of her passage through the pool of yellow light beneath the streetlamp, I isolated it: I had seen a flash of gold lamé between the lapels of her coat.

Immediately my lethargy and despondency left me. The book project started to click in my mind like a Linotype switched on. My enthusiasm retingled, my determination reared. I followed the woman's path, and stepped into the bar.

It was a dark, quiet place with only a dozen people inside. I had no trouble finding the young blonde. She was standing by herself, brow knitted over a highball glass on the bar. She looked sad. I moved to a spot beside her, and quietly ordered a beer. She looked up at me. I smiled. She frowned down at her glass, then looked back up at me. I smiled again. After a moment, she smiled too.

I do not recall exactly what I said to her in the bar, perhaps because the words were so unnatural to me that I am unable to think of them coming from my persona, in the intimate imagination that serves as memory. I do remember that we smiled, and spoke in hushed tones, and laughed once; and I recall the satisfaction I felt when she signaled that my ploy had succeeded so far, by agreeing to take a walk with me.

We strolled in the night down dark streets. She took my arm. She began to squeeze it. We whispered, smiled, cooed. I grew warm and excited as I felt the culmination of my desires drawing closer. She pressed against me as we walked. I saw flashes of gold cloth partly covering the large round breasts she rubbed against my arm. We walked, slowed, and finally stopped, on an empty street not far from a streetlamp.

She moved to face me, and gazed into my face with a tender look. I smiled, for the hundredth time, and lowered my gaze to her breasts. She moaned as though I had touched them, and rolled her shoulders slightly.

The cloth looked lovely. I was trembling with expectation. My only worries were that there was an insufficient amount, and that the fabric was too thick. I studied her shape: she was fairly plump, with a broad midsection. I tried to superimpose, in my mind's eye, the folio-sized chipboards on the breadth of her stomach and the corresponding zipper-split expanse of her back—and I calculated that the blouse would just suffice.

She whispered the name I had fabricated for myself, and inched closer to me, hands at her sides. I smiled, stared again at her breasts, and slowly placed my right hand over the left one. She groaned, and pushed the soft flesh against my palm. I softly massaged the nipple, and felt it grow hot and hard beneath my touch, beneath the cloth. The transference of texture and temperature through the fabric was almost immediate—I was certain the lamé was thin enough to serve as the binding material. I grinned in anticipation.

"Yes," she whispered, "yes, you like it, don't you? Do you like it?"

"Oh, yes," I said, "certainly. It's perfect."

She smiled coyly and stepped closer. "Maybe you ought to try the other one."

"No thank you," I said with a wink. "I only need this one, really."

She looked puzzled. I removed my hand.

"Do you . . . do you want . . . ?" She rubbed her hands tightly from her breasts to her waist, over the expanse of lamé.

"Yes," I said. "How much will it cost me?"

Her eyes widened, her jaw quivered, and she stepped back. "How . . . What do you think I . . . what do . . . why do you think . . . "

I had been afraid of this. Naturally I hoped she was not especially fond of the blouse and would sell it readily. But she was acting so offended at the prospect of parting with it that I needed to win her quickly with unction or money. Money was easier. I offered her twenty dollars.

"*Twenty dollars!*" she yelled. Her eyes were blazing. I had not counted on such fierce intransigence.

"I think twenty is generous," I said. "It's not as if the thing is new. It might even be badly worn, for all I know; plus it probably smells, and I haven't time to wash it."

She screamed and swung a fist at me. I blocked it, and she put her hands to her face and started sobbing. This was certainly more emotion than I had expected.

"Okay, look," I said, taking out a twenty dollar bill and a ten. "Here's thirty dollars. With that much, you can probably buy *two* new ones."

She jerked her head up and stopped sobbing abruptly. I waved the money. She ignored it and stared at me queerly. "Two *new* . . . ? What . . . what are you talking about?"

I sighed. "Your blouse, of course."

She gawked at me, then looked down at her torso. "My . . . blouse?"

"That's it."

"You . . . you want to buy my *blouse?*"

"Desperately."

"You brought me all the way . . . is that . . . is that why you smiled, why you picked me up in the bar? Why you asked me to come with you? Is that . . . is that why you . . . felt me? My blouse?"

I nodded. "You see—" I started to explain, but she began to laugh, and to cry, almost hysterically, sobbing and cackling, so I stopped. I was just as glad. It was getting on towards dawn, and I wanted to get the book finished.

Her laughter slowed for a moment, and I said quickly, "So, do we have a deal?"

She stopped laughing altogether and smiled at me as if I were an odd painting on a museum wall. She shook her head, then nodded. I held out the bills. Instead of taking them, she slipped off her coat and let it fall to the ground. Then, slowly, still smiling, she rolled her shoulders and reached behind her back with both hands. There was a long, tortuous sound of a zipper opening. I watched the tight cups of the blouse loosen over her breasts. Undulating slowly, she cupped her hands beneath her breasts and pulled the blouse away from them, toward me. The breasts bobbed free, and swayed in the moonlight. I reached for the blouse. She pulled back for a moment. I looked at her face. She puckered her mouth, and shimmied her shoulders, sending the large breasts into jiggling gyrations. Then she threw the blouse at my feet, snatched the money and her coat, and walked away, bare-backed in the cold.

I pounced on the lamé—a blouse no longer!—and wended my way home. On the way I examined the fabric and found it sound. I had been correct about the odor—there was a stink of perspiration in the spots beneath the arms and a whiff of cheap perfume in the breast cups, but I did not need these areas and hoped the patches across stomach and back were relatively clean.

It took me two hours to complete the stitching, gluing, snipping, and assembly. Just as the sun turned the printery windows pink, I held in my hands the marvelous object. *The Golden Notebook* was a tour de force—yes, it truly *mattered.* I knew Buzzy would appreciate it, as the manifestation of my ardor. I bore it into the house like a queen's crown before the coronation.

For a while I deliberated about how to present it to her upon her return. I finally decided that it would be best to let her find it alone. If I gave it to her by hand, the purity of her reactions would be tempered by her reactions to *me;* she would be too alert to my observation, and might miss some of the beauties she would be free to examine if left alone with the volume. Certainly, this was best.

I pulled a fine little cherrywood drop-leaf table out from our living room and set it up in the hallway, so that it would be the first thing Buzzy saw after entering. I placed the book on the flat back cushion of one of the puce chairs, and set it on the table. The gold fabric shone on the berry color like a huge square Phoenician coin on velvet. The display was glorious.

It was daytime by now, and Buzzy might be back at any moment. There was one last effect I wanted to apply. I went into the bedroom, and found a battered old anthology of ancient English poetry that Buzzy kept by the side of the bed. It is her favorite book, the only one she does not exhaust with sequential reading. Inside it, I knew, was a certain elegant bookmark I made for her from a strip of French cotton paper and sterling foil. I had printed *Buzzy's Best Book* in twenty-four-point Garamond Italic across the pale blue paper, in burgundy ink. This was the first gift I ever gave Buzzy, nearly a year ago. I took the bookmark out to the table, and propped it against a corner of the grand volume. *Buzzy's Best Book;* Toby's best gift.

I left the house. Since arranging the book, I have waited out here in my printery, passing the time by composing this little description of things at the Linotype (in ten-point Cheltenham, a reliable face). A few hours have gone by. I have grown a bit sleepy. I have a cot in the corner here, and I think I might lie down for a while. I am not worried about Buzzy—she'll come back, she'll see the book, she'll know where to find me. Most of all, she will see the book. See it, and apprehend all that I understand, about men, women, fitting together, us. She will know: it's *all* in there.

Ashputtle: or, the Mother's Ghost

Angela Carter

The Mutilated Girls

But although you can easily center the story not on Ashputtle but on the mutilated stepsisters, can think of it as a story about cutting bits off women so that they will *fit in*, nevertheless the story always begins with Ashputtle's mother, as though it is really always the story of her mother, even if, at the beginning of the story, she is already at death's door: "A rich man's wife fell sick, and, feeling that her end was near, she called her only daughter to her bedside."

Note the absence of the husband/father. Although the woman is defined by her relation to him ("a rich man's wife"), the daughter is unambiguously hers, as if hers alone, and the entire drama concerns only women, takes place almost exclusively among women, is a battle between two groups of women, on the one hand, Ashputtle and her mother, and, on the other, the stepmother and *her* daughters.

It is a drama between two female families in opposition to one another because of their rivalry over men (husband/father, husband/son), who seem no more than passive victims of their fancy and yet whose significance is absolute because it is ("a rich man," "a king's son") purely economic.

Ashputtle's father, the old man, is the first object of their desire and their dissension; the stepmother snatches him from the dead mother before her corpse is cold, as soon as her grip loosens. Then there is the young man, the potential bridegroom, the hypothetical son-in-law, for whose possession the mothers fight, using their daughters as instruments of war or as surrogates in the business of mating.

If the men, and the bank balances for which they stand, are the passive victims of the two grown women, then the girls, all three, are animated solely by the wills of their mothers. Even if Ashputtle's mother dies at the beginning of the story, her status as one of the dead only makes her position more authoritative; the mother's ghost dominates the narrative and is, in a real sense, the motive center, the event that makes all the other events happen.

The mother assures the daughter: "I shall always look after you and always be with you."

At this point, Ashputtle is nameless. She is her mother's daughter. That's all. It is the stepmother who names her Ashputtle, as a joke, and, in doing so, wipes out her real name, whatever that is, banishes her from the family, exiles her from the shared table to the lonely hearth, among the cinders, removes her contingent but honorable status as daughter and gives her, instead, the contingent but disreputable status of servant.

Her mother told Ashputtle she would always look after her but, untrustworthy, she died and the father married again, and gave Ashputtle an imitation mother with daughters of her own whom she loves with the same fierce passion as Ashputtle's mother did and still, posthumously, does, as we shall find out.

Now comes the vexed question: who shall be the daughters of the house? "Mine shall!" declares the stepmother and sets the freshly named nondaughter Ashputtle to sweep and scrub and sleep on the hearth while her own daughters lie between clean sheets in Ashputtle's bed. Ashputtle, no longer known as the daughter of her mother or of her father, either, goes by a dry, dirty, cindery nickname, for everything has turned to dust and ashes.

Meanwhile, the false mother sleeps in the bed where the real mother died and is, presumably, pleasured by the husband/father in that bed (unless there is no pleasure in it for her). We are not told what the father/husband does but we can make this assumption, that they share a bed.

And what can the real mother do? Burn as she might with love and anger, she is dead and buried.

The father, in this story, is a mystery to me. Is he so besotted with his new wife that he cannot see how his daughter is soiled with kitchen refuse and filthy from her ashy bed and always hard at work? If he sensed there was a drama at hand, he was content to leave the entire production to the women for, absent as he might be, always remember it is in *his* house that Ashputtle sleeps on the cinders, and he is the invisible link that binds both sets of mothers and daughters in their violent equation. He is the unmoved mover, the unseen organizing principle, like God, and, like God, up he pops in person, one fine day, to introduce an essential plot device.

Without the absent father, there would be no story because there would have been no conflict.

If they had been able to put aside these differences and discuss everything amicably, they'd have combined to expel the father. Then all the women could have slept in the one bed.

This is the essential plot device introduced by the father: he says, "I am about to take a business trip. What presents would my three girls like me to bring back for them?"

Note that: his *three* girls.

It occurs to me that perhaps the stepmother's daughters were really, all the time, his own daughters, just as much his own daughters as Ashputtle, his "natural" daughters, as they say, as though there is something inherently unnatural about legitimacy. *That* would realign the forces in the story. It would make his connivance with the ascendancy of the other girls more plausible. It would make the speedy marriage, the stepmother's hostility, more probable.

But it would also transform the story into something else, because it would provide motivation, and so on; it would mean I'd have to provide a past for all these people, that I would have to equip them with three dimensions, with tastes and memories, and I would have to think of things for them to eat and wear and say. It would transform "Ashputtle" from the bare necessity of fairy tale, with its characteristic copula formula, "and then," to the emotional and technical complexity of bourgeois realism. They would have to learn to think. Everything would change.

I will stick with what I know.

What presents do his three girls want?

"Bring me a silk dress," said his eldest girl. "Bring me a string of pearls," said the middle one. What about the third one, the forgotten one, called out of the kitchen on a charitable impulse and drying her hands, raw with housework, on her apron, bringing with her the smell of old fire?

"Bring me the first branch that knocks against your hat on the way home," said Ashputtle.

Why did she ask for that? Did she make an informed guess at how little he valued her? Or had a dream told her to use this random formula of unacknowledged desire, to allow blind chance to choose her present for her? Unless it was her mother's ghost, awake and restlessly looking for a way home, that came into the girl's mouth and spoke the request for her.

He brought her back a hazel twig. She planted it on her mother's grave and watered it with tears. It grew into a hazel tree. When Ashputtle came out to weep upon her mother's grave, the turtledove crooned: "I'll never leave you, I'll always protect you."

Then Ashputtle knew that the turtledove was her mother's ghost and she herself was still her mother's daughter, and although she had wept and wailed and longed to have her mother back again, now her heart sank a little to find out that her mother, though dead, was no longer gone and henceforward she must do her mother's bidding.

Came the time for that curious fair they used to hold in that country, when all the resident virgins went to dance in front of the king's son so that he could pick out the girl he wanted to marry.

The turtledove was mad for that, for her daughter to marry the prince. You might think her own experience of marriage would have taught her to be wary but no, needs must, what else is a girl to do? The turtledove was mad for her daughter to marry, so she flew in and picked up the new silk dress with her beak, dragged it to the open window, threw it down to Ashputtle. She did the same with the string of pearls. Ashputtle had a good wash under the pump in the yard, put on her stolen finery and crept out the back way, secretly, to the dancing grounds, but the stepsisters had to stay home and sulk because they had nothing to wear.

The turtledove stayed close to Ashputtle, pecking her ears to make her dance vivaciously, so that the prince would see her, so that the prince would love her, so that he would follow her and find the clue of the fallen slipper, for the story is not complete without the ritual humiliation of the other woman and the mutilation of her daughters.

The search for the foot that fits the slipper is essential to the enactment of this ritual humiliation.

The other woman wants that young man desperately. She would do anything to catch him. Not losing a daughter, but gaining a son. She wants a son so badly she is prepared to cripple her daughters. She takes up a carving knife and chops off her elder daughter's big toe, so that her foot will fit the little shoe.

Imagine.

Brandishing the carving knife, the woman bears down on her child, who is as distraught as if she had not been a girl but a boy and the old woman was after a more essential portion than a toe. No! she screams. Mother! No! Not the knife! No! But off it comes, all the same, and she throws it in the fire, among the ashes, where Ashputtle finds it, wonders at it, and feels both awe and fear at the phenomenon of mother love.

Mother love, which winds about these daughters like a shroud.

The prince saw nothing familiar in the face of the tearful young woman, one shoe off, one shoe on, displayed to him in triumph by her mother, but he said: "I promised I would marry whomever the shoe fitted so I will marry you," and they rode off together.

The turtledove came flying round and did not croon or coo to the bridal pair but sang a horrid song: "Look! look! there's blood in the shoe!"

The prince returned the ersatz ex-fiancée at once, angry at the trick, but the stepmother hastily lopped off her other daughter's heel and pushed *that* poor foot into the bloody shoe as soon as it was vacant so, nothing for it, a man of his word, the prince helped up the new girl and once again he rode away.

Back came the nagging turtledove: "Look!" And, sure enough, the shoe was full of blood again.

(The shoe full of blood. Horrible. An open wound.)

"Let Ashputtle try," said the eager turtledove.

So now Ashputtle must put her foot into this hideous receptacle, still slick and warm and wet as it is, for nothing in any of the texts of this tale suggests the prince washed it out between the fittings. It was an ordeal in itself to put a naked foot into that bloody shoe but her mother, the turtledove, urged her to do so in a soft, cooing croon that could not be denied.

If she does not plunge without revulsion into this open wound, she won't be fit to marry. That is the song of the turtledove, while the other mad mother stood impotently by.

Ashputtle's foot, the size of the bound foot of a Chinese woman; a stump. Already an amputee, she put her foot in it.

"Look! look!" cried the turtledove in triumph, even as she betrayed the secret of her ghostly nature by becoming progressively more and more immaterial as Ashputtle stood up in the shoe and commenced to walk around, squelching but proud. "Her foot fits the shoe like a corpse fits a coffin!

"See how well I look after you, my darling!"

The Burned Child

A burned child lived in the ashes. No, not really burned, more charred, a little bit charred, like a stick half-burned and picked off the fire. She looked like charcoal and ashes because she lived in the ashes since her mother died and the hot ashes burned her so she was scabbed and scarred. The burned child lived on the hearth, covered in ashes, as if she were still mourning.

After her mother died and was buried, her father forgot the mother and forgot the child and married the woman who used to rake the ashes, and that was why the child lived in the unraked ashes, and there was nobody to brush her hair so it stuck out like a mat nor to wipe the dirt off her scabbed face and she had no heart to do it for herself but she raked the ashes and slept beside the little cat and got the burned bits from the bottom of the pot to eat, scraping them out, squatting on the floor, by herself in front of the fire, not as if she were human, because she was still in mourning.

Her mother was dead and buried but felt perfect exquisite pain of love when she looked up through the earth and saw the burned child covered in ashes.

"Milk the cow, burned child, and bring back all the milk," said the stepmother, who used to rake the ashes and milk the cow, once upon a time, but the burned child did all that, now.

The ghost of the mother went into the cow.

"Drink milk, grow fat," said the mother's ghost.

The burned child pulled on the udder and drank enough milk before she took the bucket back and nobody saw, and time passed, she drank milk every day, she grew fat, she grew breasts, she grew up.

There was a man the stepmother wanted and asked into the kitchen to get his dinner but she made the burned child cook it, although the stepmother did all the cooking before. After the burned child cooked the dinner the stepmother sent her off to milk the cow.

"I want that man for myself," said the burned child to the cow.

The cow let down more milk, and more, and more, enough for the girl to have a drink and wash her face and wash her hands. When she washed her face, she washed the scabs off and now she was not burned at all, but the cow was empty.

"Give your own milk, next time," said the ghost of the mother inside the cow. "You've milked me dry."

The little cat came by. The ghost of the mother went into the cat.

"Your hair wants doing," said the cat. "Lie down."

The little cat unpicked her raggy lugs with its clever paws until the burned child's hair hung down nicely but it had been so snagged and tangled that the cat's claws were all pulled out before it was finished.

"Comb your own hair, next time," said the cat. "You've maimed me."
The burned child was clean and combed but stark naked.

There was a bird sitting in the apple tree. The ghost of the mother left the cat and went into the bird. The bird struck its own breast with its beak. Blood poured down onto the burned child under the tree. It ran over her shoulders and covered her front and covered her back. When the bird had no more blood, the burned child got a red silk dress.

"Make your own dress, next time," said the bird. "I'm through with that bloody business."

The burned child went into the kitchen to show herself to the man. She was not burned any more, but lovely. The man left off looking at the stepmother and looked at the girl.

"Come home with me and let your stepmother stay and rake the ashes," he said to her and off they went. He gave her a house and money. She did all right.

"Now I can go to sleep," said the ghost of the mother. "Now everything is all right."

The Traveling Costume

The cruel stepmother burned the orphan's face with a poker because she did not rake the ashes. The girl went to her mother's grave. Deep in the earth her mother said:

"It must be raining. Or else it is snowing. Unless there is a heavy dew tonight."

"It isn't raining, it isn't snowing, it's too early for the dew. But my tears are falling on your grave, Mother."

The dead woman waited until night came. Then she climbed out and went to the house. The stepmother slept on a feather bed but the burned child slept on the hearth among the ashes. When the dead woman kissed her, the scar vanished. The girl woke up. The dead woman gave her a red dress.

"I had it when I was your age, I used it for traveling."

The girl put the traveling costume on. The dead woman took worms out of her eye sockets; they turned to jewels. The girl put on a handful of rings.

"Sell them as you need to."

They went together to the grave.

"Step into my coffin."

She trusted her mother. She stepped into the coffin. At once it turned into a coach and horses. The horses stamped, eager to be gone.

"Now go and seek your fortune, darling."

One Holy Night

Sandra Cisneros

*About the truth, if you give it to a person, then he has power over you.
And if someone gives it to you, then they have made themselves your
slave. It is a strong magic. You can never take it back.*

—Chaq Uxmal Paloquín

He said his name was Chaq. Chaq Uxmal Paloquín. That's what he told me. He was of an
ancient line of Mayan kings. Here, he said, making a map with the
heel of his boot, this is where I come from, the Yucatán, the ancient
cities. This is what Boy Baby said.

It's been eighteen weeks since Abuelita chased him away with the
broom, and what I'm telling you I never told nobody, except Rachel
and Lourdes, who know everything. He said he would love me like a
revolution, like a religion. Abuelita burnt the pushcart and sent me
here, miles from home, to this town of dust, with one wrinkled witch
woman who rubs my belly with jade, and fifteen nosy cousins.

I don't know how many girls have gone bad from selling cucum-
bers. I know I'm not the first. My mother took the crooked walk too,
I'm told, and I'm sure my Abuelita has her own story, but it's not my
place to ask.

Abuelita says it's Uncle Lalo's fault because he's the man of the
family and if he had come home on time like he was supposed to and
worked the pushcart on the days he was told to and watched over his
goddaughter who is too foolish to look after herself, nothing would've
happened, and I wouldn't have to be sent to Mexico. But Uncle Lalo
says if they'd never left Mexico in the first place, shame enough
would've kept a girl from doing devil things.

I'm not saying I'm not bad. I'm not saying I'm special. But I'm not like the Allport Street girls who stand in doorways and go with men into alleys.

All I know is I didn't want it like that. Not against the bricks or hunkering in somebody's car. I wanted it to come undone like gold thread, like a tent full of birds. The way it's supposed to be, the way I knew it would be when I met Boy Baby.

But you must know, I was no girl back then. And Boy Baby was no boy. Chaq Uxmal Paloquín. Boy Baby was a man. When I asked him how old he was he said he didn't know. The past and the future are the same thing. So he seemed boy and baby and man all at once, and the way he looked at me, how do I explain?

I'd park the pushcart in front of the Jewel food store Saturdays. He bought a mango on a stick the first time. Paid for it with a new twenty. Next Saturday he was back. Two mangoes, lime juice, and chili powder, keep the change. The third Saturday he asked for a cucumber spear and ate it slow. I didn't see him after that till the day he brought me Kool-Aid in a plastic cup. Then I knew what I felt for him.

Maybe you wouldn't like him. To you he might be a bum. Maybe he looked it. Maybe. He had broken thumbs and burnt fingers. He had thick greasy fingernails he never cut and dusty hair. And all his bones were strong ones like a man's. I waited every Saturday in my same blue dress. I sold all the mango and cucumber, and then Boy Baby would come finally.

What I knew of Chaq was only what he told me, because nobody seemed to know where he came from. Only that he could speak a strange language that no one could understand, said his name translated into boy, or boy-child, and so it was the street people nicknamed him Boy Baby.

I never asked about his past. He said it was all the same and didn't matter, the past and the future all the same to his people. But the truth has a way of following you, of coming up to you and making you listen to what it has to say.

Night time. Boy Baby brushes my hair and talks to me in his strange language because I like to hear it. What I like to hear him tell is how he is Chaq, Chaq of the people of the sun, Chaq of the temples, and what he says sounds sometimes like broken clay, and at other times like hollow sticks, or like the swish of old feathers crumbling into dust.

He lived behind Esparza & Sons Auto Repair in a little room that used to be a closet—pink plastic curtains on a narrow window, a dirty cot covered with newspapers, and a cardboard box filled with socks and rusty tools. It was there under one bald bulb in the back room of the Esparza garage, in the single room with pink curtains, that he showed me the guns—twenty-four in all. Rifles and pistols, one rusty musket, a machine gun, and several tiny weapons with mother-of-pearl handles that looked like toys. So you'll see who I am, he said, laying them all out on the bed of newspapers. So you'll understand. But I didn't want to know.

The stars foretell everything, he said. My birth. My son's. The boy-child who will bring back the grandeur of my people from those who have broken the arrows, from those who have pushed the ancient stones off their pedestals.

Then he told how he had prayed in the Temple of the Magician years ago when his father had made him promise to bring back the ancient ways. Boy Baby had cried in the temple dark that only the bats made holy. Boy Baby who was man and child among the great and dusty guns lay down on the newspaper bed and wept for a thousand years. When I touched him, he looked at me with the sadness of stone.

You must not tell anyone what I am going to do, he said. And what I remember next is how the moon, the pale moon with its one yellow eye, the moon of Tikal, and Tulum, and Chichen, stared through the pink plastic curtains. Then something inside bit me, and I gave out a cry as if the other, the one I wouldn't be anymore, leaped out.

So I was initiated beneath an ancient sky by a great and mighty heir—Chaq Uxmal Paloquín. I, Ixchel, his queen.

The truth is, it wasn't a big deal. It wasn't any deal at all. I put my bloody panties inside my T-shirt and ran home hugging myself. I thought about a lot of things on the way home. I thought about all the world and how suddenly I became part of history and wondered if everyone on the street, the sewing machine lady and the *panadería* saleswoman and the woman with two kids sitting on the bus bench didn't all know. *Did I look any different? Could they tell?* We were all the same somehow, laughing behind our hands, waiting the way all women wait, and when we find out, we wonder why the world and a million years made such a big deal over nothing.

I know I was supposed to feel ashamed, but I wasn't ashamed. I wanted to stand on top of the highest building, the top-top floor and yell *I know.*

Then I understood why Abuelita didn't let me sleep over at Lourdes's house full of too many brothers, and why the Roman girl in the movies always ran away from the soldier, and what happens when the scenes in love stories fade, and why brides blush, and how it is that sex isn't simply a box you check M or F on in the test we get at school.

I was wise. The corner girls were still jumping into their stupid little hopscotch squares. I laughed inside and climbed the wooden stairs two by two to the second floor rear where me and Abuelita and Uncle Lalo live. I was still laughing when I opened the door and Abuelita asked, Where's the pushcart?

And then I didn't know what to do.

It's a good thing we live in a bad neighborhood. There are always plenty of bums to blame for your sins. If it didn't happen the way I told it, it really could've. We looked and looked all over for the kids who stole my pushcart. The story wasn't the best, but since I had to make it up right then and there with Abuelita staring a hole through my heart, it wasn't too bad.

For two weeks I had to stay home. Abuelita was afraid the street kids who had stolen the cart would be after me again. Then I thought I might go over to the Esparza garage and take the pushcart out and leave it in some alley for the police to find, but I was never allowed to leave the house alone. Bit by bit the truth started to seep out like a dangerous gasoline.

First the nosy woman who lives upstairs from the laundromat told my Abuelita she thought something was fishy, the pushcart wheeled into Esparza & Sons every Saturday after dark, how a man, the same dark Indian one, the one who never talks to anybody, walked with me when the sun went down and pushed the cart into the garage, that one there, and yes we went inside, there where the fat lady named Concha, whose hair is dyed a hard black, pointed a fat finger.

I prayed we wouldn't meet Boy Baby, and since the gods listen and are mostly good, Esparza said yes, a man like that had lived there but was gone, had packed a few things and left the pushcart in a corner to pay for his last week's rent.

We had to pay twenty dollars before he would give us our pushcart back. Then Abuelita made me tell the real story of how the cart had disappeared, all of which I told this time, except for that one night, which I would have to tell anyway, weeks later, when I prayed for the moon of my cycle to come back, but it would not.

When Abuelita found out I was going to *dar luz* she cried until her eyes were little, and blamed Uncle Lalo, and Uncle Lalo blamed this country, and Abuelita blamed the infamy of men. That's when she burnt the cucumber pushcart and called me a *sinvergüenza* because I *am* without shame.

Then I cried too—Boy Baby was lost from me—until my head was hot with headaches and I fell asleep. When I woke up, the cucumber pushcart was gone and Abuelita was sprinkling holy water on my head.

Abuelita woke up early every day and went to the Esparza garage to see if news about that *demonio* had been found, had Chaq Uxmal Paloquín sent any letters, any, and when the other mechanics heard that name they laughed, and asked if we had made it up, that we could have some letters that had come for Boy Baby, no forwarding address, since he had gone in such a hurry.

There were three. The first, addressed "Occupant," demanded immediate payment for a four-month-old electric bill. The second was one I recognized right away—a brown envelope fat with cake mix coupons and fabric softener samples—because we'd gotten one just like it. The third was addressed in a spidery Spanish to a Señor de la Cruz, on paper so thin you could read it unopened by the light of the sky. The return address a convent in Tampico.

This was to whom my Abuelita wrote in hopes of finding the man who could correct my ruined life, to ask if the good nuns might know the whereabouts of a certain Boy Baby—and if they were hiding him it would be of no use because God's eyes see through all souls.

We heard nothing for a long time. Abuelita took me out of school when my uniform got tight around the belly and said it was a shame I wouldn't be able to graduate with the other eighth-graders.

Except for Lourdes and Rachel, my grandma and Uncle Lalo, nobody knew about my past. I would sleep in the big bed I share with Abuelita same as always. I could hear Abuelita and Uncle Lalo talking in low voices in the kitchen as if they were praying the rosary, how they were going to send me to Mexico, to San Luis Potosí where I have cousins and where I was conceived and would've been born had my grandma not thought it wise to send my mother here to the United States so that neighbors in San Luis Potosí wouldn't ask why her belly was suddenly big.

I was happy. I liked staying home. Abuelita was teaching me to crochet the way she had learned in Mexico. And just when I'd mastered the tricky rosette stitch, the letter came from the convent which gave the truth about Boy Baby—however much we didn't want to hear.

He was born on a street with no name in a town called Miseria. His father, Eusebio, is a knife sharpener. His mother, Refugia, collects apricots into pyramids and sells them on a cloth in the market. There are brothers. Sisters too, of which I know little. The youngest, a Carmelite, writes me all this and prays for my soul which is why I know it's all true.

Boy Baby is thirty-seven years old. His name is Chato, which means fat face. There is no Mayan blood.

I don't think they understand how it is to be a girl. I don't think they know how it is to have to wait your whole life. I count the months for the baby to be born and it's like a ring of water inside me reaching out and out until one day it will tear me with its own teeth. Already I can feel the animal inside me stirring in his own uneven sleep. The witch woman says it's the dreams of weasels that make my child sleep the way he sleeps. She makes me eat white bread blessed by the priest, but I know it's the ghost of him inside me who circles and circles, and will not let me rest.

All my girl cousins here either don't talk to me or ask questions they're too young to know *not* to ask. What they want to know really is how it is to have a man, because they're too ashamed to ask their married sisters.

They don't know what it is to lay so still until his sleep breathing is heavy, for your eyes in the dim dark to look and look without worry at the man-bones and the neck, the man-wrist and man-jaw thick and strong, all the salty dips and hollows, the stiff hairs of the eyebrows and sour swirl of sideburns, to lick the fat earlobes that taste of smoke and stare at how perfect is a man.

I tell them, "It's a bad joke. When you find out you'll be sorry."

I'm going to have five children. Five. Two girls. Two boys. And one baby.

The girls will be called Lisette and Maritza. The boys I'll name Pablo and Sandro.

And my baby. My baby will be named Alegre because life will always be hard.

Rachel says that love is like a big black piano being pushed off the top of a three-story building and you're waiting on the bottom to catch it. But Lourdes says it's not that way at all. It's like a top, like all the colors in the world are spinning so fast they're not colors anymore and all that's left's a white hum.

There was a man, a crazy who lived upstairs from us when we lived on South Loomis. He couldn't talk, just walked around all day with this harmonica in his mouth. Didn't play it. Just sort of breathed through it, all day long, wheezing, in and out, in and out.

This is how it is with me. Love I mean.

Election Day 1984

Michelle Cliff

Awoman stands on a snake of a line in the back of a born-again church in a coastal town in California. In places the line is slender, in others it bunches like a python after swallowing a calf, in a shot from "Wild Kingdom." This is the polling place.

On the wall to the woman's right is a map, straight pins with colored heads indicating the positions of missionaries. She glances at the map to see if any pins are fixed to her native land. Indeed. Her island is so small that the huge blue head practically obliterates its outline.

On her left, through a glass, brightly, a Bible-study class sits around a conference table on red plastic chairs, lips moving without a sound behind a window; all are women. She begins to hate them, fights it; whatever have they done to her? God.

She recites in her head. *Though I speak with the tongues of men and of angels and have not charity I am as a sounding brass or a tinkling cymbal.* If there is a hell (which she doesn't really believe, but childhood is hard to shake) and if I am chosen to burn it will be because of this—which a teacher noted in the third grade, Palmer script flowing across the report card. *She holds herself aloof from the others.* There it was. Way back then.

"Where you from?" The woman in front of her, in a tan raincoat, a yellow fisherman's hat on her head, brown leather handbag strapped across her chest, turns suddenly to make conversation.

"New York." She answers with the place she last was, not the place she is made of. Anyhow, she belongs there no longer. Her voice would not be recognized by her people. They are background.

"How long you been out here?"

"Two months."

She is not being very friendly. The land is about to slide for Ronnie and surely this old lady is part of it, partly to blame, just as the parroting Bible class is. *Live and let live.* Her mother echoed in her head. *Slow to anger and abounding in steadfast love.* I hate their hate. *Two wrongs don't make a right. Judge not lest ye be judged.* Your father and I want for you and your brother a better life. There's no chance back there, that's all.

"How'd you get out here?"

"I drove."

"Married?"

"No."

"Alone?"

"Yes."

"You weren't scared?"

"Not really." *Liar.*

The line inches forward. People drip from unaccustomed rain. Every now and then someone says, "But we need it." And someone else nods.

"Isn't this country something?"

"Yes, it is." She does not say beautiful, desolate.

"And where did you stop?"

The younger woman begins to recite her route. Her mind glosses her spoken words. Images flash like lantern slides. As if someone dropped the tray. Out of order.

"Detroit first. I visited friends."

A rat springs across the highway and a woman in a big Buick brakes—hard. Laughing with her friends in their backyard: We brake for rats. The Heaven Hill is out of hand. She brakes hard, just like a woman. The totem pole—eagle on high—shadows them. Inside a turtle shell is sweet grass. Indians inside cities raising corn. Totems. They turn to her, serious. Has she made the right decision? She strokes the sweet grass, traces the quadrants of the turtle shell. Yes. I think so. The center fell out.

You're not running, are you? No. I don't think so. Sure?

Desert. In the distance a cluster of trailers. Wires crossing like spiders' webs. Smoke rises from thin pipes. Pickups. Children. Laundry supported on a slender thread. Everything slender, small, minute, at this distance. Nothing in the Rand-McNally. A cluster of people against red monuments, landscape laced with barbed wire. Dust cloud raised in the foreground as a roadrunner speeds by.

Labor Day parade. Union floats. Reagan in an outhouse at the back of a UAW flatbed. A woman asks for a cigarette. "Got a light too, sugar? A dime? A dollar? A house? A home, honey?

"You got a place to put your head?"

"Yes."

"You got kids?"

"No."

"God bless, sister."

River Rouge. Black Madonna. GOSPEL CHICKEN—OUR BIRD IS THE WORD! boarded up.

FREEDOM ROAD USED CARS: WE TOTE THE NOTE—rusts.

Mississippi. A plain green sign announces the King of the Waters. The Mici Sibi of the Chippewa. The river nobody wanted to be sold down. As wide as the Styx.

This is a country of waters and no water.

Glorious, ordinary the river runs.

Platte. Republican. Ohio. Little Blue. Des Moines.

In a backwater town of grain elevators and railway lines, roundhouse and old hotels, three women run a lunchroom. The wall behind the register is hung with their families. Beyond the lunchroom, the town, fields are a deep gold, pumps bow and rise, rhythm breaking the still of the landscape, in the distance a windbreak shelters a house.

She remembers from a history book in the eighth grade the photograph of a family, posed outside their sod house, amongst their valuables, chattel—Singer, piano, settee—brought into the light. *Moses Speese Family, Custer County, 1888.* That plain identification, with this opinion: *Not all Negroes were downtrodden.*

FDR smiles from a wall in a lunchroom.

In the converted bank in Red Cloud hangs a letter from Langston Hughes to Willa Cather. Upstairs a diorama illustrates the Professor's room. Ántonia's cup and saucer are found behind glass. A few streets away is the perfect small white house. A small white house with an attic room where a girl plotted and planned to get away.

1961. Small apartment over a drugstore. World map over her bed. Jam jar with babysitting geld. Lying there in the heat of a summer night, regarding France, her goal back then, the woman above them playing over and over, "I always knew I'd find someone like you, so welcome to my little corner of the world." Husband shouting to shut the goddamned phonograph off. The woman chanting. "Hit me, hit me, go ahead and hit me." Quiet then.

Farmland turns high plains.

A stone is fixed to the ground. ON THIS SPOT CRAZY HORSE OGLALA CHIEF WAS KILLED SEPT. 5, 1877.

This one will stand for the others.

She sends a postcard of the marker to her brother: Dear Bill, I'm okay. Thought you'd like (stupid word) to have this. Visited Cather's house and museum in Red Cloud. Lots of stuff. But no red carnation. Was it a *red* carnation? Love, Jess.

Salt Lake. A city set in yellow. In the tabernacle, imposing, a family, intact, divine, walks on air.

At a gas station a man throws her change at her and calls her a wetback. What tipped him off? Her speech is plain. Her skin has a tinge but could deceive the untutored eye. Her hair curls at the edges. But permanents are "in." Perhaps not in Salt Lake. She almost laughs but realizes the danger. She revs the Mustang and lets the silver rattle on the floor.

She fought the desire to call out *Adiós!* Spanish is her third language.

A tired waitress in an all-night diner serves her eggs and coffee, her skin sallow from the atmosphere. "You're not from around here, are you?"

"No."

The great white lake lies on either side of her. Black highway a thin ribbon between water and salt. Light refracting color here and there.

She turns on the tape deck and Bob Marley sings about loss and future and past and, no, woman, no cry. And she does. Her tears run salt into her mouth.

She crosses into Nevada. Stops at a restaurant on a bright Sunday morning and feeds a machine until she feels refreshed. An old man with a cup of quarters wedged in his belt feeds the one beside her. As she turns to leave, a woman in a cowboy hat, wild bird feather garnishing its rim, storms in, pushing the old man from his spinning cherries, bells, oranges. "Jesus Christ! A person can't even go get something to eat!"

"Don't mind her," the old man says, "she's just protecting her investment."

In her silver Motown prairie schooner, packed with books and all else she owns, she is driving west. She crosses into California at the Donner Pass, observes the monument to the pioneer spirit, and heads down the Sierra to the Pacific.

"My last stop before here was Reno."

"When you passed through Nebraska, did you drive through Omaha?"

"Yes. Is that where you're from?"

"No. I'm native Californian. From Bakersfield. But I was in Omaha once. In and out."

"Oh."

"Did you visit Boys Town when you passed through?"

The old woman asks this matter-of-factly, as if an orphanage was in the top ten of U.S. tourist attractions. Right beside Disneyland, Mount Rushmore, Wounded Knee.

"No."

"That's too bad. It's a wonderful place. At least it was when I was there. 1935. Of course, everything changes. That Father Flanagan was a saint. But you're probably too young to remember him."

The younger woman nods politely. She sees only Spencer Tracy, in black-and-white, on a nineteen-inch screen, getting tough with Mickey Rooney.

"I took a boy there once." The old woman declares this quietly, dropping her voice, moving closer, beckoning the stranger closer.

The younger woman is startled. Brother? Cousin? Nephew? Son? Who? She doesn't dare ask. She thinks she has met an ancient mariner, one who walks the coast, telling.

"Really?"

"Yes. Really. Like I said, it was 1935. The depth of the Depression. Just took him and drove from Bakersfield to Omaha. Almost nonstop. Didn't take that long, you know. Most of the traffic was going in the other direction." She smiles.

The child slept in the back for most of the journey. Covered with a plaid blanket. He twitched in his sleep, whimpered now and then. The desert. Her black car eating up the rays. The child remained wrapped in the blanket, suffering from a coldness, seeming not to notice the heat, light, LAST CHANCE FOR GAS BEFORE wherever. She was washed in sweat.

She sang to pass the time, to keep them—herself—company. The desert past, they crossed the Sierra. Oh, mine eyes have seen the glory of the coming of the Lord/He is trampling out the vintage where the grapes of wrath are stored. It is written in her will that they will sing it at her graveside.

She tried to get the boy to join her, but he hadn't the heart to sing. Else he didn't know the words, but she did try to teach him. The boy was too shy, frightened, to ask for food, for a drink of water, to use the bathroom. So she stopped when she thought it might be necessary and that seemed to work. It was a spinster's best solution—what did she know about children?

She stopped the car for a rest. Poured a canvas bag of water into the desperate radiator. Sitting on the running board while the car drank, they watched the people from the Dust Bowl pass them by. Each traveling band had a song. California, here I come.

"Just you and the boy?"

"Yes." Yes, me and the boy and I didn't even know his name. Finally got it out of him in Wyoming. He didn't know his date of birth, so I made one up.

"Yes. Just the two of us. We were in a big hurry, you see, so they picked me. I had the most reliable car, for one thing. And there wasn't any reason for anyone else to come along."

"Who was 'they'?"

"A group of women from my church. Baptist. Anyway, my car was pretty good, four new tires, and I was unattached and could get away at a moment's notice, and wasn't anyone to miss me. Being a single woman and all. I just put a sign on the door. Closed due to illness. I ran a small grocery store. Inherited it from my father. The kind of place you hardly ever see nowadays."

"What happened?"

"Well, we got to Omaha and I turned the boy over to Father Flanagan."

"I mean what happened before? Why did you have to take him there? Didn't anyone want him?"

She, the child-immigrant, knows intimately the removal of children. She takes the boy's part, her suspicion drenched in assumption. "Didn't you want him?"

"Wasn't mine to want, dear. Listen, it's a long story, but I've come this far. And this line is moving awfully slow—and not much at the end of it." She smiled again and the younger woman couldn't help but join her.

"He was ten years old about. He lived with his mother and father on a small ranch at the edge of town—they were tenants, not owners. Poor people. Once, when one of the church women visited the ranch with a basket for the family—which is what we need to be doing now, especially with Thanksgiving just around the corner; you can't just do it holiday time, though. Well, anyway, this was in the summer, and the church woman called on the family. She noticed, couldn't help *but* notice, that the woman who answered the door, the boy's mother, was bruised, all purple and yellow, on her face, hands, neck—everywhere not covered by her clothes. So the visitor gave the woman the basket and asked her who had beaten her—not right out, mind you, but as clear as she could make the question. And of course the woman said no one. What else could she say? The visitor told the woman that if things got so bad she couldn't stand it, she should call the minister's wife and talk to her and the minister would come and talk to the woman's husband.

"Well, the woman explained to the visitor that they had no telephone, but the visitor persisted, so the woman said, okay, if things got too bad she'd call from the pay phone at the filling station down the road. I don't think she ever intended to call on her own account. I mean, getting a minister, a stranger . . . it wasn't the brightest suggestion . . . probably would have only made things worse for her . . . anyway, the visitor left and the woman nodded and thanked her for the basket and that was that.

"Then one night the minister's wife took a call, and the voice at the other end was talking in these fierce whispers. The voice was very upset, but the woman was taking care not to be overheard. Finally, the minister's wife put two and two together. She called me and I called a couple of other women—we were the ladies' auxiliary of the church, you see. Well, we got in my car and went out to the ranch."

She paused for breath and looked around, but no one else was listening.

Her voice slowed. Each syllable carefully pronounced. "It was the damnedest sight I ever saw, or ever hope to see. Not even as a Red Cross girl, in the war, in New Guinea.

"The ranch house had a dutch door—remember those?—the kind where the top is separate from the bottom?"

The younger woman nodded. Fifties TV. A woman dressed in a frilly apron calls the boys in for brownies.

"Well, the top half was swinging wide open. On the porch, outside the door, was this man, lying on his back, his face just gone. Blowed off. Nothing.

"Inside you could see this little boy sitting on some steps, holding a shotgun, crying and wiping his nose on his sleeve. His mother was sitting next to him, face as blank as they come. Ugly red line under her chin.

"We decided then and there to get him out of town. I mean, he had his whole life ahead of him. Why should he be punished? It was an easy choice, believe me.

"It was much harder convincing these Baptists that Father Flanagan's place would be the place to take the boy. But *we* were the Baptists, Lord knows what the boy and his people were. Better there than a reform school. I told them about an article I had read in the *Saturday Evening Post* and all about Father Flanagan and him saying 'There is no such thing as a bad boy' and so on, and it was decided. And we didn't even think to call the men in on this, that was for later.

"We packed up and left that very night. We told the mother it was for the boy's own good and she seemed to agree, though she didn't say much. Shock."

"Did he say anything?"

"Hardly a word between there and Omaha. Not even when we reached the freedom road—you know, where the Mormons are supposed to have planted sunflowers along the way? I wanted to tell him what I knew, tried too, to tell him it wasn't the Mormons, it was the Indians—his people, you see."

"You didn't say they were Indians."

"Well, I think they were. They never said for sure. But I think it was a safe guess. They sure looked like it. Even if he wasn't, it was a nice story I told him. How they weren't just flowers, but holding the flower to the ground was something like a potato. Food the Indians planted during the wars on the plains. But I don't know how much got through to him all wrapped up in the back."

"Couldn't you have found out from his mother where their people were?"

The old woman sighs. "I was trying to do what I thought was best. There wasn't time, and, well, the woman wasn't talking. Indians can be difficult, but coming from New York you wouldn't know that."

The younger woman says nothing.

"I tried to tell him that if someone bullies and beats up on people they have to expect what they get—shouldn't expect no better. And he was only trying to come between his mother and another beating—or worse. Are you listening?"

"Pardon?"

"I didn't think so . . . look, better Boys Town than some godforsaken reservation . . . where he would drown in whiskey or die from TB."

"I understand what you're saying. But . . . "

"His mother wouldn't talk. He wouldn't talk—even if he knew who his people were. Even if all Indians had mailing addresses and I had all the time in the world . . . I don't know. Maybe his mother didn't talk because she thought I was doing what was best for him."

The younger woman withdraws further into silence, waiting now only for the end of the story, the end of the line.

"I don't know how much he understood of what I told him. Most of the time he seemed to be sleeping. Or I could hear him crying. Most of the time I talked—or sang. What a pair, eh!?"

She will not relinquish her reminiscence, the flavor of it, the goodness of it. And what did you get out of it? Adventure? Righteousness?

The younger woman thinks she sees the boy clearly. The tracks of children running from the Christian boarding schools, feet frozen in the snow. She's not a historian for nothing.

She asks the inevitable question: "Whatever happened to him?"

"I don't know. I never saw him after I left him at Boys Town. But the police never found out where he was either. That was good. I mean, that was the point of the whole journey. A safe place."

"What about . . . ?" The younger woman is caught up again.

"The mother? She wasn't so lucky. She went to prison for life. Manslaughter."

"Didn't she try to get away? I mean, why didn't she run?"

"And where would she go? A woman like that—traveling alone?"

They reach the voting booths, having traveled the last few yards in silence.

The Restorer

Susan Daitch

He held a pipe to the boy's mouth so he could try to smoke. Another child, a girl, stared straight at Anne. She touched the boy's shirt as he sucked on the pipe stem, running her hand down his sleeve, then she took a step back. The room was crowded with people, and all of them, in their own way, looked as if they were having a good time. A woman, dress half-untied, held her glass out, and a man, grinning, poured a stream of red wine into it. He must have been standing on a box or a chair because he was unnaturally higher than the rest. One musician played some kind of instrument Anne couldn't identify, and he, too, looked straight at her. A red parrot standing on his perch in the corner seemed the only thing not smiling, even the dog was. Anne went next door to borrow a ruler. The stream of wine had fallen in a perfect perpendicular. When she returned she held the straight edge up to it, and with a careful stroke reddened the streak of color that had begun to darken and crackle.

Red triangle: the woman's glass at the center of the painting was sharp and had resisted aging. She was afraid of the untidy woman having her glass filled. A shadow fell across her face, and the paint was badly cracked. Anne cleaned her face, but it still remained darkened and brittle looking. She lined up her narrowest sable brushes—the smallest seemed to contain only two or three hairs—but her hand stopped within an inch of her face. Nearby the face of the man who offered the boy a smoke looked lewd and distorted. She put her nose up to his. No one was watching. She was alone in her studio. Out the painted window lay the Hague or Rotterdam, perhaps. A tag read *Merry Company,* Jan Steen (1626–1679). She turned *Merry Company* against the wall.

Anne thought Steen must have been fond of oysters. Girl eating them, that painting had been sent down too. She stood very close to the canvas, then carefully cleaned a plate of oysters with tincture of lead. Anne had read that some species of oysters are hermaphroditic, others are distinctly male or female, and their gender is unknown until the shell is opened. On ocean beds scrutiny of shell is all you're allowed, tough luck. She added a blue to the antiseptic titanium white, but it turned pearly. On one bit of glass plate Anne mixed the clean white she imagined he originally used and in another corner the aged, yellowed white that remained. Silver dish, paper cone filled with pepper, broken loaf of bread, blue and white pitcher, five oyster halves scattered on a dark blue table. The girl looked furtive, as if she were stealing and had caught Anne looking at her. The paint on the glass wasn't right, but the real problem lay far in the background. A cook and a waiter or a servant, dark and murky, looked as if they were visiting from another picture, twentieth century. Either he had painted them vague and blocky on purpose, or their blurred faces were the result of deliberate overpainting by some other restorer who had worked anonymously in some other city, sometime between Steen and Anne.

Her studio was in a sub-basement. It had two doors; one was huge, chipped gray, split into two horizontal halves. That was the freight elevator, used to deliver and retrieve paintings. The pictures came from all over the world, unless they were too fragile or too valuable; then she had to go to them. Her pockets were full of metro stubs and taxi receipts.

Rembrandt seared by acid in Kassel; red paint, Guernica, Vietnam war; Velázquez cut to ribbons in London after World War I. Correggio's erotic Leda, decapitated in 1726 by a duc d'Orléans whose confessor had persuaded him of the painting's corrupting influence. It was later stolen by Napoleon, and the head repainted. By the time Anne saw Leda in Rome there was little she could do. The new head had been painted thickly, with no trace of an attempt to imitate Correggio's style. It would have been like repairing a newspaper cartoon whose image crumbles in your hands, Anne told them. A copy of the painting was said to have been made in Prague before Leda was chopped up, but no one in Rome had ever seen the copy. A soldier who had been loyal to Mussolini returned from the East with a rumor of its existence. The copy might still be in Prague or it might not be, the Italians shrugged. Back in her sub-basement Anne drew swan feathers on scraps of paper or the lid of a pizza box lying near the telephone: feathers between the legs, the way Correggio might have drawn them.

In Kassel the psychotic who flung corrosives made statements to the effect that he felt mistreated and wanted to destroy an object representative of authority. He could have held a human hostage (Volkswagen, Krupp, I. M. Farben), but he chose a quick squirt at Rembrandt, Rubens, Cranach the Elder, and Klee. Anne often didn't know whose side to take, when the slashes, acid, and red paint seemed inseparable from the canvas, and she wanted to grab a cab back to the airport.

Smashed while squads of men and dogs looked for a cache of drugs or smuggled state secrets. These were depressing jobs. Anne could understand how a viewer might feel canvas eyes staring at him or her and have to do something to make the staring stop. The damage done by the dispossessed was one thing, but the damage of the FBI, CIA, and Interpol was something else. She usually referred these jobs to another restorer. Anne wondered if this was a false posture, because she would otherwise do any job that came through the double doors. She had nothing against the Rockefellers, Japanese insurance companies, or whoever owned the objects she worked on. She had no religious or ideological ax to grind. She negated the effects of those who did.

Television. Extreme desecration can lead to a kind of celebrity conferred on the vandal, and the preservationist becomes an authority, in turn. Anne had been called once, but she felt somber and prosaic compared to the man who slashed the Metropolitan's Vermeer. He was said to have been very repentant and, like the subway vigilante who shot several people, wanted to turn back the clock and allow the cameras, lawyers, editorials, and A train to melt away. Anne saw him on the news after the story about American soldiers landing in Honduras and before the exclusive interview with the boy who claimed he murdered his girlfriend in self-defense. All this wedged between Klee and Pollock, the most difficult of all when paint starts to flake.

Sub-basement metaphors: thick-walled cell immune from vandals or catastrophe; hospital; cultural autobody shop. Black telephone, radio, Hellenic coffee cups, Chinese takeout cartons, and pizza boxes still holding a cold slice. Paint in tubes and jars, color swatches, books on chemistry, row after row of colors in various forms, dry and wet.

An emissary from the museum upstairs occasionally checked her work. *Nice job,* he would say, lightly tapping a mouth, or, *Someone stuck their umbrella in that bit?* He would carelessly poke his thumb through a hole. Horn-rimmed glasses turned away from her, faced the canvas; long back studied the damage, then returned to an office upstairs. She wondered if he had keys to her studio. Did he enter it while she was out and go through her things?

A crate of Pissarros, untouched since 1914. German soldiers had wiped their boots on paintings found in his studio in Louveciennes. Painted dirt, real mud. Anne carefully scraped one and tried to match the color of the other. A row of windows looked beyond repair. He advised his son, Lucien, to favor caricature rather than prettiness. Which Lucien chose, Anne didn't know. Yellow, for Whistler, a happy color, Lucien wrote back from England. His father gave up the apartment in Paris, gave up trips to visit his son. He kept hoping to be paid for his work; he projected sales and income and was constantly disappointed. Critics accused him of sick eyes. The illness of painters who see only blue, they said, and he quoted them to his son. *Sick eyes—* Anne imagined him lurching around Brittany wearing 3-D glasses or keeping a pornographic View-Master hidden somewhere. Anne knew she was paid more to mend the cracks in his painted rooftops than he received for a whole slew of pictures.

When Pissarro was afraid of looking at canvases he turned them against the wall. Anne's studio was full of stained, yellowed backs; dirty and reproachful echoes of what lay on the reverse. He wrote to his son that he had always thought them precious gems but feared they had turned into monsters.

Arriving from Paris, another crate. She was a waitress working in Le Lapin Agile, serving Apollinaire and Jarry. Picasso takes a cigarette wrapper from her hand when she tries to clear the table. His hands are dry and squarish. She wishes she had saved the bit of paper. The owner will say she hasn't done her job, *look at the mess you've left.* She drinks a brandy when his back is turned. Apollinaire winks at her. Anne carefully opened the crate with a hammer, packing excelsior spilled out all over the floor, and a blue Gauloise wrapper stuck out of the wooden fluff. Had it fallen off the original painting or had one of the art handlers carelessly stuffed it in the packing? The cellophane was still bound to the wrapper. The blue was too bright. It was new.

Under a self-portrait, another face emerged. Anne checked the papers. There was no mention of underpainting. As she cleaned Courbet's cheek, a second pair of eyes, a nose, and a mouth appeared. She studied the second face, referred to some books, ran up to the museum gift shop, bought some postcards and held the color reproductions up to the (two) originals. An eyelid, at first so shadowy, just under the lower lashes of the other, a nose poking through beside the mouth, mimicking the more visible one. Anne grew afraid to learn any more. Like Siamese twins with one heart or one liver, one could be saved, but the other had to be destroyed. Together, they were a freak, a restorer's nightmare of synopia. The first layer of paint could be easily wiped away or she could restore the self-portrait and obliterate the other. No one would know. She was the only witness, but she was curious about the character of the underpainting. Who was buried there? A vendetta of pigment, mute and still causing big problems. Anne turned on her television, then turned it off and left her studio, locking the door behind her.

The museum basement and sub-basement were filled with workers packing and filing. Jamaican carpenters built sculpture stands, reggae leaked from their Walkmans; temps stapled invoices; young men and women carried books and reproductions up to other floors. Sometimes their hair looked wet in the morning, and their clothes were often wrinkled or secondhand, as if the large suits and beaded sweaters had belonged to fathers and mothers who could no longer imagine why anyone would want to wear such things. Anne knew a few of the other basement workers by their first names. They were surprised to see her out during lunch hour. Usually she had food delivered.

Perhaps he had been so in love with the subject of the earlier portrait the likeness had been unbearable, and he had covered it over. Upstairs in the museum gift shop Anne spun racks of postcards as if they might answer what it meant to be in love with a portrait or even obsessed by one. Anne remembered she had spent a lot of time looking at pictures of John Lennon in 1966. To look at a photograph so long it dissolves into the flat thing it really is. She finally threw the pictures away and left home. She wished she had them now, not simply for reasons of nostalgia, but because remembering what she had thought, even stupidly, of John Lennon might shed some light on her dilemma. She rarely saw Central Park during the day but walked into it because she didn't know where else to go.

Anne returned to the mutilated Pissarros. She wanted to paint figures in the empty windows. She had to restrain herself from painting a smiley face on the murky cook in the background of the Steen. She made a small paper airplane out of the accidental cigarette wrapper.

There was a knock on the door. Delivery, Szechuan Baby Shrimp with Oyster Sauce. Anne didn't know if the face underneath was male or female. She guessed it was a woman, but she could have been wrong. She let the rice turn cold, a grainy white brick. She stuck chopsticks into the carton and drew a face on it so the thing looked like a bug.

He knocked on the door as if he were a delivery boy. He had heard there were problems with the self-portrait cleaning and restoration. She wondered if a lost child who had wandered into her studio by mistake had told someone upstairs about a picture with four eyes, but he didn't know what Anne was talking about. He insisted there had been letters, and Anne had been dawdling over the painting for months. No one had seen it, and letters had gone unanswered. What was the problem? Could he see the painting please?

He called in special photographers. The painting was X-rayed. It was on the front page of several newspapers. He kept visiting her studio in the sub-basement as if he didn't trust her, and there was nothing she could do to make him leave. None of his photographers or X rays solved the problem. He brought her grape leaves from the Greek place on Madison Avenue and half carafes of wine from the restaurant upstairs. She asked him to wipe his hands on paper towels before he touched anything. It was the only thing she could make him do.

The X rays showed a portrait of a man underneath. Anne tacked up a row of X rays, as if her studio were an oncologist's office and she were watching the progress of a cluster of cancer cells. Meetings were held, but no decisions were made about the picture.

One night, while Anne was working late, he knocked on her door. He just wanted to look at the X rays. She turned up her radio, signifying that she was very busy and he should go home. He said he had nothing to do and just wanted to look. She decided she wanted to cover up the earlier portrait. They had the X rays. You can't have everything, she told him.

He had the opposite idea and asked her to remove the self-portrait entirely. There had been plenty of photographs taken of it. There were postcards of the self-portrait upstairs. Everyone knew that. It was the right thing to do. The picture underneath was older. It should be revealed and preserved.

She told him she knew what was up. *You stare at a painting for a long time, and you begin to want to do things to it.* (The smiley faces, the figures added to windows, wiping away Dutch bourgeois grins.) *The painting seems overwhelming, and you want to take revenge. Looking is too ordinary, you're sick and tired of being careful all the time. I know all about it.*

He lined up her brushes according to thickness, arranged a row of blues from the palest icy one to the last, nearly black. He asked Anne to show him the chemicals and he'd do it. He began to go through palette knives looking for a scraper. She grabbed his knobby wrists and could feel his watch digging into her palm, but in breaking free of her he knocked into a wall of shelves and every color in the universe came crashing down. Glass jars shattered, tubes were stepped on, and in the squashing, paint gushed out of them. Dry pigment dust filled the air, clouds of cerulean mixed with puffs of rose, pools of coral spread into rivulets of amber and green. The guards rushed in. Colored footsteps were spattered all over. Waves of paint lapped the edges of frames.

The guards drew their guns. *An accident,* Anne said. *That's all. Sorry.* He ran out of the studio in his colored clothes, his footsteps led to the elevator, making a squishing sound as he ran. *Forget it,* Anne told the guards. *Let's just call the night cleaners.*

Anne looked for him in the elevator, and in the crowds wandering through the building upstairs. His name wasn't on the newly issued revised list of staff telephone numbers. The painting had been returned to the museum in Berlin, just as it was, all four eyes included. If he'd run off to Berlin Anne suspected she would have heard about it, but none of the other basement workers really knew him, and the Christmas rush was on hand.

Isabel's Sister Is Grinding Her Teeth

Stacey D'Erasmo

Isabel's sister is grinding her teeth.

Very softly, Isabel says, "Shut up, Frannie."

Frannie clicks and mumbles and shuffles her feet underneath the sheet.

Isabel has been listening to cars pass along the parkway behind their house since her dream woke her up. In the dream she was playing paralysis with her friend Leigh Ann from the old neighborhood. They used to play this game outside, crawling towards each other on their elbows, clutching at the grass and saying, "Help! I'm paralyzed! No, really." Sometimes they would grab hands, but that left only one elbow and encouraged cheating. The object was to keep their lower halves as dead weight as possible, but in the dream both she and Leigh Ann had absurdly long legs, like taffy. It made her sick to look at them. She told Leigh Ann, "I don't like for my legs to be so far away," and Leigh Ann said, "Yeah, I know what you mean." That was the only good part.

Frannie knocks one hand against the headboard of her bed but doesn't wake up.

"Be quiet, Frannie," Isabel says, and turns onto her stomach.

From the bed Isabel can see the ragged tops of trees and beyond a few dark windows of the house across the dead end. Everything looks too bright for nighttime, too big, like a movie set. Isabel wishes it were pitch-black, because then she could turn on the light and feel a real difference.

In six years, thinks Isabel, Frannie will be only sixteen, but I will be twenty. Somehow sixteen seems like less of a jump. Isabel's mother had Isabel at twenty-one, which would be five years from when Frannie is sixteen, but barely one year from when Isabel is twenty. This seems unfair, as if Frannie were getting more years.

Isabel sighs and slides one leg on top of the sheet. Although she feels slightly chilly, she turns the pillow over to get the cool side. She holds the pillow in her arms.

"None of my arms or legs touch each other now," she thinks, and shivers.

Isabel goes to sleep.

Frannie is drawing and waiting for Isabel to come home from school. She has fifty-two Magic Markers in a plastic tray next to the couch, most with frayed points and cellophane for caps. She licks them to bring their color back, although both Isabel and her mother have told her not to. Isabel said it was carcinogenic and her mother said that was going a little far, it's just not a good idea. Frannie keeps her mouth closed if either one walks into the room, and she has noticed that sometimes the purple stains don't leave her teeth for days.

Today she is drawing a large fan made of slices of different colors, and, next to that, a tremendous, indeterminately wavy shape which she is going to fill in with royal blue. In her mind she calls this shape a waddle.

Frannie is lonely in the afternoons when only she and Isabel are home. Either Isabel is in a bad mood, or she has Anna with her. If Anna is with her, they kick Frannie out of the living room so they can have the TV to themselves. At first Anna tries to be nice and asks Frannie how she is, how's school, is she excited about moving up to their school soon, but she doesn't stop Isabel from pushing Frannie out five minutes later. Then Isabel and Anna mix up cookie dough to eat raw and turn on afternoon kids' shows, like "Sesame Street." They seem to get a big bang out of these programs, Frannie doesn't know why. She hears them downstairs, screaming "F! Today's letter is F! Ffffffff!" They know all the songs, too. Sometimes they go out back to smoke Anna's cigarettes, but they leave the TV on and won't let Frannie turn the channel. Frannie never touches their disgusting cookie dough. What she likes to eat is salt, which Isabel says is bad for your heart.

Frannie gets a glass of water, dips in a Magic Marker, then squeezes it between her fingers. A nice, solid green drips from the end, but when she tries it on the paper it barely writes. She picks the silver one out of the pile on the floor.

The silver is perfect. Frannie makes the silver slice very thin and elegant. The shine of it seems gritty to her, like polished sand, and high-pitched. The brown is like hair melted down, and the black like writing in capital letters.

Frannie lays down the Magic Marker and stretches out her legs so that the page falls flat against them. From this angle her drawing looks like the aerial view of some resort, a bright tent beside a lake or Olympic-sized swimming pool. She imagines herself and Isabel there, swimming in the royal blue lake and then, dripping droplets of blue, strolling over to eat a buffet in the tent. She makes a heavy black line at the base of the fan, for the door.

When Isabel thinks about sex, she thinks of certain kinds of swift-moving phrases, like *lying down* or *standing still* or *rushing past*. She does not think of Andy, last winter's boyfriend, whose kisses seemed to take a long time and to have too many unrelated parts. Andy's kissing always brought to Isabel's mind the word *probing*, but not in the same way as in *The Godfather* when Sonny Corleone pushes the bridesmaid's wedding dress past her thighs and fucks her against the wall—a passage Celia Smith paperclipped and passed around Isabel's English class. The way that pink dress slid, quickly but also slowly, up those thighs, is how Isabel imagines sex: *sliding up.* Anna, who has been going out with a long-haired boy named Howard for six months now, says that holding Howard's penis is a little like trying to shake hands with an amputee. You keep expecting there to be something else at the end, she says, like, I don't know, fingers or something. Isabel plans to have a lot of sex, and to be thin. She wishes she had hair like Anna's, which is long and dark and cascades in tiny heavy ringlets down her back. The art teacher told Anna she looked like a Botticelli and Anna's mother told them Botticelli was a great painter, especially of cherubim. Oh, terrific, said Anna. Now I'm a fat baby. And she puffed out her cheeks. But even when Anna puffs out her cheeks she looks beautiful and complete, and it is clear to Isabel that Anna is an artist. It isn't just her pictures, especially the one of Howard looking out a window that was so exact and lonely; it is the way she picks up a pencil to draw, the way she watches how the cat walks, the way her eyes are wide and serious. Anna has an inborn authority, even over her mother, who is divorced and nervous. Isabel and Anna frequently discuss Anna's mother as if she were a reckless but unattractive third friend who dates too often for her own good and pins her hopes on obvious double-talkers. Isabel thinks it's poignant and ironic that Anna should know Howard so much better than Anna's mother knows Len, her favorite date, who takes her to concerts in the park but won't marry her. Anna's mother doesn't see the expression on Len's face when Isabel and Anna chat with him—how nervous he gets, how he doesn't know what to say, how he watches Anna hang her legs over Isabel's or lay her head on Isabel's shoulder. Isabel and Anna sit right next to each other on the couch and notice everything about him, including the way his pant leg rides up to expose his calf and the way he jiggles his drink on one knee. Isabel is glad her own parents are still married so she doesn't have to witness these charades at home, but she wonders if the divorce is what makes Anna so capable, so self-contained, and so fearless about sex. For Anna, boys are a snap; she can almost read their minds. Anna tells Isabel, "You and maybe Howard are the only people who really know me," and Isabel feels warm that Anna has told her something she wouldn't tell anyone else and that these boys will pass like so much news.

Frannie and Isabel sit, like two soldiers, on the carport roof. They are hoping for tans. Isabel insists that Frannie put suntan lotion on, even though it's cloudy, because that's when you can get the worst burn. Frannie disagrees, but lets Isabel smear some on her shoulders.

It is hot, and the top of the carport is covered with gray gravel, which makes it hotter. Isabel wishes she had worn her entire bathing suit, instead of shorts and the suit's top half. She looks at Frannie's legs dangling over the edge of the roof. Frannie is very fair and built small—her feet don't hang into space the way Isabel's do, which makes Frannie look secure and serene, levitated above the driveway in her one-piece suit like a Lycra-covered Buddha.

"Isabel," says Frannie, "let's go shopping."

"No," says Isabel. "It's too hot."

"When Mom gets home she could take us."

"No," says Isabel. Even through the towel, the gravel is biting into the backs of her knees.

"Come on."

"No."

"You're an asshole, Isabel," says Frannie and hits her hard on the arm.

"Cut it out, Frannie." Isabel scans the milky sky for a hint of real sun.

"Come *on*," says Frannie, kicking at the edge of the roof.

"No! Stop it, Frannie! You're going to fall off."

"Fuck you."

"Fuck you, too."

"Fuck you, too," Frannie repeats, mimicking her.

"I'm losing my patience, Frannie." The sun suddenly slides out from behind a cloud and hits them with the force of a strong wind.

"Did you make out with Andy a lot?"

"Cut it *out*, Frannie."

"Gretchen's older sister had an abortion."

"Gretchen's an asshole," says Isabel. "And she shouldn't be telling you things like that."

"I know what an abortion is."

"Good for you." Isabel lies down, face to the sun.

Frannie leans over to make patterns in the gravel, sweeping the sharp stones back with the side of her hand to make a tiny arena.

Underneath the stones is tar paper so dusty and worn it's almost like dirt. Frannie walks her fingers around the arena a few times, then lets her hand slump over, as if suddenly shot dead.

Isabel is ignoring Frannie, but after about five minutes clouds encroach again, and she realizes the situation is hopeless. She reaches over and takes Frannie's wrist in her hand. It is slim and warm. Isabel can feel the two delicate tendons bisecting the underside and Frannie's light pulse. With her ivory skin and her blunt hands and feet, Frannie seems to Isabel like a small but solid kite.

"Let's go in, Frannie. You're going to get burned to a crisp."

No one knows why Frannie grinds her teeth. The dentist says she is too young for orthodonture, that maybe she will outgrow the habit. Frannie tells him, But I do it when I'm asleep. The dentist smiles. A habit is a habit, he says. No matter when you do it. Frannie is quiet, thinking of bed-wetting and walking in your sleep. The dentist tells Frannie's mother to give her a little ice to chew right before bedtime. How old is she? he asks Frannie's mother and she says, Ten. Well, that's not so old, he says. If she's still doing it at sixteen, then we'll see. Can't let you worry your teeth away. Are you brushing, Frannie? Good.

Frannie secretly suspects that she grinds her teeth because of her fear of robbers. For a long time she's been afraid, it's like if a cartoon stopped and pointed its finger at you, she sees their black masks and their little caps, their thick hands gripping the windowsill. She sees an eye and part of a face edging into the window, Isabel is gone or dead asleep, and she couldn't help anyway. Frannie knows the robbers have come not to take things, but to suck out her spirit. Sometimes she holds her breath for defense. She used to run to her parents' room, but that was when she was little. Now she watches.

Isabel's mother has recently decided to clip their arguments short. She says, "Fine, Isabel. You do whatever you want." Or, "I'm sure you're right, Isabel." This tactic reminds Isabel of when you pretend to throw a ball for a dog and then snap your empty hand back to see the dog stop, bewildered, in its tracks. Isabel falls for it every time. "You're not *listening* to me," she says, despairing.

Isabel never relents, except to Anna, and she and Anna never fight. It's only when she's at home. Sometimes it's like a tornado, but more often it's like sand in her veins, or a pinching. Once it starts it doesn't stop until she's alone. Isabel's quiet father called her a shrieking harridan, and Isabel shot back that "harridan" was a stupid, faggy word no one even used anymore. He stood up, saying, If you were younger I would take you over my knee, and Isabel said, Go ahead. The longer he stood there, the meaner she felt, while inside rooms within rooms within rooms opened and filled with nothing but Isabel, safe and quiet.

When Isabel was seven she knew exactly what she was going to be when she grew up. A hippie. Hippies looked solemn, even when they were smiling, and their long hair hung straight down like sorrow. They set things on fire or marched all together carrying fake coffins and had a special, knowing look as if they had come from another planet. At eight, Isabel refused to let anyone cut her hair and thought about how much better it would be if people didn't have to wear clothes. Now that she is older, the kids who look like hippies hang out together under the trees at lunch, but Isabel is not among them. She thinks she may be a coward, or that she is lacking some vital quality. Each fall she hopes to be seen and rescued, but she doesn't really expect that this will happen, and it doesn't.

Frannie is rereading her favorite book. It is about a family who lived on the prairie a long time ago: a mother, a father, and three sisters, but the littlest sister is so little she doesn't count and Frannie skips the parts about her. Frannie is up to the middle of the book, where the oldest sister, who is wise and good and has blond hair, has been struck blind. All day now she has to sit in the corner and learn braille on a piece of leather with bumps punched into it by the father of the family. In the book everyone loves the oldest sister best and cries, in secret, over her lost future, but Frannie likes the younger, dark-haired sister, who grew up to write the book, much better. In the evenings, after chores, the younger sister leads the older by the hand around that part of the prairie where they live, describing it in detail, and helping her to count out the number of steps from the house to the barn and back. The younger sister is extremely patient and thorough in her descriptions so the older sister doesn't miss anything. Frannie knows that if it were her, she might be afraid of the clear, oblique blue of her sister's eyes and maybe restless in her sister's new, fierce grip, but she would not let go of her sister's hand. Without faltering she would walk her out to the road, and down to the river, and home.

Vito Loves Geraldine

Janice Eidus

Vito Venecio was after me. He'd wanted to get into my pants ever since tenth grade. But even though we hung around with the same crowd back at Evander Childs High School, I never gave him the time of day. I, Geraldine Rizzoli, was the most popular girl in the crowd, I had my pick of the guys, you can ask anyone, Carmela or Pamela or Victoria, and they'll agree. And Vito was just a skinny kid with a big greasy pompadour and a cowlick and acne and a big space between his front teeth. True, he could sing, and he and Vinny Feruge and Bobby Colucci and Richie De Soto formed a doo-wop group and called themselves Vito and the Olinvilles, but lots of the boys formed doo-wop groups and stood around on street corners doo-wopping their hearts out. Besides, I wasn't letting any of them into my pants either.

Carmela and Pamela and Victoria and all the other girls in the crowd would say, "Geraldine Rizzoli, teach me how to tease my hair as high as yours and how to put eyeliner on so straight and thick," but I never gave away my secrets. I just set my black hair on beer cans every night and in the morning I teased it and teased it with my comb until sometimes I imagined that if I kept going I could get it high enough to reach the stars, and then I would spray it with hairspray that smelled like red roses and then I'd stroke on my black eyeliner until it went way past my eyes.

The kids in my crowd were the type who cut classes, smoked in the bathroom, and cursed. Yeah, even the girls cursed, and we weren't the type who went to Church on Sundays, which drove our mothers crazy. Vito was one of the worst of us all. He just about never read a book or went to class, and I think his mother got him to set foot in the Church maybe once the whole time he was growing up. I swear, it was some sort of a holy miracle that he actually got his diploma.

Anyway, like I said, lots of the boys wanted me and I liked to make out with them and sometimes I agreed to go steady for a week or two with one of the really handsome ones, like Sally-Boy Reticliano, but I never let any get into my pants. Because in my own way I was a good Catholic girl. And all this time Vito was wild about me and I wouldn't even make out with him. But when Vito and the Olinvilles got themselves an agent and cut a record, "Teenage Heartbreak," which Vito wrote, I started to see that Vito was different than I'd thought, different than the other boys. Because Vito had an artistic soul. Then, on graduation night, just a week after Vito and the Olinvilles recorded "Teenage Heartbreak," I realized that, all these years, I'd been in love with him, too, and was too proud to admit it because he was a couple of inches shorter than me, and he had that acne and the space between his teeth. There I was, ready for the prom, all dressed up in my bright red prom dress and my hair teased higher than ever, waiting for my date, but my date wasn't Vito, it was Sally-Boy Reticliano, and I wanted to jump out of my skin.

About halfway through the prom, I couldn't take it anymore and I said, "Sally-Boy, I'm sorry, but I've just got to go over and talk to Vito." Sally-Boy, who was even worse at school than Vito, grunted, and I could tell that it was a sad grunt. But there was nothing I could do. I loved Vito and that was that. I spotted him standing alone in a corner. He was wearing a tux and his hair was greased up into a pompadour that was almost as high as my hair. He watched me as I walked across the auditorium to him, and even in my spiked heels I felt as though I was floating on air. He said, "Aay, Geraldine, how goes it?" and then he took me by the arm and we left. It was like he knew all along that one day I would come to him. It was a gorgeous spring night, I could even see a few stars, and Vito put his arm around me, and he had to tiptoe a little to reach. We walked over to the Gun Hill Projects, and we found a deserted bench in the project's laundry room, and Vito said, "Aay, Geraldine Rizzoli, I've been crazy about you since tenth grade. I even wrote 'Teenage Heartbreak' for you."

And I said, "Vito, I know, I guessed it, and I'm sorry I've been so dumb since tenth grade but your heart doesn't have to break anymore. Tonight I'm yours."

And Vito and I made out on the bench for a while but it didn't feel like just making out. I realized that Vito and I weren't kids anymore. It was like we had grown up all at once. So I said, "Vito, take me," and he said, "Aay, Geraldine Rizzoli, all *right!*" He had the keys to his older brother Danny's best friend Freddy's car, which was a beat-up old wreck, but that night it looked like a Cadillac to me. It was parked back near the school, and we raced back along Gun Hill Road hoping that Sally-Boy and the others wouldn't see us. Even though Vito didn't have a license, he drove the car a few blocks away into the parking lot of the Immaculate Conception School. We climbed into the backseat and I lifted the skirt of my red prom dress and we made love for hours. We made sure I wouldn't get pregnant, because we wanted to do things just right. Like I said, I was a good Catholic girl, in my own way. Afterward he walked me back to Olinville Avenue. And he took out the car keys and carved "Vito Loves Geraldine" in a heart over the door of the elevator in my building, but he was careful to do it on another floor, not the floor I lived on, because we didn't want my parents to see. And then he said, "Aay, Geraldine Rizzoli, will you marry me?" and I said, "Yeah, Vito, I will." So then we went into the staircase of the building and he brushed off one of the steps for me and we sat down together and started talking seriously about our future and he said, "Aay, you know, Vinny and Bobby and Richie and me, it's a gas being Vito and the Olinvilles and singing those doo-wop numbers, but I'm no fool, I know we'll never be rich or famous. So I'll keep singing for a couple more years, and then I'll get into some other line of work and then we'll have kids, okay?" And I said sure, it was okay with me if he wanted to sing for a few years until we started our family. Then I told him that Mr. Pampino at the Evander Sweet Store had offered me a job behind the counter, which meant that I could start saving money right away. "Aay, Geraldine, you're no fool," he said. He gave me the thumbs-up sign and we kissed. Then he said, "Aay, Geraldine, let's do it again, right here in the stair-case," and he started pulling off his tux, but I said I wasn't that kind of girl, so he just walked me to my door and we said good night. We agreed that we wouldn't announce our engagement until we each had a little savings account of our own. That way our parents couldn't say we were too young and irresponsible and try to stop the wedding, which my father, who was very hot-tempered, was likely to do.

The very next morning, Vito's agent called him and woke him up and said that "Teenage Heartbreak" was actually going to get played on the radio, on WMCA by The Good Guys, at eight o'clock that night. That afternoon, we were all hanging out with the crowd and Vito and Vinny and Bobby and Richie were going crazy and they were shouting, "Aay, everyone, WMCA, all *right!*" and stamping their feet and threatening to punch each other out and give each other noogies on the tops of their heads. Soon everyone on Olinville Avenue knew and at eight o'clock it was like another holy miracle, everyone on the block had their windows open and we all blasted our radios and even the angels in Heaven had to have heard Vito and the Olinvilles singing "Teenage Heartbreak" that night, which, like I said, was written 'specially for me, Geraldine Rizzoli. Vito invited me to listen with him and his mother and father and his older brother Danny in their apartment. We hadn't told them we were engaged, though. Vito just said, "Aay, Ma, Geraldine Rizzoli here wants to lis-ten to 'Teenage Heartbreak' on WMCA with us, okay?" His mother looked at me and nodded, and I had a feeling that she guessed that Vito and I were in love and that in her own way she was saying, "Welcome, my future daughter-in-law, welcome." So we sat around the kitchen table with the radio set up like a centerpiece and his mother and I cried when it came on and his father and Danny kept swearing in Italian and Vito just kept combing his pompadour with this frozen grin on his face. When it was over, everyone on the block came pounding on the door shouting, "Aay, Vito, open up, you're a star!" and we opened the door and we had a big party and everyone danced the lindy and the cha cha all over the Venecios' apartment.

Three days later "Teenage Heartbreak" made it to number one on the charts, which was just unbelievable, like twenty thousand holy miracles combined, especially considering how the guidance counselor at Evander Childs used to predict that Vito would end up in prison. The disk jockeys kept saying things like "these four boys from the streets of the Bronx are a phenomenon, ladies and gentlemen, a genuine phenomenon!" Vito's mother saw my mother at Mass and told her that she'd been visited by an angel in white when she was pregnant with Vito and the angel told her, "Mrs. Venecio, you will have a son and this son shall be a great man!"

A week later Vito and the Olinvilles got flown out to L.A. to appear in those beach-party movies, and Vito didn't even call me to say goodbye. So I sat in my room and cried a lot, but after a couple of weeks, I decided to chin up and accept my fate, because, like Vito said, I was no fool. Yeah, it was true that I was a ruined woman, labeled forever as a tramp, me, Geraldine Rizzoli, here I'd gone and done it with Vito Venecio, who'd turned out to be a two-faced liar, only interested in money and fame. Dumb, dumb, dumb, Geraldine, I thought. And I couldn't tell my parents because my father would have taken his life savings, I swear, and flown out to L.A. and killed Vito. And I couldn't even tell Pamela and Carmela and Victoria, because we'd pricked our fingers with sewing needles and made a pact sealed in blood that although we would make out with lots of boys, we would stay virgins until we got married. So whenever I got together with them and they talked about how unbelievable it was that skinny little Vito with the acne and the greasy pompadour had become so rich and famous, I would agree and try to act just like them, like I was just so proud that Vito and Vinny and Bobby and Richie were now millionaires. And after a month or two I started feeling pretty strong and I thought, okay, Vito, you bastard, you want to dump Geraldine Rizzoli, tough noogies to you, buddy. I was working at the Evander Sweet Store during the day and I'd begun making out with some of the guys in the crowd in the evenings again, even though my heart wasn't in it. But I figured that one day someone else's kisses might make me feel the way that Vito's kisses had made me feel, and I'd never know who it would be unless I tried it.

And then one night I was helping my mother with the supper dishes, which I did every single night since, like I said, in my own way, I was a good Catholic girl, when the phone rang and my mother said, "Geraldine, it's for you. It's Vito Venecio calling from Los Angeles," and she looked at me like she was suspicious about why Vito, who'd been trying to get into my pants all those years when he wasn't famous and I wouldn't give him the time of day, would still be calling me at home now that he was famous and could have his pick of girls. When she'd gone back into the kitchen, I picked up the phone but my hands were so wet and soapy that I could hardly hold onto the receiver. Vito said, "Aay, Geraldine Rizzoli," and his voice sounded like he was around the corner, but I knew he was really three thousand miles away, surrounded by those silly-looking bimbos from the beach-party movies. "Aay, forgive me, Geraldine," he said, "I've been a creep, I know, I got carried away by all this money and fame crap but it's you I want, you and the old gang and my old life on Olinville Avenue."

I didn't say anything, I was so angry and confused. And my hands were still so wet and soapy.

"Aay, Geraldine, will you wait for me?" Vito said, and he sounded like a little lost boy. "Please Geraldine, I'll be back, this ain't gonna last long, promise me you'll wait for me as long as it takes."

"I don't know, Vito," I said, desperately trying to hold onto the phone, and now my hands were even wetter because I was crying and my tears were landing on them. "You could have called sooner."

"Aay, I know," he said, "this fame stuff, it's like a drug. But I'm coming home to you, Geraldine. Promise me you'll wait for me."

And he sounded so sad, and I took a deep breath, and I said, "I promise, Vito. I promise." And then the phone slipped from my grasp and hit the floor, and my mother yelled from the kitchen, "Geraldine, if you don't know how to talk on the phone without making a mess all over the floor, then don't talk on the phone!" I shouted, "I'm sorry,

Ma!" but when I picked it up again, Vito was gone.

So the next day behind the counter at the Evander Sweet Store, I started making plans. I needed my independence. I knew I'd have to get an apartment so that when Vito came back I'd already be ready for him. But that night when I told my parents I was going to get my own apartment they raised holy hell. My mother was so furious she didn't even ask whether it had something to do with Vito's call. In fact, she never spoke to me about Vito after that, which makes me think that deep down she knew. The thing was, whether she knew or didn't know, seventeen-year-old Italian girls from the Bronx did not leave home until a wedding ring was around their finger, period. Even girls who cut classes and smoked and cursed. My parents sent me to talk to a priest at the Immaculate Conception Church, which was right next door to the Immaculate Conception School, the parking lot of which was where I gave myself to Vito, and the priest said, "Geraldine Rizzoli, my child, your parents tell me that you wish to leave their home before you marry. Child, why do you wish to do such a thing, which reeks of the desire to commit sin?"

I shrugged and looked away, trying hard not to pop my chewing gum. I didn't want to seem too disrespectful, but that priest got nowhere with me because I had my own spiritual mission which had nothing to do with the Church. I was waiting for Vito.

The priest told my father that the only solution was to chain me up in my bedroom. But my mother and father, bless their hearts, may have been Catholic and Italian and hot-tempered, but they were good people, so instead they got my father's best friend, Pop Giordano, who'd been like an uncle to me ever since I was in diapers, to rent me an apartment in the building he owned. And the building just happened to be on Olinville Avenue, right next door to my parents' building. So they were happy enough. I insisted on a two-bedroom right from the start so that Vito wouldn't feel cramped when he came back, not that I told them why I needed that much room. "A two-bedroom," my mother kept repeating. "Suddenly my daughter is such a grown-up she wants a two-bedroom!"

So Pop gave me the biggest two-bedroom in the building and I moved in and Pop promised my father to let him know if I kept late hours, and my father said he'd kill me if I did, but I wasn't worried about that. My days of making out with the boys of Olinville Avenue were over. I would wait for Vito, and I would live like a nun until he returned to me. And I didn't intend to call Vito or write him to give him my new address. He'd be back soon enough and he'd figure out where I was.

And I began my wait. But a couple of weeks after I moved into the apartment I couldn't take not telling anyone. I felt like I'd scream or do something crazy if I didn't confide in someone. So I told Pop. Pop wore shiny black suits and black shirts with white ties and a big diamond ring on his pinky finger and he didn't have a steady job like my father, who delivered hot dogs by truck to restaurants all over the Bronx, or like Vito's father, who was a construction worker. I figured that if anyone knew the way the world worked, it was Pop. He promised he'd never tell, and he twirled his black mustache and said, "Geraldine Rizzoli, you're like my own daughter, like my flesh and blood, and I'm sorry you lost your cherry before you got married but if you want to wait for Vito, wait."

So I settled into my new life and I waited. Pamela married Johnny Ciccarone, Carmela married Ricky Giampino, and Victoria married Sidney Goldberg, from the Special Progress Accelerated class, which was a big surprise, and they all got apartments in the neighborhood. But after a year or two they all moved away, to Yonkers and Mount Vernon, and I'd visit them once or twice with gifts, but it was like we didn't have much in common anymore, and soon we lost touch.

And Vito and the Olinvilles kept turning out hits, even though Vito never wrote another song after "Teenage Heartbreak." In addition to the doo-wop numbers, Vito had begun letting loose on some slow, sexy ballads. I bought their 45s and I bought their albums and every night after work I would call up the radio stations and request their songs, not that I needed to, since everyone else was requesting their songs anyway, but it made me feel closer to Vito, I guess. And sometimes I'd look at Vito's photograph on the album covers or in the fan magazines and I'd see how his teeth and hair and skin were perfect, there was no gap between his front teeth like there used to be, no more acne, no more cowlick. And I kind of missed those things, because that night when I gave myself to Vito in the backseat of his older brother Danny's best friend Freddy's car, I'd loved feeling Vito's rough, sandpapery skin against mine and I'd loved letting my fingers play with his cowlick and letting my tongue rest for a minute in the gap between his front teeth.

So, for the next three, four years, I kind of lost count, Vito and the Olinvilles ruled the airwaves. And every day I worked at the Evander Sweet Store and every night I had dinner with my parents and my mother would ask whether I was ever going to get married and have babies and I'd say, "Come on, Ma, leave me alone, I'm a good Catholic girl, of course I'm gonna have babies one day," and my father would say, "Geraldine, if Pop ever tells me you're keeping late hours with any guys, I'll kill you," and I'd say, "Come on, Pa, I told you, I'm a good Catholic girl," and then I'd help my mother with the dishes and then I'd kiss them goodnight and I'd go visit Pop for a few minutes and then I'd go upstairs to my own apartment and I'd sit in front of my mirror and I'd tease my hair up high and I'd put on my makeup and I'd put on my red prom dress and I'd listen to Vito's songs and I'd dance the lindy and the cha cha. And then before I went to sleep, I'd read through all the fan mags and I'd cut out every article about him and I'd paste them into my scrapbook.

Then one day, I don't remember exactly when, a couple more years, maybe three, maybe even four, all I remember is that Carmela and Pamela and Victoria had all sent me announcements that they were on their second kids, the fan mags started printing fewer and fewer articles about Vito. And the radio stations were playing Vito and the Olinvilles less and less often and I had to call in and request them more often because nobody else was doing it, and their songs weren't going higher than numbers 15 or 20 on the charts. But Vito's voice was as strong and beautiful as ever, and the Olinvilles could still do those doo-wops in the background, so at first I felt really dumb, dumb, dumb because I couldn't figure out what was going on.

But I, Geraldine Rizzoli, am no fool, and it hit me soon enough. It was really simple. The girls my age were all mothers raising kids, and they didn't have time to buy records and dance the lindy and the cha cha in front of their mirrors. And the boys, they were out all day working and at night they sat and drank beer and watched football on TV. So a new generation of teenagers was buying records. And they were buying records by those British groups, the Beatles and the rest of them, and for those kids, I guess, an Italian boy from the Bronx with a pompadour wasn't very interesting. And even though I could still fit perfectly into my red prom dress, I had to face facts too. I wasn't a teenager anymore.

So more time went by, again I lost count, but Pop's hair was beginning to turn gray and my father was beginning to have a hard time lifting those crates of hot dogs and my mother seemed to be getting shorter day by day, and Vito and the Olinvilles never got played on the radio at all, period. And I felt bad for Vito, but mostly I was relieved, since I was sure then that he would come home. I bought new furniture, Pop put in new windows. I found a hairspray that made my hair stay higher even longer.

But I was wrong. Vito didn't come home. Instead, according to the few fan mags that ran the story, his manager tried to make him into a clean-cut type, the type who appeals to the older Las Vegas set. And Vito left the Olinvilles, which, the fan mags said, was like Vito had put a knife through their hearts. One mag said that Vinny had even punched Vito out.

And then Vito went and got married to someone else, a skinny flat-chested blonde model from somewhere like Iowa or Idaho. A couple of the fan mags ran little pieces, and they said she was the best thing that had ever happened to Vito. Because of his love for her he wasn't depressed anymore about not having any more number-one hits. "Aay," he was quoted, "love is worth more than all of the gold records in the world." And I cried. I kicked the walls. I tore some of the articles from my scrapbook and ripped them to shreds. I smashed some of his albums to pieces. I was really, really angry, because I knew that it was me, Geraldine Rizzoli, who was the best thing that had ever happened to him!

Soon after that, Vito's mother and father died. A couple of the fan mags carried the story. They died in a plane crash on their way to visit Vito and his blonde wife in Iowa or Idaho or wherever she was from. I didn't get invited to the funeral, which was in Palm Beach. Vito's parents had moved there only six months after "Teenage Heartbreak" became number one. Five big moving vans had parked on Olinville Avenue, and Vito's mother stood there in a fur coat telling everybody about the angel who'd visited her when she was pregnant with Vito. And I'd gone up to her and kissed her and said, "Goodbye, Mrs. Venecio, I'm going to miss you," and she said, "Goodbye, Carmela," like she was trying to pretend that she didn't remember I was Geraldine Rizzoli, her future daughter-in-law. The fan mags had a picture of Vito at the funeral in a three-piece suit, and the articles said he cried on the shoulder of his older brother Danny, who was now a distributor of automobile parts. There were also a couple of photos of his blonde wife looking bored.

Then I started to read little rumors, small items, in a few of the magazines. First, that Vito's marriage was on the rocks. No surprise to me there. I was surprised that it lasted an hour. Second, that Vito was heavy into drugs and that his addiction was breaking his blonde wife's heart. Really hard drugs, the mags said. The very worst stuff. One of the mags said it was because of his mother's death and they called him a "Mama's Boy." One said he was heartbroken because of his breakup with the Olinvilles and because Vinny had punched him out. And one said he'd been doing drugs ever since Evander Childs High School, and they had the nerve to call the school a "zoo," which I resented. But I knew a few things. One, Vito was no Mama's Boy. Two, Vito and the Olinvilles still all loved each other. And, three, Vito had never touched drugs in school. And if it was true that he was drowning his sorrows in drugs, it was because he missed me and regretted like hell not coming home earlier!

Soon after that I read that his blonde wife had left him for good. Then I pretty much stopped hearing about Vito altogether. And that was around when my father, bless his heart, had the heart attack in the hot dog truck and by the time they found him it was too late to save him, and my mother, bless her heart, followed soon after. I missed them so much, and every night I came home from work and I teased my hair at the mirror, I put on my makeup, I put on my prom dress, I played Vito's songs, I danced the lindy and the cha cha, and I read through the fan mags looking for some mention of him, but there weren't any. It was like he had vanished from the face of the earth. And then one day I came across a small item in the newspaper. It was about how Vito had just gotten arrested on Sunset Strip for possession of hard drugs, and how he was bailed out by Vinny of the Olinvilles, who was now a real estate salesman in Santa Monica. "I did it for old time's sake," Vinny said, "for the crowd on Olinville Avenue."

The next morning, Pop called me to his apartment. He had the beginnings of cataracts by then and he hardly ever looked at the newspaper anymore, but of course, he'd spotted the article about Vito. His face was red. He was furious. He shouted, "Geraldine Rizzoli, you're like my own daughter, my own flesh and blood, and I never wanted to have to say this to you, but the time has come for you to forget Vito. If he was here I'd beat the living hell out of him." He flung the paper across the room and sat in his chair breathing heavily.

I waited a minute before I spoke just to make sure he was going to be okay. When his color returned to normal, I said, "Never, Pop. I promised Vito I'd wait."

"You should marry Ralphie."

"Ralphie?" I asked. Ralphie Pampino, who was part of the old crowd, too, had inherited the Evander Sweet Store when Ralphie Sr. died the year before. It turns out that Ralphie Jr., who'd never married, was in love with me, and had been for years. Poor Ralphie. He'd been the kind of guy who never got to make out a whole lot. I'd always thought he looked at me so funny because he was constipated or had sinuses or something. But Pop told me that years ago Ralphie had poured out his heart to him, and how until this moment he'd never betrayed his confidence, but that Ralphie had his own spiritual mission. He was waiting for me. I was touched. Ralphie was such a sweet guy. I promised myself to start being nicer to him. I asked Pop to tell him about me and Vito, and I kissed Pop on the nose and I went back upstairs to my apartment.

The next day, Ralphie came over to me and said, "Geraldine Rizzoli, I had no idea that you and Vito . . . " and he got all choked up and couldn't finish. Finally, he swallowed and said, "Aay, Geraldine, I'm on your side. I really am. Vito's coming back!" and he gave me the thumbs-up sign and he and I did the lindy together right there in the Evander Sweet Store and we sang "Teenage Heartbreak" at the tops of our lungs and we didn't care if any customers came in and saw us.

But after that there wasn't any more news about Vito, period. Most everyone on the block who'd known Vito and the Olinvilles was gone. And I just kept waiting. Just around that time an oldies radio station, WAAY, started up and it was pretty weird at first to think that Vito and the Olinvilles and all the other groups I had spent my life listening to were considered "oldies," and I'd look at myself in the mirror and I'd think, "Geraldine Rizzoli, you're nobody's oldie, you've got the same skin and figure you had the night that you gave yourself to Vito." But after a while I got used to the idea of the oldies and I listened to WAAY as often as I could. I played it every morning first thing when I woke up and then Ralphie and I listened to it together at the Evander Sweet Store, even though most of the kids who came in were carrying those big radio boxes turned to salsa or rap songs or punk and didn't seem to have any idea that there was already music on. Sometimes when nobody was in the store, Ralphie and I would just sing Vito's songs together. There was one DJ on the station, Goldie George, who was on from nine in the morning until noon and he was a real fan of Vito and the Olinvilles. The other DJs had their favorites too. Doo-wop Dick liked the Five Satins, Surfer Sammy liked the Beach Boys, but Goldie George said he'd grown up in the Bronx just two subway stops away from Olinville Avenue and that he and his friends had all felt as close to Vito as if they'd lived on Olinville Avenue themselves, even though they'd never met Vito or Vinny or Bobby or Richie. One day Goldie George played thirty minutes straight of Vito and the Olinvilles, with no commercial interruptions, and then some listener called in and said "Aay, whatever happened to Vito anyway, Goldie George, he was some sort of junkie, right?"

"Yeah," Goldie George said, "but I'm Vito's biggest fan, like you all know, because I grew up only two subway stops away from Olinville Avenue and I used to feel like I was a close buddy of Vito's even though I never met him, and I happen to know that he's quit doing drugs and that he's found peace and happiness through the Chinese practice of t'ai chi and he helps run a mission in Bakersfield, California."

"Aay," the caller said, "you tell Vito for me that Bobby MacNamara from Woodside says, 'Aay, Vito, keep it up, man!'"

"I will," Goldie George said, "I will. I'll tell him about you, Bobby, because, being so close to Vito in my soul when I was growing up, I happen to know that Vito still cares about his loyal fans. In fact, I know that one of the things that helped Vito to get through the hard times was knowing how much his loyal fans cared. And, aay, Bobby, what's your favorite radio station?"

"AAY!" Bobby shouted.

And then Goldie George played another uninterrupted thirty minutes of Vito and the Olinvilles. But I could hardly hear the music this time. I was sick to my stomach. What the hell was Vito doing in Bakersfield, California, running a mission? I was glad he wasn't into drugs anymore, but Bakersfield, California? A mission? And what the hell was t'ai chi? I was so pissed off. For the first time I wondered whether he'd forgotten my promise. I was ready to fly down to Bakersfield and tell him a thing or two, but I didn't. I went home, played my albums, danced, teased my hair, and closed my eyes and leaned my head on my arms. Vito was coming back. He just wasn't ready yet.

About two weeks later I was behind the counter at the Evander Sweet Store and Ralphie was arranging some Chunkies into a pyramid when Goldie George said, "Guess what, everyone, all of us here at the station, but mostly Vito's biggest fan, me, Goldie George, have arranged for Vito to come back to his hometown! This is Big Big Big Big News! I called him the other day and I said, 'Vito, I grew up two subway stops from you, and like you know, I'm your biggest fan, and you owe it to me and your other loyal fans from the Bronx and all the other boroughs to come back and visit and sing "Teenage Heartbreak" for us one more time,' and I swear Vito got choked up over the phone and he agreed to do it, even though he said that he usually doesn't sing anymore because it interferes with his t'ai chi, but I said, 'Vito, we love you here at AAY, man, and wait'll you hear this, we're going to book Carnegie Hall for you, Vito, not your grandmother's attic, but Carnegie Hall!' How about that, everyone? And just so you all know, the Olinvilles are all doing their own things now, so it'll just be Vito alone, but hey, that's okay, that's great, Vito will sing the oldies and tickets go on sale next week!"

And I stood there frozen, and Ralphie and I stared at each other across the counter, and I could see a look in his eyes that told me that he knew he'd finally lost me for good this time. Because Vito was coming back. He may have told Goldie George that he was coming home to sing to his fans, but Ralphie and I both knew that it was really me, Geraldine Rizzoli, that he was finally ready to come back to. Vito worked in mysterious ways, and I figured that he finally felt free of the bad things, the drugs and that boring blonde wife from Iowa or Idaho and his own arrogance and excessive pride, and now he was pure enough to return to me. I wasn't wild about this t'ai chi stuff, whatever it was, but I could get used to it if it had helped Vito to get better so he could come home to me.

Ralphie sort of shook himself like he was coming out of some long sleep or trance. Then he came around the counter and put his arm around me in this brotherly way. "Geraldine Rizzoli," he said really softly, "my treat. A first-row seat at Carnegie Hall."

But I wouldn't accept, even though it was such a beautiful thing for Ralphie to offer to do, considering how he'd felt about me all those years. I got teary-eyed. But I didn't need a ticket, not me, not Geraldine Rizzoli. Vito would find out where I lived and he'd come and pick me up and take me himself to Carnegie Hall. He'd probably come in a limo paid for by the station, I figured. Because the only way I was going to the concert was with Vito. I went home after work and I teased my hair and I put on my makeup and I put on my red prom dress and I danced and sang.

All week Goldie George kept saying, "It's unbelievable, tickets were sold out within an hour! The calls don't stop coming, you all remember Vito, you all love him!"

On the night of the concert Pop came by. He sat across from me on the sofa, and he said in a raspy voice, "Geraldine Rizzoli, I didn't ever want to have to say this, but you're like my own daughter, my own flesh and blood, and as long as Vito wasn't around, I figured, okay you can dance to his albums and tease your hair and wear the same clothes all the time and you're none the worse for it, but now that he's coming home I've got to tell you he won't be coming home for you, Geraldine, if he cared a twit about you he would have flown you out to L.A. way back when, and I'm sorry you let him into your pants and lost your cherry to him, but you're a middle-aged lady now and you're gonna get hurt real bad and I'm glad your mother and father, bless their souls, aren't around to see you suffer the way you're gonna suffer tonight, Geraldine, and I don't wanna see it either, what I want is for you to drive down to Maryland tonight real fast, right now, and marry Ralphie, before Vito breaks your heart so bad nothing will ever put it together again!"

I'd never seen Pop so riled up. I kissed him on the nose and told him he was sweet, but that Vito was coming. After Pop left, I played my albums and I teased my hair and I applied my lipstick and I danced the lindy and the cha cha and I waited. I figured that everyone in the old crowd would be at the concert. They'd come in from the suburbs with their husbands and their wives and their children, and even, I had to face facts, in some cases, their grandchildren. And just then there was a knock on my door and there he was. He'd put on some weight, but not much, and although he'd lost some hair he still had a pompadour and he was holding some flowers for me, and I noticed that they were red roses, which I knew he'd chosen to match my prom dress. And he said, "Aay, Geraldine Rizzoli, thanks for waiting." Then he looked at his watch. "All *right,* let's get a move on! Concert starts at nine." And I looked in the mirror one last time, sprayed on a little more hairspray and that was it. Vito took my arm just the way he took it the night I gave myself to him in the backseat of his older brother Danny's best friend Freddy's car, and we went downtown by limo to Carnegie Hall, which was a real treat because I didn't get to go into Manhattan very often. And Carnegie Hall was packed, standing room only, and the crowd was yelling, "Aay, Vito! Aay, Vito! Aay, Vito!" and Pamela and Carmela and Victoria were there, and all the Olinvilles came and they hugged Vito and said there were no hard feelings, and Vinny and Vito even gave each other noogies on the tops of their heads, and everyone said, "Geraldine Rizzoli, you haven't aged a day." Then Goldie George introduced Vito, and Vito just got right up there on the stage and he belted out those songs, and at the end of the concert, for his finale, he sang "Teenage Heartbreak" and he called me up onstage with him and he held my hand and looked into my eyes while he sang. I even sang along on a few of the verses and I danced the lindy and the cha cha right there onstage in front of all those people. The crowd went wild, stamping their feet and shouting for more, and Goldie George was crying, and after the concert Vito and I went back by limo to Olinville Avenue and Vito gave the limo driver a big tip and the driver said, "Aay, Vito, welcome home," and then he drove away.

And ever since then Vito has been here with me in the two-bedroom apartment. He still does t'ai chi, but it's really no big thing, an hour or two in the morning at most. Pop died last year and Vito and I were with him at the end and his last words were, "You two kids, you're like my own son and daughter." Vito works in the Sweet Store now instead of me because I've got to stay home to take care of Vito Jr. and Little Pop, who have a terrific godfather in Ralphie and a great uncle in Vito's older brother, Danny. And, if I'm allowed to do a little bragging, which seems only fair after all this time, Vito Jr. and Little Pop are very good kids. They go to Church on Sundays and they're doing real well in school because they never cut classes or smoke in the bathroom or curse, and Vito and I are as proud as we can be.

Suzanne Gardinier

She is sitting in the kitchen alone drumming on the tabletop, ♫ ♫ ♫ ♫, Evensong Alison Maritime Monahan Caribou Respirate Barbara Carousel Carolyn Marilyn Marjorie. The accents alternate between hands and her head sways back and forth to follow them. Below the waist her body is still as the furniture. Her legs hang over the chair edge and her feet don't touch the floor. A tightness in her chest and jaw and temples eases as she crests the hill of each triplet; when she hears the geese hahonking over the water she pulls from their chaotic crying triplets, triplets from the wind they ride over the trees, triplets from car engines on the narrow curved road, ♫ ♫ ♫ ♫, 1-2-3, 1-2-3, 1-2-3, 1-2-3. It's morning.

The gods of the household are asleep. Their door at the top of the stairs is closed. Before daylight she broke free of a nightmare and climbed up in the dark, past the door, propped ajar, and burrowed her arms and shoulders and face into her mother's warm, sleeping skin, while her father snored on his back, a continent away. Her bare feet were cold as she stood by the bed, and the backs of her knees started to tingle and numb; she locked them and did not pull away until her mother murmured, "Okay? It's okay. Go to sleep now," and opened her arms' warm circle. She walked back downstairs, wide awake, watching her white feet walk and walk, and lay in bed with the light on, making whales from the cracks in the ceiling and turning the pages of books until morning came.

Now the door is closed and she can't remember the dream or the trip upstairs or the trip back down or the stories or the whales. She does remember the letters, black and inviolable, stepping across the pages; she leaves the triplets and climbs the alphabet for a while, singing to herself the song of the letters' names, tracing them on the table.

Z, Z, Z, she slashes, like the masked bandit on television, who cuts it into things with his sword. The screen door shines open and slaps shut and the orange tiger lily blossoms in the scrabbly garden are almost touching the ground. She loops one stem, then another with her thumb and first finger, pulls each upright, holds it, lets it fall. The orange sun is climbing the eastern haze and already the heat beats in her hair and reaches under her clothes. She squats in the dirt righting the lilies; weeks ago they were crushed by half of an old silver maple that split and fell in a big-winded storm. Bees start to crowd the roses along the dirt path to the water; she crouches close enough to feel afraid and buzzes softly along with them, watching them hover over the spread pink blossoms and push their faces in.

Hungry and thirsty and whine slap again and she climbs the counter for four cookies and brings a jug of cold water out to the back step. She twists each sandwich apart, licks down the sweet cream, and piles the bare chocolate halves beside her. When the cream is gone she eats the covers, in two bites each. Then water until the skin across her stomach is taut and pushes out the shirt with umbrellas on it. When she stops chewing and swallowing the silence shoulders in again.

Still no sound from them. From outside by the lilies she can see the white curtain over their window suck in and out with the wind. On the tabletop she writes a quick note with her finger: DEAR DEAR GONE TO THE BEACH COME, as she's seen her mother leave notes for her father on pads embossed with his name.

Past the bees in the prickly bushes wood planks bridge a marsh pond, part slickened green with algae, part clear. She sits on the hot wood, lets her feet dangle, and watches the turtles' streams of bubbles rise through the black water. One beaked head surfaces, water rolling from its forehead and open eyes, then disappears. She sings its name to herself: tur-tle, tur-tle, then faster, like a train, *turtleturtleturtleturtle,* and waits for it to climb the bank and lie still so she can lift it, as she has before, jogging the living weight back and forth in her hands, fingers prodding for the head and clawed feet pulled deep inside the shell.

Just before the dirt path gives onto sand the shade is deepest, the earth cool and damp underfoot. As she walks she has been singing, "We Are Marching to Pretoria" and "All Aboard for Blanket Bay." In the shade she stops, thirsty and tired; she rubs her eyes roughly and lies down, her cheek against coolness, fingers knit in the grass at the edge of the path. Before she falls asleep a fly lands on the back of one leg, then the other, crawling a short distance over her skin, flying up, landing again; her arms are too heavy to brush it away.

The dream she's been carrying takes its time unfolding, but does, after the bees and the moving curtain and green hills over which she runs in great looping strides. In a room of tall porcelain statues the sound of water hisses from the walls; streams of it pour into the basin and bathtub and rush down the toilet hole and away. On one wall, papered with anchors, is a painting, high above her head, green and blue and gold; she hears the sound of waves coming from it, and the bars of wave color move. She is bouncing the long soft notes of "All Aboard" off the shiny walls and holding her satisfying stomach in her hands and then no more or speak or any sound from her and feet not floor and open enough and open enough but small and please and please and the fallen maple branches rasping her cheeks and must swallow must breathe must breathe and all the water inside her rushing out and she loves someone who is there and someone who is not.

When she wakes up on the ground the fly is still tracing the backs of her legs and she smells piss, soaking and darkening her shorts and the dirt. As she stands her heart knocks in her neck; she brushes her clothes and looks toward the cove, where a strip of blue tops a rise of sand. She walks back in the direction she came from, across the board bridge and in the back door, trying to keep her legs apart and the wet cotton away from her skin.

The gods are still sleeping. She scratches where the burning itch is and the smell on her fingers is acrid, dear, disagreeable, interesting.

She tests wisps of it with her nose and listens for any sounds of stir-ring. *Tick Tick* from the floors and walls. The house swells under the sun. The cove water is shallow, she's allowed to walk there alone, and she considers going back and lying down up to her neck to hide the stain and cover the smell and cool the burning. She wants her mother to be there when she arrives, in a low chair half in the water, brown feet plowed into the wet sand, reading those paperbacks with guns and coiled ropes and knives on the covers, her hair gathered at the back of her neck. There will be bologna and ketchup sandwiches. There will be lemonade. There will be cautions and sun protection lotion and no swimming for an hour after lunch and applause for the dead man's float and dives. Under plastic sunglasses there will be her mother's eyes, resting on her head, wherever it goes.

In the kitchen she takes off her clothes—even the bottom of the umbrella shirt is wet—and wads them in a corner behind a chair. Naked, she holds her arms and legs spread, like an astronaut in a padded suit. She bobs around the kitchen, slowly touring the moon-scape of overflowing ashtrays, dishes caked with egg, beer bottles, bread box, the brown and yellow linoleum squares. If she takes off her mask in this alien world she will be unable to breathe and will die. Her body is cradled deep in the clumsy costume she maneuvers across the floor. Earth is green and blue gold and very far away.

She floats into her room and covers herself with a green shirt and green shorts and is no longer an astronaut. Her stomach stirs and her bowels swell and she tightens herself against them. She wants to save every supper she has ever had, to grow large and permanent and extravagantly full. There's a knock at the back door.

"Collecting," says the boy behind the shimmering screen. The wide orange strap of the newspaper bag is bright on his sturdy right shoulder. She opens the door and takes the paper from his other hand.

"They're asleep," she says. His eyes scan her face. "I don't have any money."

"Your mom said today. She owes me. Can you ask her?"

"They're sleeping."

"C'mon."

"Say please."

"C'mon."

"Okay. See you." She starts to turn away, and he hooks one thumb angrily into a belt loop.

"Okay. Please," he says, surveying the yard.

"Say pretty please."

"Pretty please."

"Say Zorro."

"What? C'mon, just go. Just go ask her. I said please."

"Say Zorro."

"*Zorro. Okay? Zorro.*"

"Say her name."

"Mrs. Monahan."

"No. Say her name."

"That *is* her name."

"Nope."

"What's her name?"

"Marjorie. Say Marjorie."

"Marjorie."

"Three times."

"Marjorie Marjorie Marjorie! Ask her!"

"No," she says. "No. They're sleeping."

"What are they sleeping at twelve o'clock for?"

"None of your business. Run along, Bri." It's a phrase used among the neighborhood kids as a taunt, a flag thrown down on the ground.

Brian sets his jaw, slouches the bag off his shoulder, and sits down on it a few paces from the door. "She owes me. She said. I mean it. I'm waiting."

"Run along, Bri. They're sleeping." What she has hoped for all morning—the sight of them, giants, rumpled, in bathrobes, snapping short sentences and filling tall glasses with Alka-Seltzer and tomato juice—she now dreads, Brian's eyes on them and his standing by the table with his cap bill folded in his back pocket while her mother bends over to find the pocketbook and the wallet and the change. Brian interlaces his fingers behind his head and leans his face into the sun.

It starts slowly, her foot against his bag, small kicks, and him back at her, nudging her foot with his sneaker, not too hard, and then him standing and the two of them squared, him two inches taller and pounds heavier but her short pushes edging his shoulder back, then his hers, sharp, bringing the color to their faces, then closer and closer and his nostrils flaring and the upclose grass smell of his hair and her arm muscles itch and twitch and ache to cut the Zs into his shirt and shut his eyes with fists.

"Faggot," she spits at him, "faggot, you faggot, get out of here," and they are locked, growling, then shouting, his fingernails leaving two red trails and then his head vised in her arms tighter tighter one fist pounding her side below the last rib until she knows she will puke or piss again or die but tighter tighter and he is choking his neck fluttering making those grabbing sounds with his throat and she listens drawing them through her ears into a cavity in her chest her teeth ground together until her jaws ache and she thinks maybe that and not the fading punches will force her to let go and fall—

—and then Brian is a child crying and she has become a god, looking down at his body shaped like a C on the ground, the back of the green shirt gathered in a fist several times the size of his, the fist of a god, her father, awake, in his knotted bathrobe swearing, smelling of angry sweat, holding her suspended like a fish in the claws of a bird over her vanquished opponent, who from this great height looks equally like a friend. Her father kicks senselessly at the sack of papers and stalks her inside under his arm, where already she rides limp and mute, searching for the anchors on the wallpaper—left fluke, right fluke, single center shank—as they cross the threshold of her room.

The door is slammed shut and the bed is narrow and as he raises his hand again and again words pour from his red mouth in a language she doesn't understand but plans to study someday. She will learn to draw his words on paper she will be their scholar and the black letters will march across the page with the same rhythm he is filling the house with they are filling the house with it together she must learn the letters' names she clings to the paper anchors and blurts the letters first to the pile of green clothes on the floor then to the red with flashes of yellow and black that comes when she closes her eyes.

From the bed from a great distance she hears Brian's small strangled coughs and goes to the window to see him holding one hand to his throat while accepting a glass of water from her mother, who crouches on the grass facing him. She is wearing a white cotton shift, and her legs are folded and brown under it. From the clasp at the nape of her neck wisps of hair slip and fall. Brian stammers in a parched hilly voice like the beach sand high up near the dunes, and her mother's voice and her hand smoothing back his hair are the cool cove waves, firming, soothing, erasing. Brian shoulders his bag and her mother rises and comes quickly into the house, the familiar fall of her bare feet sweep past the closed door, then out again with bills in her hand, transferred to Brian's. Even this doesn't console him; from the window she can see the fear still shadowing his face. As he leaves the yard she watches his battered sneakers and wishes they were on their way somewhere together, to exchange folded newspapers for money, or to ring doorbells and by the time the neighbors answer be gone.

The door slaps shut and the yard is empty and she smells bacon and cigarette smoke and knows that the hands on the skillet and crockery are hers and his those on the burning and the tall red glass. She looks out at the blue and green and orange yard, tracing on the windowsill the masked man's slashing signature, in three strokes, the end of everything, *Z, Z, Z.*

Joe Louis Was a Heck of a Fighter

Jewelle Gomez

Gilda was more than alive. The 150 years she carried were flung casually around her shoulders, an intricately knit shawl handed down from previous generations, but distinctly her own. Her legs were smooth and mocha brown, unscarred by the knife-edge years spent on the Mississippi plantation and strengthened by more recent nights dancing in speakeasies and discos. The paradox did not escape Gilda. Her power was forged by deprivation and decadence and the preternatural endurance that had been thrust upon her unexpectedly. Her grip could snap bone and bend metal, and when she ran she was the wind, she was invisible and alone.

Tonight, going home to Effie, she walked easily, gazing at the evening skyline. The tree-shrouded park sloped gently downward from the city street to the sluggish river. The soft flowing of the water played in her ears, obscuring the city sound. Ahead of her through darkness Gilda saw a man leaning against the park fence, hidden from the streetlight by the shadows of a thick maple tree. Her body tensed but she felt no fear. He was in his twenties, strongly built and obviously up to no good. But he was only a man, while she . . . well, she knew the ropes.

What she did feel was anger, something she'd only recently learned could be hers. Her mother, Fulani features hemmed into a placid gaze, had not been allowed that luxury. She had been a slave, admonished to be grateful. As a child Gilda had not understood; the master who owned all and was responsible for everyone never showed anger; his wife, whom he pampered and worshiped oppressively, was angry all the time. As was the overseer who regularly vented his anger on black flesh. But the blacks were not thought to have anger any more than a mule or a tree cut down for kindling.

The young man stood under the maple, his intentions leering out from behind an empty grin. As she walked past he spoke low, almost directly in her ear, "Hey Mama, don't walk so fast."

Gilda continued on, hoping he would take his loss and shut up. He didn't. "Aw Mama, come on be nice to me."

The anger speared her, leaving a metallic taste in her mouth. Where were the words for what she felt? Gilda stopped and turned to him, smiling as she remembered the words of an irate Chicago waitress in 1949: "I am not your mama. If I were I would have drowned you at birth."

She walked on. He caught up again. "Why you bitches so hard. Come on sistuh, give me a break!"

She walked on.

"Come on little girl, let me see that smile again." With that, he seized her arm in what he thought was a viselike grip. She shook free easily, leaving him off balance. Without another word he snatched at her close-cropped hair, hoping to pull her into the shadows.

A low moan sounded in the back of Gilda's throat. She could almost see her slim fingers clenched around his neck, snapping the connection to the spine. She replaced that vision with the memory of a hot night in Florida in 1950. She'd been sitting in an after-hours club watching the fighter show how he'd whipped a Tampa boy who said boxing was just a "coon show." Gilda smiled again as she raised her fist and smashed it into the man's jaw. He fell unconscious to the cracked pavement, half-sprawled on the thin city grass. Gilda lifted him from the street so he sat against a tree; she knelt low, hiding them from the traffic, and smoothly sliced the flesh behind his ear with her fingernail. She took her share of the blood swiftly, enjoying the warmth as it washed over her. Then she held her hand to seal the wound and felt the man's faint but steady pulse.

As she rose to leave, Gilda was glad she had such a good memory. "Yeah, Joe Louis was a heck of a fighter!" she said aloud, then turned swiftly, and disappeared inside the wind blowing off the river.

P Not Q

Todd Grimson

It was the best job he'd ever had. Way out in the middle of nowhere, in an underground lab beneath the desert—he didn't know if the site was in New Mexico, Arizona, Utah, or Nevada . . . but it didn't matter, because he had no desire whatsoever to come up and out into the air.

Pavel was supposed to be in charge of security, and he slept there, surrounded by the video monitors of the console. The place was incomplete, funding had never been approved to finish construction or fill in the rest of the staff. Pavel sat, looking off into the cool darkness of the huge chamber, his cot and hot plate on a raised platform in a warehouse-like space empty but for giant spools of cable, scaffolding, and wooden crates of unknowable equipment, and he petted his cat, drank his tea, and was content.

In another section, there was some activity, some scientists and scientific types, but Pavel rarely came in close contact with them. To take a shower or fetch food from the pantry, he had to go through their area, and he nodded at them, they knew who he was, but he was not here to socialize. He got enough of their conversation from surveillance devices, voice-activated microphones, and the like.

For some reason, when the engineers had built the showers, they'd built them outscale, so that the cubicles were some fifteen feet deep and the water cascaded down from twenty feet or so up in the air . . . although the controls had been installed at a reachable level, perhaps as a last-minute stopgap. Pavel loved these showers, loved the smooth turquoise tiles: it was the kind of shower in which Aztec sacrificial victims would have washed themselves, with aloe vera soap, before climbing the steps of the pyramid to joyfully give their red hearts to the beating sun.

He waited, sometimes, until he was pretty dirty, to make the clean feeling more intense. He and his cat, a Siamese, communicated by a rough telepathy—rough in that sometimes it did not work—and Pavel waited, the distant ceiling a hundred feet above his platform, no lights up there, waited as his animal stalked mice and other small prey. He had an arsenal, but he hadn't cleaned any of the guns in months. He had submachine guns, tear gas, stun grenades, and a rocket launcher he'd built from a kit.

He made no effort to keep track of the days and weeks and months. He read no books, magazines, or newspapers, listened to no radio, watched no television . . . unless, of course, his monitors counted as television . . . as no doubt they did, in some sense, as he did watch them, if intermittently and erratically . . . those images formed on his retina, and were registered there, and back on through the nervous circuitry into his brain—though to what end, or, if waiting for something, waiting for what, he could not have said.

He had his irregular routines. Certain tunnels to explore, leading off into the old mine shafts; his austere meals to prepare; his tea; his important naps; time spent following his cat about. Time was like a viscous clear fluid, and if specks of matter changed shadow or shape within this fluid, metabolizing or undergoing metamorphosis, still the fluid was indistinguishable from what it had been before, even if there seemed added some faint sense of flavor, or tang.

So, when the terminal suddenly came to life with a clatter and printed a message, Pavel wasn't sure how to respond. Certainly he was prepared to obey, to run through the drill, whatever the drill might turn out to be, but there was a good moment during which it seemed he had forgotten how to read.

Then the message organized itself into: P NOT Q. ACTION TO TAKE: PICK UP SCHULTZ AT AIRPORT, 0900. QUERY?

He had none. Since it was not the Q protocol, there was really nothing to ponder. The next morning, he would have to ascend and drive in. He could remember Schultz, but just barely. There was no reason to set an alarm. At 0600 he was up and about. None of the scientific crew seemed to be awake.

He took the elevator to ground level, and was not surprised that the battery in the pickup truck was dead. He fixed this, filled up with gas, and set out. The sun was on the horizon, the morning sky lavender, leaving shadows of tangerine and rose upon the peach-hued land-scape of sand, rock, and dust. He left a big plume of dust behind him as he headed toward the mappable roads. When he pulled onto the well-worn asphalt highway his mind was clear and clean, he saw a big truck pulling a double silver trailer that said PIKE'S, and he went the other way, caught up in the minute, instantaneous tensions of driving, trying to drive *rightly* as if judged by some higher law of harmony between vehicle, traffic, and road.

Pavel witnessed an early-morning shining lake mirage, and this blended into a real memory, the first in a while . . . he was in the dis-tant mountains at the festival of Gobardan, with its displays of colored lights and huge puppets, the children begging candy. If you didn't have any, they would sing a jeering little song at you, and harass you as much as they could, tolerated and even abetted, with laughter, by the adults. The cattle were painted, and decorated with garlands of flowers. Many people wore elaborate animal masks, and took part in various dances and rites. There was one ceremony that had made a tremendous impression on Pavel—in a sense he had been trying to figure it out ever since. He couldn't get it out of his mind. There was a young mother, incidentally pretty, nude, with short dark hair . . . and she was lying down, in good humor, her belly rubbed with crimson ocher, and she drew up her knees as a tame male roebuck came and stood there in front of her, in a symbolic position, and all of this was taking place in a cavern, lit by hundreds of candles, the walls painted with figures—Pavel could still remember some of the music, the women's chorus in the thin air outside, as they all came out, Pavel spellbound, under a baroque profusion of stars, all blinking and coun-terblinking, in clusters and bunches, lively and shining, and he had caught the eye of the girl, the young mother, her dark eyes had looked into his, he couldn't hold her gaze and looked down to the shark's-teeth necklace she was wearing, it couldn't have been shark's teeth so far from the ocean, more likely wolf or panther—and somehow, witnessing the shining lake mirage and recalling the ceremony made him realize, today, that an intention, or capacity of intention, was forming within him, that the muscle of will's contraction was all but spent, ready to spring back . . . and, alert, he caught a glimpse of a roadrunner amid the flat sands and cacti, the spiky flowers and rock formations, rocks turning carnelian or dried-blood red with iron, greenish with malachite, gray or bleached like bones.

Civilization: telephone wires, power lines, road signs, the occasional service station, a billboard or two, more and more automobiles—Pavel saw that he was nearing the airport, outside the city, and he looked at his watch and saw he was on time.

When Schultz deplaned, the last passenger to do so, Pavel nodded, and Schultz recognized him too. Schultz was a big, heavy man, with glasses, a round, almost piggish head, receding dark hair, and red, meaty lips which seemed to evidence a need to eat and drink and talk. He would not have been an attractive man to women, but he nevertheless held himself with a certain arrogance, or spoiledness; and Pavel had seen this type before.

Soon they were in the vehicle, heading for the project, and Schultz reached over to turn on the radio: a country weeper commenced. They continued, but in a few minutes Schultz interrupted Pavel's reverie by a question.

"What do you think about vengeance?"

Pavel considered this seriously, then saw that there was no reason for a serious answer, and said, "Why do you ask?"

"Oh, I don't know," Schultz said. "I was just thinking about that song." And as if in afterthought: "It's hard to be sinless, no matter where."

Pavel had no comment, and the DJ spoke for a while; another song came on, whereupon Schultz said,

"So how're things going? I mean, how is the work?" The familiarity seemed forced.

"As I understand math," Pavel replied, "if we had twice as many people, we could get the same job done in half the time."

"Correct," Schultz said. "Or: approximately."

And nothing else was said for many miles.

"You know," Schultz began, perspiring, loosening his tie, "when people commonly believed in witches, there was an overwhelming body of evidence that seemed to support this, support belief in magic and witchcraft."

Pavel didn't see what he was getting at. But Schultz seemed disturbed, with something on his mind. There was air conditioning, but he seemed to be becoming increasingly warm.

"Opposites attract," he went on. "This is what causes perpetual motion. Destruction is good, and goodness destructive. That kind of thing." He was looking out the window, squirming around, developing a tic in his neck and shoulders and head.

"Where are all the animals?" he asked. "I thought I'd see some Gila monsters, or deer."

In a few moments he began to suffer a sort of seizure, gasping and trembling and contorting, and Pavel pulled over to the side of the road, pushing Schultz away once when the man clutched at him with hot hands.

His body settling down, Schultz spoke, slumped against the door, in an unusual voice. It sounded as if he said his name was Slog. The tic continued, and he said, having difficulty getting it out, that he was from a distant planet, and that he controlled part of the brain of Schultz.

Pavel listened, demonstrating his attention, aware of the loaded .38 he had at his disposal in a little holder under the seat. The easiest thing might be to have Schultz dig his own grave, then put him in it. After all, this wasn't really Schultz. It was the wrong Schultz.

"What planet did you say you were from?"

"Arco," it sounded like, and Pavel recalled that that was the last service station they'd gone past.

"We have to go back," he said. "The airport's as far as I can take you."

Schultz seemed to be regaining his earthly composure somewhat, as though perhaps a load was off his mind. In a more normal voice—still twitching a bit, however—he said, "You have no idea how much better you'd feel if you could escape from gravity for a few years. Just no idea. Pull over, pull over here!" he shouted, and Pavel braked, alarmed, but saw the solitary phone booth Schultz was pointing at—and as soon as he could, Schultz ran out, slamming the door, running to this phone booth out in the middle of nowhere. Pavel followed, holding the .38.

"Hello? Hello? Yes. Right. Absolutely. You're right."

The phone had not been ringing before Schultz answered it. Pavel observed him. When the conversation was concluded, Schultz simply threw the receiver down to dangle, swinging back and forth, at the end of its cord. With a sudden movement he bent over, coming up— much to Pavel's surprise—with a live, wriggling rattlesnake, which he held right behind the head, chuckling evilly, hissing back at it, looking it in the face.

For a moment, in the near delirium of this scene, Pavel thought he saw a halo of flames around the fat man's head.

Then Schultz flung the serpent away from him, mightily, and returned, now docilely enough, satisfied, to the truck.

Pavel wanted the gun near at hand, but he was afraid that if he sat on it, he might accidentally blow off one of his buttocks. Left in his lap, it might do more unpredictable harm. So he put it back under the seat.

"Let's go get a sno-cone," he said, as he started the engine and shifted into gear.

"Sounds fair," said Schultz, and he didn't speak again all the way back into town. Rather, he hummed and tapped his fingers in a manner that kept Pavel nervous, waiting for some further act to which he might have to respond.

It wouldn't do, he decided, just to send Schultz back on the next plane. And from here he couldn't exactly send him to Mars, or wherever Schultz would imagine he wanted to go. But still, he needed to be someplace, and that someplace was not the underground project, where he'd be a security risk and a pain in the ass.

True to his word, Pavel stopped and bought Schultz a sno-cone, almond flavored, and managed to consume one himself as he drove out to Madame Rosa's, where he might be able to bunk Schultz for a few days.

It was a big house, long and low, and Pavel took the ignition key and his gun up to the front door, leaving Schultz in the passenger seat, finishing his sno-cone, trying to get every last bit of syrup from the folded paper, sticking out his big, strong bovine tongue.

A Hispanic girl, young and skinny, answered the door with ill will, looking tired, saying, "What are you doing here?" She was adorned with an interesting necklace, but it wasn't made of any teeth.

It looked like a ranchero he'd seen once in a cheap vampire movie. In fact, it was almost certainly the same place.

"My friend needs a place to board for a couple of days. Top dollar. Madame Rosa has dealt with our account before."

"Yeah, well, we're not working right now."

"Why not?"

"We're on strike," she said, and then clarified, with less spite, "We're all sick."

"That's okay," Pavel said. "Do you have any drugs you could give him? You know, to relax him. He's been working too hard."

"Just a place to rest? That's all?"

"Right. Someplace quiet and secure."

"We could put him in the dungeon," she said, friendlier still, thinking it over, and Pavel agreed, "That'd be great."

She laughed, and Pavel went and fetched Schultz, who cooperated but looked a little bit as if he was thinking of going off on another interplanetary jag pretty soon. That was okay, Pavel thought. They'd know how to handle him.

All the long ride back out to the project, he knew he'd done the right thing. They could come and get Schultz anytime they wanted. He'd be safe there. It was better than locking him in a bathroom somewhere, which had been his alternate plan.

So now he drove, listening to that same country station, going past the Arco sign, hearing that same slow song about revenge. Steel guitar, a Southern accent, accusations of misconduct and the bad consequence foretold. Yeah.

When he went down, the scientists asked him, "Where is he?" and he shook his head and said, "It was the wrong Schultz." They realized they weren't going to hear more.

In the showers, he got a big surprise: someone had wheeled in metal carts of dead bodies, just piled them up, unbelievably pale and violet tinged, shaved bald—and then Pavel saw that they were crash dummies, they looked so real they'd given him a scare. Why had they brought them in here? And why today, of all days?

They must have had their reasons, he supposed, forgetting about it as the water began to fall down on him from high above, splashing off his body onto the turquoise tiles.

The Complete Works

Gary Indiana

He's written the thing, he's sending it off. *Why didn't you love me,* it says, *when I was the only one who loved you.* He considers the events that have not taken place since he became a celebrity, acquired money and opportunities, proved to his French Catholic, diminishing family that he exists. He hasn't forgotten about Nino. He hasn't learned how to purchase clothes. He doesn't own a duplex. The one he entertained great hopes about, the one with whom it was finally going to work out, has written to say that something truly unexpected has occurred.

The agronomist showed him her bees. She put the net-encased bonnet on his head and showed him how to light a smoke pot. He stuffed the smouldering burlap into the creased tin chamber, snapped the lid down.

"They almost never do anything," she said. "It depends entirely on their mood." She paused while locking the shed. "Is it *mood?* That is the English word?"

He opens his address book and notices that on a single page three names are those of dead people and two are of people he no longer speaks to.

What about my scars, he asked his artist friend, the one he'd begun to love after calling him an asshole. The artist had flinched then, as if he'd been hurt by someone he cared about. Brett seldom realized that people cared about him until he hurt them.

Don't you think everybody notices my scars, he said.

Most people don't notice anything, the artist said. Most people can't see shit from Shinola.

Later the same day he said to Elizabeth, Don't people think of the SS when these kids turn their parents in?

Elizabeth said: You think they know what the SS was? They don't know shit from Shinola.

"The white wine has to be bottled during the quarter moon," the agronomist said, stroking the hair of her eldest, fiercely attached son. "And then for the red, the three-quarter moon. The children do it. They like to do it."

I'm glad if you're happy, he's written, as if they were a pair of bumper stickers. *But I can't help feeling*— Yes, he thinks, when you feel something, it surprises you. But actually, you can't help it.

I called, his mother said, because I have . . . a little bad news.

He knows before the pause that she has a lot of bad news. There are voices one knows so completely that they could read the phone book and one would still hear *Phaedra*. After almost four decades, the words she has for his father dying are: a little bad news.

At the age of thirty-seven he realized he'd never play mah-jongg with Robert Lewis, who had expressed interest, three years before, in forming a mah-jongg group. On the strength of this Brett had bought a two-hundred-dollar mah-jongg set. He had learned from elderly Chinese in the Chinese ghetto in Bangkok how to play fast, fast, fast. He'd thought Robert Lewis was going to be his friend forever but he'd lost Robert Lewis to heroin, a little differently than he'd lost Nino to heroin. Robert Lewis's loss had been gradual and dignified. It was, in fact, still going on. He would probably be losing Robert Lewis in bits and pieces for the rest of his life, but he lost Nino over two days of incredible ugliness, permanently.

"We'd like to be the kind of people who—"

"We'd like to pretend we're the kind of people who—"

Get together for mah-jongg once a week. Order dinner in from the local whatever. Still fuck.

The funeral, the wake. Open casket at Pilsudski's Funeral Home. No one in this family knows what to do with death. Cry, at least. He's gone. He was a good person. And now he looks so dead. You brought me into the world and now you've gone out of it and I'll never get anything straight with you, will I. Never did, never will. But if you were still here we'd both be laughing about the flowers. Death means never having to respect your allergies.

"Mama, what are you going to do?"

"Well, I was thinking about that."

His brother and sister-in-law are trying to look natural, nursing the gin and tonics they never allow themselves in Washington because Roy has to fly at six in the morning and it sets a bad example for the kids. Roy missed the runway by three inches with a senator's wife on board six months ago, no fault of his own, they'd redirected to a smaller landing strip for security reasons. The plane touched down okay, but taxiing across the field Roy thought they had eight feet leeway, and they didn't. Three days of urine tests and psychological examinations and finally, uncharacteristically, a call from the White House to lay off.

"I think I'll have this room done over. You know, Ames has a good deal now on pile carpets. I could take up this and put a new one down and then do something about those draperies."

You're the second person I talked to today who used that expression, Brett said to Elizabeth.

Oh yeah? Who was the first?

You know who.

Oh. Well, it doesn't surprise me that he says that too. I say it all the time. The trouble is, most people don't know what Shinola is anymore, either.

A childhood that he can't remember: does that mean it was happy, or just the opposite? He waits on line at the bank machine, while an uninteresting young woman talks to her uninteresting young man in a loud voice, for the benefit of the other customers. All these people whose voices tell you that nothing will ever really happen to them: they talk louder than the others, hoping their banalities will seem glamorous to people whose lives are even less their own.

The machine spits out forty dollars, less than he's asked for. Words appear on the screen: I'm sorry, I can't handle your transaction now.

His bank machine tells him it is sorry.

His bank machine talks just like Nino.

The only time he ran into Nino afterward had been at the corner of St. Marks and Third Avenue. Brett was twenty minutes late for his appointment. Nino did not know what to do with his face, and the other junkie who had stepped in to pick up the pieces after Brett threw Nino out stood glowering at the encounter like a mother snake protecting a new litter.

"Small world," Nino said, in a jittery voice. He smiled quickly, his eyes darting to his snake-companion for assurance. As if a momentary reconnection with the past might be enough to snap their bond of Krazy Glue.

"Not if you have to clean it," Brett said, looking at Nino's friend. He continued walking.

I can't handle your transaction now.

I'm sorry.

Even a machine can say "I" and offer sentiments.

He's noticed that people quite often say "thank you," now, when you haven't done anything for them: if you hold the door for just an extra second until their hand catches it, instead of letting go as soon as you've passed through. Maybe people are so desperate for civility that even the hope of it makes them say "thank you."

It's only because Danny was there, Nino told him over the phone. If Danny hadn't been there it would've been a lot different. I still love you, Brett.

Danny was always there, Brett told him.

Not when I was with you, Nino said. When I was with you I felt strong enough to stay away from him.

You were never with me, Brett said.

They had to burn the peaches and the figs and the plums, incinerate all the vegetables, destroy the milk.

"I'm not *so* worried about the iodine and cesium; they decay quickly," the agronomist said. "But. The strontium. A problem. Especially with respect to the soybeans. Because. We're having to plant soybeans in the next year, or pay a special tax. Because of the corn surplus. I worry about the strontium. In the soybeans. You say soybean, in English?"

I still love you, but I can't handle your transaction now.

Have a nice day.

He wondered if the awful couple—the tennis player and the feminist artist—who hired Nino to work in their loft knowing that Nino and Danny had burgled his apartment, had a sign in their car window that said CHILD ON BOARD. They were the kind of people who would, he thought. He thought the precisely appropriate reward for their largesse would be if Nino and Danny kidnapped the baby and sold it to buy crack.

If I can't be the one, I can at least wish you every happiness: I can, he thinks, and I do. All the happiness in the world. Which is to say: not all that much.

"Over easy," the dealer's wife explained, encouragingly, to the English-impaired Swedish waitress, illustrating the idea with a graceful flipping motion of her hand. "Kiss the pan?"

The waitress looked at the dealer's wife incredulously.

"You want over easy," she said, penciling the order on her pad.

"They don't know 'kiss the pan' in New Jersey," the dealer scolded when the waitress left. "It's a Manhattan term."

"It's not a Manhattan term at all," replied his wife. "It's an egg term."

I don't love you any more. Sad.

I can't handle your transaction now.

But I wish you all the happiness, you know: all the happiness in the world.

The Palace of Marriage

Karen Karbo

No Soviet emigrates for any real reason. Okay, Solzhenitsyn, Sharansky. But they are movie stars of emigration. No usual émigré has their problems. Usual émigré leaves because one night he starts drinking. He is drinking and he is sad. He is in bad news with his boss, let's say, or some friend has disappeared forever into psychiatric hospital. No American can understand such sadness. This man is a bathtub drain with bathwater swirling down it all at same time.

For my wife Bella Bellinka and me it was one February midnight. Heat and light vanished from our apartment without warning. Such cold is impossible to remember. In Los Angeles we do nothing but perspire and squint; heat and sunlight are always here, careless, competent, extravagant, like Americans.

But that February night we huddled in bed wearing every clothes we could get on. We boiled potatoes for our pockets and socks. I had a cold; tears of ice formed at end of my dripping nose. We drank and drank.

Bella and I talked until our throats hurt about what we wanted. A lot, it was, for people who had next to nothing. It started with heat, then bloomed into things fantastic. Bella wanted clothes, shoes, stockings, mascara, manicures, bedroom slippers, highball glasses, mail-order catalogues, marzipan, super-absorbency Tampax, *Vogue*, a subscription to *Vogue*, a job at *Vogue*, things of which I had never even heard.

I wanted a garden of cactus and a baby. First American Bogoga. Ernest Bogoga. William Bogoga. F. Scott Bogoga.

Bellinka humored me. My wishes were few and simple. Harmless dreams. But we were so stirred up. We got going. Our breath turned hot and thawed two small patches on window above our bed. I mashed a few potatoes still in my back pocket. Now I realize this sudden passion was sparked by thoughts of possibilities, not love.

One thing leads to another. Is most cruel fact on earth. *A* is one thing, *B* is other thing. *Leads to* is part no one can see or name. No one can say, "I am now living *leads to*." *Leads to* is how whole world winds up at *B*, biggest sins and mistakes.

Suddenly I am making applications for visas. I am sitting in offices, waiting for signatures. I even say I am Jew to emigrate. Jews then they were letting out. Can you imagine, saying you are Jew to get out of persecution? But there I am. I have become Bogogowicz.

Then we are on airplane, sixteen hours out of Vienna, ten in New York, finally soft, hot air of Los Angeles, palm trees as tall as skyscrapers, going, going, going, ending way up in mustardy haze. Cars like stars, splattering galaxy of black asphalt streets. Fantastic.

Every morning our neighbor does things naked on her terrace. Yoga, toenail polishing, needlepoint. Today it is leg shaving.

Our apartments mirror each other across narrow driveway. Both are second floor. She supposes her pots of bushy ferns, avocado plants, and camellias hide her. But no. She is betrayed; I am one who is hidden. From bedroom window I watch. I watch her pink plastic shaver sail up her shin, over her knee, and beyond.

At 6:30 a.m. every day I hear her sliding door open, close. Out of bed I stumble, fumbling, putting on my glasses. At night I leave our bedroom curtain open.

Early morning is only reasonable time in Los Angeles in September. After around 9 a.m. wind comes. Wind is hot, dry, as though someone put entire city in clothes dryer. People get bloody noses. Houses in Hollywood Hills burst into flames for no reason. Every day smells like campfire. At night faces and car windshields are coated with thin layers of soot.

Our neighbor lifts her head, sniffs. Air is already brown-orange with smoke from fires burning all night. But now is pleasant. She enjoys herself. She squirts on shaving cream, whistles Chopin. She is our first American neighbor: happy, cultured, clean, her nipples dark and flat as the discs underneath our living room chairs. They are for prevention of dents on wall-to-wall carpet, these discs. My Bella Bellinka loves them. They always seem to be on sale somewhere and she buys more than we will ever need. Same with air fresheners. All my clothes smell now like pine trees. I have not seen one pine tree since we left Soviet Union.

My wife, my sweet Bella Bellinka, is asleep. Only her back rising up and down says she is breathing and still alive. She sleeps flat on her face. This is to keep her hairstyle from mussing.

When we became émigrés Bellinka's hair became art. Every Thursday afternoon now she returns home from a person named Roger, her head balancing a high, bright, curled tower of hair. It comes before me, and makes her wary of performing wifely duty. She is afraid I will damage her curls, despite my promises.

Real reason is not her hair, of course. I see her eyes glimmer at night while watching couples in love wrestle on television. Simple fact is I am ugly and I am old. Not age old, but life old. I am fifty-four, Soviet, bald, and nearly blind. All I want in life are cactuses for my terrace, and a son.

I stand ogling my neighbor long after my interest goes. My leg gets a cramp. I love my Bella Bellinka. I ogle only to make Bella jealous a little. I believe things might improve between us if, first thing she opens her light gray eyes, she is faced with my interest in another woman.

Instead, Bellinka is irritated. "Yuz, shame on you! People call police for this here!" She whips curtains closed, swats my arm. Her low stern voice reminds me how she used to reprimand a dog we had in Moscow. This old dog was incontinent, and loved our only rug.

"She is there in plain sight!" I say. "I am still a man. Don't dish me over the coals. Please, Bella Bellinka, I beg of you!"

"Oh, Yuz." She goes into bathroom.

Outside, palm trees lining our street are shaken awake by burst of wind. It starts already. It is said this wind, known as Santa Ana, makes people crazy. The fronds creak and groan in unison. I have never heard a tidal wave, but this is what I imagine it sounds like.

Bella and I argue violently about silly things. Where to buy ice cube trays. What is cable TV and do we need it. Which bus goes where. How to keep our apartment cooler. We avoid arguing about things upon which we truly disagree. We are afraid. Now we are in America, there is no reason for our marriage.

In Soviet Union we married for reasons of housing. Bella I met only once. She was cousin of fellow worker at laboratory, willing to do anything for permanent residency permit in Moscow. She was too talkative, overweight, provincial. As a man mostly from Moscow, my advantage was clear. Somehow I was taller than her then.

She always carried around a *Vogue* magazine she got on black market. It got rained on, snowed on so often it disintegrated. Bella wept, as though she had lost her eyesight. I found her odd but beautiful. And I was forty-eight years old, never in love, with a twelve-by-nine-foot apartment in central Moscow I inherited from my grandfather.

When we met on steps of Palace of Marriage for ceremony, Bella didn't recognize me. She passed right by and tapped on shoulder of a much taller, much younger man. Corrected, she blushed, strangled her bouquet in embarrassment. I perspired, over-forgave her. She asked how big was apartment again. Thirteen by ten feet, I said. I invented a large kitchen, in case seeing me in cruel gray daylight changed her mind.

Accounting entered our young relationship there and then. Yuz forgives; Bella is forgiven. Yuz has Moscow apartment; Bella has nothing. Bella wants to emigrate; Yuz loses good job in applying for visas. Yuz wants a child; Bella falls asleep instantly. Bella is forty. I know what is happening. She is waiting to shift blame from herself to biology.

Yuz loves Bella; Bella tolerates Yuz, remembering all she owes him.

Every person who tries to emigrate loses his job, first thing. I worked in special research laboratory as operator of machine that washed and sterilized laboratory instruments, Petri dishes. This was special lab in dull green building, huge and unmarked, on Kropotkin Street. It was place for researching in vitro fertilization.

My Petri dishes grew humans. Or tried to. They were old dishes, warped a little. They appeared to seal properly but actually allowed all kinds of things to grow inside. Humans never got so far. There had never been a baby from that place yet. Either egg and sperm never got along, or women who came for implantation had so many abortions that no embryo could get good hold. Crude jokes went around.

Once, at end of my shift, near my last days there, when all instruments and dishes were clean, slick, and steaming, I found incubator where special Petri dishes were kept. Light shining on them was yellow warm. Culture medium was scab color, dishes looked innocent, empty. But I knew, I knew. Here were racks and racks of potential Soviet citizens. Dumb cells being coaxed along for eventual implantation, birth, then what? Thirty years washing laboratory instruments for lucky ones.

I went home right away. Bella was packing her china, her most beloved thing. She thought she could take it with her, even though I tried to persuade her we would never be able to get it out.

I said, "If we ever get to America we must have child." Bellinka, so anxious to emigrate, so afraid it would not happen if she made trouble, promised me yes. She says now she only said she'd think about it.

But that cold dull day is scar on memory. The rusty red discs glowing under their artificial sun, the humble worried face of my wife, her nod. A cracked tea cup in her hand. A baby, yes. Frank Bogoga. Don Bogoga. Brooke Bogoga.

I cook breakfast while Bella prepares to go to work. She is TA, teaching assistant of beginning Russian at university. I do not know what this is, but I know she brings home paycheck and takes classes in Advanced Russian Syntax. Neither of us have ever heard of Syntax before this job. It sounds like something to do with space.

I drop icy hard waffles in toaster. Eggo they are called. Syrup in *babushka*-shaped bottle. Instant Tang. I also open package of Sno-balls, chocolate cake with pink coconut-flavored foam outside. All American food looks like it could be sold in toy stores.

I said this once to Claire Davis, secretary at Department of Slavic Languages where Bella teaches. Her laugh was like bullets, *ha! ha! ha!* She is making fun, or what? No, she said I was a stitch.

What it is, a stitch? Why is food funny? I never know if America is serious or joking.

Outside our kitchen window is something I will never understand. A billboard higher and bigger than any I ever see. Is several blocks away, looming over all smaller buildings between us. On it is red-headed girl in sunglasses standing, one hip jutted out. She has tight, fierce green pants, breasts the size of hot air balloons floating up under black T-shirt. This is all, except TEENA spelled in big glittery plates that reflect sunlight. In middle of night I come into kitchen for water and she is there. Lights from bottom of billboard shine on her all twenty-four hours. Through our thin curtains her legs look like two green smoke stacks colliding. Who she is? Does she advertise a movie, beer, car telephones?

Bella scuttles in, sandals in hand. "What does Teena advertise?" I ask.

Bella laughs. "Teena is fantastic."

"What it is for, Teena? She actress?" I make a butter sandwich of my Eggos. I like my Tang straight from jar with no water added.

"Who knows. Not so much butter, Yuz. Bad for heart."

"How can she be fantastic if you do not know what she is? Is wasteful, all that paint. She is fantastic and no one knows what she is for? Is ridiculous."

"No," says Bella. "You are ridiculous. She is pretty, that's all. Please just to go with it, okay?"

"*Go* with it? What is that? With what am I supposed to go. You copy Americans like a big talking Russian bird."

"You are hopeless," she says. "I am not big." She pushes her waffle aside, begins applying her makeup. She does this at breakfast table so to have benefit of natural daylight. All her ladies' fashion magazines say makeup is best applied this way, in this light, and so she does.

I stare at her. I am like a television channel changed. She is not angry or even flustered. She sips coffee from one of her china cups. She dragged them through after all. They are cheap, homely white. When she opened carton, second day we arrived, all handles were broken off. Broken and stolen, for they were nowhere.

Bella Bellinka is like these cups. An empty one. Broken, but still able to float. Floating upon America. She is tiny and fragile, the ocean immense, but she soars in the sunshine, up one tall wave, down another, never sinking. She goes with it. I know this expression. Never would I use it. We are not so American as she likes to imagine.

"Perhaps emigration was not right," I say. "Is so difficult in Los Angeles. So difficult for Yuz."

"Yuzushka, please. You have job. We both do. Soon we will have car. Is heat making you upset? I will make you more Eggos. But no butter! Promise Bella." She hurries around kitchen. She pours me more coffee, even though I have some.

My job is as photocopier. Los Angeles motto is no place you can walk to is worth working at, but is not true. Captain Copy is eleven blocks from our apartment. Is air-conditioned, decorated with pink fishing nets, painted starfish with glitter. Free coffee on all day.

Today, as I walk, a red sun sits on my bald head. The sky is thick and yellow. I have my hat, but I will not wear it in public. Is a white sailor hat, with YOOZ ANDREYEVICH sewn in blue thread. Except owner, everyone at Captain Copy must wear these hats. The first one they gave me said USE. I made them do over. New one said YOOZ, a clown name, even worse. Bogogas have dignity, I insisted. My name is Yuz. My heart slugged against my chest. They refused to try again. I forced them to add ANDREYEVICH. They called me a stupid old pinko. What is that, a fish? Wind rolls an empty garbage can down middle of street against traffic. Cars swerve to miss it, but no one gets out to turn it right. My lips, they are so chapped.

I have one friend in Los Angeles: Pak, a square, wavy-haired Korean. He works at Captain Copy seven years. He has had three hats, all of them misspelled PACK. Most of our business is screenplays for movies. Fast rich people in shorts come in, jiggle their legs, their keys, while waiting.

When no one is there we photocopy body parts. We read screenplays. Pak is teaching himself English this way. "CUT TO—Lunch," he says when he goes out at noon. "CUT TO—The Next Day," he says every morning.

We tell each other everything, but as with Americans I don't understand all. Pak has problems with his car, he stole it or had it stolen. There is some tube situation also. Either inside his wife or the television set.

Today, boss is on vacation in Mexico, some place that starts with X. I sit by coffee maker and eat spoonfuls of coffee whitener. I have somehow gotten on subject of cactus. Pak photocopies without putting down lid. Every few seconds a white flash bleaches his face. I think he may go blind. I tell him. He nods and grins.

"I want garden, Pak. Is only matter of going, putting down $2.89, taking my Bunny Ears, my Baby Toes or Aloe and starting, right? But what if I spend every monies on Powder Puffs and Silk Pincushions, only to discover I want Organ Pipes and Prickly Pears? Too much choice. My wife says is typical Soviet fear."

"CAMERA ZOOMS IN ON YUZ," says Pak. "He is a burned-out shell of a man, but has quite a way with the ladies. Think young Burt Reynolds."

I make Pak sit down. I think perhaps hot Los Angeles wind dries up his brain.

Evening comes. Wind stays. Bella Semyonovna and I ride bus to Department of Slavic Languages for special get-together party. Invitation says we are gathering to welcome all new faculty and students. It takes forty-five minutes to go twelve miles from our apartment to university. Smells of urine, melting plastic bus seats. Bella complains her thighs are sticking. She has a new dress, new silver high-heel shoes.

We pass bank sign saying 6:30, temperature 101. A man at front of bus steals wallet from woman's purse. Her blind eye dog licks his shoe. People are desperate. Sky is blotted with sulfurous smoke. Fires wink in the hills. Like Russian steppes, Los Angeles sometimes seems emptied of weather. All clouds, rains, frosts, and fogs are scooped out, leaving only this monotonous wind. I say this to Bella. She shrugs. Is better than freezing rain. She is reading one of her magazine articles: "Make Your Love Making Aerobically Efficient!" A picture shows two tan people in bed wearing sweat bands and stop watches.

"Huh," I say, "why you reading that?"

She shuts magazine, pretends she hasn't heard.

Slavic Department is small and crowded. I drink four or five vodkas just so I can speak. There are mostly professors, a few students. They huddle in circles that keep breaking apart and reforming, the way low-level life forms reproduce. They sweat, swab their suntan faces with their hands.

Bella has propped me by food table, so she can mingle. I eat hard-boiled eggs, their yolks suffocated by black caviar. One after another I eat.

These people mean much to Bella. Her dimples work overtime. I hear her across room, through chinks in party noise, giggling and calling people *Cookie*. She never says *Cookie* at home.

Claire Davis, secretary to Slavic Department, arrives. She says she stopped for ice. She is tall. Her face is like loud music. Freckles, moles, wild eyebrows, green-gold-brown eyes all going at once. She is not Slavic. She says when she took this job she thought Slavic was inventor of artificial heart. She only works here because she wants to write. She is illiterate, then, or what? She wants to write Russian?

She reaches over and pinches my side. "How's it going, Yuz?"

"Good, good," I mumble, my mouth full of egg.

She throws herself down in a folding chair. She wears shorts. I am drunk. Her knees stare up at me. Two doorknobs wrapped in silk, sprouting tender blond hair. "Yuz, now that is a cool tie. It looks like Las Vegas."

I look down. My tie is deep green, tiny saguaro cactus stitched on, stems bent like arms. I found it one day in dumpster behind our apartment.

"I call it my Cac-tie," I say.

"Ha! Ha! Ha!" Her bullet laugh. She loves this. She pulls over a tall thin boy. His bony jaw chewing looks like machinery. He wears a T-shirt that says TOO MEAN TO MARRY. "Pencil Neck," she says to him, "check this out. It's his Cac-tie."

"Booooooo!" says Pencil Neck, but he laughs too.

People are interested. They stop by food table for crackers, more vodka, and stay to admire. They love that I found it among garbage. Jim Spaniel, Assistant Professor of Soviet Society and Culture, says he admires my audacity. I say I thought audacity was some medical procedure. I am going in for an audacity. People laugh. Claire refills my glass. You are *something*, she says.

Dr. Vera Omulchenko, Department Chairman, says, "Yuz, Bella never told us you were such a wit." She has arrived late, giving car trouble as reason. However, I notice she comes with Sergei Lublinsky, famous émigré writer. Lipstick is smeared around her lips, her eyes a little sleepy. Those lovers are around the age of Bella and me, I think.

"That tie is . . ." Sergei Lublinsky wags his finger at it, thinking, " . . . camp."

"Camp!? Only camp I know is where my father lived almost his whole life."

"Your father was in a concentration camp?" Claire's smile drops. She leans closer.

"Magnitogorsk. Labor camp. Fourteen years he lives on soup of rotten cabbage and garbage parts of animals. In deepest winter his shoes were scraps of rubber tied to his feet with wire. And what for? Stealing food ration card from dead neighbor's body."

"You guys," says Claire. "I can't imagine. I have a trauma if I can't get a new outfit." She looks at me, waiting.

I go on. Vodka is kind; it numbs you before reopening all those deep old wounds. I speak to Claire's knees.

"My father was a thermostat. This is real. Commissar had greenhouse. Is built of cypress, greenhouse. These days all are plastic, but in Soviet Union in 1937 they are cypress. Each morning my father goes up to fire boiler for heating, takes care of opening and closing of ventilation. Imagine, at labor camp, tiny greenhouse of birds of paradise, hibiscus, camellias. No prisoner was to know of greenhouse. Those who found out disappeared.

"Once, there is no electricity. Greenhouse goes dark, cold, snow blows inside vents, things freeze. But succulents grow, even there, even then. They huddle near ground, keep all nourishment inside. Surviving is what they do.

"My father was a cactus himself. White hair out like so, fierce expression and tough skin, tough short barrel man. Like me, you know, only better eyesight and not so bald. He manages to get his clothes patched with newspapers so he can read up on latest propaganda. He even gets friend on woman's side of camp. He never sees her face but finds loose board at back of compound near latrines. He can reach through, feel her slim ankles, her breasts—" I have never talked so much to an American in my life. Waves of memories crash through my head.

"Hi Cookies." Is Bella. She pats back of her hair. I realize no woman in this room has hair like hers. It looks like a dessert. "Has Yuz been folding your ear?"

Claire laughs. "Bending our ears. No, this stuff's great. I mean, awful. Incredible."

Bella looks at her a little icy. "Time to go," she says to me.

"A few minutes more," I say. "They like my tie."

"Yes? We purchase at downtown Bullocks department store. My friend Cricket, she is salesgirl of sportswear, instructed us. Is chic, you know."

Claire raises an eyebrow at Jim Spaniel. He has taken some notes on my story, on a tiny pad of paper with a tiny pencil. They begin to laugh. Is low, chugging laugh of people who are tired and hot. I join in. Laughter feeds laughter. We cannot stop.

Bella folds her arms, grows furious, "Yuz Andreyevich, you are laughing at me?"

"We are," I say.

I go home alone.

Claire gives me ride. Wide black streets are empty. The night smells charred. Another bank sign. Time 11:45, temperature still 101. I ask how can it be? Sign must be broken. Claire says she heard it was going to get hotter. She drifts from lane to lane. Driving by braille, she calls it. Braille part is when she bumps over reflective lane markers. Tonight she's had six vodkas and a peach. She says she's on a diet.

Claire's car is air-conditioned. I lean my head against the window. I have never driven alone in a car with an American. A fire truck speeds past, lights whirling but no siren. She tells me about woman she read about who was denied artificial insemination because she wanted a baby on her own. She hated men but loved babies. Claire says this woman used turkey baster. She got some guy who was willing, then impregnates herself. And it worked. Could I believe it?

"Sure," I say. "They have dog psychologists here." I roll down my window. Claire is too young, too foreign. Breathing, even in her air-conditioning, is like inhaling gauze.

We stop in front of my apartment building. I get out. "*Spasiba,* Claire. You are good girl. Say, I mean to ask. Who is this Teena?" I point to billboard. Giantess Teena leers down at us from nighttime sky. Her lips are pink and full. Merciless.

Claire doesn't even need to look. "Nobody. That's her thing."

"She is an actress, singer?"

"She's on billboards. It's a gimmick. You know what a gimmick is? She doesn't do anything. She's a personality."

"She is famous? For doing nothing?"

"Sort of. Yeah, I guess."

I know what is turkey baster. I know because Bella Bellinka went to garage sale down our street and bought an entire drawer of kitchen instruments for fifty cents. We have this drawer sitting on our kitchen counter. At bottom of it under bottle openers, corkscrews, spatulas, and many other mysterious things is decal of person named Barney Rubble. Bellinka and I plan to use turkey baster for our first Thanksgiving. But I will use it now. Robert Bogoga. Madonna Bogoga. Sly Bogoga. Garage sale was being given by a woman who was going to prison.

I fill turkey baster while leaning against kitchen counter.

I am drunk, sure, but what is that? I was forty-eight when I met Bella, and am a drinker since age thirteen. I am saying I have performed this very thing while drunk for many cold decades. I still have on my tie. My mind provides its old slide show. With one hand I push open kitchen curtain. Teena Teeninka, American saint of nobody and nothing, spurs me on.

The lights of Los Angeles reflect off its smoky, smoggy ceiling, giving our bedroom a murky glow. Bella is asleep on her back, her arms and legs tossed away from her. Heat has driven her to this. Curtains and windows are open. I sit on bed edge. The bulb of turkey baster is greasy. Our neighbor is having a party. Music, a fan whirring. Someone yells *Addis Ababa!* A few people applaud. Clark Kent Bogoga. James Bond Bogoga. I know I cannot stop. To stop is to think. Outside, wind has died but still shrieks around inside my head.

I move Bella's leg.

Suddenly, her eyes click open. "Yuz?"

I throw myself on her. She doesn't yell. She growls Russian curses. She smells of toothpaste, vodka, cheese. She grabs my ears. Her nightgown slides up. "How many eyes does an earthworm have?" says someone across the way.

My hands land on her hairdo. She pulls on my ears, kicks at my thighs.

"You filthy Cossack!" she screams. She hates me. She says I am stupid old man. I rub her curls flat. This is what I've wanted, I know it now, yes! They are stiff. They crackle at my touch.

Finally, I stop. I stand. My turkey baster and future progeny have rolled behind bed, to join their fate with lint and lost shoes.

"I am sorry," I say. Sweat blinds me. My shins ache.

"You are disgusting drunken stupid man," she says. She rubs her neck. "Claire is not impressed with you, she feels sorry for you. She listens to your stupid stories from pity."

"Bellinka, I am sorry."

"You are joke to them, those Americans."

"We both are," I say.

She is so stunned to hear this she nods. "Yes, but at least I know this! I have my feelers open. I am no stupid."

"Is so hot," I say.

And, quiet, suddenly. Like many people holding their breath. I look out bedroom window. Our neighbor, standing on her terrace, among her jasmine and dwarf orange trees, watches. She is with a man and another couple. They hold wine goblets, bob their heads around to see. Behind them, in living room, colorful board game is laid out on coffee table. I try to imagine my wife with these tall, brown, fun people; a thick, simple cactus lost among lilies.

"What are you looking at!" Bella moves behind me, crosses her arms over her chest.

One of the men asks us if everything is all right.

"They're Russian," my neighbor says.

"Oh, I didn't know."

"What, that explains it?" Bellinka says to him. "As though we are only people to do crazy things?"

"Los Angeles is to blame," I say.

From habit Bella pats her hair, even though it stands up like weeds.

I close the curtains.

Elvis's Bathroom

Pagan Kennedy

On Elvis TV specials they tell you he "passed away," makes it sound like he died in bed. Truth is, Elvis died on the can, then he fell on the floor and curled up like a bug. Great, huh? The king of rock and roll dead on the floor with his pants around his ankles.

I never would've found out about that, or any of the cool stuff I found out about, if I hadn't got my tattoo. We'd just hitched to New York, my bullet-headed boyfriend and me, out two days of school to see a band play. Before the concert we were hanging out in the park and I fell asleep—must've been the shit pot we'd bought. I had this dream about an upside-down Jesus hanging on an upside-down cross. Jesus's lips were all covered with spit and blood and I thought he was saying, "You got to stop ignoring me, Spike."

After the concert, me and my boyfriend went down by the docks— where the slaughterhouses are and it smells like fish—and into one of those all-night tattoo places. Underneath the eagles and naked ladies and anchors hung up over the counter is this tall guy with his eyebrows grown together.

I said I wanted that one on the wall, the cross, only upside-down and with no Jesus on it.

He goes, "Look, kid, I only do what you see up there. I ain't no artist." Then he started telling me what a bitch a tattoo is to get off—but actually that's why I wanted one. When I had the dream, I knew this upside-down Jesus was my Jesus, and he wanted me to do the coolest stuff, like stay in New York and be in a band instead of hitching back to New Hampshire the next day, where I would be bored as shit in high school.

But I couldn't figure out how to stay in New York, cause I didn't know anyone. So getting the tattoo was like a pact with the upside-down Jesus.

The guy's hand was on the counter, and I put my hand on his and went, "Aw, mister, aw, pretty please?"

So he finally said okay, and let me up on the chair, which looked like a dentist's chair, except it was all stained with dark brown spots, maybe dried blood. The guy worked slow, one dot at a time and each one felt like a tiny cigarette burn on my arm. The tattoo didn't look like anything at first, but when it was finished it was just like I wanted. And I was thinking that's how my life would be if I followed the upside-down Jesus—one cool thing after the other, and later I'd see how all along it'd fit together.

A year later, when I'd just gotten out of high school, I was thinking I'd try to move to New York. Then this friend of mine who went to my high school in New Hampshire, but a year ahead of me—Oona—called. She was living in the seedy part of Boston, place called Allston, where the hardcore and garage scene was. She said they needed someone in her house.

I went down for a day to look and the place was just my style: graffiti with the names of bands like UFO Baby and Reptile Head (Oona said they used to practice in the basement), stolen gravestone leaning against the banister on the staircase, big plastic Santa with gas mask out on the porch, and in the kitchen a bunch of chairs they obviously got off the sidewalk on trash day.

For all my life, if I put my feet up on the table or my cigarette out in a glass I was always getting yelled at. Not even yelled at, but worse, just Mom saying "Sarah," in that math teacher way of hers. In this house I could throw up on the floor, tear a hole in the wall, or slit my wrists for kicks to splatter blood on the ceiling, it was all okay.

When Oona and me got to the bathroom, I saw this upside-down crucifix hanging from the chain you pull to make the toilet flush. Seeing that made me realize I wasn't supposed to go to New York.

I went, "Oona, check it out—just like on my arm," and I showed her my tattoo. I wanted her to see that this was something amazing, cause for me it was a sign that I should live in this house.

She went, "That's all over Allston. It's a witchcraft thing." She wasn't freaked out like me. Oona's never freaked out by anything. She's great—a real curvy girl with long black hair, wears old lace dresses, smells sweet as a graveyard.

She started telling me about the house. What really freaked me out was that Juan Hombre, who used to be with The Benign Tumors, still lived in the living room. They didn't make him pay rent cause he was a celebrity. Even living up in New Hampshire, I'd heard of the Tumors. They'd do covers of songs like "Going to the Chapel," first straight, like they were a fifties lounge band, and then they'd let loose on their own version and everyone watching would tear each other apart. Just when they were starting to get airplay, they broke up.

They put out one record, which I had. I couldn't even believe I owned it, it was so cool. On the back of the jacket was a picture of each Tumor. In Juan Hombre's picture, he was jumping off the stage, twisted up in the air like a wrung-out rag—a skinny guy with heavy cheekbones, dark skin, and wild black hair. He was the coolest-looking one of all of them. And when I thought of that picture again, I realized he looked like the upside-down Jesus in my dream.

I met him the day I moved in; there he was, sitting at the kitchen table eating bread and reading the *New York Post*. He looked like a vampire, skinny as hell with dark circles under his eyes.

I told him I was the new girl moving in and sat down. I went, "I loved that record you guys put out."

"Thanks," he said, but he seemed embarrassed. I go, "So, is your name really Juan Hombre?"

He said, making fun of himself, "No, that's my stage name. My real name's Mark Martinez, and I'm not even Spanish, just a Portugee boy."

I go, "What?"

"Portuguese—you know, sausages, sweet bread, cork farmers."

I was spending a lot of time in the kitchen, wailing away on this African drum I had.

Juan would come in there a lot to get things—a beer or something—but then he'd sit down at the table and we'd start talking.
Mostly we talked about Elvis. Me and Juan didn't give a shit about the
early Elvis; we were into the late Elvis, like what he ate—fried peanut
butter, bacon and banana sandwiches—and all the pills he took.

Before I met Juan I didn't even know anything about Elvis. I
thought he was supposed to be like Pat Boone. But we'd sit there at
the kitchen table, and Juan would tell me Elvis stories. When Elvis
didn't like a TV show, he'd take his cool-looking gun out of his belt
and shoot out the TV; he stayed in this hotel in Vegas where they
brought him new TVs all the time. He could swallow sixteen pills at
once. He'd get all these girls to strip down to their underwear and
wrestle on top of his bed, and he'd sit on the floor watching. He called
his dick "Little Elvis."

The weirdest shit was about how Elvis died: like, when they did
the autopsy on him, they practically found a drug store in his stomach, but the thing is, though, creepy thing is, none of the pills were
digested. What I'm saying is, Elvis didn't die from pills like everyone
thinks; he died from something else.

Right before the end, he did a lot of reading—right there on the
can. He got real religious, but in an Elvis way, reading stuff about
UFO cults, Voodoo, Atlantis, raising people from the dead, same time
as he was reading the Bible and considering himself some kind of big
Christian.

Anyways, just after Juan told me about how Elvis died, I had this
dream about him sitting in the bathroom reading—this book just like
the Bible only it's the other Bible, and it tells about Elvis's own Jesus.
Elvis says some words out loud from the book and this other Jesus
comes in through the door. He's a skeleton, with flames all around his
bones and skull. The skeleton-Jesus touches Elvis on the forehead
with one flaming finger, and that's when Elvis dies.

I said to Juan, "I want to go to Graceland. I feel like if I could
just see his bathroom, I'd have this revelation or something." I was
afraid to ask him to come, but then he said, "Yeah, let's do it. When

do you want to go?" Our trip to Graceland—we talked about it a lot, but I think it was really just a way of saying we wanted to sleep together.

A couple days later, Juan asked me out on a "Date With Hombre," as he called it. We went to Deli-King—the diner where all the punks and street people hang out—and it was amazing being in there with him. We could barely get to a table, what with at least six people going, "Hey, Juan, where you been? We missed you, man," and they all want to talk to him. The only ones who didn't recognize him were the real hard-core street people—only thing they talk to is their coffee.

Meat Hook, crazy fucker who was thrown in the bin for trying to cut off his own dick, and also the former star of UFO Baby, stood up and clapped Juan on the back. He was tall and skinny, with his hair in a greasy ponytail and a skull tattooed on his forehead. "Juan," he said, "we got a room open in our house. You want to live over on Ashford?"

"Right now I'm okay," Juan said as we sat down. Juan was so cool I could practically see an aura around him; I couldn't believe it was me there in the booth with him. He was wearing a leather jacket someone had given him, just like that, cause they liked the Tumors. His hands stuck out of the sleeves, brown and bony with scars all over them from his job in this lab hauling boxes of radioactive waste. I thought how his hands would feel like sandpaper sliding over my skin.

He started telling me Deli-King stories, like the time him and Kirk were in there and tried to steal one of the little pictures of the Parthenon off the wall. That was a few years ago.

"You sure've been here a long time—the way everyone knows you and shit," I said.

Then he came as close as I'd ever seen to getting annoyed. He said he was planning to move to New York real soon. He was fucking sick and tired of Allston—he couldn't get any good band going here cause he already knew everybody and he knew he didn't want to play with any of them.

Nothing happened on our date, except that we came up with an idea for a band. I was already just starting as the drummer in a hard-core band called Train Wreck, but I didn't see why I couldn't do a band with Juan, too. It was going to be called Elvis: What Happened? I was going to be the Elvis impersonator and Juan would play guitar. We'd do the music that Elvis would have done if only the Colonel hadn't put him in all those corny movies. Juan was sure that if it weren't for the Colonel, Elvis would've gotten together with Jimi Hendrix, so he was going to play his guitar like Jimi would've.

I said to Juan, "This is a good idea and all, but something about it seems weird. I mean, everybody talks about what Elvis would've been like, but I've been thinking that you couldn't have an Elvis without a Colonel Parker. That's just the way it works, you know?" I was kind of kidding, but in another way, I wasn't. I said, "It's like, see, at the cosmic level there's an Elvis force and a Colonel Parker force, and the Elvis force is everything young and cool and the Colonel force is everything old and mean and moneygrubbing. But they're two sides of the same thing; they're the same person."

Juan was laughing at me, which made me kind of mad, but then he said, "That'll be part of Elvis: What Happened? We'll start with a dimmed light, and you'll walk out in your Elvis costume and explain that." Maybe that's why Elvis: What Happened? never got off the ground. Right from the beginning it was too conceptual.

Well, actually, the other problem was Juan. He kept playing out of my singing range, so I go, "Come on, you're only playing in B flat. I can't sing that low."

He goes, "I can't help playing in B flat. That's my key. I'm just a one-key Portugee."

And every time I fucked up, Juan seemed to take it like a sign that the whole thing would never work out. He'd hunch up over his guitar more and maybe run up and down the scales once, like he was already thinking about something else.

I kept going, "Juan, I know it sounds like shit now, but it'll get good if we practice."

This guy in Train Wreck used to play with Juan and he tells me, "Juan's a nice guy, and an amazing guitarist when he was with the Tumors. But he was so depressed when I tried to play with him that I had to drop him." I was wondering if maybe Juan was too good of a guitarist for all of us.

One day we went to a party at Timmy's. Timmy and her friends are the fashion kind of punk, like with dyed hair that hangs just right over their eyes, antique clothes, and pointy English shoes—and always look like they just took a shower.

Me, I'm tall, and I was muscular then because I worked at UPS throwing boxes onto trucks. Plus, I had a crew cut. This particular day, I was wearing what I always wear: combat boots, jeans, and a muscle shirt so my tattoo showed.

All the fashion punks were ignoring me. To top it off, Juan was kind of ignoring me too. He was talking to Timmy mostly and I was wondering whether they'd ever slept together. She had on this sixties miniskirt that showed just how toothpicky her legs were. I couldn't take it. I was sick anyways, so I told Juan I was leaving.

I walked home and got in bed—had chills and was lying under all my blankets shivering. I nodded out in that weird way you do when you get a fever, but woke up when I heard Juan come home. I was thinking, "Is he going to come up to my room?" and he did. He stood in the doorway for a minute, looking at me lying there.

"My face is numb," he said. "I can't understand it; I only had two drinks." He walked over to my bed like he was walking in a moving subway car, hands out in front of him. He looked around for a minute like he didn't know what to do, then he sat on my bed, his hip on my stomach through the covers. It reminded me of the way my Dad would sit on my bed sometimes.

I was sure they'd put 'ludes in his punch, the way he could barely stand up a minute ago but could still talk—which is 'ludes, not booze. I didn't want to waste this opportunity of having him wasted, so I go, "Juan, tell me something. How come people are always saying you were different when you were in the Tumors? And how come you guys broke up?"

He said, "I don't know. After a while it wasn't clicking. One day I walked out of practice and didn't come back. When the band broke up, I realized I was just some moron who carts around radioactive waste for a living."

I couldn't understand how he could think he was a failure. I go, "You're the best guitarist in Boston. You could play with any band you wanted. And, besides, what about New York? You're going to move to New York."

"I'll never get there," he said. "I can't even get a band together here."

"What about our band?" I said.

He massaged my shoulder, "Yeah, well, what we're doing is okay, but it's a joke, a joke band."

When he first came in my room, the sun was just setting, and I'd been watching the sky out my window going from reddish to purple. It was getting to be twilight, but I didn't turn on the lamp next to my bed. It looked like the air in my room was turning purple too. I couldn't see Juan's face anymore. He goes, "Spike," and rakes one drunk hand through my crew cut.

Then Juan, just a shadow, lies down next to me.

"Are you crazy?" I said. "I'm sick. You're going to catch my disease."

"I don't care," he says. Then he kisses me. The way he does it is sucks, like he's sucking all the air out of me and my lungs will collapse. But then his hand on my stomach is real gentle, and he's sweet and calls me Priscilla. And soon all the light fades and it's night in my room.

Later that night I woke up and saw Juan was sitting up in bed with his head leaned against the wall. I thought maybe he was watching me sleep. But when I asked him what he was doing, he said, "Just thinking."

I started thinking how when I was fourteen and didn't even know what punk was, he was hanging out with Meat Hook and all those guys.

I sat up beside him. The moon was over the electric plant out my window, and his chest was lit up white, with shadows where his ribs were. I stretched out my arm, twisting it around so he could see my tattoo. "Know why I got this?" I said. I told him about the upside-down Jesus. I said, "In my dream he looked like you."

"As handsome as Juan Hombre?" he said.

"I'm serious. Promise me you won't laugh at me?"

"No," he said.

But he didn't really mean it, so I said, "It seems like everybody who's really cool knows this secret. You know it; I can tell you do. I want to know what it is more than anything."

"Spike, that doesn't make any sense. Believe me, if there was a secret I would tell you what it was." But I thought he was just saying that cause I wasn't cool enough to know it: the secret was what Juan knew in that picture where he's screwed up in the air; what Meat Hook knew when he tried to cut off his dick; what Elvis knew, sitting on the can, when his own Jesus touched him on the forehead, right where his third eye would be.

"Look, it's now or never," I said, cause I was getting a week off from UPS soon. In a week, I figured, there wasn't time to hitch or even drive. We'd have to fly. I had the money, cause UPS paid good.

"Okay," said Juan. He said okay but I'd have to lend him some cash.

I was fine now—I always get well right away—but Juan was sick as a dog. He was coughing and sneezing and he slept even more than usual. He'd been sick for weeks, but he wouldn't go to the doctor. He wouldn't even take aspirin; all he'd do is pop downers once in a while. It was like he just wanted to lay there and suffer.

But he said he'd go to Graceland anyways. My UPS job was driving me crazy and I felt like if I didn't go somewhere, I'd go insane.

Besides, I guess I had some idiot idea that things would be better if we were traveling. We hadn't fucked since that first time, maybe cause Juan was sick. We'd fool around, but then he'd say, "I'm sorry, Spike, I'm tired now."

This might sound stupid, but once we were in the airport and not in Allston, he looked different. I mean, nobody recognized him here as Juan Hombre, and when I saw him kind of slumped in his airport chair, coughing, looking older even than thirty, for the first time I saw him like he probably saw himself.

Plus, we were on this crappy, cheap airline probably just set up for punks and people like that who don't really give a fuck if they crash.

And Juan, he hadn't even bothered to take Contac or anything. We take off and suddenly he gets quiet, just sitting there with his head in his hands, going, "My ears, oh shit," cause his ears couldn't pop since they were all clogged.

We got to Graceland by afternoon. They make us line up outside, and the fat people with the IT'S HARD BEING THIS SEXY, BUT SOMEONE'S GOT TO DO IT T-shirts are giving me the eye. I tried to tone down my act for Graceland—sneakers instead of combat boots—but I still stuck out way more than in Boston.

This perky Graceland tour girl makes us file through the door all in a line. Juan and me were laughing at her accent cause when she told us to stay with the group it sounded like she was saying for us to stay with the grape.

Inside, in front of every room, was another Barbie-doll zombie tour guide who said stuff and when you walked to the next room you could hear them saying exactly the same thing all over to the next people.

The stairs are right there when you walk in, but we didn't see them at first cause we went with the herd over to the dining room. Then Juan grabbed my arm, going, "Spike, look." The stairs were roped off.

I was pissed, fucking pissed. I went up to one of those Barbie dolls and said, "Are we going to get to go upstairs and see the bathroom where he died?"

"No, I'm sorry, Ma'am," she said.

"This sucks. I can't believe this." I started raving about how pissed off I was, right there in Elvis's living room where he probably did a lot of ranting and raving himself. The difference was at least he got to see the bathroom.

We did it all, every last idiotic Graceland thing—toured the Lisa Marie and the Hound Dog, his airplanes; watched a corny movie called "The Dream Lives On"; took pictures in front of the grave.

When Graceland closed, we sat on the sidewalk of Elvis Presley Boulevard waiting for a bus to come and take us somewhere to sleep—a motel, a park, whatever. Even though it was six, the heat was still blowing off the highway, blasting us every time a bunch of cars passed.

Not having seen the bathroom, man, I still felt so burned I had to smoke a joint and mellow out. I told Juan he shouldn't cause of his cough but he did anyways.

We were leaning against the wall around Graceland, which had writing all over it. I started walking up and down, reading; each stone had one message to Elvis written on it like "Motor City Hell's Angels Know Elvis Is Still the King," or "Freddie from Alaska came here to see you 3/12/84." I found an empty stone and wrote, "Elvis I came here to see the toilet you died on but they wouldn't even let me upstairs."

When I sat down again, I noticed Juan had kind of fainted. His head was leaned up against the wall and his eyes were slits.

I hit him on the shoulder, "Come on, Juan, man, you can't sleep here."

He said, "Spike, I feel like shit," which was weird, cause in all the time he'd been sick, he hadn't complained once I don't think. He looked all pale under his dark skin, and when he coughed he sounded like an old man in a bus station. I slid my eyes over his way, wondering what in the hell I was doing there with him.

It was starting to get dark and he'd fallen asleep leaned against the wall when this purple Pontiac, with fins and everything, pulls up to the gate in front of Graceland. A black lady gets out and, real businesslike, opens a vial, pouring white powder in a line across the road, right in front of the gate.

I got up and ran over to her. "Excuse me," I said, "do you know when the downtown bus comes by here?"

"Ain't no buses after six o'clock," she said. She had hair all stiff and wavy, like a wig, and was wearing a cotton dress with little flowers on it. She was old, about my mom's age, I guess. She looked at me for a minute, then said, "If you want a ride somewheres, get on in back."

"Wait a sec. Let me get my friend." I went and waked up Juan. He said, "You got us a ride? You're great, Spike," then limped along behind me and we got in the back seat of the car. I was kind of ashamed for her to see me with him, some old sick guy.

She already had the car running, and when we got in, she backed out onto the highway. I said, "If you could just drop us off downtown, like anywhere, that would be great."

"Don't you children want some dinner? Let me fix you some."

I looked at Juan, but he had his eyes closed. I go, "Sure, that would be really nice. Do you live in town?"

She half turned her face to me, only for a second, but I thought I saw a design of dots on her forehead, darker than her skin. "No, honey. I live way out in the country."

When she said that, it was like one part of me started freaking, imagining all kinds of ax murder scenes in this house of hers. But this other part of me knew it would be okay.

After a while, she turned off the highway. It was dark now, and I could tell we were in the boonies, cause all I saw in the light from her headlights was trees and mailboxes—tin boxes on top of sticks along the road.

Finally, she turned onto a dirt road and parked. We got out and followed her up this hill all covered with weeds and dead-looking bushes. On top was her house, which looked like a dark, big box blocking out the stars.

"You live alone?" I said. It kind of occurred to me that she could have a son who would beat us up.

"My husband, Henry, he's over at the Night Owl watching the game on TV. That gets him out of my hair once and a while," she said, kind of laughing. The door wasn't even locked. We walked in and it was dark in there and smelled perfumey, like incense. She turned on a lamp and said, "Now you sit here and I'll get us something to eat."

We were in a living room all crammed with weird shit—a big framed picture of JFK with ribbons hanging down from it, baby dolls, Christmas lights, a deer-head trophy with designs painted on its fur, a Buddha with a red lightbulb on top of his head, and a hubcap with a crucifix in the middle of it. Juan and me sat down on this couch the color of a tongue. Juan had waked up some and he said, "Looks like home," meaning our house in Allston.

The lady came back with bowls on a tray, and sat down in a chair opposite us. She handed me a bowl and I started eating this hot, spicy stew.

She said, "Now tell me how come you children are down here?"

I told her about Graceland, about how I wanted to see the bathroom where Elvis died cause of my dream about him. She laughed. "I shoulda known." Then she went off on a wild story. She looked at me when she told it, like Juan wasn't there.

"This is a secret," she said, leaning forward. "In the few years before she died, my mamma ministered to Elvis's hairdresser. Mamma was a spiritualist, born with a veil over her face. She lived here with us, and when the hairdresser came for love potions and such, I'd hear all kinds of things, cause he was so fond of talking about Elvis.

"Towards the end, Elvis, he was studying Voodoo. He goes down to Schwabs, the five-and-dime on Beale Street, and buys all of them fake books on Voodoo. He reads all them books and thinks he knows everything, like he's some kind of swami, even took to wearing a turban, I hear.

"Mamma, she tells the hairdresser to warn him; she just knows something bad is waiting to happen to him if he keeps this up.

"A few days later that hairdresser comes back and what do you think? He says Elvis told him he had a funny dream. He dreamed Jesus was standing over his bed looking at him. This Jesus got a crown of flames and he's holding keys.

"Mamma says, 'That ain't Jesus, that's Pappa Legba, king of the dead. Tell Elvis not to mess with Voodoo anymore. Tell him to stop taking them pills.' By now Elvis wasn't just reading the five-and-dime stuff; he'd got ahold of the real thing—bought it from some bad Voodoo men for near five hundred dollars. Listen, honey, if you go making money off Voodoo, that's black magic you're doing. Likewise if you make a spell that hurts anybody else. Those men, they stand down by the river at the end of Beale Street. They sold Elvis a book, spells on how to kill people, how to make folks do what you say.

"And a week later, Elvis died. He was reading a book, the bad Voodoo book. I found out from the hairdresser. And you know what page it was on?"

The lady leaned forward and I leaned forward, even though I thought she was bullshitting me. "What?" I said.

"It was open to a spell—a few words you say, that's all—for summoning up Pappa Legba. Now anybody with sense knows you can't make Pappa Legba do anything; only reason you call him up normally is so you can ask his advice kind of, cause sometimes things here get out of line with the spirit world."

I was playing along, since it was her house and her food. "Don't you wonder what Elvis asked him to do?"

"Yes, I do," she said, real serious. "Elvis must of told him to do something, then Pappa was mad and struck him dead. Or maybe that's what Elvis wanted in the first place—to be dead."

I looked at Juan. He was still eating, his spoon shaking when he held it to his mouth. He smiled at me, even though I don't think he'd been listening to her really. I was hoping the lady didn't notice how out of it he was.

I thought she was trying to fake me out, so I said kind of sarcastically, "How come you're telling us all this? Isn't it a big secret?"

She said, "I thought you should know, since you got the cross of Legba on you."

She was looking at my arm—at my tattoo I realized. "My tattoo is the cross of Legba? Well, then it's just some kind of coincidence, cause I didn't know that when I got it," I said.

She goes, "Ain't no coincidences. You're a child of Legba."

She goes into telling me about him. Says he watches over crossroads and thresholds—that's why the keys. When people die he comes to get them and if you want to talk to spirits, you got to go through Pappa Legba. He's like the bouncer of the spirit world, I guess.

And I had the same feeling I did when I saw the upside-down cross in the bathroom in Allston—like everything was falling into place, and would keep on falling into place as long as I didn't fuck it up.

Viv—that was her name—said to Juan, "Here, take this pill." She was standing over him, and he took it from her and put it in his mouth, before I could say anything. Juan, that guy never thought twice before taking a pill.

He looked up at her leaning over him and goes, "Do you mind if I lie down?"

"Not at all, sweetie, stretch your legs out," she said, and I stood up so he could put his legs where I was sitting. I took off his shoes for him. They were black lace-ups, the leather all cracked and scratched, with a hole on the bottom of each.

She showed me the extra room where Juan and me could stay after she made the bed. Like the rest of the house, this room was just full of stuff. There was an old wood cabinet with glass shelves and through the glass I could see all these amazing things, like a little mosaic bird made out of colored mirrors and something that looked like someone's cut-off hand.

She goes, "This was to be my baby's room, but she died before she was even out of me."

I was afraid to say something wrong, so I kept my mouth shut.

"It's okay," she said, "it was eighteen years ago—I've come to live with it." I was freaking, cause I was eighteen. I wanted real bad to look in that room, but already we were walking down the dark hall to the kitchen, and we ended up sitting in there. She brought us each a glass of lemonade. I start to drink it, but she laughed and said, "Hang on there," and poured something from a flask into each of our glasses.

The kitchen was all dark, and the floor was crooked, which made me kind of seasick. There were plants, herbs I guess, hanging upside-down from the wooden beams in the ceiling.

I ended up telling her practically my whole life story. She listens like she's heard it before. Her dark skin shines blue sometimes and I like that. Every one of her fingers has a ring on it, like Liberace's. While I talked, I heard her breathing in and out the way she breathes.

Sometimes when I said something she goes, "Ummm-hmmmh." When she heard my story, she said, "Most bad children are just bad, but some few are the children of Legba. They're bad cause they've got power but don't know how to use it, so it gets all gummed up inside them. Never happened to me, cause my mamma knew what to do, how to keep the power running through me. She used to sprinkle dirt from a graveyard on me when I was asleep."

"God," I said, "I wish someone'd done that for me, man. My child-hood sucked."

Somehow we started talking about Juan. "He's not always such a mess," I said. I told her what he was like when he was in the Tumors.

She goes, "The more power you got, more can go wrong."

I said, "What about your mom? Didn't it go wrong with her?"

She leaned forward, even closer than before. She said, "She knew how to hang onto it. It ain't a secret, it's a science, something you got to follow at every turn and keep learning every day." She sat up straight again. "We women pass that science down one to the other cause you sure can't trust a man with the power. They spend it like money for booze, but we know how to keep it till we're all sucked up and old. Not that I have anything against men. They start out pretty, and when they're past that, they can work and earn you money, like my Henry. But they sure cannot understand about power, honey."

We were still talking an hour or two later when Juan walked in. He said, "I was wondering if you have any Kleenex?"

"There's paper napkins on the shelf there," she said.

"Thanks." He took one and blew his nose until he'd used up the whole napkin. "Thanks for your help. I'm feeling much better." He can be real polite sometimes.

"You ready for a real bed now?" Viv said.

"Yeah," he said. It was only about ten, and Viv said she was staying up to wait for Henry.

After Viv finished the bed and left the room, I took a look in that glass cabinet. What I thought was a bird made out of colored mirrors turned out to be the edge of a picture frame. I pulled it out: it was a square made of clay with colored mirrors and gold stars and silver moons all stuck in it. Inside the square was a picture of a black girl. It was all old and faded, and the girl was wearing a black dress, which didn't seem like a dress on her cause she was so muscular.

Juan had been sitting on the bed while I looked around. I sat next to him. "The plane leaves tomorrow," I said.

"It's been a great trip, Spike. I'm glad you got us down here." He was always sweet like that, giving me the credit.

"I don't think I'm going to go back right now. Viv said I could stay here."

I expected him to freak out, but he said, "I thought maybe you were going to say something like that." He put his arms around my waist and leaned his head on my shoulder. "I always knew you were too cool for Allston. You're so cool, Spike." I guess that in his own lazy, half-assed way he loved me.

"I'm coming back to Allston," I said, kind of weirded out. "I'm just staying here for a week or something, not forever."

"Yeah, right," he said. "I don't know about that."

And then, by way of saying good-bye, we did it for a long time, real gentle. Later, middle of the night, I wake up and see he's staring at the floor where the moonlight, coming through the window, makes six squares.

"What are you thinking about?" I say.

"What I always think about. I'm trying to figure out where I fucked up." The hollow of his neck has a few beads of sweat in it, like a cup with only the last few drops of a magic potion inside. I lean over him to lick out each last one.

Mutti

John L'Heureux

The eight-o'clock bell had already rung, but Anton stood on the footbridge anyway, watching the dark water. The bridge was off limits during school hours; nobody was around to see him now, though, and Anton liked the feeling he got leaning over the bridge, so he stood there, waiting. It was cold, and getting colder, but there was no ice on the stream yet. There would be ice on the way home.

A boy in the lower school had drowned in the stream a year ago; that was why the bridge was off limits.

Anton watched a patch of leaves pull away from the bank and eddy out into the middle of the stream. He squinted, turning the leaves into a brown jacket, his own, floating toward him as he stood above, watching. There was a small rock directly beneath where he stood. If he could make the leaves float toward the rock, touch it, he would have the picture of his own dead body, face down, floating there beneath him. Drowned. He concentrated hard, willing the patch of leaves to drift toward him. But the leaves caught for a moment against a branch and spun in a full circle, trailing behind them a dark green patch, slimy, changing the shape of everything. Then, suddenly, for no reason, the leaves broke free of the branch and came to rest against a rock. Anton smiled. Perfect. The back of his head was just visible above the water, the dark brown jacket moved in the stream, washed by it, softly, easily, and Anton inhaled the cold water deeply. Drowned. Dead.

He could not leave the bridge so long as his body lay there in the stream. It was getting late. He always missed the eight o'clock bell, but he did not want to miss the eight-ten and the end of homeroom period. It was Friday, and if Mr. Hollister were to call him in again, it would be today. If he called him in, he would skip gym. If he called him in, he would get through the morning all right, and then maybe the afternoon. And then there would be the stones, and his mother, and all Saturday and Sunday with nothing to be afraid of.

Move, then, he wanted to say to the body beneath the bridge. At once the leaves broke away from the rock. Again Anton smiled. It was going to be a safe day.

In the corridor outside homeroom everything was silent. He peeked through the little glass window and saw Miss Kelly pacing up and down in front of the room. She was wearing her Friday sweater, green-blue and baggy, and she was mopping her nose with a tissue. She always had a cold.

The principal was making the morning announcements and his muffled voice came in little spurts through the heavy door: PTA, cheerleading, speech club. Anton opened his locker and put away all his books except American History; he would need that for first period. He hung up his coat, his cap, his scarf. He looked both ways for a moment and then quickly, in a single hurried motion, he took off his face and hung it on the side hook, so that only his profile showed. And then he slammed the locker door, ready, as the eight-ten bell rang for first period.

"You're late, Anton," Miss Kelly said at the classroom door. "Go to the office and get a Pass. Oh, and here's a note. Mr. Hollister wants to see you in the Guidance Office during your first free period. So please don't be late for him. You're always late, Anton, I don't know why that has to be." Miss Kelly hugged herself in her green-blue sweater. "Can you tell me why that has to be? That you're always late?"

Anton said nothing.

"Well, I've had a little talk with Mr. Hollister about you. I've told him you're doing very well in English, your written work, but you don't talk enough. You don't contribute. Don't you think you could contribute more?"

Students had begun to drift in for Miss Kelly's English class and some of them were listening, Anton knew.

"We both like you, Anton. Mr. Hollister and I, both. I want you to understand that. We're just concerned about you. You're just so ... "

But Anton was not listening to her. He was listening to the fat girl in the front row who was saying to her girlfriend, "We're concerned about you, Anton. We love you, Anton. We adore you. Oh, Anton!"

"Very well," Miss Kelly said, seeing that he was not listening to her, seeing his face redden. "Please see Mr. Hollister during study. And *please* be on time." Brisk now, all business, she said to the class, "All right, people, please settle down. We are still on Chaucer and it is already December and we are a full century behind."

Miss Kelly was in love with Mr. Hollister, Anton knew, and he knew too that Mr. Hollister would never return her love. Mr. Hollister loved him.

He got through American History and Algebra and Art without having to say anything. As always, he knew the answers, but he kept silent even when he was called on. He preferred that the others think him stupid and just ignore him. He didn't want them to look at him or talk to him or even talk about him. He wanted not to exist. Or to be invisible. To escape. So he waited.

Even in art class he waited. Art was an elective and Miss Belekis had seen at once that he had a real gift for draftsmanship, so she had loaned him books on anatomy and told him to draw whatever he wanted. She had praised his first drawings—fat peasant women knitting or praying or peeling apples, imitative stuff—and he had liked her praise, but he saw the danger of being noticed. And so for Miss Belekis he drew the same peasant women again and again, trying to make the drawings seem less finished each time, trying to conceal his growing mastery of craft. After a while, he just gave her the same old drawings. She stopped commenting, but she continued to loan him the books.

Years later, as a famous sculptor working in marble and stone, he would remain just as secretive, a mystery to his agent and the galleries where he showed. He was a recluse. He saw almost nobody. And though he always sculpted from life and, in time, went through three wives and a mistress, he claimed he just didn't like people. He merely sculpted them from stone.

But now, in high school, he had no choice. He was forced to see people. Still, he could keep them from seeing him. At nights and on weekends, he made good progress with the human figure, drawing it over and over in every imaginable posture, and always nude. This did not embarrass him. This was art, and it had nothing to do with life.

In life, he was terrified at the idea of a nude body. This was why he cut gym class repeatedly. All the boys taking off their clothes in front of each other, looking, some of them even wanted to be looked at. And Coach Landry encouraging it all. It made him want to run and hide. And they looked at him, too.

Only last night he had been drying himself after his shower, when he noticed a few dark brown hairs, down there, and he realized he would never be safe again. He squatted on the bath mat and covered himself with both hands, squeezing tight, and praying, "Oh no, God, please don't let me get big there, and have hair that shows, and be like the others. Please don't let me ever be a man." But even as he prayed, he knew it was hopeless. He took his hands away and the dark hairs were still there. It would happen to him, too. Nothing would stop it. Not prayer. Not anything.

"Anton, my friend. Come right in," Mr. Hollister said. "Have a seat. Go on, sit down. Now tell me. How are things going? Things going okay?"

"Yes." Anton looked down. Mr. Hollister was wearing his red turtleneck. His blond hair was long and floppy. He crossed his legs wrong.

"Good. Good. So how are you doing? Oh, well, we've done that, haven't we. What I really mean, Anton, is that as your guidance counselor I'm concerned about you. I mean, you're a really bright young man, but you're always late for everything, and your teachers say you don't contribute in class, and, gosh, I've noticed myself that you're, well, you're . . . let's say independent. Some might say a loner. Some might even say antisocial. But I understand that. I do. I was a private kid myself. Like you, in a way. You know?"

Anton looked up at him and resolved to tell him nothing. He would break in. He would destroy.

"You're thin, Anton. Do you eat enough? I mean, do you have a good appetite?"

"Yes."

"Good. Good. Well, frankly, what I really want to ask about, express my concern about is . . . the bruises. The cuts on your hands, your face sometimes, that broken wrist you had. I mean, Anton, how do you have so many accidents, for instance? I wonder if you could tell me about that."

"I'm clumsy. I'm not careful."

"Well, Anton, I was wondering about your folks. Your mom and dad. Do you get along with them okay? I mean, they never hit you or anything, do they?"

"No."

"I mean, those bruises aren't from them. Your father doesn't hit you or anything? Even once in a while? You could tell me, you know. I could make sure he'd never hurt you again."

"He never hits me."

"No, of course not. We just have to check, you know. And your mother, neither? No?"

"No."

"Well, let's see. I know quite a lot about you," Mr. Hollister said and flipped open a manila folder on his desk. "We know quite a lot about each other, I mean." He leafed through several sheets of paper.

What he knew was that Anton was fourteen, an only child, male. He was born a United States citizen, of Russian and German parents. His father was a translator of Slavic literature. His mother was a housewife. They had lived in this small Massachusetts town for less than a year. What he knew was that Anton was alone.

"Don't we," Mr. Hollister said.

"Don't we what?"

"We know quite a lot about each other, I mean."

Anton waited for a moment and then looked him full in the eyes. "Yes," he said.

Mr. Hollister cleared his throat and uncrossed his legs and looked again at the sheets of paper in the folder. Slowly his face began to color. When he raised his eyes, he found Anton still looking at him, waiting. He lowered them again.

"Well, any time you want to talk, Anton, you feel free to just come in here and see me." His voice was different now. "I'm concerned about you, as you know; about all the kids. So you just come ahead any time. Okay?"

"Thank you," Anton said. He lowered his eyes finally, and then he stood up to go.

"Any time," Mr. Hollister said.

Mr. Hollister and Coach Landry were prefecting at the West End stairs when the crowd started down to the lunchroom. Seeing Anton approach, Mr. Hollister said, intending to be heard, "I'm concerned about that Anton fellow. He's a fine young man, I think." And Coach Landry, not intending to be heard, but heard nonetheless, said to him, "Just keep it in your pants, Hollister."

Anton drifted with the crowd downstairs to the lunchroom, and then slowly, almost aimlessly, walked on past it and, once out of sight, moved quickly down the corridor to the gymnasium area and the boiler room. Nobody ever came here except to get to the gym.

Anton ate his lunch in a stall in the men's room, or rather, he ate the apple, having thrown away the sandwich and the cake as soon as he left home this morning. He was safe here. The walls and the cement floor were painted dark green and the massive stalls were made of oak and coated with many layers of varnish. There were no windows, and only a single small bulb lit the room. It smelled like church. There was a new men's room on the far side of the gym, with white walls and tan metal booths and lots of light. The boys used that place all the time, but nobody ever came here. Anton sat on the high toilet in the abandoned men's room and ate his apple.

So, it was almost over. And he had made it this far. Only two more classes. Tomorrow he would spend all day drawing. And Sunday, too, if he wanted. He finished the apple and continued to sit there, his hands folded in his lap, waiting.

The rest of the afternoon passed slowly. He was called on three times in French class and twice he gave the answer quickly, almost eagerly. The third time, though, he caught himself, and pretended he didn't know the answer.

He had slipped earlier today with Mr. Hollister, coming out from behind his school face to look at him, and he had almost done it again in French. He would have to be more careful. He could see Miss Pratt looking at him the way she looked at the others, encouraging him to risk an answer, right or wrong, enticing him out. He thought of his real face hanging downstairs in the green locker. When Miss Pratt called on him again, she would find he was not even there. The bell rang. Only one more class to go.

Miss Kelly was crazier than usual today. She kept sniffing and mopping at her nose and hugging herself, but at least she did not call on him. She seemed, in fact, to be deliberately avoiding him. "The Prioress's Tale," she was saying, raises the most interesting problems of anti-Semitism in Chaucer's Middle Ages. The Jews, of course, had been driven out of England in 1290. Which means that Chaucer was probably writing about Jews, and about anti-Semitism, from an accepted tradition rather than from any actual experience of his own. Did they see what this implied about the Christian world view of that time? Somebody raised his hand to contribute. Anton turned and saw that it was Kevin Delaney, who said that he used to live in Bridgeport and he knew some Jewish kids there and they were just like anybody else; they weren't like New York Jews at all. This got Miss Kelly all upset, though she pretended that he had made an interesting contribution, and then she tried to get them to talk about prejudices and stereotypes in their own lives. Everybody had something to say about this, and they all began to talk at the same time. Anton smiled to himself; they'd do anything rather than read Chaucer. Finally the bell rang and Miss Kelly thanked everyone for an interesting and profitable discussion. In three minutes he would be free.

But instead of just piling her books and papers while they waited for the final bell, Miss Kelly signaled him to the front of the room. She turned her back to the class and edged him around so that nobody would hear her. There was that interested silence. "You can talk quietly, class," she said loudly, and when finally there was a whisper or two, she said, "I hope you found that discussion period helpful, Anton. You see, we all have strange notions about other people sometimes, and sometimes all of us feel that we are outsiders. Do you see? I hope you see that."

Anton began to blush. What a fool the woman was. They were all looking at him, every one of them. He wanted to kill her; she was killing him. But he only stood there, his eyes lowered.

"I had a little talk with Mr. Hollister, you see." She paused for a moment, but Anton said nothing. "Did you have a good talk with Mr. Hollister? Mr. Hollister is a very unusual man. He has the ability to care. He is a feeling person who feels for others. Mr. Hollister . . . "

She wasn't talking to him. She was just talking.

Anton raised his eyes and stared at her. He was thinking he could say simply, "He doesn't love you. He will never love you," and she would die, right there, in front of the classroom.

Suddenly Miss Kelly stopped talking and looked at him. "What?" she said. "What is it?" Anton said nothing. "Why are you looking at me that way?" she said. "Stop that. You stop that right now."

It seemed hours before the bell finally rang.

Anton braced his books under his left arm and walked across the footbridge without looking at the water on either side. There would be ice on the stream by now, at least along the edges. And there would be ice in the clay bank. He walked with purpose, but not too fast. He didn't want the others to walk with him or to offer him a ride—not that anyone ever had. But he was careful just the same.

After half a mile, Anton turned off High Street onto Putnam Road and he was completely safe at last. He had a two-mile walk down Putnam, past the woods and the old mill and the clay bank, and then another half mile and he would be home. His mother would be in the kitchen, watching television and sipping her muscatel; his father would be out in the cabin working on Gorky. He would show her the bruises and cuts and she would console him, and at night he would lock his bedroom door and draw the things he had felt while she cradled him in her arms. And then he would fall asleep and dream of dying.

He broke a branch and used it as a walking stick. He was an old man taking little steps, propped up by a cane that bent beneath his weight. He walked this way up to the twenty-fifth tree. For the next twenty-five he walked like his mother. And for the next, like his father. He hugged himself, sniffing, and said, in Miss Kelly's voice, "I had a little talk with Mr. Hollister today, Anton." And then for a long time he walked like himself, thinking of Mr. Hollister and how he crossed his legs wrong, and of Miss Kelly. Both of them had seen him with his real face. It was getting harder to hide. He wanted to say real things. He wanted to refuse. But mostly he wanted not to be noticed. And now he was getting hair down there, and he would get big like all the others, and he would be like them in every way except inside, where he could be just himself, and terrified.

He thought of that picture of the old woman on a bridge, screaming. Was it called *The Scream*? He saw the blackness of her open mouth, and he shaped his own mouth like hers, and in a moment he heard the long high wail coming and it would not stop. But finally it did stop. He was dizzy then and black spots sparkled behind his eyes, but he had done it and he felt good. And he had passed the old mill without looking at it once. In a minute he would be at the clay bank.

He rounded a turn in the road and there it was, a cliff of clay thirty or forty feet high, half of it chewed away by some huge machine, so that you could see the layers and layers of red and brown and gold and blue gray. You could spend hours staring at it and never succeed in counting all the colors. He would never paint in color until he could paint this, he thought. He would never risk it. But then what was he thinking, since he knew he would never paint at all.

There were ice patches here and there, and frozen chunks of clay, and some good patches of shale. Anton took off his mittens and quickly, expertly, slashed at the knuckles of each hand with a small slab of stone. The blood came slowly, but he was patient and waited before slashing again. He did not want to go too deep.

And then, somewhere inside, he heard himself think, But what if I don't die. "What if?" he said aloud, and at once he saw himself naked, walking down the school corridor. He was big and hard and he had hair down there. Miss Kelly and Mr. Hollister turned away from him in disgust, and the others all laughed at him, but he did not care. He walked through the corridor and out the front door and down the hill to the little footbridge. He looked back at the school, but nobody had followed him, nobody cared anymore. Without a pause, naked in the cold, he dove into the icy water and swam.

No, he could not let it happen that way. The old way was better. Death would happen if he just waited.

He looked down at his hand and saw that the blood had begun to flow nicely. He made a quick slash vertically across the back of it, and then he was done.

On the edge of an ice puddle he found the right piece of frozen clay. It was a silver blue, the color and weight of steel, and it fitted his palm perfectly. He tossed it in his right hand a few times, got the feel of his fingers around it, and then gathered his books for the short walk home.

He thought of the picture he would draw tonight. A naked man, old, emaciated, tied to something—a dog, a horse, something dead— and out of his mouth small birds come flying.

And as he walked, making up his picture, he beat his right cheek with the frozen piece of clay. He beat it slowly, rhythmically, making the cold flesh swell a little, making the bruise settle into the skin. His cheek grew red and redder, veins surfacing slowly and breaking, preparing the flesh for the purple and black that would follow later.

Anton closed the kitchen door and stood there waiting for his mother to notice. But there was no need to wait; she seemed to have expected it.

"No, oh no," she said, crying. "They've beaten you again, my poor Anton, my poor baby." She held out her arms and he came to her. She cradled him in her lap, whispering over and over, "This is a terrible place, a terrible place. But Anton, my baby, Anosha, you've got your Mutti. You'll always have your Mutti. Your Mutti loves you."

He could smell the sweet wine on her breath and feel her strong arms around him and her soft breasts warming, protecting him. He abandoned himself to the luxury of her grief.

Country Cooking from Central France
Roast Boned Rolled Stuffed Shoulder of Lamb (Farce Double)

Harry Mathews

H ere is an old French regional dish for you to try. Attempts by presumptuous chefs to refine it have failed to subdue its basically hearty nature. It demands some patience, but you will be abundantly rewarded for your pains.

Farce double—literally, double stuffing—is the specialty of La Tour Lambert, a mountain village in Auvergne, that rugged heart of the Massif central. I have often visited La Tour Lambert: the first time was in late May, when *farce double* is traditionally served. I have observed this dish being made and discussed it with local cooks.

The latter were skeptical about reproducing *farce double* else-where—not out of pride, but because they were afraid the dish would make no sense to a foreigner. (It is your duty to prove them wrong— and nothing would make them happier if you did.) Furthermore, they said, certain ingredients would be hard to find. Judicious substitution is our answer to that. Without it, after all, we would have to forgo most foreign cooking not out of a can.

The shoulder of lamb itself requires attention. You must buy it from a butcher who can dress it properly. Tell him to include the middle neck, the shoulder chops in the brisket, and part of the foreshank. The stuffing will otherwise fall out of the roast.

In Auvergne, preparing the cut is no problem, since whole lambs are roasted: the dish is considered appropriate for exceptional, often communal feasts, of a kind that has become a rarity with us.

All bones must be removed. If you leave this to the butcher, have him save them for the deglazing sauce. The fell or filament must be kept intact, or the flesh may crumble.

Set the boned forequarter on the kitchen table. Do not slice off the purple inspection stamps, but scour them with a brush dipped in a weak solution of lye. The meat will need all the protection it can get. Rinse and dry.

Marinate the lamb in a mixture of 2 qts of white wine, 2 qts of olive oil, the juice of 16 lemons, salt, pepper, 16 crushed garlic cloves, 10 coarsely chopped yellow onions, basil, rosemary, melilot, ginger, allspice, and a handful of juniper berries. The juniper adds a pungent, authentic note. In Auvergne, shepherds pick the berries in late summer when they drive their flocks from the mountain pastures. They deposit the berries in La Tour Lambert, where they are pickled through the winter in cider brandy. The preparation is worth making but demands foresight.

If no bowl is capacious enough for the lamb and its marinade, use a washtub. Without a tub, you must improvise. Friends of mine in Paris resort to their bidet; Americans may have to fall back on the kitchen sink, which is what I did the first time I made *farce double*. In La Tour Lambert, most houses have stone marinating troughs. Less favored citizens use the municipal troughs in the entrance of a cave in the hillside, just off the main square.

The lamb will have marinated satisfactorily in five or six days.

Allow yourself three hours for the stuffings. The fish balls or quenelles that are their main ingredient can be prepared a day in advance and refrigerated until an hour before use.

The quenelles of La Tour Lambert have traditionally been made from *chaste,* a fish peculiar to the mountain lakes of Auvergne. The name, a dialect word meaning "fresh blood," may have been suggested by the color of its spreading gills, through which it ingests its food. (It is a mouthless fish.) It is lured to the surface with a skein of tiny beads that resemble the larvae on which it preys, then bludgeoned with an underwater boomerang. *Chaste* has coarse, yellow-white flesh, with a mild but inescapable taste. It has been vaguely and mistakenly identified as a perch; our American perch, however, can replace it, provided it has been caught no more than thirty-six hours before cooking. Other substitutes are saltwater fish such as silver hake or green cod. If you use a dry-fleshed fish, remember to order beef-kidney fat at the butcher's to add to the fish paste. (Be sure to grind it separately.)

To a saucepan filled with 2½ cups of cold water, add salt, pepper, 2 pinches of grated nutmeg, and 6 tbsp of butter. Boil. Off heat, begin stirring in 2½ cups of flour and continue as you again bring the water to a boil. Take off heat. Beat in 5 eggs, one at a time, then 5 egg whites. Let the liquid cool.

Earlier, you will have ground 3¾ lbs of fish with a mortar and pestle—heads, tails, bones, and all—and forced them through a coarse sieve. Do *not* use a grinder, blender, or Cuisinart. The sieve of La Tour Lambert is an elegant sock of meshed copper wire, with a fitted ashwood plunger. It is kept immaculately bright. Its apertures are shrewdly gauged to crumble the bones without pulverizing the flesh. Into the strained fish, mix small amounts of salt, white pepper, nutmeg, and chopped truffles—fresh ones, if possible. (See *truffle*.)

Stir fish and liquid into an even paste.

Two hours before, you will have refrigerated 1 cup of the heaviest cream available. Here, of course, access to a cow is a blessing.

The breathtakingly viscid cream of La Tour Lambert is kept in specially excavated cellars. Those without one use the town chiller, in the middle depths—cool but not cold—of the cave mentioned earlier. Often I have watched the attendant women entering and emerging from that room, dusky figures in cowls, shawls, and long gray gowns, bearing earthenware jugs like offerings to a saint.

Beat the cool cream into the paste. Do it slowly: think of those erect, deliberate Auvergnat women as they stand in the faint gloom of the cave, beating with gestures of timeless calm. It should take at least fifteen minutes to complete the task.

At some previous moment, you will have made the stuffing for the quenelles. (This is what makes the stuffing "double.") It consists of the milt of the fish and the sweetbreads of the lamb, both the neck and stomach varieties. (Don't forget to mention *them* to your butcher.)

The milt is rapidly blanched. The sweetbreads are diced, salted, spiced with freshly ground hot pepper, and tossed for six minutes in clarified butter. Both are then chopped very fine (blender permitted) and kneaded into an unctuous mass with the help of 1 cup of lamb marrow and 3 tbsp of aged Madeira.

I said at the outset that I am in favor of appropriate substitutions in preparing *farce double:* but even though one eminent authority has suggested it, stuffing the quenelles with banana peanut butter is not appropriate.

The quenelles must now be shaped. Some writers who have discoursed at length on the traditional Auvergnat shape urge its adoption at all costs. I disagree. For the inhabitants of La Tour Lambert, who attach great significance to *farce double*, it may be right to feel strongly on this point. The same cannot be said for families in Maplewood or Orange County. You have enough to worry about as it is. If you are, however, an incurable stickler, you should know that in Auvergne molds are used. They are called *beurdes* (they are, coincidentally, shaped like birds), and they are available here. You can find them in any of the better head shops.

But forget about bird molds. Slap your fish paste onto a board and roll it flat. Spread on stuffing in parallel half-inch bands two inches apart. Cut paste midway between bands, roll these strips into cylinders, and slice the cylinders into sections no larger than a small headache. Dip each piece in truffle crumbs. (See *truffle.*)

I refuse to become involved in the pros and cons of presteaming the quenelles. The only steam in La Tour Lambert is a rare fragrant wisp from the dampened fire of a roasting pit.

We now approach a crux in the preparation of *farce double:* enveloping the quenelles and binding them into the lamb. I must make a stern observation here; and you must listen to it. You must take it absolutely to heart.

If the traditional ways of enveloping the quenelles are arduous, they are in no way gratuitous. On them depends an essential component of *farce double,* namely the subtle interaction of lamb and fish.

While the quenelles (and the poaching liquid that bathes them) must be largely insulated from the encompassing meat, they should not be wholly so. The quenelles must not be drenched in roasting juice or the lamb in fishy broth, but an exchange should occur, definite no matter how mild. Do not *under any circumstance* use a Baggie or Saran Wrap to enfold the quenelles. Of course it's easier. So are TV dinners. For once, demand the utmost of yourself: the satisfaction will astound you, and *there is no other way.*

I mentioned this misuse of plastic to a native of La Tour Lambert. My interlocutor, as if appealing for divine aid, leaned back, lifted up his eyes, and stretched forth his arms. He was standing at the edge of a marinating trough; its edges were slick with marinade. One foot shot forward, he teetered for one moment on the brink, and then down he went. Dripping oil, encrusted with fragrant herbs, he emerged briskly and burst into tears.

There are two methods. I shall describe the first one briefly: it is the one used by official cooks for public banquets. Caul (tripe skin) is scraped free of fat and rubbed with pumice stone to a thinness approaching nonexistence. This gossamer is sewn into an open pouch, which is filled with the quenelles and broth before being sewn shut. The sealing of the pouch is preposterously difficult. I have tried it six times; each time, ineluctable burstage has ensued. Even the nimble-fingered, thimble-thumbed seamstresses of La Tour Lambert find it hard. In their floodlit corner of the festal cave, they are surrounded by a sizable choir of wailing boys whose task is to aggravate their intention to a pitch of absolute, sustained concentration. If the miracle always occurs, it is never less than miraculous.

The second method is to seal the quenelles inside a clay shell. This demands no supernatural skills, merely attention.

Purveyors of reliable cooking clay now exist in all major cities. The best are Italian. In New York, the most dependable are to be found in east Queens. (For addresses, see *Appendix.*)

Stretch and tack down two eighteen-inch cheesecloth squares. Sprinkle until soaking (mop up puddles, however). Distribute clay in pats and roll flat until entire surface is evenly covered. The layer of clay should be no more than one-sixteenth inch thick. Scissor edges clean.

Drape each square on an overturned 2-qt bowl. Fold back flaps. Mold into hemispheres. Check fit, then dent edge of each hemisphere with forefinger so that when dents are facing each other, they form a three-quarter-inch hole.

Be sure to prepare the shell at least forty-eight hours in advance so that it hardens properly. (If you are a potter, you can bake it in the oven; if not, you risk cracking.) As the drying clay flattens against the cheesecloth, tiny holes will appear. Do *not* plug them. Little will pass through them: just enough to allow the necessary exchange of savors.

Make the poaching liquid—3 qts of it—like ordinary fish stock (q.v.). The wine used for this in Auvergne is of a local sparkling variety not on the market; but any good champagne is an acceptable substitute.

By "acceptable substitute," I mean one acceptable to me. Purists have cited the fish stock as a reason for not making *farce double* at all. In La Tour Lambert, they rightly assert, the way the stock is kept allows it to evolve without spoiling: in the amphoralike jars that are stored in the coldest depths of the great cave, a faint, perpetual fermentation gives the perennial brew an exquisite, violet-flavored sourness. This, they say, is inimitable. *I* say that thirty drops of decoction of elecampane blossoms will reproduce it so perfectly as to convince the most vigilant tongue.

Fifteen minutes before roasting time, put the quenelles in one of the clay hemispheres. Set the other against it, dent to dent. Seal the seam with clay, except for the hole, and thumb down well. Hold the sphere in one hand with the hole on top. With a funnel, pour in *hot* poaching liquid until it overflows, then empty 1 cup of liquid. This is to keep the shell from bursting from within when the broth reaches a boil.

Be sure to keep the shell in your hand: set in a bowl, one bash against its side will postpone your dinner for several days at least. In

La Tour Lambert, where even more fragile gut is used, the risks are lessened by placing the diaphanous bags in woolen reticules. It is still incredible that no damage is ever done to them on the way to the stuffing tables. To avoid their cooling, they are carried at a run by teenage boys, for whom this is a signal honor: every Sunday throughout the following year, they will be allowed to wear their unmistakable lily-white smocks.

Earlier in the day, you will have anointed the lamb, inside and out: inside, with fresh basil, coriander leaves, garlic, and ginger thickly crushed into walnut oil (this is a *must*); outside, with mustard powder mixed with—ideally—wild boar fat. I know that wild boars do not roam our woods (sometimes, on my walks through Central Park, I feel I may soon meet one): bacon fat will do—about a pint of it.

You will have left the lamb lying outside down. Now nestle the clay shell inside the boneless cavity. Work it patiently into the fleshly nooks, then urge the meat in little bulges around it, pressing the lamb next to the shell, not against it, with the gentlest possible nudges. When the shell is deeply ensconced, fold the outlying flaps over it, and shape the whole into a regular square cushion roast. Sew the edges of the meat together, making the seams hermetically tight.

If the original roasting conditions will surely exceed your grasp, a description of them may clarify your goals.

In Auvergne, the body of the lamb is lowered on wetted ropes into a roasting pit. It comes to rest on transverse bars set close to the floor of the pit. Hours before, ash boughs that have dried through three winters are heaped in the pit and set ablaze: by now they are embers. These are raked against the four sides and piled behind wrought-iron grids into glowing walls. The cast-iron floor stays hot from the fire. When the lamb is in place, a heated iron lid is set over the pit. The lid does more than refract heat from below. Pierced with a multitude of small holes, it allows for aspersions of water on coals that need damping and the sprinkling of oil on the lamb, which is thus basted throughout its roasting in a continuous fine spray. Previously, I might add, the lamb has been rapidly seared over an open fire. Four senior cooks manage this by standing on high stepladders and manipulating the poles and extensible thongs used to shift the animal, which they precisely revolve over the flames so that it receives an even grilling.

Thus the onslaught of heat to which the lamb is subjected is, while too restrained to burn it, intense enough to raise the innermost broth to the simmering point.

Carefully lower the lamb into a twenty-five-inch casserole. (If you have no such casserole, buy one. If it will not fit in your oven, consider this merely one more symptom of the shoddiness of our age, which the popularity of dishes like *farce double* may someday remedy.) Cover. You will have turned on the oven at maximum heat for forty-five minutes at least. Close the oven door and lower the thermostat to 445°. For the next five hours, there is nothing to do except check the oven thermometer occasionally and baste the roast with juices from the casserole every ten minutes. If you feel like catnapping, have no compunctions about it. Do *not* have anything to drink—considering what lies in store for you, it is a foolish risk. The genial cooks of La Tour Lambert may fall to drinking, dancing, and singing at this point, but remember that they have years of experience behind them; and you, unlike them, must act alone.

One song always sung during the roasting break provides valuable insight into the character of the Auvergnat community. It tells the story of a blacksmith's son who sets out to find his long-lost mother. She is dead, but he cannot remember her death, nor can he accept it. His widowed father has taken as second wife a pretty woman younger than himself. She is hardly motherly toward her stepson: one day, after he has grown to early manhood, she seduces him—in the words of the song, "she does for him what mother never did for her son." This line recurs throughout as a refrain.

It is after the shock of this event that the son leaves in quest of his mother. His father repeatedly tries to dissuade him, insisting that she is dead, or that, if she is alive, it is only in a place "as near as the valley beyond the hill and far away as the stars." In the end, however, he gives his son a sword and a purse full of money and lets him go. The stepmother, also hoping to keep the son from leaving, makes another but this time futile attempt to "do for him what mother never did for her son."

At the end of three days, the son comes to a city. At evening he meets a beautiful woman with long red hair. She offers him hospitality, which he accepts, and she attends lovingly to his every want. Pleasure and hope fill his breast. He begins wondering. He asks himself if this woman might not be his lost mother. But when night falls, the red-haired woman takes him into her bed and "does for him what mother never did for her son." The son knows she cannot be the one he seeks. Pretending to sleep, he waits for an opportunity to leave her; but, at midnight, he sees her draw a length of strong, sharp cord from beneath her pillow and stretch it towards him. The son leaps up, seizes his sword, and confronts the woman. Under its threat, she confesses that she was planning to murder him for the sake of his purse, as she has done with countless travelers: their corpses lie rotting in her cellar. The son slays the woman with his sword, wakes up a nearby priest to assure a Christian burial for her and her victims, and goes his way.

Three days later, he arrives at another city. As day wanes, a strange woman again offers him hospitality, and again he accepts. She is even more beautiful than the first; and her hair is also long, but golden. She lavishes her attentions on the young man, and in such profusion that hope once again spurs him to wonder whether she might not be his lost mother. But with the coming of darkness, the woman with the golden hair takes him into her bed and "does for him what mother never did for her son." His hopes have again been disappointed. Full of unease, he feigns sleep. Halfway through the night he hears footsteps mounting the stairs. He scarcely has time to leap out of bed and grasp his sword before two burly villains come rushing into the room. They attack him, and he cuts them down. Then, turning on the woman, he forces her at sword point to confess that she had hoped to make him her prisoner and sell him into slavery. Saracen pirates would have paid a high price for one of such strength and beauty. The son slays her, wakes up a priest to see that she and her henchmen receive a Christian burial, and goes his way.

Another three days' journey brings him to a third city. There, at end of day, the son meets still another fair woman, the most beautiful of all, with flowing, raven black hair. Alone of the three, she seems to recognize him; and when she takes him under her roof and bestows on him more comfort and affection than he had ever dreamed possible, he knows that this time his hope cannot be mistaken. But when night comes, she takes him into her bed, and she, like the others, "does for him what mother never did for her son." She has drugged his food. He cannot help falling asleep; only, at midnight, the touch of cold iron against his throat rouses him from his stupor. Taking up his sword, he points it in fury at the breast of the woman who has so beguiled him. She begs him to leave her in peace, but she finally acknowledges that she meant to cut his throat and suck his blood. She is an old, old witch, who has lost all her powers but one, that of preserving her youth. This she does by drinking the blood of young men. The son runs her through with his sword. With a weak cry, she falls to the floor a wrinkled crone. The son knows that a witch cannot be buried in consecrated ground, and he goes his way.

But the young man travels no further. He is bitterly convinced of the folly of his quest; he has lost all hope of ever finding his mother; wearily he turns homeward.

On his way he passes through the cities where he has first faced danger. He is greeted as a hero. Thanks to the two priests, all know that it was he who destroyed the evil incarnate in their midst. But he takes no pride in having killed two women who "did for him what mother never did for her son."

On the ninth day of his return, he sees, from the mountain pass he has reached, the hill beyond which his native village lies. In the valley between, a shepherdess is watching her flock. At his approach she greets him tenderly, for she knows the blacksmith's son and has loved him for many years. He stops with her to rest. She has become, he notices, a beautiful young woman—not as beautiful, perhaps, as the evil three: but her eyes are wide and deep, and her long hair is brown.

The afternoon goes by. Still the son does not leave. At evening, he partakes of the shepherdess's frugal supper. At nighttime, when she lies down, he lies down beside her; and she, her heart brimming with gladness, "does for him what mother never did for her son." The shepherdess falls asleep. The son cannot sleep; and he is appalled, in the middle of the night, to see the shepherdess suddenly rise up beside him. But she only touches his shoulder as if to waken him and points to the starry sky. She tells him to look up. There, she says, beyond the darkness, the souls of the dead have gathered into one blazing light. With a cry of pain, the son asks, "Then is my mother there?" The shepherdess answers that she is. His mother lives beyond the stars, and the stars themselves are chinks in the night through which the fateful light of the dead and the unborn is revealed to the world. "Oh, Mother, Mother," the young man weeps. The shepherdess then says to him, "Who is now mother to your sleep and waking? Who else can be the mother of your joy and pain? I shall henceforth be the mother of every memory; and from this night on, I alone am your mother—even if now, and tomorrow, and all the days of my life, I do for you what mother never did for her son." In his sudden ecstasy, the blacksmith's son understands. He has discovered his desire.

And so, next morning, he brings the shepherdess home. His father, when he sees them, weeps tears of relief and joy; and his stepmother, sick with remorse, welcomes them as saviors. Henceforth they all live in mutual contentment; and when, every evening, the approach of darkness kindles new yearning in the young man's heart and he turns to embrace his wife, she devotedly responds and never once fails, through the long passing years, to "do for him what mother never did for her son."

The connection of this song with *farce double* lies, I was told, in an analogy between the stars and the holes in the lid of the roasting pit.

When your timer sounds for the final round, you must be in fighting trim: not aggressive, but supremely alert. You now have to work at high speed and with utmost delicacy. The meat will have swelled in cooking: it is pressing against the clay shell harder than ever, and one jolt can spell disaster. Do not coddle yourself by thinking that this pressure is buttressing the shell. In La Tour Lambert, the handling of the cooked lamb is entrusted to squads of highly trained young men: they are solemn as pallbearers and dexterous as shortstops, and their virtuosity is eloquent proof that this is no time for optimism.

Slide the casserole slowly out of the oven and gently set it down on a table covered with a thrice-folded blanket. You will now need help. Summon anyone—a friend, a neighbor, a husband, a lover, a sibling, even a guest—so that the two of you can slip four broad wooden spatulas under the roast, one on each side, and ease it onto a platter. The platter should be resting on a soft surface such as a cushion or a mattress (a small hammock would be perfect). Wait for the meat to cool before moving it onto anything harder. Your assistant may withdraw.

Meanwhile attend to the gravy. No later than the previous evening, you will have made 1½ qts of stock with the bones from the lamb shoulder, together with the customary onions, carrots, celery, herb bouquet, cloves, scallions, parsnips, and garlic (see *stock*), to which you must not hesitate to add any old fowl, capon, partridge, or squab carcasses that are gathering rime in your deep freeze, or a young rabbit or two. Pour out the fat in the casserole and set it on the stove over high heat. Splash in enough of the same good champagne to scrape the casserole clean, and boil. When the wine has largely evaporated, take off heat and add 2 cups of rendered pork fat. Set the casserole over very low heat and make a quick roux or brown sauce with 3 cups of flour. Then slowly pour in 2 cups of the blood of the lamb, stirring it in a spoonful at a time. Finally, add the stock. Raise the heat to medium high and let the liquid simmer down to the equivalent of 13 cupfuls.

While the gravy reduces, carefully set the platter with the roast on a table, resting one side on an object the size of this cookbook, so that it sits at a tilt. Place a broad shallow bowl against the lower side. If the clay shell now breaks, the poaching broth will flow rapidly into the bowl. Prop the lamb with a spatula or two to keep it from sliding off the platter.

Slit the seams in the meat, spread its folds, and expose the clay shell. Put on kitchen gloves—the clay will be scalding—and coax the shell from its depths. Set it in a saucepan, give it a smart crack with a mallet, and remove the grosser shards. Ladle out the quenelles and keep them warm in the oven in a covered, buttered dish with a few spoonfuls of the broth. Strain the rest of the liquid, reduce it quickly to a quarter of its volume, and then use what is left of the champagne to make a white wine sauce as explained on p. 888. Nap the quenelles with sauce, and serve.

If you have worked fast and well, by the time your guests finish the quenelles, the lamb will have set long enough for its juices to have withdrawn in the tissues without its getting cold. Pour the gravy into individual heated bowls. Place a bowl in front of each guest, and set the platter with the lamb, which you will have turned outside up, at the center of the table. The meat is eaten without knives and forks. Break off a morsel with the fingers of the right hand, dip it in gravy, and pop it into your mouth. In Auvergne, this is managed with nary a dribble; but lobster bibs are a comfort.

(Do not be upset if you yourself have lost all desire to eat. This is a normal, salutary condition. Your satisfaction will have been in the doing, not in the thing done. But observe the reaction of your guests, have a glass of wine [see below], and you may feel the urge to try one bite, and perhaps a second ...)

It is a solemn moment when, at the great communal spring banquet, the Mayor of La Tour Lambert goes from table to table and with shining fingers gravely breaks the skin of each lamb. After this ceremony, however, the prevailing gaiety reasserts itself. After all, the feast of *farce double* is not only a time-hallowed occasion but a very pleasant one. It is a moment for friendships to be renewed, for enemies to forgive one another, for lovers to embrace. At its origin, curiously enough, the feast was associated with second marriages (some writers think this gave the dish its name). Such marriages have never been historically explained; possibly they never took place. What is certain is that the feast has always coincided with the arrival, from the lowlands, of shepherds driving their flocks to the high pastures where they will summer. Their coming heralds true spring and its first warmth; and it restores warmth, too, between the settled mountain craftsmen of La Tour Lambert and the seminomadic shepherds from the south. The two communities are separate only in their ways of life. They have long been allied by esteem, common interest, and, most important, by blood. Marriages between them have been recorded since the founding of the village in the year one thousand; and if many a shepherd's daughter has settled in La Tour Lambert as the wife of a wheelwright or turner, many an Auvergnat son, come autumn, has left his father's mill or forge to follow the migrant flocks toward Les Saintes-Maries-de-la-Mer. Perhaps the legend of second marriages reflects a practice whereby a widow or widower took a spouse among the folk of which he was not a member. The eating of *farce double* would then be exquisitely appropriate; for there is no doubt at all that the composition of the dish—lamb from plains by the sea, fish from lakes among the grazing lands—deliberately embodies the merging of these distinct peoples in one community. I should add that at the time the feast originated, still another group participated harmoniously in its celebration: pilgrims from Burgundy on their way to Santiago de Compostela. Just as the people of La Tour Lambert provided fish for the great banquet and the shepherds contributed their lambs, the pilgrims supplied kegs of new white wine that they brought with them from Chassagne, the Burgundian village now called Chassagne-Montrachet. Their wine became the invariable accompaniment for both parts of *farce double;* and you could hardly do better than to adopt the custom. Here, at least, tradition can be observed with perfect fidelity.

It is saddening to report that, like the rest of the world, La Tour Lambert has undergone considerable change. Shepherds no longer walk their flocks from the south but ship them by truck. The lakes have been fished out, and a substitute for *chaste* is imported frozen from Yugoslavia. The grandson of the last wheelwright works in the tourist bureau, greeting latterday pilgrims who bring in wine. He is one of the very few of his generation to have remained in the village. (The cement quarry, which was opened with great fanfare ten years ago as a way of providing jobs, employs mainly foreign labor. Its most visible effect has been to shroud the landscape in white dust.) I have heard, however, that the blacksmith still earns a good living making wrought-iron lamps. Fortunately, the future of *farce double* is assured, at least for the time being. The festal cave has been put on a commercial footing, and it now produces the dish for restaurants in the area all year round (in the off season, on weekends only). It is open to the public. I recommend a visit if you pass nearby.

Eat the quenelles ungarnished. Mashed sorrel goes nicely with the lamb.

Serves thirteen.

Manhattan on the Rocks

Michael Musto

They do, I watch. They dress, scream, carouse, screw, I take notes.

I am the ringleader, the mirror to their marauding, the reflection of their cavalcade. Someone swings from a chandelier, and I muster a wry smile. A woman squirts milk from her bosoms at a nightclub audience, and I nod knowingly and involuntarily reach for my pen. I am neither over- nor underwhelmed, just whelmed. I don't have sex, I don't drink, I don't do drugs. I don't do. I watch.

As publisher of *Manhattan on the Rocks*—yes, a dread "counter-culture magazine"—I've become friend to the zanies, sycophant to the stars, and anathema to anyone wearing Ralph Lauren. Printing my gut reactions to all things bright and beautiful without much regard for advertiser appeasement or social climbing has made me Someone—Someone to distrust, Someone to loathe, Someone for press whores to line up for a visitation with and plead with for a mention, any mention, as long as the proverbial spelling is correct and it's in boldface, preferably fourteen-point Optima boldface (press whores know these things). These people adore me; as a former English lit major, my spelling is as flawless as my way with a new-wave polka at five in the morning for an audience of one. That much I'll do.

Since dropping out of Dartmouth in the second half of my fifth year (still a junior, because of silly things like credits), I've been on a circular party coaster that stops only so I can compile my magazine and occasionally read it, with bodily functions an annoying but only intermittent interruption. Dartmouth was too American-provincial, the frat parties I now and then deigned to attend reeked depressingly of impending beer bellies, an English lit degree is ultimately as useful as Mace, and finally I started resenting the mornings I had to race cross-campus to exams without quality time to stop and learn the Oscar nominations and other crucial info that could cement my education. Proust suited me fine, but Robert De Niro's self-imposed weight fluctuations were even more fascinating. Stendhal was nifty, but more important, was Cher really going to wear that hairdo and be a serious actress at the same time?

As someone who studied Simon and Garfunkel lyrics as poetry in the not very esoteric New York City public school system, I was ill prepared for the required battery of Greek and Roman classics, which most of my blue-eyed classmates could recite with the same élan with which I could list Johnny Depp's film credits (did you know he was in *Platoon*?) and all the Hollywood Squares who'd ever had prescription-drug dependencies. The *Enquirer* became my Monarch Notes to a world of glitz and scandal that was so much realer than those in any English lit classic. The Scarlet Letter A was never to be emblazoned across my chest; I was getting C+s.

So I split. I always suspected the school had only let me in to fulfill their quota of people from Queens (one) anyway. To the chagrin of my family of well-fed Italians—a family that had never been to college, just weddings—I crash-landed back in New York, past Cerberus and into the gates of Kips Bay (Manhattan's forgotten, thank God, neighborhood). No one has discovered Kips Bay and no one ever will, so it's a perfect watching ground, from which you're under no one else's scrutiny. It's the only audience left in New York—everything else is onstage begging for applause.

My parents didn't want me to leave my liberal arts training in the first place. My father would have been far happier had I followed his footsteps and joined the DiBlasio's illustrious line of pharmacists—a dynasty of shameless drug dealers (no Squares, but numerous Mafia princesses, served). My mother, meanwhile, wanted me to take *her* lead and become a professional neurotic, wringing hands and biting lips for a living. But since I'd weaseled into one of the top six of the eight Ivy League schools and had already used up so much of their hard-earned money on expenses, it wasn't so perverse of them to want me to follow through with it and be a college-educated pharmacist-slash-neurotic. "My son, the dropout" became my new verbal tattoo, my designation in the Who's Who of bridge-and-tunnel hell.

I was never going to please them, a reality made all the more horrifying because I'm their one and only, and they don't even have pets, just those stickpin rhinos my mother cranked out once in a fit of community-workshop obsession. To a family of failures, I was the biggest failure of all; they weren't even wannabes, just contented cows gleefully chewing their cud in the urban backyard of Astoria, but I—I was a could-have-been. I could have been the best pharmacist they ever produced, I could have been the biggest professional neurotic that ever lived. And here I was, a dropout, a runaway, a party boy with scads of carelessly groomed facial hair. They wanted me to die brutally. How it pained them, then, that their own *Enquirer* worship made me some kind of family prodigy. My mother, the Rupert Pupkin of Astoria, begged me once for Peggy Lee's lipstick imprint or a swatch of Don Ho's hair—"from anywhere," she said, "even his nose." "Fuck you," I shrieked. "I wouldn't go *near* his nose."

To push the folks' heads even deeper into the mud trough, I was going to become the most famous, most compulsive partygoer in the highly competitive world of full-time partygoers. Schmoozing it up with the people who never sleep, I partied with uptowners, I partied with downtowners, I partied with drag queens with bigger pudenda than both my parents had in their prime, I partied with every ounce of that four-and-a-half years' worth of pent-up Ivy League libido until each night's parties seemed to segue seamlessly into the next night's, and there were no exams to grill me on who wore what and whether their shoes matched their colostomy bags. The Spanish Inquisition, WASP version, was over. Unlike "Jeopardy," where even the answers have to be phrased like questions, I was playing a game where there were only answers—who, what, when, and how they were spelled—and I was drowning in them, eating them up like a social ringworm on an endless sucking-and-gloating mission.

Anxious for something more demanding to do than "working the room"—an art which, once you've mastered it, you can only repeat—I founded *Manhattan on the Rocks,* a publication designed as a shrine to all that information, told my way. I write most of the columns, do the layouts, and even buy copies to inflate sales statistics, relying on others only to take pictures (I can't focus) and sell ads (too tedious for words). For backing, I used money left me by my favorite fat Uncle Vito (out of two fat Uncle Vitos)—the one who got stuck in the closet and had to be crowbarred out by police amid much embarrassment by my family, many of whom are still fuming that I got his entire lump-sum savings and property in Queens, but weren't too mad to ask me for lipstick imprints of *their* favorite stars.

Uncle Vito liked me because I'd sit and watch porno movies with him and speculate about why the female star had a penis. He liked me because I didn't patronize him, and I only joke about the closet incident now because I know he would have found it amusing had it happened to someone other than himself. If *I* were to get stuck, I'd find it hilarious, because I always feel as if the things happening to me are really happening to someone else and I'm just watching. I feel like I'm a character in a movie I paid to see. If I were to get hit by a car, I'd laugh, because I love action movies.

My favorite fat Uncle Vito is still subsidizing my career down here in Satan's playground, and I just know he's chuckling up in the big, overstuffed closet in the sky, laughing those big, blowsy laughs that could knock you down a flight of stairs. All other expenses are covered by the comp syndrome that goes hand in hand with my entitled way of life. I go to clubs free. I eat at free buffet events and drink rivers of cranberry juice at open bars. Other people pay for my cabs. (That "I only have a twenty" routine works every time.) I buy fashion off the street, and I delouse it by soaking it in salad dressing, then rinsing clean. The only things I'm not "on the list" for are rent and newspapers, but I've found certain newsstands where you can read the essential columns without them yelling "Hey, this isn't a library" in five languages. And once *Manhattan on the Rocks* started turning a profit, I convinced myself, I'd be living in block-long limos with wet bars and VCRs and maybe even conference calls, and wouldn't have to worry about rent at all. ("Only in My Dreams," as the very annoying Debbie Gibson sings.)

Meanwhile, I live from hand to mouth, from party to party. Blessed with the social conscience of a flea, I find all the turmoil at my doorstep just a loud and ugly incentive to party harder and throw larger confetti. As more and more crack hotels open two blocks away on fashionable Park Avenue—the kind of residences you can only approach holding an umbrella, because a baby is methodically thrown out of a window about every twenty minutes—I find it a persuasive argument for staying out till dawn with nary a thought in my mind. As enough homeless people stagger down my street to make it look like a Black Hole of Calcutta version of the set for *Ironweed,* and seemingly costumed-by-Equity extras go so far as to perform intricately thought-out rap songs to ensnare your attention ("I'm not gonna steal—your watch—and hock it/If you would just insert some coins into my pocket . . ."), I can only long for the party crowd, who could never summon the brainpower to come up with a rap song and are therefore not nearly as intrusive to my own private walls, the tower I've constructed around myself to ward off anything too ugly or demanding.

As AIDS keeps adding to the city's devastation with pain and anger and depression, I want to forget, to ignore, to dance—the dance of a person who *chooses* not to care, because a life of constant caring is draining and demoralizing and ultimately doesn't change anything. In the world of glitter balls and fake celebs, you can change things, turn a mental knob and make it quieter, louder, more intimate, or more frivolous at whim. By magnifying a relatively trivial world and making it earthshaking, you never have to worry about anything more important than the next outfit, the next invite, the next hangover remedy (two Nuprin and a Vitamin B-complex pill work just fine for me lately—all right, I do occasionally accept substances when forced, but I still consider that a passive activity). You're always OK until the last streamer is tossed and then you just find another party. You are never homeless.

News

Max Phillips

There were five yellow post-its on the front window of the closed restaurant when I got there at nine to meet my friend News. The first said that she was sorry, the second said that she was stupid, and the last three gave directions to a nearby café she swore would be open. I peered through the smoked glass between News's notes. The chairs were piled in the back under a plastic shroud, and sections of the floor had been pried up. The restaurant looked as if it had been closed for a long time. I smoothed my chin and adjusted my tie in the dark glass. I could just see my new haircut. I had black, wavy hair, parted on the left and swooping over my right eye down to my shoulder, like Veronica Lake. Below the part, the left side of my head was shaved down to blond fuzz, and I felt the cold wind move over it in a different and surprising way.

The hairdresser had been recommended by News. She bent my head over the basin and told me, "I wouldn't suggest this concept to just any of my clients, but you have the sort of Burne-Jones face. A guy like you could make it work."

"Maybe you mean Botticelli," I said. "Burne-Jones people had big square jaws."

"You know," she said. She turned my chair away from the mirror before she began to cut. "You'd only get upset if you saw this before I get it finished."

"I'm probably not going into this with the right attitude. I guess I worry I'm just giving people something else to misconstrue. You know, sometimes everything you let anyone see seems like, I don't know, evidence. To be used against you."

"Hold still," she said.

People kept coming into the salon, staring, and then looking quickly away.

News's directions were clear and accurate, strangely enough. Soon I was looking around the café for her. The hostess came up to me, a plump woman with spiky black hair and pointed black booties. "Can I help?" she said. "Just tell Alina what you want, and she'll take care of you. Whatever it is, you've come to the right place. We'll fix you up." She took me by the shoulders and turned me toward the diners. "You see these people? These are all happy people. That's because Alina takes good care of them. Talk to me, honey, and we'll make you happy too."

I said, "I'm looking for my friend News. She's supposed to be here.

"Um, her full name is Newport News," I said.

"News, name. Name, News," Alina muttered. "Okay, no problem. We'll have this cleared up in a minute. You just hold tight, honey, and everything's going to be fine. Just a moment." She disappeared into the kitchen.

I hung around for a while, then decided to wait outside. It was dark. I could smell the cold river. Cabs went by every few minutes, and I craned my neck to see if News was in one of them. Then a silver BMW pulled up to the curb. A slim black woman with a very long neck got out and looked me over, hands on hips. I was wearing an antique wool cutaway, gray silk harem pants, and orange Keds. My legs were very cold. "Uh-huh," she said.

"I'm waiting for a woman named News," I told her.

"That's right," she said. "That's okay. News sent me to get you." She opened the door for me. "My name's Nancee." She spelled it. "Come on."

Nancee drove very fast, using the manual shift with a lot of skill. Her fingers were long and looked hard. She wore a black Kansai jacket with cloth-of-gold numerals down one sleeve, which I thought was kind of a bad idea. "Where are we going?" I asked.

"Someplace nice," she said.

We parked in front of a loft building. There was a metal sidewalk in front, patterned with thick glass plugs that glowed with light from below, suggesting big doings underground. I followed her up three long flights of stairs. She opened a steel door. "This is my place," she said. It was a huge room, full of people in gray business suits, and the music was very loud. Nancee had a way of shoving people aside that seemed like perfect manners. She led me to the far end and into a narrow, twisting hallway, stopping in front of a lighted niche with a low pedestal. The sculpture or whatever had been removed, probably to keep it from getting broken.

She turned to me and rubbed her hard thumb over the fuzz on the side of my head. "Sweet," she said. "That is really something. Did you sort of feel you had to do that?"

"I guess News is somewhere around here," I said.

"Uh-huh," she said. She moved up and kissed me, backing me onto the pedestal in the little niche.

"Well," I said. She took hold of the back of my head and kissed me again. Her tongue was extremely smooth, as if she didn't have any tastebuds. With the other hand, she undid my pants and handled me. Then she stepped back to survey the effect, her head to one side. "Better," she said. "Much better. Just a moment," she said, and disappeared around the corner.

I stood there. A man in a gray business suit came by, holding a drink. He nodded. "That's right," he said. "We're all just here to have a good time. Right?"

"That's right," I said.

He left, and I did up my pants and went back into the party. Nobody was dancing. I figured News would be easy to spot. Her bicycle-reflector earrings, for instance. The snail tattoo on her left cheek. I moved through the crowd until I reached the opposite corner of the room, where I saw two marines in fresh crewcuts and green fatigues, sitting on a bench by the wall. The bigger one saw me and grinned. "Hot damn," he said. "Another fag. Come on over and sit by me, boy." He thumped the bench beside him. "I been waiting all evening for some *ro*-mance."

I went over, and he pulled me down next to him on the bench. He had a big carton of chocolate milk in one hand. "We must a done wrong to get here," he said. "The nigger woman come by in a little car and tell us to get in. She backs me into a corner over there and starts in to monkey me. Next thing she's gone." He shook his head. "We been in New York two days now and I don't think it's so great."

His friend smiled sardonically. The big marine hooked an arm around my shoulders and studied me. His breath was sweet with chocolate milk. "Do you know," he said, "that you are prettier than any woman I ever fucked?"

"Probably," I said.

"A sense of *humor*," he said. "Now that's fine, but y'all stay nice and don't become hurtful. Remember I'm sensitive."

His friend laughed. "Wylie," he said, "I had a look at your dossier. They got you down as chronically violent, a discipline problem, and a possible sociopath."

"That's what I'm saying. I'm sensitive."

"I'm looking for a woman named Newport News," I said. Wylie looked at me, aggrieved.

"Talk nice," he said. He put his head back and seemed about to howl like a dog. Then he snored deeply. He kept hold of his chocolate milk.

"Now would be a good time to go," his friend said.

I nodded and moved off diagonally through the crowd until I came to the bar. There was a long row of chocolate milk cartons, and piles of fruit pies, chocolate milk, and crumbcakes in brightly colored cellophane wrappers. I was pretty hungry by this time, and I had a few. There was no alcohol, and everything seemed to be in sealed individual packages except an enormous bowl of M & M's. I picked this up to see what it weighed—easily thirty pounds—and a girl's voice by my ear said, "Maybe you should leave some for the rest of us."

She had cropped brown hair and a fake mole. "I mean, you should follow your impulses," she said, "but there's also the thing of not developing an acquisitive head, which is bad for you. That's what got us into the war in China."

"Vietnam," I said.

"Yeah. I like your hair, by the way."

"Thank you. I like your dress." She bent her head and examined it. It was a yellow vinyl minidress with magenta and orange ovals. The vinyl against her flesh made tiny sucking noises, like masking tape being peeled off of glass.

"This is mostly a nostalgia thing for me," she said, still staring at her dress, "but I also think the whole 1968 thing is ready to come back again, the whole Aquarian ideal. You know, the sharing and the peacefulness."

"Well, I suppose. I was two years old in 1968. How old were you?"

"I was born in '71," she said frostily, "so like I said, for me this is mostly a nostalgia thing."

"I'm looking for a woman named Newport News," I said.

"I'm sure," she said, and left.

I took some chocolate milk and wandered through the party until I found another door. It was slightly open. I went in. Nancee was curled up on the bed inside. Several skirts were spread out neatly on the floor in front of her. She was wearing her jacket and red pumps. Aside from that, she was naked. She picked up her head when I came in, said, "Oh. Hi," and let it drop again.

I sat down beside her. "Hi. Um, I'm still looking for my friend, News."

She spoke into the sheet. "Did you ever just go along, not really knowing what sort of mood you were in? And then some little thing happens and decides you? I don't know anybody named News," she said sadly. "She sounds nice."

I patted her bare hip, which was also unnaturally smooth, and went back out. For some reason, I had trouble finding the front door, but I did find a small door like a service hatch, which I had to stoop to get through. It opened onto a dim, cramped corridor lit by mercury-vapor lamps that glowed powder blue with a red halo. I worked my way around coils of cable and dusty sheets of chipboard until I came to a spiral staircase in a cage of steel mesh, which I thought must lead to the back door.

The stairs seemed to go down a very long way before they let out into a low concrete tunnel. I kept walking along, waiting for the sounds of traffic or the smell of garbage. Eventually I found myself between two rows of buildings in a narrow alley roofed over with the same steel mesh, through which I could see a narrow strip of stars. They seemed very bright, the way stars are supposed to seem from the bottom of a well. After about five minutes, the alley widened into a little sunken courtyard, with a crowd of people standing behind a velvet rope. They were all wearing gray business suits. There was a door in the corner through which I could hear electronic dance music, sounding like bird calls and muffled punches in the belly. A big guy was standing by the door. I went up to him and said "Excuse me."

He put a hand on my chest. "Simmer down, Honeysuckle Rose. These people have all been waiting."

A woman with a clipboard appeared behind him and said, "Is there a problem?" She looked at me intently over her half-glasses. She was wearing a ruffled salmon dress, paisley tights, and brogues.

"We have a situation here with Honeysuckle Rose," he said. "I doubt he's on the list, Valerie."

Valerie didn't take her eyes off me. "Corliss, this young man will always be on my list. Always. Let him through, please." Corliss looked stonily ahead, and I said "Thank you" and walked quickly into the club. It was decorated with brocaded sofas and junked cars, and someone was burning incense in a big way.

Valerie, at my elbow, said, "I hope you'll make allowances for Corliss. He's the owner's idea of a credible deterrent. But a boy like you shouldn't have to cope. Has anyone given you a drink card? Here you are. Oh, that is some hair." She straightened the hair over my eye and ran her nails through the blond fuzz around my ear. "There's nothing I admire more than an uncalculated risk. Oh, you're dessert, that's what you are. And sensitive too, am I right? I'm wrong of course. I'm making you up from scratch. You're nothing but a trick of the light, I guess. You're nothing but a beautiful dream. Just a moment," she said, and disappeared into the crowd.

I waited. I took a sip of the drink in my hand—it tasted like canned fruit punch, no liquor—and then realized that someone had just put it there. He said, "Hi. I really like your necktie." I was wearing a Cub Scout neckerchief with a bear's-head slide I'd whittled myself to earn a woodcraft merit badge. I always thought it came out well, except the bear looks slightly drunk, but there was something else I couldn't do and I never got the badge. I said, "Thank you. I'm just here to have a good time."

He was wearing a gray business suit and smiling a great deal. He said, "This is a pretty neat place. I come here to keep up with you avant garb young people. And the new music." They were playing Spandau Ballet's "Age of Blows," which came out when I was still working toward my woodcraft badge. The man in the suit took my shoulder and brought me over to sit in one of the junked cars, saying, "Over here we won't be in the way of the dancers." I looked around. Nobody was dancing.

I said, "I really can't stay. I'm looking for a woman named Newport News. We were going to have dinner. She's a friend, but she's also being represented by my gallery. I mean, she'd like to be represented, and I'm doing what I can. It's not my gallery in the sense that I own it, of course. I'm only the receptionist. I really think you should take your hand off my leg."

"In a minute. I swear I'll take it away in a minute. Come on," he said anxiously, "you're a faggot, aren't you?"

I said, "Let me get back to you on that one."

Valerie, standing by my shoulder, said, "Neutral corners, everyone. Kennebeck, don't pester this child or I'll feed you to Corliss."

"Thank you for the drink," I said, getting up. "Goodbye, Valerie, I really have to go. I'm looking for a woman named Newport News."

"Lucky gal," she said sadly. "Come with me and I'll see what we can do."

She took my arm and led me through the crowd and into the kitchen. There were huge steam tables, one of which held a whole goat, including the horns, and stocky Asians with glistening, squarish heads were hammering away at it with knives. She opened a sliding door behind the walk-in fridge. "Take the first left all the way," she said. "Can't miss it." She gripped the back of my neck and kissed me. "Be good," she said, and walked off, waving her clipboard at the steam.

The tunnel was no wider than the gigantic pipe just over my head, which thrummed, radiating heat, and was covered with scales of rust that kept catching my hair. When I came out the other end, I was on the uptown platform of the Prince Street 6. A train was coming into the station. Well, I thought. News would certainly have given up by now, even assuming she hadn't forgotten her own directions to the café. In either case, she'd probably be with her boyfriend Beaumont. When the doors opened, I got on.

Beaumont's building was on 84th near the park. The doorman was turning slowly under the heat lamps in the awning, like a chicken on a rotisserie. He nodded and pushed open the door. I told him, "I'm looking for Newport News." The lobby was done in white travertine and those mirrors that are patterned with a sort of golden eczema. Upstairs, nobody answered the bell. I've got a key to Beaumont's place from all the times I've helped him set up for parties, so I opened the door and went in to leave a note.

Inside, it was all beige, blond wood, and chrome, which I was having Beaumont get rid of as quickly as possible. The living room was a welter of gray business suits, scattered over the furniture and floor for his housekeeper to take to the cleaners. Beaumont's TV is never turned off, because News thinks this will help scramble the ratings and fool the networks into putting on more very bad shows, which she really likes. It was showing a concert in a ballroom somewhere. Nobody was dancing.

I went to the desk for paper. There was a photo of News on it in a heart-shaped frame. She was naked and, except for the tattoo, looked about twelve. Next to that was the desk blotter, on which Beaumont had written:

lev/bnd mtg fri 11 Morgan
         need to see   several lack of matter I cant
genetech 36.8 U carbd 104(harris?)
    testicles/TENTACLES?   never simply
News News News News News News News

Below this he'd written my name, and then:

  fag/not?   major hair ... NEWS?!
News/noose(nu?)
        burne-jones[?]
  sensibly   other shirt

At the very bottom, he'd written in tiny script:

<u>hurts all over</u>

Next to this was a gold-filled fountain pen with the cap off. Next to that, a packet of condoms. I decided against leaving a note and went back downstairs. It was drizzling when I got outside, and I was wondering if I could spare money for a cab when a gun-metal Turbo Carrera hissed up to the curb and Wylie the Marine poked his head out. "It's the fag!" he said happily.

He got out and hugged me, then wiped the hair back from my face. "I been thinking," he said. "Dudn't your hair keep getting in your mouth? I bought this car here with some money this lady give me. She wants me to hurry right back. I bet you still looking for your friend."

"That's right. But it's always a pleasure, Wylie."

"Well, shit. I been in New York two days now and you the only one's been nice to me. Get in and I'll take you where you want to go. Well, come on in out of the wet, boy. Sweet as you are, you'll prob'ly melt."

Wylie insisted that if we stayed by the river we'd travel fastest, and we wound up in Fort Lee, then Riverdale, then Queens Village. It was nearly two when he let me off in front of News's building on East Third across from the men's shelter. There were three residents standing by her steps, hunching and weaving in the cold like slow boxers. They watched with no special expression as I went in. I climbed to the fifth floor, crunching long shards of green paint under my feet, and rapped on News's door. I heard her tape deck blaring away inside. Just then I noticed that her name plate had been replaced by one reading: "Carol Heitzer/Attorney-at-Law." The door swung open. It was a long, sinewy woman in a strapless green ball gown, with a corsage climbing her bare shoulder. She had very large biceps, and her eyes and lips were bright.

"I'm sorry," I said. "I'm looking for a woman named Newport News."

"Uh-uh, honey," she said. "You been looking for me."

It was close to dawn when I got back on the street. The lights were out in the men's shelter. The sidewalks were empty. The drizzle had lifted into an opaque, grainy sky, which trembled and strained with dim light. I could feel the faintest breezes against my bruised mouth. I'd left my socks in Carol's apartment and I was cold.

I walked to the middle of the street and stood there. All the windows were pale gray, going blue. I let the wet breeze run against my face.

An old baby carriage rolled out of an alley across the street and bumped to rest at the curb. I went over and looked in. It was empty except for a gold candy box. The box was empty too. As I put down the lid, there was a scream, tapering into a giggle, and then an engine roared, and a gray limousine skidded around the corner, barely missing me, and took off toward the west.

I stood there. I waited.

I heard the engine again, and the tires squealing. The noise was working its way back toward me, on streets behind streets. I got braced.

An old Plymouth with orange patches of body putty slewed around the corner and jerked to a halt in front of me. The back door popped open. Her black hair seemed wet. She was wearing a gray business suit, and under that, a Spiderman T-shirt. Under that, her narrow chest moved rapidly.

"Hello, News," I said.

"You're late," she said. "Get in."

I hesitated. The driver was an older guy I'd never seen, with a long scar down his cheek. And he was wearing a neckerchief with a slide just like mine, which seemed ominous. But after a moment, I got in without asking any questions. I didn't want to make things more difficult than they already are.

Big Sky

Noel Ryan

I had a stare that could make you wild. I could stare the violence out of you, stare you into fists and your teeth closed tight and you would need to beat or kick at the staring.

In Montana, standing on the side of the mountain above our farm, you look far, far to the mountains on the other side of the valley, and then you see the river there, and you look down beyond where the river slinks out across a far, wider valley, and you follow that until you are utterly lost in all that space, those endless shadowy valleys and shaley-black mountains piled across mountains and sky and clouds. It was supposed to make you think of God and thrill and inspire you to religion. It did not thrill or inspire me. It frightened me, that hugeness, the long and the high and the upward and the ageless and the impossibility of breaking it into words or even thoughts.

I stared at people as if they, too, were those wordless valleys and soprano mountains I know here in Montana, as if they, too, were huge spaces with something ancient aching at them. I looked at them and between my eyes and theirs looking back or not, there was the unanswered, that immensity where words back up into themselves like a train or spiral out like hunting hawks until they are gone into the sky. People are immensities—like skies. I see it in the space between us, between our eyes and our words.

It got so that I couldn't hear words. When I was sixteen or seventeen is when it happened. It wasn't a physical thing, not as if the fluids in my eardrums dried up or the little hearing hairs inside died—it became so that I couldn't hear words, just the hail and thundercrack of sound, big storms of sound, downward sweeping torrents and cloudbursts of sound, noise, but sometimes unscrolling into a music. I would sit in the classroom and listen to the nuns up at the blackboard and their voices would come out like singing, but like opera singing, and I would sit and watch them with their pointers tapping a fraction or a Latin verb, but what I heard was the singing, like a Gregorian chant or the Indian praying you hear at night from the reservation. The meaning of words slipped off the edge of the sound, like spaghetti from a fork, and I would hear only the music, the sound, nothing that made a word or caused a feeling I recognized.

At first it was just in school, but soon enough after it moved all over my life. I had a job in a grocery store for a while and the old couple who owned it, friends of my mother, would give me all kinds of directions, but I couldn't make out what they were saying. Here a quack, there a quack, everywhere a quack quack. It got so they would explain one thing and I would do it and then another thing and I would do it. But you can't run a store that way, so they let me go. They were the ones who told my mother that I had problems.

My mother especially I could not understand. But then she never gave me directions. She just yelled. She just called names. "You little . . . " and I would stare at her and her words would fire into a hard brick, a weapon. Sometimes she would shake her voice over her head like a Zulu shakes his spear. My mother said she knew that look on my face, that defiance, and she would beat it out of me, that stare. She would show me. And the beating would happen.

I got good marks in school because our tests were based on what was in the books, not what the nuns said. But I had to be taken out of school anyway. And it was not because Joseph Greycloud kicked me in the head with his ice skate. It was because I talked to myself. I couldn't help it or stop it. But it wasn't for Joseph Greycloud kicking me with his ice skate. I wouldn't even notice I was yelling until the class stopped and everyone would be looking at me and I would be saying things out loud that teenage boys in Catholic schools weren't supposed to say, or even think. I shouted obscenities at the end. It was my sex hatching, I suppose. Something had to be done. The beatings didn't stop. My mom thought she could beat it all out of me because the nuns were afraid of me.

My brother Don had this friend, Eleanor, who went to Vassar. That was really something for Helena, a Helena girl at Vassar. She went off to Vassar with a load of responsibility. It was as if all of Helena were attending Vassar with her, that whatever she achieved was a collective achievement. Helena is like that. People think they have a say in your life.

Eleanor graduated from Vassar with honors. She was going on to the University of Virginia to law school. Her parents gave a big welcome-home party for her out at the golf course. They rented the clubhouse and hired caterers and strung Japanese lanterns out across the ninth fairway and along the stream and over the wooden bridge. They hired the Shenanigans, a country western band with Irish singers and a comedian. Don was Eleanor's date.

In the mail, hand-addressed, came my gold-embossed invitation, as formal as a wedding invitation. Inside the invitation was a smaller printed envelope and a card you filled out saying whether you would attend or not and how many guests would be in your party. You could bring anyone you liked. I brought my school friend Kent. I had this crush on him.

At the bottom of the invitation was printed this phrase—"*Répondez, S'il Vous Plait.*" RSVP. I liked that phrase very much and I used it on everyone as if I could speak French. I had tried to teach myself the French language once. It was fun sometimes to be very haughty and say "*Noblesse Oblige.*" I thought about writing a letter to my father and leaving it at the boardinghouse where he moved after he left us. In the letter I would tell him how I was doing in high school. I might send him my report card. Three As! I would tell him I was getting so good at the piano that I could play Chopin waltzes (but not the polonaises) and some Bach. Imagine, Pop (I would write), you have a son who can play Bach on the piano! *Répondez, s'il vous plait!* Respond, if you please. The French aren't afraid to be what they are, say what they think, make demands. Respond, please. If you please.

One of the As I got in seventh grade was in declamation class. We were to give a memorized reading from literature and tell something personal, an anecdote about ourselves. I memorized "Friends, Romans, Countrymen" from Shakespeare's *Julius Caesar.* For my personal story I told about the time my father took me up into the Continental Divide on the sheep hunt. I told about seeing the moose.

Loretta was in our declamation class. Her family came to Montana for a while and then moved on. They were poor and brown and came and went and no one really noticed them. Loretta was silent and didn't stay around long enough to have friends. In the declamation class, she stood up and recited *Old Ironsides* by Oliver Wendell Holmes. Then she told her anecdote about herself and her little sister. The family had moved to Montana from Louisiana, where Loretta's father had worked in the oil fields. But one day, in Louisiana, Loretta and her sister went out by a river to go swimming. Loretta's little sister jumped into the river first, but the backwater was nested with water moccasins and they killed her. The classroom glittered with the pointed tails of serpents. Loretta told this story in a soft, two-note voice, as if she was saying something very polite to a grown-up.

After that I used to stare at Loretta until she complained at me. I used to stare, wondering how a person could be normal when such terrible things had happened to them. I used to think terrible things made you tormented and theatrical, like Heathcliff or King Lear. There was nothing about Loretta to indicate she had known such horror. Sometimes I think once you know horror, then that is all you are ever able to know. Nothing else is real enough.

My mother said it never happened about the window upstairs. Once she came to the mental hospital out at Warm Springs to visit me and started calling me names and I told her I didn't like her talking to me that way, that my doctor said I didn't have to let people talk to me that way. And then I said (Oh brother, had I been waiting for a long time to say it!), "and you had no right to push me out of that window that time. No right. You could have killed me!"

She went mad. Deadly. "No such thing ever happened!" she shouted. "You made that up. Some story to tell that doctor to make me look bad! Everything you say is made up! You're a filthy liar!"

She was wearing a silk bandanna, and she untied it and ran it against her nose. "If you only knew what this was doing to me. I didn't drive over MacDonald Pass and then another fifty miles to sit here and be told I am a liar! You just shut up, *mister!*" I could see her throwing herself uptop her rage like a bronco buster, a pony—she'd ride that rage until they both were still and bent and winded. "I hope you never live to know what misery you have caused me!" is what she shouted at me.

I told my mother very sarcastically that the rules of the hospital were that you couldn't shout or use bad language or get violent or they would put you into the locked ward, sometimes for a month.

No threat like that ever stopped my mother. "*I* am not a patient here!" We were sitting out at the picnic benches in the park. I saw a nurse on the porch look up, look over at us.

I stared at my mother. Her shouting silenced my mind, froze it up like gears in winter. She knew my look, but out here with the nurse watching she couldn't hit me. "You are just exactly like your father!"

The window happened. It happened. She was just too ashamed of what happened. What she did was push me out the window. When I was little. About six, I guess. It was during the time when my father still lived with us but would come home drunk all the time. He came home drunk the day she threw me out the window. I wonder where my three older brothers were that day? I wonder why I was home all alone with my mother the morning she threw me out the window?

We had no money. By the time I was thirteen, fourteen, my older brothers had found girls, married, and gone. They each moved out and went to college. My brothers studied in the sciences and each is, today, a kind of scientist—pharmaceuticals, biochemistry, metallurgy—working as a technician here in the Northwest.

I was alone at the farm with my mother and we had no money, just that empty farm, and when Snarge died my mother said, "No more dogs. That's it." My mother worked as a secretary in a federal government office, Internal Revenue, or maybe it was the Federal Reserve. She was a GS4—a secretary. On Sundays I would ask her for fifty cents to go to a movie but she would say no, there was no money for movies when I couldn't get out and hold down my own job. I had been fired from the grocery store. There were no jobs for thirteen- and fourteen-year-olds in Helena at that time.

I would walk in town and go down by the train station to my father's boardinghouse. He was not often there, but I always hoped and took the chance. I was afraid to call him up. He could say no over the phone but when I got him face to face he would give me something. He got jobs out of highway crews, so often he would be gone—off to places like Chinook or Havre or West Yellowstone. I would rap on the screen door of the boardinghouse, and usually someone would be in the living room listening to the radio or playing cards. They would usually tell me that my father had gone off, but if he was there they would go upstairs and get him. He was never gruff with me. He would come out on the porch smelling like whiskey. I would ask him for fifty cents for the movies and he would give me a dollar. We never talked about anything. He didn't know who I was except that I was his youngest son. I gave him no excitement in that.

Movie musicals on Sunday afternoon. You wouldn't think something like that could mean so much to someone. In Montana movies weren't supposed to mean that much to a guy. I should have been out playing baseball, my mother said, but I couldn't do that. I went to the show like my mother went to Mass—for hope. Movies were like some future that lay ahead, a suggestion that there was more and at least something other to life. Give to airy nothing a local habitation and a name. That's Shakespeare. I knew I would rather die and go to MGM than to Jesus's heaven.

I know why she threw me out the window. I don't know why she pretended it didn't happen, but then she got hurt that day pretty bad herself. My father came home that morning drunk. He had been out all night and just ran out of places to go and be and was left with his home and his family. Home and family were hell for my father, just simply hell.

I knew he was violent when he was drunk, but he never hurt us kids, just her. "Get help!" she screamed. She had locked him out and he was at that moment downstairs breaking the kitchen door window and jiggling with the chain lock. "Go get someone!" She tried to push me out my bedroom window but I hung on. I was screaming—No! It was a long drop from that second-story window. There was nothing but a few bushes. "Get help!" She bent my fingers back from the windowsill and then hit me with her palm on my forehead and I just dropped. I landed in the bushes and rolled onto the lawn and then I took off howling down the road. There were some people, drifters who had rented a cabin down the lane from us. I ran into their cabin without knocking and the lady saw the blood on me from my nose and the man bolted toward our house and the woman kept me there with her, though I was crying and hysterical and my blood scared me. They put my mother into the hospital with a broken arm (my father had tackled her in the front yard) and my father in jail for a couple days to cool him off. My brothers and I stayed at home. My aunt Tess from Butte came and stayed with us, keeping a rifle propped near the kitchen door in case my father came back unexpectedly.

Eventually my father did move back home, but he didn't stay long. There were more fights and finally he left. I was eight years old when he left for good. I think finally he gave up. I think he saw there was nothing at this place for him. Sell the junkers. Do whatever you like, he said. It was just after he left for good that my father came back out and took me on the sheep hunt and we saw the moose. I think he wanted to be friends but then he was almost fifty years older than me.

The farther into Montana you go, the farther you get from ideas. I first knew that when my father took me on the sheep hunt and we saw the moose.

In Helena, the capital of Montana, you get all the ideas up at the legislature and the church. From the mountainside near our farm you can see Helena built down there in a pocket of the mountain in what was a gold-mining gulch, Last Chance Gulch. I spent most of my time up on the mountainside the first summer I couldn't go into town. I couldn't because I did something dumb. I kissed my friend, ex-friend, Kent at Eleanor's party. There will never be an end to that. If there is an idea of me down there in Helena, well, that's where they got the idea.

You go back into the mountains and you get away from ideas. And you go up beyond that, into the actual wilderness where there aren't even any trails, just mountains and forests and the deer and bear, the moose and the mountain lion, there you find no ideas at all except those you brought with you. I can stand on the mountainside above our farm and say "I've changed." I can go down to Helena and stare at those people like I would stand in a cemetery and stare at the stone angels. Those people are their own tombs and they do not frighten me any longer. I got good help at the hospital and I see a therapist two times every week. I have to take lithium for stability, but I read and I go to school two nights a week up at the college. I am studying literature. I am changing. They are not, those people there in the town. The miracle that had happened to me is no less than if you found a way to make stones burn.

Eleanor's party took place out on the grand lawns of the golf course on an evening when hot moonlight pressed against you, a blue pressure with only one answer in it. Walking out in that night with my friend Kent was like crawling in pain across the bottom of a sea, because I loved him.

We were too young to be given drinks by the white-coated bar-
tenders. Older boys sneaked us a few. Kent and I were not at
Eleanor's party to socialize. We were too young. We had conspired
beforehand that we would get drunk. I saw my chance when all the
guests, standing out there under a great canopy like a circus tent,
turned toward Eleanor's father, who was saying something proud. I
stole a bottle of champagne from one of the washtubs behind the bar.
Kent and I were off across the bridge and down the ninth fairway. We
sat in the sand trap near the seventh green. There was that moonlight
and me circling Kent like some doomed planet. We popped the bottle
and drank it. We laughed, we were silly. And then we wrastled a bit
and it was then I put my hand *there* and I kissed him, hard and serious. I thought that was what we both wanted. I thought that was the
quotient of us—some kind of love. Kent pushed me off him and ran
away. I think he ran all the way home from the golf course. I don't
think he told his parents. I think for a while he didn't tell anyone.

I called him up next day but he wouldn't talk to me. I called a few
more times and he would never come to the phone, always had his
mother or father or sister lying for him.

Then I knew I had done something very wrong. I knew I had better
stay away from town. Something in me turned dark. Sunday I would
go in town to the movies. No one ever was around town on Sunday
afternoon. Empty streets full of dust and beer smells. One Sunday I
saw Kent at the movies with a group of boys. They didn't see me. I
was sitting in the back on the side. I wanted to sit with him and his
friends but the thing that had turned dark and hard inside me said no,
said beware. I was fifteen then.

They put my father in the Veterans' Hospital at Fort Harrison, a few
miles outside of Helena. I couldn't go visit him. They had rules about
children and I wasn't yet eighteen and couldn't go on the wards. Who
knows what you might see. My brothers went out and visited my
father. They said he had had some kind of breakdown, a physical
breakdown from work, a breakdown from exhaustion. I would always

tell my brothers, "Say hello to Dad for me." And they would come back very depressed and evasive and I would ask if they said hello for me and they would say yes, they'd told him. That's all they would ever say. My mother walked around like some triumphant empress with her cruelty dragging at her face and contorting it. No one said anything about my father dying. His sickness didn't seem to have anything to do with dying. They were afraid to tell me he was crazy.

I like to ice-skate. I like Montana when winter comes. Winter occupies the mountains like a foreign army. You don't argue with it. It has its own rules. It has its own force.

I loved to ice-skate then. I used to skate alone. It was the only truly graceful physical thing I could do. The sailing in the wind, the white chill and the gray sky, your body feeling its joy in being a mortal thing, moving swiftly in the elements like only birds and fish can move.

The skating rink was actually a big, natural pond in the city park—and that was where Joseph Greycloud and his friends surrounded me. They caught me by the far fence and his friends stood around as if they didn't notice what was happening, shielding Joseph Greycloud. He sneered first at my girly way of skating, and then he said things like he had heard I was a queer, and his friends all looked at me with dead eyes and with their jaws clamped. Joseph Greycloud did all the talking and I just stared at him. He couldn't get an answer out of me or a plea or fear. His fists closed. He knocked me flat. I had hoped at first it was just horsing around but then I was on my knees and I saw as I looked up from the ice, saw the pleasure and the vengeance in Joseph Greycloud's eyes, that this licking had been all planned out. Joseph Greycloud just said one word—"Queer!"—and shoved me back flat across the ice. Then he kicked me in the head with his ice skate. There was blood all over and they skated quickly away and left me there. I went to the warming house. One eye was closed already because the blood was filling it. Blood all over me. They took me to the hospital. I had eight stitches. I still have a slight

scar, a white line. It healed very well. No one asked me what happened. At school the boys said sarcastically, "Fell down, uh? Fell
down and hit your head, uh? Shouldn't be skating so fast." Everyone
knew what happened. Everyone knew about Kent and me on the golf
course. Everyone knew everything.

It was as if I was the only one in Helena, Montana, who knew what
happened to me and there was no one on my side. I think my father
would have been on my side, even if he knew the truth. But that winter he was out at the military hospital and I couldn't go see him.

No one mentioned the scar. Then or ever. Not even my brothers. It
just wasn't there.

I couldn't go into the military hospital because I wasn't old enough. I
went out there with my brothers and waited around in the garden while
they were inside visiting. The hospital had a veranda going all the way
around the second floor. The building was painted yellow, pale yellow,
and the veranda had shutters like venetian blinds that hung down and
opened sideways. I sat on a stone bench and my brothers wheeled my
father out to the veranda. They were standing around him while he sat
in his wheelchair in light blue pajamas that looked as if they had a
paisley design and a bathrobe, a white bathrobe, thick toweling it
looked like. His white hair was slicked back. He had probably just
been given his bath. He stretched his head and looked out and down
at me, smiled and waved his hand. He turned his head and spoke with
my brothers and they gathered around him and lifted him up out of the
wheelchair and they opened one of the veranda blinds and held onto
him and he stood there wobbly and leaning out and calling to me.
How ya doin'? he called, and I told him I was doing just fine and
asked him how he was doing. He said he was doing just great. And
then we looked at each other smiling and waiting for one or the other
to shout something. Are ya still practicin' the piano? he called and I
said yes, I would play something for him when he got out. Good, Good,
he smiled. He certainly had gotten old quickly. He seemed so fragile
and trembling. We'll go see a picture show when I get back on my feet,

he called, and then he let out a big, sad sigh. OK? Sure, Dad. OK. They settled him back down into his wheelchair and took him away from the window and the last I saw of him was his hand waving up over the window ledge. For me. Goodbye son.

I had been shouting too much. The staring had turned to shouting.

They got some of the older boys from the senior class to come to the classroom and they were real friendly to me. None of the older boys were friendly to any of us. There were three of them, plus Sister Mary Benedict. They all talked very politely to me, asking me how I was doing and had I seen this or that movie and whatnot, walking me out of the school and across the schoolgrounds and behind the church and then on to the rectory where Monsignor Wilkens had been called.

Bill, my oldest brother, got there and sat in the rectory with us. Bill drove me home to get my things. I asked if I could come live with him and his wife but he said I needed something more than that right now. He was very kind to me. My mother stayed in her room and wouldn't talk to me. She had a big argument with Bill. I heard her tell him I would do anything to cause trouble for her. I was just like my father. Late that evening Bill drove me across the mountains to the mental hospital at Warm Springs. I was there the first time for three years. I've been back twice, when things get strange on me. A few years went by and I spent six months there again and a year later about four and a half months. In between I've been able to get some schooling. The stays at Warm Springs get shorter because I'm getting better. I am changing. That is the key. Changing.

All the day of my father's funeral she was on the phone. I have never known anyone so indifferent to death as my mother. She kept calling people and asking them advice about wills and probates and community property and social security payments and military benefits. She had half the town pitying her and supplying her with information. She wanted to sell the farm right away and move to Phoenix with her sister. It wasn't until a week or so after the funeral that she found out my father had left his rights to the farm to us kids and not her. So we were co-owners and for the first time ever she got real nice to me, but I didn't then and I won't ever sell my interest in this farm. My brothers, they don't care. The property isn't worth a thing. Good for nothing, but it's part mine and she isn't going to use it to buy herself a red Impala so she can cruise around Arizona. She hates me now. Absolutely hates me. She went off to Phoenix when I had gone back into the hospital for the second time. She sent me a letter saying she wanted me to come live with her in Phoenix with my aunt. Fat chance!

I didn't sit in the first pew at my father's funeral because my brothers and their wives were there and two of them had babies so they needed the whole front row. My mother sat there center stage looking as if she were weathering an ocean gale, her lips pulled into a tight little knot, screwed into place just like her hair. I was kneeling behind her all during the Mass. And at some moment or another she leaned her butt back on the pew and was looking for something in her purse (not a hankie, that's for sure, probably a Chiclet). She was fiddling there, turned half-around, looking deep into her purse, when I saw her whole face change. Her eyes, her mouth, changed completely. I saw the look there on her face, like someone pulled the plug down at the bottom of her heart. She got a smirk on her of the merciless, of triumph. It was the look Joseph Greycloud had on his face the day he kicked me with his ice skate. Now she could get away with anything.

I live alone here on the farm. I have cleaned the place up quite a bit. I sold Dad's junkers. They are gone and tall grass covers the field at the back of the house. My brothers have suggested that I rent a few rooms out to the college people. My brothers would like to see me prosper a bit. I will rent some rooms, I believe, though living here with strangers will be awkward at first, no less for them than for me. But then, I am also now a college person, two nights a week.

I spend time at school and I have a part-time job through the state rehab. I work at the historical library out at the state capitol. I shelve

books four hours a day. I am learning to catalogue books, give them a
number and a letter. I love looking through the new acquisitions, the
stiff, clean volumes about western history. Frontier artists did not por-
tray the violence. They painted the survival. I could spend a whole
day just looking at the original paintings of Charlie Russell. What a
sense of humor old Russell had!

I often walk the upper trails on the mountain. I am quite close to
the town, yet frequently, in the mornings and especially in the snow, I
see footprints of deer, of bear, of smaller clawed creatures, the great
regal stamp of the moose like something Henry the Eighth might use
to seal a letter.

From the mountainside you can see far out into the valley, and
there, if you know where to look, you can see the cemetery. It is in a
woods. There is a stone wall around it and an iron gate you pass
through.

Now and then in winter I walk the five miles to the cemetery. I cannot have a driver's license because the medication I take puts me in
danger of having a seizure behind the wheel. I do not go to the cemetery in summer since there are always families there laying flowers, or
worse, funerals taking place. In the winter there is no risk of running
into families, but I do call the funeral home and ask if there are any
services that day and if there aren't then I am safe. I don't like people
staring at me when I am at my father's grave.

My father had been dead for a couple of years before I went out to
visit the grave. That first visit was a bad day for me at the cemetery. I
got there and walked to where I thought my father's grave was but I
couldn't find his stone. I was among a thousand stones there, sticking
up in the pine woods covered with snow, and I had to walk on hundreds
of graves and brush the stones off until I could read the names. Still, I
couldn't find my father's grave. It was as if he was hiding from me.

After a good hour of stomping around in that snow in the graveyard
and getting more and more angry and frustrated, I heard my shouting.
I usually heard it after it had been going on for a while. I looked
around quickly but I was still the only one out there in the graveyard

so no one heard me and no one would call the police. Nevertheless, I was in a rage and I sat down on the steps of one of those mausoleums and started to cry and then the whole, stone-filled load seemed to need crying for. I couldn't find my father's grave. Oh, I simply howled.

But my doctors had told me some practical things to do. *Think it through,* they said, *just get yourself quiet and think it through.* And so I just sat there and had some coffee and smoked a cigarette and calmed myself down and tried to remember my father's funeral, coming out here behind the hearse and just being there again, living through it. Not the sorrow, just the scenery. And then I knew where he was buried. I was way off. I remembered where I was standing and what I was looking at as they lowered the casket.

It only took me ten minutes to find it. So it worked. Proof that I am changing, that I can control my life, one moment at a time, if I must. One day it will be natural to me. One day it will no longer be fear. I stood by my father's grave and talked to him about that. I don't know if he was anywhere listening. But it was a good moment there, thinking that I was talking to him, and telling him what was going on with me and that I had found him and he could be proud of me.

I would like to write a book about my father. I would have to make most of it up because I never have known much about him. I would like to write about the sheep hunt and the moose.

It was a morning, no, it was still night, 4 a.m., but even in the night in Montana at wintertime the snow glows as if some kind of supernatural light were shining there beneath it. He woke me when the sky was clear, clear and still and moonless, the stars frozen in multitude. We drove up onto the MacDonald Pass and then followed a somewhat cleared trail off and farther up into plateaus of snow. We came to the sheep ranch and there were many hunters, but I was the only child. A bottle of whiskey was passed around and the men poured themselves some in their coffee cups as we stood out near the sheepfolds awaiting instructions from the sheep rancher. No one questioned my being there. My father just told me to stay close and if

I got tired to follow our tracks back to the ranch. He must have trusted me a lot to say that.

It was time to round up the sheep from the surrounding mountains. What we had to do was go in a great circle, up canyons and down ridges, and bring the scattered flocks down to the ranch so they wouldn't starve and freeze. Already some had been found stranded and dead. Frozen. So we set off, my father and four or five others in our group, heading out into the mountains and ringing those copper bells and shouting. There were clumps of sheep around trees and they turned their woolen foreheads and snouts and weak black eyes at us and we sent them down the mountain and went on upward. The wind was stiff and grainy with snow. On the higher fields we found many sheep, shooed them together and got them moving down. The trees thinned higher up; we could see a hundred miles across the landscape in every direction, the snow-covered mountains and the lonely, frozen valleys and the timber there, the white and coal blue of the world, the heavy silver sky, seamless with the day pushing down behind it. From those deep, lonely valleys we could hear the *baaa* and the clonk of the sheep bells as the animals heard us coming. The men went into the woods. I could hear their old dented copper bells and their shouting and whistling to one another, so it wasn't likely I would get lost. I know now my father was keeping an eye out for me. We went into the woods again. And on the slopes and in the darkness of the forest, I could hear the men and the sheep moving across the snow.

My father was leading up a ridge where the trees were thick. He went around one side of some trees and I went around the other. Then I was standing against a pine tree—under its lowest branches where the brown pine needles formed a cleared, damp circle and the earth was black—and out there in a clearing was a moose. I could have touched him, this large, muscly, thick brown-coated moose standing still and listening to the movement around him. He lifted his long potato-shaped head back a little and those immense antlers reached up like ocean waves, so bony and gray and ridged, touched the tree limbs ten feet up. The moose lowed like a cow but with a

227

high, frightened, warning pitch to its voice. Its mate was probably nearby hidden in the trees. I crept back behind the tree but stopped because my father was standing right behind me and he put his hands very gently on my shoulders as if pressing me to stop, pressing me until I stood still in the snow, and he pulled me back against him and we stood there and respected the moose. We kept our distance and stayed silent as snow while the moose turned and passed before us and onto one of its trails, knowing we were there yet knowing we were unarmed, not hunters.

I could smell cigarettes and whiskey on my father and the close, snowmelt heat of his wool coat. I could feel the strength in his arms as he held me pressed to him and he crossed his gloved hands down across my chest and kept me safe. I laid my head back against his big winter coat and we stood in absolute silence, as if struck there in marble, watching and so close to something very rare, and my father was, I suspect, as wonderstruck as me, and the moose moved through the snow and into the shadows to gather his love to himself and then lead on into the mountain fastnesses and farther up, into its safety and into its life.

The Swimming Team

Lynda Schor

At this moment, who could possibly think I'm not a good mother, sitting next to my four-teen-year-old daughter and her friend on the number 7 train at din-ner time, taking them to the YMCA all the way out at the end of Queens for a swim-team tryout, as that is the only YMCA in the entire city of New York with an Olympic-sized swimming pool. But any congratulatory feelings on my part are curtailed when I picture my two little sons, whom I've had to leave home, if they've ever arrived there, where they'll have to let themselves in with their keys, if they haven't lost them, and who have no dinner waiting for them, but will most likely eat all the junk they can find around while star-ing glazedly at television, in between fights during which they will not only injure each other, but will break everything in the apartment including the plants.

During this time my husband will arrive home, but it's useless to imagine that he'll make dinner either for himself or the children, whom he may not even notice unless he has to tell them to lower the TV and/or stop fighting so loudly so that he can play punk rock on his new Tandberg stereo without too much distraction.

It may appear that he's terribly negligent, but he's not the chil-dren's father. He's never had any of his own and has no idea how to take care of them. He's never pretended to me that he wanted to take over the role of father to my children; moreover, perhaps because he's Japanese, he's not accustomed to preparing his own dinner and most likely wouldn't eat at all if there wasn't someone around to prepare and serve it. Furthermore, he's quite a bit younger than I am. Not even old enough to be my daughter's father, Hiro adds an interim gen-eration to our family.

Although Hiro won't be a father, he's my lover, and is wonderfully diligent, imaginative, and joyful about it, as if by pumping alive our ever smouldering sexual obsession with each other he could flatten my real-life family out of existence.

Perhaps I'm not really a good mother, choosing a lover for myself rather than a father figure or a family-type person. The children's real father doesn't want to be a father either. Older than I, he quits work every five months and collects unemployment so he can go on six-month-long trips in a camper he can afford because he never pays any child support, and during which he eats only nuts and granola and gets to use his large assortment of Swiss army knives.

Because Hiro has a profession he loves, and takes pride in his work, I imagined I was choosing someone quite different this time, until I had a dream in which both Hiro and my former husband, Jim, stood side by side on a bleak hill, next to one empty swing, at a hotel in the Catskills. I recall remarking in the dream that they looked exactly alike, although one of them is Jewish, the other Japanese. When I woke I realized with horror that they do resemble each other in many respects. Neither of them is tall and each possesses a delicate and slender frame. They both have thin legs, and their large heads are supported by delicate necks topped with thick, unkempt hair. When seen from any distance they look like youths.

Alexandra, my daughter, may be teen-sized forever. Her friend Adina, more than a year younger, is already taller and more voluptuous than I. Their long, stringy hair falls around newly broadened womanly shoulders. When they aren't whispering to each other, as now, I entertain the suspicion that my proximity is hampering the free flow of conversation. I wonder what they're thinking, staring into space, neither speaking nor looking at anything in particular, but not wishing to recall my own teenage dreams, amply interwoven with nightmares, I stop speculating.

"Look at that," I say, removing my eyes from Adina's mature breasts to point out the window at the panorama of all Queens and part of the Manhattan skyline laid out below in the bronze of sunset, as we curve in the air, like a roller coaster, an airplane, a high-wire artist, on this tenuous elevated track. Both girls look up and out the far window, not even bothering to turn their heads, then, unimpressed, resume staring straight ahead like catatonics.

I imagine the entire train, as it curves around, falling off the track, beginning with the car we're in. We move slowly as the train takes the turn. Our car tilts to the side, the ancient track trembles, vibrates, accentuating awareness of how high we are. Suddenly we tilt even further, too much I'm sure, causing people to slide slightly, shopping bags and newspapers moving away on their own. From my window it appears that our car is extended from the track like a loop, hanging suspended, yet I don't want to become alarmed if it's only some sort of optical illusion created by the angle of the curve and the setting sun, which, reflecting off distant roofs and windows, is nearly blinding.

I once more attempt to make conversation.

"Do you still like Larry?" I ask Adina, knowing she has a crush on our downstairs neighbor.

"He has another girlfriend." She giggles, embarrassed, perhaps sad. I don't know what to say.

The train, making a grating noise, seems to be starting, but instead the slight movement appears to be sideways, as if we're slowly falling farther off the track. At that moment, glancing into a neighbor's eyes, it is possible to see everyone doing the same, perhaps to see fear reflected there too, validated. As the car makes a deep lurch sideways, a tough youngster, terrified, swings from the hand support in a complete circle. The other hand supports all swing forward with a clang, like empty trapezes.

"Oh my God," says an old man, falling into Adina's lap. I search desperately for a trainman, a conductor, to tell us what's happening, to reassure us, as I do even when a train I'm riding on stops between stations, or whenever I smell smoke in a tunnel, but, as usual, it's impossible to find one.

Hanging over the void, expecting at any moment to fall, I almost wish we'd get it over with in one comprehensive crash instead of this slow, nerve-wracking slipping. I can hear the sirens of fire engines, police cars, and ambulances far below accentuating, making absolute, a danger which, because of their distance, appears to be somewhere else.

An elderly man, the only person still calm, moves carefully through the car, seemingly reassuring people, telling them to remain still, not to panic. When he comes closer I notice that he's quite handsome, his gray hair shades lighter than his elegant suit. He places his leather briefcase beside me on the slanted seat and studies the scene outside. Following his gaze I see fire trucks and city cranes congregating below in a tension of unexpressed possibility. Looking through to the next car, I see it's tilted too. Who knows how long the train can hang on before the entire thing hurtles off the track, killing its passengers and whoever might still be below.

The man fixes me for one moment with deep blue eyes, then addresses everyone, the three weeping women, the nail-biting tough, the shrieking-and-clinging-to-each-other Adina and Alexandra, myself.

"Let's not panic," he says in tones of modulated authority. "May I suggest that we all try to remain on the upper side of this car, where our combined weight may help us remain on the track until help arrives."

Those in any state to respond huddle on the raised side of the car. As we work together breaking windows open, I feel warm, capable hands touch my own trembly ones. Slowly, like an apparition, an incredibly tall bright yellow crane appears outside. The man, gazing into my eyes, takes my scratched, dirty hands in his and, putting out his tongue, licks the blood off a cut finger.

It isn't too long before we've found our way through the labyrinthine Y to the registration room, which is filling with teenagers. Alexandra and Adina, fidgety and bored, both of them impatient types who give up easily, force me to relinquish the gray-haired fatherly fantasy husband (or future husband) image I conjure up when overcome by desperation or fear. Unlike either my first husband or Hiro, who require constant capable nurturing, he's handsome in a teddy bear way. Capable of incessant cuddling, sometimes he's very tall, large enough to bear any burden, mine or his, that comes along, enormous enough to completely enwrap me, a home I can securely live in. I never imagine us making love.

I picture Hiro in the bathtub, tiny tan legs shiny with unrinsed soapiness, submerged, only slightly rounded knobby knees sticking out. A small, ribby, hairless chest under a long, vulnerable neck which supports a head that's heavy but slightly flat in back like a baby's who's been put to sleep on his back too often, also rises from the water. Perspiration moistens his unruly hair and runs down his face, with its large wide-set eyes, sweet unformed blob of a nose, and soft sweet fat lips a bit turned up at the corners, tiny, tiny teeth underscored with a few hairs of a sparse oriental beard. I wash his minute golden shell ears carefully with a soapy washcloth, and when I rinse, by wringing the cloth out over him, water runs down his hair, which, when wet, adheres to the back of his neck and shoulders. The pool is enormous, grandstand seats like Shea Stadium. The room, hot and humid, smells of chlorine and moisture. Light appears to be emitted by the pool, which is pale blue at one end, fading into a frightening green at the deep side, and which paints a shimmering illumination on the wall and ceiling, creating the sensation that the entire room is floating.

Children slowly straggle from the locker rooms, towels around necks or hips, while mothers, neat in polyester, congregate at the lowest grandstand railing, leaning over, imparting last-minute instructions, imploring that they pull down the bottoms of their suits, fix their straps, comb their hair. I pull my fingers through my own long curly mass of hair and guiltily open the book I always carry in my purse. Alexandra and Adina haven't come out yet.

"Do good and I'll get you Carvels," the woman beside me screams.

She nudges me. "How long has your kid been taking the swimming classes?"

"We didn't know there were classes." I realize now that my daughter and her friend will be competing against children who have been specially trained. "Even if she makes the team," I tell her, "I don't know how I'd get her to the practice sessions. She's kind of young to travel so far herself, and I have two younger children at home."

She nods. "Do you live nearby?" I ask.

"We live all the way out in New Jersey. But my husband will pick up my other one from school, give her a snack, take her to dance class, and then come for us in the car and take us all to McDonald's. Carvel for dessert."

I lift my eyes from my book in time to see Alexandra and Adina below, walking so close together they might be holding hands. When they reach the edge of the pool, they separate and slip into the cerulean. Alex, dwarfed by the pool, practices a stroke, which nevertheless seems smooth and mature, I think, hoping it can suffice against the pure bulk and strength of many of the others. She searches for me in the grandstand, as she has done all her life, as if I'm a security amulet without which she can't function, then placing me, proceeds with a strong, sweeping breast stroke.

The instructor, a stocky man in loose shorts and sleeveless shirt, gray chest hair curling back over the edge of the armholes like lace trim, carries a clipboard. He is holding in his mouth a whistle that looks like a huge pacifier. When he blows this whistle, which reverberates shrilly, its echo illusorily rippling in synchronicity with the dancing light, the remaining tardy teens issue out.

While the instructor and a few of the youngsters test the electronic timing equipment, I look at the young boys and almost automatically, as if in slow motion, close my book. I look around to see whether anyone has noticed that I'm blushing, embarrassed and disturbed that I'm so affected by their youthful good looks, sexuality explosively apparent in all their extreme self-consciousness. Slim or muscular, in the tiniest trunks, each is tempered and tanned. Their shoulders, newly enlarged, taper sharply to taut, tight, rounded buttocks, to firm muscular legs. Their hair, thick and neat, has been combed so often the ridges are visible in the grandstand. Their amazingly concave bellies, emphasized by tufts of hair, dark or golden, rise to protuberant pubic areas.

I seek my daughter for guidelines. How does she deal with such exuberantly explicit, if embarrassed, sexuality? She and Adina, not having heeded the whistle, are in the middle of the pool, flailing in a weakening backstroke. A glance at the other mothers is enough to prove that I'm the only one attracted by the almost palpable aura of pubescent sensuality.

While the instructor divides the entries into heats according to age and dispenses instructions, I find myself walking, breathless and barefoot on the damp tile floor, coming from the lockers, where I've rapidly and unobtrusively strewn my clothes, in my black satin teddy, short but slightly flabby white legs flapping. Everyone watches as I approach the instructor anxiously twisting up my long curls, which are already slightly streaked with gray.

"You forgot to call my name," I say in the ensuing silence.

The instructor stops staring. "What is your name?" He riffles through his cards twice but gives me the benefit of the doubt. "I must have lost it. You can fill out a new one later." He instinctively assigns me to the oldest heat.

My daughter looks at me and wonders whether she recognizes me. In order to verify her suspicions she searches the grandstand for my supporting presence, which is no longer there. It is then that she knows for sure that the woman in the black satin underwear is her mother. She smiles at me tentatively, and I can see that she's both pleased to see me participating for a change in something she's interested in and embarrassed because it's pretty clear that this isn't any parent-child venture. I wink at her awkwardly.

It appears that the younger kids are occupying one bench, the teenagers the other. I try to seat myself unobtrusively, naturally, but squeeze in beside an attractive young man who emerges from the blur of generalized sensuousness. Perhaps that's his girlfriend on my other side, whose long firm legs reluctantly shove, whose short blond hair surrounds a well-sculpted and faintly annoyed face.

As I watch the first heat composed of younger children swimming backstroke across the pool in a silence broken only by the watery sounds of splashing and spitting, I feel the youth's warm, lightly hairy thigh against mine as my flabby ones settle flatter on the bench, and wonder whether he can feel the perspiration beginning to form between our legs, tickling lightly, merging, linking us.

My daughter is somewhere at the end of this bench, but I can't see her without bending over conspicuously. Fortunately she's not in my heat, as I haven't begun, and don't want, to think of the ramifications of competing with her.

When I hear my name and line up at the front of the pool next to the same boy, I realize, too late, that I don't know how to dive. As the instructor says, "One, two," and blows his whistle, I attempt it, trying not to think, landing hard and flat with a large and loud splash that creates a wide wake which everyone else floats up and down in, losing speed, yet I've managed to get myself far out, where I begin my fairly proficient crawl. My concern that perhaps I'll be upset, humiliated for Alexandra if she fails, is gone. Now I'm concerned that I'll be humiliated for myself, or that she'll be embarrassed for me—still, I'm too excited to care that much.

I also don't know how to somersault off the edge of the pool for a speedier return, so, crouching, pushing off with my feet in a flurry of chlorine water, I'm a bit behind. Holding my breath and climbing out as the timekeeper calls the time, I'm relieved to notice one small person climbing feebly out behind me.

Drenched, chest aching and shaking, I manage to crawl back to my bench, pressed against the same boy. Perhaps we've absorbed water, expanded. Sitting in his puddle, my own dripping drops melting into his, I quake and shiver. But there's no time to rest. Now it's the butterfly stroke. This time I don't attempt to dive, but jump neatly, as far as I possibly can, regaining some ground and some composure; a sensation of more control. Hands butterflying tantalizingly in my neighbor's wake, I purposely move into his range, my hands, finally, on the downstroke, fluttering along his upper torso all the way down to his penis. It's impossible to tell whether or not he's noticed. In his zeal to win, his zest for speed, he hasn't slowed down at all, and soon he's out of reach.

I no longer notice timing, or care whether I'm winning or losing, or how I look to anyone. Caught up in the sexual atmosphere I've created, I wonder whether my chosen object is aware, is with me. I must have a sign from him, yet wish to obtain it extremely subtly for fear of being repugnantly overt, frightening to him in his sexual inexperience and youthful romanticism.

My legs feel like jelly; my shivers are absorbed by the bench, which rattles fitfully on the tiling. My youth has gooseflesh too; it rubs coldly against my finer-grade bumps like sandpaper. Wordlessly he offers me his wet towel. The cropped blonde girl looks at me directly for the first time. Is this the sign I'm seeking?

By now I can only fall weakly into the pool, my nose filling instantly, painfully, with the sharp chlorinated water. My head feels as if it will burst. Still somewhat submerged, the last thing I feel is my young man's entire body cover mine as he mistakenly dives directly on top of me.

The next thing I'm aware of is lying poolside on my abdomen, everyone crowded around observing, Alexandra in the foreground, shivering, legs bowed with fear, the top of her suit awry, stringy hair dripping into her towel, the edges of which she regressively sucks.

By process of elimination, I ascertain that it's indeed my friend who's sitting across my upper thighs, applying splayed strong and technically perfect former babyfingers to my back lower ribs, exerting a firm, soothing pressure, which he releases peristaltically, rhythmically, to some litany he intones in a deep yet shaky adolescent voice. The instructor objectively examines and corrects technique, but I'm aware of nothing but the feel of buttocks on my upper thighs, right under my own backside, which can also feel, so subtly, the press of his chest whenever he leans forward. Am I breathing on my own? I don't care, so fantastic does it feel to give myself up to this.

"I don't think I can allow you to continue," the instructor says, as soon as I can stand unsupported. For a moment I feel mortified, as if I've failed, and tears burn in my already wet and reddened eyes, as if I were really one of the kids, until I realize that I'm being rescued from making a complete fool of myself.

A matron opens the girls' locker room for me, where I sit resting, relieved, until I decide what to do. Then I sneak to the locker entrances. The matron is no longer there, so I try the men's locker room door. It's open. I enter slowly, deciding that if anyone questions me I can always pretend to be in the wrong place unknowingly.

I can hear the shower running, and enter the steamy room. Unable to see, I rip off my soaking teddy. I can feel the hot, luxurious needle spray warm and rejuvenate my exhausted body as I turn and twist under the stream, lifting my hair, my arms, so I can feel it all over. When the steam lifts, I see my friend in here already, also luxuriating in the shower, turning under it, upraised arms revealing patches of thick, surprisingly dark hair, and below, water running around and streaming down the sides of a penis already erect. His arms enfold me gently, firmly, on their downward movement as he senses me join him, first unobtrusively, then so closely no stream of water can flow between us, but must course around us like a river around a rock. I soap him all over as we fall foaming onto the shower floor, hot water spraying over us in fine needles.

He's amazingly potent and proficient, I think, surprised, trying not to seem a corrupting or gross influence on his youthful innocence by exhibiting too much passion, when suddenly I have a view through the doorless shower stall of the entire locker room, bodies lying everywhere, pulsating in a peristalsis of pullulating passion, as my virile teenager moans, "Good mama, good mama . . ." holding me close, gyrating firmly within me.

The End of a Somewhat Less Than Noble Season

Sharon Thompson

The distorting processes of history and communication have encoded the memory of the species in metaphor, fiction, projection, also displacement, and you may think or feel that you remember, or you may experience an illusion of memory derived, in actuality, from current evidence, perhaps not as narrative but as sensory intuition. It was near the end of the last cycle. Like Jehovah, the planet administered the warnings at the outset. (An accurate rendering would reverse this formulation, but we must work to some extent with culture and language as they come down to us.) Hiroshima, Nagasaki, Chalk River, Troy, Windscale, Santa Susana, Savannah River, Idaho Falls, Detroit, Morris, Monticello, Browns Ferry, Three Mile Island, Chernobyl, Orissa, Hanford. Plenty of chances, honey.

The brain was the same, endowed with the familiar capacity to mistake metaphors and fables for the rules themselves, those written on the face of the earth—preserve, destroy, balance. So, yes, they persuaded and coerced each other to live by magic—consort with the other gender only when fertile, pray during the rains, never drink milk—and they forgot the originating text. They could, theoretically, have been awakened by the creations of imagination or fantasy in their own time, but they ignored them, with the exception of those to do with milk, which was forbidden and enjoyed a brisk underground market. To balance toxicity and radiation during maturation, childhood became the age of journeys. So many urban dwellers took up aerobic forms of locomotion—as if preparing to run en masse off the planet—that DOT closed a strip on every highway over four lanes. The general sense of irony sharpened to such a degree that *Roget's Thesaurus* listed *sentimental* and *ironic* as synonyms.

But this story takes place earlier, during the five-year period between the destruction of the podzol, where the richest humus on earth lay, and that of the eastern seaboard of North America. No one was staying in out of the rain; bottled-water sales had leveled off. The thyroid guy had sold out his supply of potassium iodide for the third time, and wasn't laying in any more than his family would need. French and Italian wines were selling again internationally and so were brie and romano. Some people still drank Evian and Perrier, hoping the minerals and purity would outweigh the effects of strontium 90. The feeling of grace had worn off too—the blessed sense that never had there been so sweet a planet, such spicy and tantalizing breezes, such clear, light, cool rain. The sunsets were, of course, suspicious. Too much chartreuse and Prussian blue in them. But oh my.

They slept in Billie's loft like burrowed mice, hugging lumps of down comforter and afghan, surrounded by newspapers and magazines, wine glasses spotted with dried circles of burgundy, sticky tea cups, dried teabags on mottled silver spoons, curled lemon rinds. Lena wound as tight as a compress around Billie, who reached in her dreams for the ladder's curved rail and looked, at dawn, as if she had begun to flee from Lena's embrace just as the hot lava poured.

The backup alarm in the kitchen went off at half past five, startling Lena, who released her grip. Billie sprang for the ladder as Lena raised her head, auburn waves matted, dry lips a faint pucker heading for Billie's throat. The air whooshed mildly away as Billie went down the ladder. Whirlpool, current. They always missed each other now.

In the first weeks of their affair, they assumed that the high excitement they generated in each other would explode into passion. It never did. Billie has wondered if the warmth of their embraces used up desire. Still amazed to be in a woman's arms, Lena has wondered why embraces aren't enough. (Lena was one of those women who come out after thirty-five, partly because it takes that long for them to get over their first horrendous lesbian affair—the one with their mother—but also partly because age unmans them.) Billie has concluded that for her there has to be a great deal of sex in a relationship or none. Lena has thought this a rigid dichotomy. Billie has agreed. "Still, have you ever been with someone who went to sleep before you came?" Lena has had no idea what Billie is talking about. To her, disappointed anticipation is incomprehensibly subtle. Lena has argued that the circumstances of her life preclude frequent sexual experiences. Tension and ritual can make up for hurry and hiatus, Billie has accommodated. Lena has insisted that sex should come amiably and naturally. Billie has not felt like talking about it anymore. Lena has asked again if Billie has another lover. Billie has smiled as if she did. This sometimes worked. (Lena always wants to play if there is a game going.) No wonder that, in place of passion, irritation caught fire. Anger. The hardest bond to break.

Billie came back kaleidoscopic in orange, red, purple, and green, handed Lena a bright mug of milky coffee. "We're late," a strategic half-truth to inspire urgency in Lena, who seldom slept more than four or five hours but went into a coma when she stayed with Billie.

Lena drank half the coffee and leaned back into the feather and foam mounds. "You used to be so neat," she wondered, then dozed off. Lena's complexion had a grainy sepia cast in the murky light. She aged five years or more during an assignment. Billie smoothed the lines and blotches; the slither line of a zipper—the sleeping bag?—ran skeletal across one temple, over her forehead. Lena—flushed, surprised—made one of her soft baby shrieks, crooked fingers of both hands toward Billie, who shook her head and disappeared down the ladder.

"If we'd planned to leave at a reasonable hour, you needn't have come over here last night."

Lena climbed down. "What about a day without rules?" She smiled as if they were a cute couple she used to know, slipped on a tangle of socks on the last rung, and catapulted forward. "You've missed me," she declared.

"I've been busy."

Sure of her point, Lena didn't respond. One part journalist, one part pol, residing somewhere between the speeds of light and sound, Lena reached for the phone first thing in the morning, hung up well past midnight. She went to Washington more often than Billie went across town. Billie taught high school art (hardly a big drain on energy or intelligence, in Lena's judgment). And then she had her art projects—the contemporary fossil project, the nest project. The kind of thing you might do in an old-age home. This was one of their silent fights.

As Billie got ready, Lena wandered through the apartment, nonchalance a transparent camouflage for avidity. The big room was as orderly as the bedroom used to be. The last thing Lena had expected was to lose Billie to work. In bad fights, Lena attributed Billie's apparent youth to her refusal to arrange for success—which Lena called becoming "responsible." Billie returned the insult by accusing Lena of the gifted-child syndrome. "You could have anchored the news at age six," Billie shouted. Lena wept. How could Billie be angry at her for the tragedy of her life. An only child, she watched kids, puppies, sunsets, couples making out in the movies, even her own body, the way aliens watch TV: with an involuntary, drastic suspension of disbelief.

"You *have* been busy," Lena called to Billie over the sound of running water. "Have you finally decided to break through?"

Billie only knew she had begun to feel time running out. Fresh pine shelves lined the walls, the bottom ones filled with clay of graduated hues, the middle with trinkets from Billie's love life. Completed fossil sculptures lined the shelves. Billie photographed their stages, then sent them away for burial. "Where's the nest project?" Lena called. "Texas. Everything's in Texas now."

Lena drove. Billie stared blindly at the road. She couldn't see in the dark at all anymore. Older by several years, Billie would say that age counted, and that Lena was the child—"daughter" was how she put it. But Billie looked like the kid. No one over fourteen had hair like hers and not since the 1940s. Country yellow, curly at the ends. Billie tied it back with crimped paper ribbon. Her clothes didn't help either.

Pima blouses with lace-edged round collars—buttons every color down the front. Billie's face *was* aging in a country way, flesh drying around the bony structure of her character—her open-eyed steady stare, half innocent, half seen-everything, all stubborn. Apple dolls look like that after a while.

The two met almost four years before. Lena had just finished a book and suddenly realized she hadn't replaced her husband. The sight of Billie made her think "vacation." Billie said she never worked hard enough to need one. Lena sent postcards from every stop and felt as if she had a companion. When she got back to town, she was madly in love. Billie thought, I'll ride this one out. It won't last long and it might be a nice change from my usuals.

Her usuals: janitors who quoted Sylvia Plath, wrists like expressway cloverleafs, drug dealers who managed the habits of MTV megastars, arthritic dancers who cooked organic for drunken novelists, political idealists gone merc and cynical, mercs gone idealist and romantic. These flames had come to her bed with hair reeking of garbage, fingers icy with snow, hot with dynamite; to go down under the covers on them was to come up drunk or stoned or speeding, the taste of danger on her tongue. She showered before she lit the stove, for fear she might explode. When people talked of traveling, she was perplexed: Why leave your bed? Now she knew why. To get away from the screams.

If they suited each other in nothing else, they were equal challengers. No Roman emperor ever chose a better match. Neither was after territory: they had righteousness in common. That made it worse. Contradictions lay from the highest to the lowest ground of their relationship. To stay together, one or the other would have had to change entirely. Lena, with her reformer's optimism, didn't see any problem.

In the beginning, they imagined mitigating factors. Lesbianism would shift the balance; women were the more social and fair half of the species after all. Billie know lesbianism better, but she counted on Lena's bourgeois side as a cooling factor, and agreed to buy a summer house with her. The house became the reason to stay together. Or was it just Factor 1 in a hidden maternal agenda. For a while things got worse because they tried to make them better.

Billie cherished the child in herself and fought to salvage the child in Lena. Lena defended her own adulthood, and dreamed of a child to take the pressure off—a stuntwoman for herself, a stand-in to play with Billie. In the meantime, she escalated her rhetorical habit: as she took off her wool gabardines and silks, she fretted about the Mideast; as she unhooked her bra, drought took on biblical proportions. No sooner did her eyes open after she came than she trilled toxic wastes and nuclear catastrophes, inflation, unemployment, the underclass. Billie called Lena repressed, a precocious dead-heart adult. Those sickening fights were still not as bad as the ones that came later, when, stupefied, they lost the mercuric silver lines of interest. Then Lena took Billie's refusal to raise a child with her as rejection, and Billie took Lena's desire for a child and her global obsessions as infidelity; then the really horrible battles came.

They stayed in the city through the summer, fighting on the telephone. Around mid-September, they grudgingly gave each other honorable discharges. (They hadn't cheated on each other, they hadn't lied, they hadn't faked anything. They would love each other forever but see each other as little as possible.) Lena got a lover briefly—a party member in Cuba. Perfect, thought Billie with finality. Lena was grateful that Billie held her tongue. It spared her defending the affair, which made it easier to drop it. Nothing left to do now but what they were doing—close the summer house that had stood empty all season.

Lena pulled off at a bagel shop in Queens, a ritual stop. They both went in. "What are you two doing out so early?" said the guy behind the counter. He winked Billie's way. Lena flushed with pleasure and ordered two dozen assorted. Billie said they'd get stale. Lena said, "We'll freeze them." Billie said they were going to turn the freezer off. Lena said, "So we'll freeze them in the city." Billie said Lena was in the city about one day in ten and she could get fresh bagels a block from her apartment. "So I'll give them to you. Let me give you some bagels." Billie said she hated bagels. Lena said then maybe they shouldn't get any. Billie said she was hungry and this was the last reasonable food between here and the house.

"Compromise," suggested the guy behind the counter. They all laughed and, they hoped, something broke. In the car, they chewed peaceably, and joked about all the fights they'd had, as if this were their first trip out together and they were becoming acquainted by talking about former horrible relationships.

Billie said she'd drive now. Lena lowered the back of the cushy seat until she was almost flat out and went to sleep. The horizon opened to the white sun; opalescent clouds stretched thin.

Billie turned the tape deck on low, and forgetfully ran her fingers through Lena's hair. Sweet Honey filled the car. The further out, the more sky to land: a dried finger of sand and earth, spindly defoliated trees. Lena woke when they turned off the stretch of highway between the main access route and the country road that led to the house, but she was uncharacteristically quiet. She wondered if she would become more like Billie after she recovered from the break. Woods interspersed with clapboard houses. Sandy lanes leading back to secreted developments.

The open farm stand had a deserted air. Everything seemed to these days. A girl sixteen or so shivered behind the counter in a red and black lumber jacket, poring over a chemistry textbook. A quartz heater radiated her woolly back. A few lopsided pumpkins on the bare shelves, dark green ribbed squash with orange hot spots. Big purple kale, limp around the edges. Cauliflower flowerets stained brown. Some dried flowers. Everything dies, Lena wanted to say, but she didn't want to hear Billie's riposte. I'm getting better, she thought. She didn't say that, either. They bought a swollen bottle of fizzy cider. Bubbles bit their tongues as the bitter scent of chickens blew in their direction. The flower garden plot to the east had dried furrows, chrysanthemums cut down to stubs against their stakes.

A cream Oldsmobile crunched the gravel, curved around them, and stopped in front of a table heaped with dried corn. The driver, robust in knickers and a tweed jacket, camel's hair cap, opened the trunk and pulled three brace of Muscovy ducks out by the feet. Deep blue-green throats curving toward the gravel, they swung with his march rhythm as he carried them to the stand. "When Johnny comes marching home again, hurrah, hurrah." Lena heard children's voices behind the chicken shed, and went to watch them. Billie followed, irritated.

Three little girls lay under a sheet of plastic suspended by fruit crates. Pressing the length of their bodies against the perimeter, legs bent at the hip, arms stretched above their heads, they held four plastic sides tight. They had plastic bags over their heads and hands and feet. They barely stirred. Lena stood back at a Norman Rockwell distance (she wanted her own child but had no interest in getting close to those of others) while Billie, predictably handling it all in reverse, walked over, hands in her pockets, casual, smiling. The girl whose torso held down the eastern flank pinched the foot of the northern guardian. "Shall we help them?" her voice muffled through the bag and the plastic walls. Northwest shook her head and looked away.

The guardian of the south began to sit up and lift the plastic. North tried to kick her without letting go of her wall of plastic. "You can't act unless we all agree." South lay back, deadweight on her edge of the plastic. Billie came closer. North began to pummel the ground. "No, no, no, no. Go away." The guardian of the south held her face against the plastic. Her nose and lips squashed flat against the surface. The green lines and arrows on the bag striped her forehead. "I'm sorry," she breathed.

"What are you playing?" said Billie.

"Guess," said North.

"House," said Billie.

"Sort of," North grimaced and East began to howl, "Owwwwww." They all chimed in, writhing on their perimeters. "Oh no. It can't be. Owwwwwwwwwwwwwwwwwwww."

North became explosive: "Pow. Whoosh. Phroooooomm. Owwwwwww, I am burning up, owww, owwwwww, owwwwwwwwwww."

Her comrades screeched and expired.

"Bomb shelter," said Billie.

"You're way behind the times." North, stern.

"Nuclear disaster."

"We're safe in here," East confided. "You were caught outside the house when it happened. You are getting more irradiated every second."

"Well," said Billie, "there's no point in our coming in then, is there? I mean if we're irradiated already."

"There might still be time." South turned to her comrades. "They might be okay if they had a bone transplant."

"Then they'd irradiate us. We'd have to have one too." (North.)

East began to cry. "Transplants hurt," North added. Her point carried. "And who wants new bones? Where will they get enough new bones?"

"Well, go without them then," Billie recommended. "Like stuffed animals." East smiled mildly. North turned her back.

Billie brushed her hands free of bits of gravel and dust. She got in the car and hit the gas till the engine drowned out the kids.

They were driving through the woods. "You made them up anyway," said Billie.

The last stretch was little more than driveway. The house down a dirt road behind a mansion the Dominicans turned first into a convent, then into a home for unwed teen mothers. Lena almost mentioned wanting to do a piece on ecclesiastical adaptations to the changing role of women. Caught herself in time. Bordering the salt marsh, their place, framed in pin oaks, with a climbing rose on one side of the doorway, wisteria on the other. Thanks to Lena, the fishing shack it began as now formed an entranceway to two peak-roofed studios.

A housekeeping urge always overtook Lena when they got to the country. It lasted till morning, when the need to capture history hit her again. Now she wanted to make a fire. Billie objected. Lena dropped her hands as if she were letting their relationship fall. Maybe it was really over.

Billie went to find the hose to drain the pipes. When she came back, Lena had two logs on the hearth and some sticks and paper. A flame leapt up from the back of the hearth. "Just a few sticks," Lena said. "It won't burn long. It'll take the chill off." Billie made coffee. She had given up. It wasn't like her. Maybe it was a good sign. As the fire died down, Lena took a typewritten sheet from her pocket and began to read the instructions to herself.

Billie brought over the two wastebaskets and settled in to watch, legs dangling over the vinyl-tile–covered trap (squares of green and black, neo-Depression). Lena dangled the short piece of black rubber hose over the bucket. Being in the country was good for her. She looked ten years younger than she had in the morning. Her hair even seemed more auburn. It wasn't all the light.

The job took an hour and a half.

"That it?" (Billie.)

Lena only smiled like that when she had gotten away with something.

"What?"

"I forgot antifreeze. An accident, I swear."

Lena was rummaging through the cupboards for soup when Billie decided to try the convent. She followed the strains of "Ave Maria" to the chapel, where the choir seemed to be arranged by the size of the singers' bellies.

The last drain was filled with the electric blue liquid. This was it, then. The sky looked threatening. Storm blowing in. The sky looked like a close-up of kale. They were sweaty, overheated. "Jesus," said Billie. "What did they make this place? R-70?"

Lena said that every time she woke up in strange weather she assumed there had been a nuclear disaster. Billie said this was hurricane weather, not nuclear winter. "You always get like this when you get enough sleep. Some people can't drink milk, you can't tolerate your dreams." Lena started to cry. Billie apologized. She said that waking up together put her unconscious on red alert. "It probably thinks we're back together. It's shouting, 'Don't do it, don't do it.' " "Why not," Lena bawled, flinging her arms around Billie. Billie bent over Lena, stroking her wet hair back from her forehead, blowing on her temple, pulling her between the curve of her arm and her breast, patting her shoulder. Lena snuggled in and began to kiss the side of Billie's breast in small wet sucks that made vacuums, popped in the air.

"Stop that," Billie batted at Lena.

Lena inched back slightly for a better view. Behind Billie the sky looked peculiar, a sizzling blue.

"We'd better get back." They had said the same thing at the same time. Knock on wood. It was a first.

They drew the curtains and checked the faucets. Locked the front door and embraced, leaning their heads on each other's shoulders like babies nodding off, safe, warm, high above rough ground.

They parted, went out into the blue air. It felt warmer. They got in the car. Lena was going to drive. They reached the paved road. Heading for the highway, they imagined they were in separate cars. Billie turned on the radio. They didn't know they heard the announcement, but they turned around. The wind chime was moving slightly. Bing, ping. The sky was black, blue, and silver. Billie put the keys in her fingers at the ready, got out of the car, closing the door quickly. Lena moved over to Billie's seat. Screen door ajar, Billie unlocked the kitchen door. Closed it, but with her hand on the knob ready to open up. Lena slid out of the car, slammed the door; Billie opened the kitchen door and Lena dashed in. They shut the door and locked it twice as if they feared the terrible swirl beyond gravity.

As if they were hired to, they went through the house, from east to west, pulling down the thermal shades, pressing Velcro lips in place. Billie looked under the sink for bottled water. Pulled up one gallon of distilled, one of Great Bear. In the pantry, there was a liter of Perrier and one of Evian. A six-pack of Classic Coke. Diet Pepsi. Some ale. Two bottles of champagne for the lobsters that Lena considered the only acceptable beach food before she did the story on dumping off the continental shelf and gave up shellfish.

They stood empty-handed in the kitchen. Shrugged. "Do you think we could sleep through this?" They knocked the windowsills to stave off bad luck. Went upstairs to bed again, wide awake now. Curled together. At last their bodies said, at last. They knew each other so well.

"After Harrisburg," (Billie pulling Lena into her arms) "when I went to bed, I thought, Winds, if you are blowing my way, I am lying here in orange and copper sequins. Blowtorch my nipples."

"You're lying." (Lena tightening her legs.)

"No. All the time I was thinking, here's your chance again, protozoa and radiolaria, annelids, dendroids. Crinoids and starfishes, you will have another day. Blastoids and scorpions, get ready. Centipedes, come forward one more time, you terrific evolutionary advance. Schizopoda and syncarida, here it comes—your ideal level of background radiation. Pterodactyls crowded the skies like blimps on Armistice Day as I came. Turtles and crocodiles arose. Goblin sharks, cretaceous birds, orbitoids, dogfishes."

Lena slowing her hips and looking fondly at Billie.

"When I opened my eyes, I thought, the background radiation will decline. Next time I want to be a radiolaria. Schizopoda wouldn't be bad."

"It could go forward some the next time." (Lena pecking Billie's cheek.) "The social history could be somewhat different. DNA could vary infinitesimally. We might evolve into a generous and collaborative species."

"That's what you always say," said Billie.

"Don't ruin this." (Lena.)

They lay waiting, one imagining desire, the other death. "Do you think we might have just entered menopause together?" Lena whispered. Desire, anxiety, and fury explode.

Billie pushes herself up over Lena. Giving in at last. Her arm swings far out behind her to gain momentum, returns, hand fisted, between Lena's legs. Lena jerks back, catches herself, presses her elbow close to her ribs, clenches her fingers, punches her ring into

Billie's solar plexus. Coughing, Billie rolls diagonally across the mattress, left leg bent, knee forward on Lena's right side, Billie's right leg scissoring across Lena's abdomen, Lena sliding between Billie's legs to the floor. Swift jabs, stopping short, around the room, paying strict attention not to break the barrier.

Propelled by light alternating jabs, left left right right, they revolve to a sliding door that opens on a narrow deck. Lena pulls the curtains open. The sky is blue fire and swirling with white satin ribbons imprinted with every memory, possibility, and material reality that does or ever has existed in the galaxy, the room is packed with simulacra, squashed one against the other, sweating radioactive iodine. Billie and Lena are coming just from the pressure. "I always hoped I'd come without a vibrator before I died," says Lena blissfully. They are still coming, they are flying, they are splitting and multiplying, a loop in the universe sucking them in until they are along the underbelly of a satin cosmic string, infinite Billies and Lenas and tin cans and Toyotas and cups of tofutti and dildos and pizzas and Statue of Liberty T-shirts and two-dollar hot-pink earrings and bolts of Korean silk and lobsters and power plants and poodles and microchips and oil rigs. All the scientists at Brookhaven and Oak Ridge go speeding by flat as pancakes with their Geiger counters going ratatatat ratatatat—and all the salad bars and condominiums and personal computers, and the pope flying by and Ronald Reagan and the Margarets Atwood, Fuller, and Thatcher, the Georges Bush and Washington, Jesus, Buddha, Wright, North, Hedda, everyone and everything flat, blue, and turning in the rush of nothingness inward, as the universe takes a deep breath, yawning with boredom, reel after reel spinning backward back into the belly of the whale, pressed flat beyond flat, beyond air beyond matter, I, the first to go, we next, this and that then, and other next to last and all finally.

The meltdowns of that era took place in too orderly and rational a series to have been merely accidental. Astroarchaeohistorians deduce that the workers designed these occurrences as periodic warnings—

initially every five years, then three, then one, then six months, before concluding that it would be better to destroy the planet than to endure the unbearable process of destruction. That afternoon seven melt-downs occurred on the eastern seaboard, and the states of New York and South Carolina disappeared from the face of the earth.

Millions of years passed. In the deepest recesses of the vacuum, the shrunken loop began to radiate with the irritation that had so long ago and far away usurped desire. The formation of their matter began once more.

Small Pleasures

Lynne Tillman

LONDON: Some people keep diaries or journals so as not to go mad. A man I knew insisted this was true, then stopped keeping his, and voluntarily committed himself to a mental hospital. Jessica writes copious letters home. Early in the morning and late at night I hear her banging away on her typewriter. Apparently she has many friends, along with a large family. Secretly she could be hard at work on the great American novel, although no woman I've ever known has ever used that phrase, one that's ridiculous to me, and I can't imagine Jessica engaging in that notion. But you never know what people contain within themselves, if anything at all, and Jessica might just have a vast life were I able to crack her open and look inside. I prefer to think that she does. For instance, I'd like to read her deliberate movements as emerging out of a fully conceived sense of herself as being anyone from Cleopatra to Merle Oberon, to that woman who used to be a Republican representative from New Jersey, Millicent Fenwick. Which would have been a great name for Jessica, except she herself is far from being a Republican and left the U.S. because of Vietnam and stayed away after Watergate. Her family are staunch conservatives with ancestors dating back to the American Revolution. Some of Jessica's aunts are active in the D.A.R. Jessica has escaped that, yet has a kind of grand dame quality to her, something that carries over into her present incarnation as an American Buddhist. She sits across from me at breakfast, a tiny Buddha, spreading orange marmalade over cold toast with a seriousness and grace usually reserved for bigger things.

I don't have many fantasies. Perhaps I lack a fantasy life entirely, although you could consider my interest in other people's lives entirely fantastic, even a little crazy. I do keep a diary, though. Not a "good" one, but sufficient to remember the days that pass, my own soap opera.

I tell Jessica that I want things plain. When I read a book I'm suspicious of elaborate description. An excess of adjectives bothers me, as if the writer were attempting to overcome me, to finesse me like a bridge player. Or to seduce me. I don't mean I don't like details. "Some people like excess and elaborate descriptions, some even like to be seduced," she says almost haughtily, and I imagine her in the throes of a great excessive sexual passion, Charles planting tiny wet kisses at her wrist, his mouth moving up to her shoulder and neck, and in profile Jessica's mouth is slightly open, as in perfume commercials. She hurriedly drinks more coffee, looking at me as if she knew what scene was playing on my tiny stage, or launching pad, so to speak. She's reminded of a man she knows, back home, whose vocabulary was so rich, no one understood him, whose stories were so elaborate, by the time he reached the point, you felt exhausted and as if you didn't care. Jessica could just be speaking about excess and elaboration or she could be speaking about us, or me, in some subtle way.

It helps that we're both reading Henry James. She's on *The Europeans* and I've got *The American,* which seems apropos. Conversation with Jessica, and nearly anyone else, leaves me confused, because like the proverbial river that is never the same, all conversation leads from subject to subject, a horse that trots, canters, then gallops away from one's initial point of departure. I don't ride horses; I did once, as a child, but Jessica rides them and they're in my mind now.

My hotel room, plain and verging on ugly, is easy to ignore. The landscapes on the wall, inoffensive, the fake wood bureau, serviceable. The room is cleaned by women I never see. I don't want to see them, because my sense of privacy will be violated if I know the people who come into this space. Sometimes I don't let them in, we've all seen that in movies, and then I hear muttering outside my door. But it stops. Sometimes I wait until everyone has left the floor, and only then do I go out of the room. Adventure creeps into this mundane event, and I remember my father talking about someone's being out of his element, which is, I suppose, one way to put it, my trips in foreign places. But I can't write my father a postcard because he's dead. Sometimes I forget that.

Jessica's good about death. She doesn't avoid discussions about it and seems to think it's a suitable subject for analysis rather than a morbid preoccupation of mine or others. Similarly, she can discuss Charles as if he hadn't abandoned her. Her equanimity appears endless, making her a kind of metaphysician about even her own life. Jessica had wanted to be many things, a veterinarian, a physicist, an opera singer, a biologist, even a missionary during an early Protestant awakening, as she put it. She had come, emerged full-blown, from a long line of people used to doing good. But she became a poet, an antiquarian bookseller, and a Buddhist and suffered from being missionless, an ennui I don't have, not having come from people like hers. Insanity roamed through her large Midwestern tribe, cloistered in proverbial dark closets in gabled houses in areas of the country where no one else lived for miles and miles, as if openness and lack of contact outside the family provided the most fertile ground for a certain kind of American psychosis. But Jessica loved that same fertile intemperate ground, the depopulated landscape, and communed with nature, noticing trees and naming them, saving leaves and drying them, until her hotel room resembled, with its Buddhist altar and woodsy decor, a certain kind of diorama, from my point of view. To Jessica anything natural inspired awe and was beautiful, whereas what people made in order to look beautiful or to look at beauty was always and forever tainted. I tell her I can't see the trees for the people.

One of whom is Charles: I feel I've tainted her life with my report that Charles had not dropped off the face of the earth but was seen walking around in an underground tunnel and an Istanbul hotel. Perhaps she would have preferred him living as a monk in a monastery, separate from the human race, disconsolate, or she'd rather have him dead and with the angels. Jessica believes in angels. Then she could have held on to him in memory. That's what I do, hold on to memory. You relive memories, you develop them, you make them bigger and better and add a touch here and there, like a dab of perfume at the throat of a memory. Death gives you a reason to remember, to put it all together. To put together a new body, of evidence, of evidence of love, of evidence of something solid to withstand the ephemeral. People always say you shouldn't live in the past, but that's so stupid because it's not a matter of will, it's not voluntary. A person without a past is like a nation without history. It's impossible. Jessica says things like, I must get on with my life, and I think of *Goodbye, Mr. Chips*. She's unquestionably and remarkably good about death.

When we discuss Charles, I try to recall for her, and for me, those few conversations he and I held in the hotel and in the tunnel. Now it seems important to take the pieces of dialogue that lie strewn in that tunnel and pile them on top of each other. And like the jigsaw puzzle that always comes to mind when someone says my life is in pieces, one wants to fashion a whole, something like a personality or a character, but I never finished those giant puzzles when I was a kid, and the way I pick up the pieces and display them for Jessica must be nearly useless. He said, I say, "I'm not much good at anything." "I hate London." "I think I'll travel for a while. Just read and think. Maybe learn to play the clarinet." He talked, I report, about Anthony Blunt and the Cambridge spies, then segued to Suleiman the Magnificent, the sixteenth-century sultan of Turkey, who patronized the arts, particularly those craftsmen who worked with gold, because that was the trade he knew. Ottoman emperors had to learn a trade, which was the kind of thing my father would have appreciated, I told him then. Charles said, I can't do anything with my hands. Then he held his hands up in front of his face and wiggled them but as we were underground they were covered by shadow and I couldn't really see them. He, I supposed, knew what his hands looked like and the gesture, now that I think of it again, is entirely unreadable and not at all in character with the character I'm remembering for Jessica. He has become, to me, like the underground man, a nihilist full of despair, who tests the limits of rationality whenever possible. For example, perhaps he left her for no reason at all. This is not what I tell her. Just as I don't tell her that I sometimes feel like a female version of the underground man, which would make Charles and me transnational siblings. In my imagination, anyway.

It's possible that Jessica intuits how Charles and I are alike, and likes me because I'm like him, if I am. Now I think I am, though I didn't when I talked with him in Istanbul, which leads me to think that one remembers even the recent past imperfectly and so much in relation to oneself that every object is skewered upon one's own identity, like a kind of shish kebab. I can feel like any number of people, though, people I've met briefly or have known over a longer period of time. Everyone is just as chameleonlike, personality fragile as old glass in the windows of historical houses or, like dust, easily shaken from a very dirty mop.

Thinking of dirty mops, I can't really imagine Charles and Jessica having sex together. Jessica seems as much out of her body as in it, and Charles, I can barely recall his body at all, just his large head and those pale bluish round eyes that stared into dark spaces along with mine. I imagine many people couldn't dream of sex with me or imagine my having sex with others. This doesn't stop me from applying unyielding and unimaginative standards to them.

Before going into our separate rooms which are next door to one another, Jessica said, putting her key into the lock, I'm not sure though what importance beauty has, except for the peace it gives me. But is that enough? Not to worry, I say to her, borrowing one of her phrases which is already borrowed from the English. A transplantation of a sort. Easy to do. Simple. Quite simple. In bed I feel like a body claimed by a name. Then a name claimed by a body. A thing, a human thing, small and powerless. I don't confide these thoughts to her. Beauty has never had much importance to me.

Morning. Outside there's shouting, yelling. It's a fight between two men which I watch from my hotel window. I enjoy watching fights, as if I were a participant fighting my own dark and dirty battles. I don't like to fight. The two men don't look English, and their angry sounds are twice removed, male and foreign. Foreign also to the English who stand on the sidewalk, also watching. They're arguing about money. One could be the other's father. The younger man shouts: I worked all day yesterday, all day, I want some money. The older man bellows: Work? Work? I worked too, you'll only spend it on drugs. They're standing close to each other, the public scene grotesquely intimate. The younger man slaps the older man across the face and pulls a black wallet from his back pocket which he brandishes, as if it were a sword or handkerchief, waving it in front of his adversary's face. The younger man then strides to the center of the street, looks around, walks back to the sidewalk, and throws the wallet down in front of the older man. The older man, who had been standing on the sidewalk as if he too were an observer at the spectacle, picks up the wallet almost casually and marches off, unruffled, a briefcase in one hand, the wallet in the other. Neither man looks back as they get farther and farther from each other, both turning a corner at the end of the street, leaving each other behind without a second glance.

The fight is much less conclusive, though one got the wallet from the other, than, say, a prizefight or baseball game in which there is a winner. It's much more like fiction.

I could never do that—or haven't yet—leave someone behind without that second furtive glance. What was that song? "I was looking back to see if she was looking back to see if I was looking back at her."

The street returns to its ordinariness, and the passionate battle, familial or otherwise, is forgotten on a summer's day. It's at moments like these I relish most being away, and am almost happy about having been an only child. Almost happy to be in a country different from my recently widowed mother's. This scene from my mother's eyes would have been edited differently. She used to work as a film editor in Hollywood and New York, but she started as a script supervisor. In those days she was called a script girl. But that's a different story. One I've heard and told a million times. "You can't right history," my mother would say, "but you can rewrite it and then edit the hell out of it."

My favorite place near the hotel is a small French café off Queensway, an international street filled with Middle Eastern, Greek, and Italian restaurants and shops, and a tremendous mixture of nationalities, in which I feel comfortable. There's a transitory Times Square feeling to the street, not down-and-out, just a way station. The people who will stay here forever, I feel, might get stuck in a kind of limbo, a not-London, a not-anywhere. Voluntary and individual diaspora is a luxury.

Depending upon whether I think I deserve it or not, I'll stroll over to the French cafe, for a café au lait and a small pastry. A small pleasure. Small pleasures could be the title of a film I'd want to go to or a store I might work in, or only what it is now, a moment in my life. But why not, I think, title these moments in a life?

The café is nearly empty. There's a sign outside it which reads Morning Coffee, leading a visitor like me to suspect a difference later in the day. As I walk in, Claudia, the proprietor and coffeemaker, announces, We're having an English summer. It's early June and this statement strikes me as preemptive or at least premature. Also it's an entirely new idea—an English summer. An elderly man and woman smile knowingly, almost as if Claudia had divulged a secret or told a dirty joke, then they bite into pastries that ooze from all sides. Claudia's Italian, born in Bologna, a Common Market European, but she's been in London long enough to be a kind of hybrid, and I wonder if that will be my fate too, as it appears to be Jessica's. Watching Claudia, I'm thinking about the English summer, hybridization, and the elderly couple who are engaged in an animated discussion about the time their currency, not that long ago, either, changed from shillings, half-pennies, and sixpences to its present decimal system, more or less making the pound like the dollar. Everything got more expensive "right off," the woman remarks, everything changed overnight. She recalls a discussion on a bus, where complete strangers, dismayed, sought conversation about this radical move by the government. She doesn't say radical. She says horrible. Life changed overnight, she repeats. Became less English, the man notes, and they both nod. Claudia smiles at me.

Concepts like less English and English summer weigh oddly. I imagine a New York summer—I can't imagine an American summer, which instantly says something about size of country, I suppose, different climates everywhere, the variety of groups, ethnic groups, and my own experience: I'm not sure I feel like an American, except that I do love baseball and Westerns. A New York summer: New Jersey tomatoes, ballgames on TV, air conditioners, a city that feels empty on the weekend, beaches covered with garbage and bodies, heat, tension, uncontrolled tempers on the subways or streets, a fear of indiscriminate violence, the fear of violence born of discrimination, people hanging out, open windows in poor neighborhoods, kids shouting for other kids to come out. These images come to mind almost without thinking, a rush of associations as vivid and disturbing as those from my childhood. Just as personal.

Claudia's small and her hands are well formed, muscular, full of definition. I generally look at hands and teeth. She's got small teeth that look as if they've had some care. All her movements are economical; she wastes nothing, reminding me of sayings like "waste not, want not," as if she were a Puritan daughter rather than a Tuscan, proud of Bologna's Communist government, history, and people. I once told her, twelve café au laits back, that I'd been in Bologna and instantly I was transformed into a special customer. I like to watch her. There's a precision to her like a wonderful Italian design, a small fast car or a lamp so simple it's profound. No doubt I romanticize Italians, or anyone who appears to contain that which I do not, and how I perceive these abundances must be by the light of my lacks, a curious contradiction that I exist with. We've already discussed Anna Magnani and Rossellini's *Una Voce Umana*. We've talked about his leaving Magnani for Bergman, which was, according to her, a national disgrace. I don't actually report on my stay in Bologna.

BOLOGNA, ITALY: Signor Mancini—"Not related to Henry," he tells me jovially the day I arrive at Pensione Mancini—wears a black suit every day. His white shirt is frayed at the collar, which leads me to think business is bad or that he's deeply depressed. He's old enough to have not only lived through World War II but also to have served in it. Since this is Bologna, I'm certain he was a Communist partisan or someone like Marcello Mastroianni in *A Special Day*, the Communist homosexual newscaster that Sophia Loren, a lonely housewife, makes love with on the day Hitler comes to meet Mussolini in Rome.

In the courtyard of this old pensione, Signor Mancini moves from breakfast table to breakfast table, taking orders in a measured and friendly manner. He is sober and serious. I remember my father telling me that waiters in Europe were proud of their work. According to my father, everyone in Europe was proud of his or her work. A shoemaker, he'd say, has pride in the product he turns out, a baker, a butcher. And so on. He'd list several other occupations, talk about the glory of work, and return to his office with a sigh, as if going to certain defeat.

Signor Mancini looks like my father. What's left of his hair is dirty blond, he's got greenish eyes, small and hard like marbles, and lightly tanned skin. Even so he looks sad. Usually having a tan makes anyone look happier but not Signor Mancini and not my father, who railed against the deadly effects of the sun and lay in it whenever he could. "I don't understand," he'd say to my mother, "how anything natural can be bad. It doesn't make sense."

The arches around the square where my hotel is located allow the Bolognese to stroll in the shade, drink an espresso, and sit for hours watching the pigeons, reading the paper, talking and arguing. I find one restaurant that caters to the family and I go there every day for lunch. At least it seems to cater to the family. I'm the only solo at a table, and I order three courses merely to drag things out. Soup, pasta, a meat dish or fish, while families of eight gesture, chew, laugh, and sometimes even cry in a performance better than any theater. I'm positive they know I'm watching, and no doubt they feel sorry for me, all alone, in a beautiful city, a signorina without a signor or bambini. Or maybe they think I'm a widow or divorcée. On different days I try to act differently. Eat with downcast eyes or eagerly read a book or newspaper. I don't like reading the *Herald Tribune* in public anymore.

The restaurant owners expect me by now, and there's a flourish when I walk in. The maître d' waves his table napkin and I enter. This is one of the reasons I go there. I need a sense of order and a sense of being known. The familiar, I discover, is readily available, can be constructed quickly merely by returning to the same place more than twice. Two times can be chance, three times is habit. Maybe monogamy got started in just this way. I know people who never want to go to the same restaurant twice. One, a man, is never monogamous, can't seem to be; the other, a woman, loves eating well and can be monogamous, but expects men not to be. I hope they never get involved. Pondering this, I roll the spaghetti onto my fork. I'm still not sure if I'm eating it correctly, but my efforts cannot go unnoticed by my hosts and the other diners.

Signor Mancini is behind the desk when I return from lunch a little drunk. I ask for my key and when he hands it to me our hands touch slightly.

You have a letter, Signorina, he says soberly, and I wait for a death sentence. It's from my mother. Mia mama, I tell him to satisfy what I think is his curiosity. Ahh, he says, and pats my hand, this time deliberately, then points above the desk to a picture of a small rotund woman. Mama, he says sadly. I wonder if I'll ever have a desk with a picture of my mother prominently displayed above it that I'll point to and say Mama. I think of cloth monkey mothers, dummies, and baby dolls. Saying mama in Italy resonates—not at all like saying it anywhere in America, where there's no prevailing sympathy behind it. There was *I Remember Mama* but that, I smile to myself, was in television's infancy.

I place the letter in my pocket, say grazie meaningfully, and retire to my tiny room, where I read my mother's letter, asking me when I'm coming home, and listen for a good part of the night to cats in heat and an argument in Italian coming from the square.

LONDON: When Claudia asks me about Bologna, if I visited such and such, I have to say no. I took walks, I say. I looked in store windows.

So many shoes. We make shoes in Bologna, she states, and with her hand slices the air for emphasis. I think of more Italian films, and passion, and how she impossibly resembles Monica Vitti and Vittorio Gassman. I think of her lover who's Irish and has a wife. I think of the Irishman at the hotel who works behind the desk. Does he have English summers? I stare as Claudia empties cups and cleans the table where the elderly couple were just sitting. I feel that I must regain her respect. I say, I stayed at the Pensione Mancini. Her gray eyes shift from right to left. Do you know Signor Mancini? Yes, Claudia says. She tells me, her mouth a downward curve, that everyone knows the Mancinis at home. A casa. That the family was once rich and important. The pensione was, in fact, once their home. Then the war came. Brother fought against brother. Which side was Signor Mancini on, the one I know? He was a fascist, she says. After the war he spent time in jail. They never spoke again. Then the brother died. And his mother? I ask. A saint. Claudia crosses herself. Mama Mancini died years and years ago. She never really recovered.

Walking on Queensway I'm carrying a container of hummus and a bag of tomatoes. I like the way they sell tomatoes here: hard ripe English tomatoes. Hand-lettered signs or shouts from the people hawking them. Women and men with bright red swollen hands. I imagine Claudia and Jessica meeting. I don't think Jessica would be taken by Claudia the way I am, or perhaps I don't want her to be. Actually I don't want to get to know Claudia better. There's a perfection to the incomplete way in which we know each other.

Should I have known, have guessed, about Signor Mancini, I wonder as I stare at the wallpaper in my room. This wallpaper, were it in my apartment at home, would drive me crazy. But here it doesn't matter, like not being bothered by a city council election you couldn't vote in anyway. It passes right by, and I'm unencumbered, clipping my toenails and placing the small hard pieces in the ashtray that reads Inverness Terrace. Small hard pieces of American toenails, Americana of a sort. Some people might burn them. I love the way Claudia says Ciao.

Jessica's at my door. She's found a place to live and will leave our home away from home, her safe place from Charles. She once described her previous flat as having too many ghosts, a not unusual thing to say, except that she believes in ghosts the way she believes in angels. In fact a ghost to her is an angel without a resting place. Today's *Guardian* has a paragraph on angels. The Vatican says they exist. Jessica isn't amused or surprised. Her small sharp eyes (the eyes of a knitter, my mother would say) find their way into some secret part of me. Jessica thinks that, and I'm beginning to believe her. She also believes that no one should have any secrets and that everyone knows all secrets already. To her nothing is secret, everything is sacred.

Moving from one street to another or one city or country to another requires just about the same amount of energy, and when Jessica left the hotel, I decided to return to Amsterdam and to hold my London life in suspension, a bit of fluff caught in a solution, or hold my life in suspense, if suspenseful could be used to describe my life in London.

Certainly life is filled with everyday mystery, we're given answers to questions that answer nothing, and no doubt life goes on without me, and things don't remain the same, but can "I" ever know that? This question, like so many others, being insoluble, I boarded the boat-train for the Hoek of Holland and was violently ill on what's considered a mild crossing. My father was also prone to seasickness in calm waters, though this is hardly comfort when you're collapsed in a gray toilet. And why should being like someone else be comforting anyway? I'm often amused at how I or others bring arcane tidbits into conversation, for reassurance, that on further reflection should not be.

On the train to Amsterdam from the Hoek, I sat in a compartment with other foreigners, one a Pakistani man, one an English girl of seventeen, one a Belgian man, all of us headed in the same direction for different reasons. The Pakistani and I engaged in one of those fitful conversations in which neither is able to make clear what one wants to say. Finally we stood in the compartment passageway and talked about the neon lights on buildings, that blaze of created energy that gives color to our nights. Beauty, he said to me, artificial beauty. Yes, I agreed. Why, he said, are you not married? I don't want to be. Ah, he said, scrutinizing me, then may God be with you. I thanked him. The rest of the journey he and I were noticeably silent, as if something portentous had occurred. When we detrained at Centraal Station at dusk, the Pakistani shook my hand seriously and I bowed slightly, an atavistic gesture that brought Charles to mind, but one just as grave as his handshake. With a doleful expression he took his leave, and I'm sure he watched me throw my bag into the taxi and shook his head, certain I was meant for tragedy.

Amsterdam doesn't seem a suitable place for tragedy, but place—the city, for instance—is as much a mental space as a physical one, and its physical boundaries, its history, are much less concise than any term such as "city" might lead one to think. Am I headed for tragedy, I wonder as the cabdriver brings me to the hotel. And are conversations with strangers necessarily uncanny?

They give me the same room. It still doesn't have a television and I'm embarrassed to ask for one. The breakfasts are also the same, which pleases me enormously. Eat the same thing every day and you won't go mad. Also said to me by the friend who insisted upon keeping a diary for the same reason.

I think I understand why so many English plays take place in the breakfast or sitting rooms of hotels. Apart from the cheapness of their production, any aggregate of people, drawn or thrown together and involuntarily in each other's company, poses dramatic possibilities. It's not that you expect anything very fantastic to happen—the American woman called Joy is not going to do a strip in the breakfast room, the Englishman called Pete is not going to sing an aria just because he feels like it, the German Gregor will not fall to his knees and confess some terrible crime—there will be no orgy. We are all remarkable for our constraint. If something like that did happen—if Olivier, the Frenchman, exposed himself to me in front of my fellow diners—the course of playwriting would have been altered, as would the site of the hotel. And I would not now be playing at eating this raisin bun, or krentebollen, in the breakfast room. I'd be in a state beyond words, blood racing, or I might be laughing nervously. Olivier merely smiles at me, a sly, guarded slash of a grin, throws his book (Truffaut on Hitchcock) into his leather satchel, pushes his wire-rimmed glasses up onto the bridge of his nose, and strides past me, brushing against my arm ever so slightly. Why do I feel I've seen this scene before? And will I "end up in bed" with him? Is my life as predictable as it sometimes appears?

After stints as a teacher, book editor, actress, dancer, choreographer, and carpenter, M. MARK became arts editor, and later executive editor, of the *Village Voice*. In 1981 she founded the *VLS*, a monthly journal devoted to publishing criticism, cultural commentary, and fiction. In 1988 the *VLS* became a national magazine.

KATHY ACKER is the author of *Hannibal Lector, My Father; Empire of the Senseless; Great Expectations; Blood and Guts in High School; Don Quixote;* and *Literal Madness*, which consists of three short novels. She lives in San Francisco.

DOROTHY ALLISON is the author of *The Women Who Hate Me*, a book of poetry; *Trash*, a collection of short stories honored by two Lambda Literary Awards; and *A Bastard out of Carolina*, a novel. She lives in San Francisco.

RUSSELL BANKS is the author of eleven books of fiction, most recently *Affliction* and *The Sweet Hereafter*. He lives in Princeton, New Jersey, and upstate New York.

BLANCHE MCCRARY BOYD's third novel, *The Revolution of Little Girls*, was recently published. She is the author of a book of essays, *The Redneck Way of Knowledge*, and her articles have appeared in *Vanity Fair, Esquire, Premiere, Vogue*, and the *New York Times Magazine*. She teaches writing at Connecticut College.

BRUCE BROOKS is the author of four novels: *The Moves Make the Man, Midnight Hour Encores, No Kidding*, and *Everywhere*. He has also written three nonfiction books, about birds, predators, and animal architecture. He lives with his wife and son in Maryland.

ANGELA CARTER was born in 1940. Her last book was a collection of short stories, *Saints and Strangers* (1986), and her new novel, *Wise Children*, will be published in January, 1992. She lives in London.

SANDRA CISNEROS is the author of *Woman Hollering Creek*, a collection of short stories; *The House on Mango Street*, a novel; and two collections of poetry, *My Wicked Wicked Ways* and *Bad Boys*. She lives in San Antonio, Texas.

MICHELLE CLIFF's most recent publications are *Bodies of Water*, a short-story collection, and *No Telephone to Heaven*, a novel.

SUSAN DAITCH is the author of *L.C.* and *The Colorist*. She teaches at Sarah Lawrence College and lives in New York City.

STACEY D'ERASMO is a senior editor at the *VLS*. She lives and works in New York City.

JANICE EIDUS is the author of *Vito Loves Geraldine*, a collection of short stories, and *Faithful Rebecca*, a novel. "Vito Loves Geraldine" won a 1990 O. Henry Prize. She is a native New Yorker, now living in midtown Manhattan.

SUZANNE GARDINIER is the author of *Usahn: Ten Poems and a Story*. She teaches writing and lives in Sag Harbor, New York.

JEWELLE GOMEZ is the author of *The Gilda Stories*, a novel. She is the Director of Literature at the New York State Council on the Arts. Originally from Boston, she's now a Brooklyn girl.

TODD GRIMSON's stories have appeared in *BOMB*, *Between C & D*, *The Quarterly*, and elsewhere. He is the author of a novel, *Within Normal Limits*. He lives in Portland, Oregon.

GARY INDIANA is the author of two short story collections, *White Trash Boulevard* and *Scar Tissue*, and *Horse Crazy*, a novel. He lives in New York City.

KAREN KARBO is the author of *Trespassers Welcome Here* and *The Diamond Lane*. She divides her time between Portland, Oregon, and Los Angeles.

PAGAN KENNEDY writes about books for the *VLS* and *The Nation*. She has won a grant from the Massachusetts Arts Council for her fiction; her stories have been published in *The Quarterly*, *Prairie Schooner*, *StoryQuarterly*, and other magazines.

JOHN L'HEUREUX's most recent collection of stories is *Comedians* and his most recent novel is *An Honorable Profession*. Next year he will publish a new novel, *The Shrine at Altamira*.

HARRY MATHEWS is the author of several books of poetry and fiction, among them *Armenian Papers: Poems 1954–1984* and *Cigarettes*. He divides his time between Paris and New York.

MICHAEL MUSTO writes "La Dolce Musto," the weekly nightlife and entertainment column in the *Village Voice*. He is the author of two books, *Downtown* and *Manhattan on the Rocks*.

MAX PHILLIPS is a writer, graphic designer, and illustrator whose stories and poems have appeared in publications ranging from *The Atlantic* to *The Antioch Review*. The recipient of a 1991 NEA Creative Writing Fellowship, he has just completed a story collection, *People I Would Not Ordinarily Kiss,* and is at work on a novel. He lives in New York City.

NOEL RYAN has published stories in the *VLS, Christopher Street,* and *The Alternate,* and the anthologies *Aphrodesiac; First Love, Last Love;* and *Men on Men 3.* He lives in Helena, Montana.

LYNDA SCHOR is the author of *Appetites* and *True Love & Real Romance,* two books of short fiction; a forthcoming novel, *Wet Dream;* and a forthcoming book of short stories, *Love Takes Off Its Shoes.* She lives in New York City and Baltimore.

SHARON THOMPSON is coeditor of *Powers of Desire: The Politics of Sexuality.* She is currently finishing a book on teenage girls' narratives about sex, romance, and pregnancy.

LYNNE TILLMAN is a writer and filmmaker. She is the author of *Haunted Houses, Motion Sickness,* and *Absence Makes the Heart;* she codirected and wrote the independent film *Committed.* She lives in New York City.

Subscribe
**to the literary magazine
that broadens your mind
and tickles your fancy.**

VLS
VOICE LITERARY SUPPLEMENT
Venturesome. Lively. Surprising.

Recently published by Serpent's Tail

Who Was That Man? A Present for Mr. Oscar Wilde, by Neil Bartlett
"Neil Bartlett has grabbed history by the collar and made bitter love to it. He has embraced what was alien and criminal or merely clinical and loved it into poignant life." —Edmund White

Voices from the Plains, a novel by Gianni Celati
"His quietly understated glimpses of those sobered, stunned lives has a moving, cumulative power."—*Philadelphia Inquirer*

The Seven Deadly Sins, a fiction anthology edited by Alison Fell
"If these women are so sinfully excessive, bizarre, manic, viruently premenstrual, bitchy, etc., why do they remind us so much of you and me?"—*The Nation*
Contributors: Kathy Acker, Michèle Roberts, Zoë Fairbairns, Alison Fell, Agnes Owens, Sara Maitland, Leslie Dick

Count Julian, a novel by Juan Goytisolo
"Magnificent beauty and perfect craftsmanship only adds to the power of his invective against his 'harsh homeland.' "—Carlos Fuentes, *The New York Times Book Review*
Also available: *Marks of Identity* and *Juan the Landless*

The Passport, a novel by Herta Müller
"We can feel the overwhelming burden of life under a totalitarian regime."—*Chicago Sun-Times*

The Variety Artistes, a novel by Tom Wakefield
"A charming story of a warm and memorable character. And it does much-needed damage to damaging stereotypes of older women."
—*The New York Times Book Review*
Also available: *Lot's Wife* and *Forties' Child*

Serpent's Tail books are available at quality bookstores.